Praise for *Dangerous Illusions*

"The suspenseful conclusion and believable romantic element will leave readers eager for the next installment."

Publishers Weekly

"Hannon delivers a new romantic suspense series that starts off slowly but then races full speed ahead, spinning out a twisty plot. The author's many fans will devour this work."

RT Book Reviews

"Hannon is at the top of her game. *Dangerous Illusions*, the first in the Code of Honor series, will satisfy any suspense reader."

Christian Market

"Hannon's latest novel is a page-turner that will keep the reader up late at night, trying to finish the book and uncover the truth."

Christian Library Journal

Books by Irene Hannon

HIDDEN PERIL

IRENE HANNON

Revell

a division of Baker Publishing Group
Grand Rapids, Michigan

Published by Revell
a division of Baker Publishing Group
PO Box 6287, Grand Rapids, MI 49516-6287
www.revellbooks.com

Printed in the United States of America

Library of Congress Cataloging-in-Publication Data
Names: Hannon, Irene, author.
Title: Hidden peril / Irene Hannon.
Description: Grand Rapids, MI : Revell, a division of Baker Publishing Group, 2018.
   | Series: Code of honor ; 2
Identifiers: LCCN 2018008486 | ISBN 9780800727697 (pbk. : alk. paper)
Subjects: | GSAFD: Mystery fiction. | Christian fiction.
Classification: LCC PS3558.A4793 H53 2018 | DDC 813/.54—dc23
LC record available at https://lccn.loc.gov/2018008486

ISBN 978-0-8007-2777-2 (cloth)

18   19   20   21   22   23   24   7   6   5   4   3   2   1

To my father, James Hannon—
who encouraged me to write suspense.

Thank you for the countless tea-and-scones
sessions at Starbucks to brainstorm story ideas,
reminisce . . . and solve all the world's problems!

Your love, support, and generosity
have enriched my life in ways too numerous to count.

No one could have a better father—and friend.

PROLOGUE

Why was a light burning in the workshop at midnight?

Suppressing a shiver, Brother Michael Bennett peered at the sliver of illumination seeping under the bottom of the heavy wooden door at the end of the long, vaulted passageway.

There could be only one explanation.

The monk who'd closed up the shop for the day had forgotten to flip a switch.

He wiped a hand down his face and leaned a shoulder against the rough stone wall. That wouldn't have happened on his watch. Last chore before he left each night, he extinguished all the lights.

Eyeing the door, he gauged the distance. Could his legs handle the detour? Questionable. The bug that had felled him at noon had left his muscles wobbly as Jell-O. If his parched throat wasn't screaming for some chipped ice, he wouldn't be making this taxing trek to the kitchen.

Fuel for the workshop generator, however, was expensive.

And they had better uses for the funds entrusted to their care.

Shoring up his waning strength, he pushed off from the wall and trudged down the drafty passage, the February chill creeping into his Florida-born-and-bred bones . . . as it always did in winter.

Yet not once in the past ten years had he regretted his decision to join this simple religious community in the shadow of the Qalamoun Mountains. Christianity had flourished amid the harsh beauty of this high desert for centuries, and it was an honor and privilege to make a contribution to that tradition . . . no matter how small or insignificant.

Life might not be easy here—but it was good.

Tonight, however, he could have done with a few luxuries.

Like room service.

And heated hallways.

Another shiver rolled through him. It wasn't as cold in here as it was outside, where the temperature was probably hovering near freezing—but it couldn't be much above fifty.

Then again, no one was supposed to be wandering the halls at this hour.

He picked up his pace.

At the door to the workshop, he paused to catch his breath. All he had to do was flick off a light, continue to the kitchen for his ice, and return to his warm bed.

The sooner the better.

He twisted the knob . . . pushed the door open . . . and froze.

A dark-haired man was hunched over a workbench against the far wall, a high-pitched whine abrading the midnight stillness. It was impossible to identify him from behind.

But whoever he was, he shouldn't be here.

A prickle of unease skittered through him, and he gripped the edge of the door to steady himself. "Hello?"

His raspy greeting was no more than a hoarse whisper.

He raised his voice and tried again, wincing as the words scraped past his raw throat.

8

The whirring noise stopped abruptly, and the man spun around.

"Khalil?" Brother Michael stared at the refugee who'd arrived on their doorstep two years ago, one of the many desperate souls who'd lost everything in this war-ravaged land. He switched to Arabic. "What are you doing here?"

Beads of sweat broke out on the twenty-six-year-old's forehead. "I'm working."

"At midnight?"

"I wanted to finish a . . . task."

God knew the small contingent of brothers needed all the help they could get to keep the place running, and Khalil was a hard worker. That was one of the reasons he'd been allowed to stay on as a volunteer in exchange for room and board.

But no one expected him to toil at the expense of sleep.

"You don't have to put in nighttime hours. You more than earn your keep as it is." Brother Michael leaned a shoulder against the doorframe. "This can wait until tomorrow."

"As you wish. I'll just clean up before I leave." The man gave a slight bow, his back brushing against the workbench.

A flutter of shavings drifted to the floor.

Too many, given the nature of the work they did here.

Odd.

And what had produced that whine he'd heard when he'd opened the door?

Certainly none of their usual equipment.

Brother Michael's pulse quickened.

Something wasn't right.

He needed to check that workbench.

"I'll help you with the cleanup." He forced himself to walk toward the bench, each step a supreme effort.

"No." The sweat on the man's forehead glistened in the overhead light. "You're sick. I'll take care of it."

"I insist." The workshop was his responsibility—as was Khalil.

When you pled a refugee's case with the abbot and other monks, it was your duty to ensure he abided by the rules. If the man was using the space for questionable purposes after hours, the issue needed to be addressed.

He continued toward the bench, stopping a few feet away, waiting for his protégé to give him access.

For several seconds they locked gazes. A parade of emotions darted through the younger man's eyes. Panic . . . fear . . . resignation. And then resolve.

Without a word, Khalil moved toward him, stepping aside as they exchanged places.

Now that he had a clear view of the bench, Brother Michael scanned the items on the wooden surface. Added them up. Gripped the edge of the worktable.

Dear God!

How could he have made such a terrible mistake?

Khalil wasn't here to support their mission.

He was here to . . .

A shattering pain exploded in the back of his head, and Brother Michael staggered.

Groped for the edge of the bench.

Missed.

Legs crumpling, he slumped to the stone floor.

And in the scant few moments before the darkness swirling around him snuffed out the light, he sent a silent, desperate plea to the Almighty.

Please, God, let someone—somewhere—discover the truth and put a stop to the evil deception that is defiling this holy place.

1

Brother Michael was dead.

Kristin Dane gripped the edge of the corrugated, travel-worn shipping carton that had logged more than six thousand miles on its journey from Syria to St. Louis, blinked to clear her vision, and forced herself to reread the letter.

Dear Ms. Dane:

I am pleased to send you the 50 pillar candles you ordered from our humble workshop here in the cradle of Christianity. We are grateful for your willingness to support our humanitarian work by selling the labor of our hands in your shop. As you know, every dollar we receive is used to help victims of the terrible violence here, Christians and Muslims alike. We continue to be amazed at the resilience and strength of the remarkable Syrian people, who have suffered so much.

And now I must pass on some sad news. Brother Michael has, quite suddenly, gone home to God. On February 22, he grew ill and took to his bed. The next morning,

11

we found him on the floor in the workshop. We believe he rose during the night and went to the shop for some reason. It appears he tripped, or perhaps grew dizzy, and fell backward, hitting his head on the corner of a workbench.

I know this will be a shock to you, as it was to all of us. Our American brother spoke often of your kindness to him when you met three years ago while he was visiting your city.

Here at the monastery, we are already missing his selfless work and the deep spirituality and trust with which he lived his life. And we grieve the shortness of his days. Forty-four seems far too young to die.

Please pray for the repose of his soul, as we will continue to do here in the land he adopted—and loved.

> *With gratitude in Christ,*
> *Abbot Jacques Gagnon*

"Kristin?"

From a distance, a voice penetrated her shock.

Refolding the single sheet of paper, she lifted her chin. Susan Collier was standing in the doorway between WorldCraft's stockroom and the retail section of the shop.

"Are you okay?" The woman took a step toward her.

"No. I'm trying to . . . to absorb some bad news." She relayed the contents of the letter to her part-time clerk.

"I'm so sorry." Sympathy deepened the lines at the corners of the other woman's eyes. "From everything you've told me, he was a fine man."

"The best. A saint among us." She traced a finger over the hand-lettered label on the box. "Meeting him was an amazing experience. He had an incredible ability to draw people in."

"Some men are very charismatic."

At the hint of bitterness in her words, Kristin looked at her. "I meant that in a positive, spiritual sense. Brother Michael exuded holiness. Not all men are like your ex."

"I know." Susan's features relaxed a hair. "I keep reminding myself of that. Brother Michael sounded like one of the good guys." She motioned toward the box. "Do you want me to put those on the display for you? I know you usually like to do it yourself, but you're already cutting it close for the wedding."

Shifting gears, Kristin checked her watch.

Her clerk was right.

In less than three hours, the bride would be walking down the aisle. And since she was one of the two people standing up for the groom, she couldn't be late.

Letting Colin down wasn't an option.

"Yes, thanks." Kristin set the letter from the abbot on the desk wedged into one corner of the stockroom. "If you need me for anything later today or Monday while I'm at the small business seminar, call or text."

"I'll be fine."

"I know." She summoned up a smile. "In the year you've been with me, I've come to rely on you for much more than clerking duties. You've been a huge asset to WorldCraft."

Cheeks pinkening, the mid-fortyish brunette smoothed a renegade strand of hair back into the sleek chignon at her nape. "Thanks. I appreciate you giving me the job. If it hadn't been for you and Kate Marshall, I don't know where I'd be."

Kate Marshall . . . Kate Marshall. Oh, right. The director of New Start, the agency where Susan had gone for career counseling after she finally walked away from her abusive marriage.

"You would have been fine. With your background in retail, someone would have snapped you up."

"I don't think so. My skills were rusty after being on hold for two decades."

"Not true. Your volunteer work with the handicraft co-op kept them fresh—and dealing with that kind of merchandise was perfect background for the fair trade goods I sell here." She retrieved her purse from the desk drawer. "Now I'm off to be best woman."

"You earned that title in my book the day you hired me."

"Don't give me so much credit." She squeezed the woman's arm. "I just recognized talent when I saw it. Thanks again for working extra hours on Monday to cover for me."

"No problem. Have fun at the wedding."

"I'll give it my best shot."

But as she left by the rear door and crossed to her Sentra, even the sunny skies on this second day of April couldn't chase away the pall hanging over her.

Brother Michael was dead.

Not from militant bullets or bombs or blades as she'd always feared, but from a tragic accident.

Why would God take a man who'd left everything behind to do desperately needed work in a dangerous land?

It didn't make sense.

And it felt all wrong.

But as Colin always reminded her when she raised such questions, trying to understand the mind of God was an exercise in futility. You had to trust in his goodness and accept that he saw the bigger picture, even if your own lens was murky.

Bottom line, at some point you had to let questions like this go.

Depressing the auto lock on her keychain, she closed the distance to her car in a few long strides, slid behind the wheel, and started the engine.

This was one of those times—at least for the next few hours. She couldn't allow her gloom and grief to ruin the biggest day of Colin's life. She and Rick owed their best bud total support and focus.

So she'd fix her hair, do her makeup, slip into the knockout black dress she'd splurged on for this event, and smile for the world.

Even if her heart was aching.

. . . . .

Plate of hors d'oeuvres in one hand, drink in the other, Luke Carter surveyed the elegant room at the country club. Appetizing food was displayed at various stations. Tables for eight and tall cocktail rounds were draped in white linen, with candles and flowers in the center of each. A string quartet played in the background to the accompaniment of tinkling glasses and the laughter of the animated reception crowd. Outside, lanterns twinkled on the terrace, where some of the guests were taking advantage of the unseasonably balmy weather.

It was a first-class party in a beautiful setting.

And he did *not* want to be here.

But when one of your new colleagues went out of his way to invite you, not showing up would have been rude—for the reception, anyway.

The church ceremony?

Different story.

Besides, no one in this crowd would have noticed his absence for the exchange of vows.

Nor would anyone miss him if he ducked out fast tonight. Except for Sarge and a few other detectives seated at two adjacent tables across the room with spouses or girlfriends, everyone was a stranger.

And he wasn't in the mood to socialize with coworkers or make small talk with people he'd never see again.

Skirting the crowd, he kept out of his colleagues' line of sight. No reason to sit. He wasn't staying that long. The minute he was through eating, he'd track down the bride and groom, pass on his best wishes, and beat a hasty retreat.

As he hugged the fringes of the group, he gave the place a sweep. He needed an out-of-the-way spot to deposit his plate and glass so he could chow down.

An empty cocktail table in a shadowy corner caught his eye. Perfect.

He made a beeline for it.

Ten feet away, he saw an older gent approaching it as well.

Before he could decide whether to fade back into the crowd or lengthen his stride to claim the table first, the elderly man spotted him and grinned.

"Don't even think about it, young man. You may be faster than I am, but this cane hanging off my arm can be a lethal weapon. However, I'll be happy to share."

The corners of Luke's lips flexed. The guy appeared to be good-natured, and it might not be a bad idea to take him up on his offer. Other guests might think they were together and leave them alone.

He finished the short walk and set down his plate. "Sold."

"Happy to have the company." The man held out his hand. "Stan Hawkins."

"Luke Carter." He returned the gent's firm shake.

"Friend of the bride or groom?" Stan speared a meatball with a toothpick.

"Groom. But I'm more coworker than friend. I've only been in town since January, so I'm still learning the ropes and getting acquainted."

"Ah. Another detective. You boys do good work."

"Thanks. We try. What about you?"

"I retired long ago. From accounting. It was a pleasant, steady job—but crunching numbers isn't as exciting as tracking down criminals."

Luke stifled a smile. "I meant, do you know the bride or the groom?"

"Oh. Well, of course you did." He dabbed at the corner of his mouth with a napkin. "Both—now. But I knew Trish first. I live across the street from the house where she grew up. I had a little hand in getting the two of them together, you know."

"Is that right?"

"Yep." He squinted toward the front of the room, where the newlyweds were posing for a photo by the cake. "I'll have to get a piece of that to take home to my wife. She was real disappointed to miss the wedding, but she had one of her arthritis flare-ups this morning."

"I'll be happy to get a couple of pieces for you after they cut it." Luke finished a stuffed mushroom and moved on to a crab cake. As soon as he was done, he'd exchange a few words with the bride and groom, fetch Stan's cake, and slip out the exit that was mere steps away from their table.

He ate faster.

"That's very thoughtful of you. Navigating through a crowd is tricky with that nuisance." He waved a hand toward the cane he'd propped against the wall. "It's tough getting old—but better than the alternative, as they say." The man winked at him. "So are you here by yourself?"

"Yes." He downed his last toasted ravioli in one bite and took a swig of his drink. "I'll go get that cake for you now."

"I'll save your place."

Keeping the bride and groom in his sights, Luke circled the perimeter of the crowd and crossed to the couple.

"Luke! I'm glad you made it." Colin shook his hand. "Let me introduce you to my bride." He drew the woman beside him closer and went through the formalities.

It wasn't as hard as Luke had expected to utter a few

pleasantries. Probably because they didn't look like a traditional bride and groom. Colin was in a suit, and the bride wore a fancy knee-length pale blue dress. Other than the sprig of flowers tucked into her hair and Colin's boutonniere, they could be any couple at any cocktail party.

Except . . . the love between the bride and groom was almost palpable. As it should be on a wedding day.

As it had been on his.

Swallowing past the lump in his throat, he wrapped up the conversation, snagged two pieces of cake and some paper napkins, and retreated to his table. At least talking with Stan wouldn't dredge up any painful memories.

Only the older man wasn't alone anymore.

Luke's step faltered as he approached the tucked-away spot.

A woman had joined their twosome.

Her back was to him, but he could see she was much younger than his new friend.

He gave her a quick head-to-toe. Blonde hair cut in a longish shag. A black dress with skinny straps and a low-cut draped back, the fabric molding her curves. A pair of killer legs showed off to perfection by high heels, each of which sported a small bow on the back.

So much for the safe haven he'd staked out.

Maybe he could ask one of his colleagues to deliver the cake and . . .

Stan leaned around the woman and waved him over.

Blast.

He was stuck.

But it didn't have to be for long.

He'd hand over the cake, make small talk for a minute or two, and offer some excuse to escape.

Armed with that plan, he returned to the table and set the cake and napkins in front of Stan.

"Thank you, young man. I saw the best woman wandering around and invited her to share our cozy corner."

Best woman?

He turned his attention to their new tablemate.

The front view of the thirtysomething woman was equally arresting. Intelligent blue-gray eyes. Strong chin. A tad-too-thin nose. Prominent cheekbones.

She wasn't beautiful in a classical sense. Her features didn't have perfect proportions. But her face was . . . . intriguing. Distinctive. Filled with character.

It was the kind of face that would age well. Long after the Hollywood-type beauties among her peers faded, this woman would continue to draw second looks from men.

All at once, he realized she was holding out her hand.

Uh-oh.

He must have missed Stan's introduction.

Grasping her fingers, he offered the first excuse that came to mind. "Sorry. The background noise is getting louder. Your name was . . . ?"

"Kristin Dane."

"Luke Carter." He squeezed her hand and released it. "Did I hear Stan say best woman?"

"Yes." She picked up a prosciutto-wrapped spear of asparagus. "I shared the honors of standing up for Colin with another friend. The three of us have been tight for more than twenty years." She tilted her head. "Weren't you at the wedding?"

"No. I, uh, was working a case today." Only in the morning, though. He could have attended the ceremony if he'd wanted to be there.

"Luke's a detective too, like Colin." Stan folded a napkin around the first piece of cake.

"Oh?" Curiosity sparked in her eyes. "I don't recall Colin mentioning your name."

"I'm new in town."

"That might explain it."

Stan finished wrapping the second piece of cake, stacked it on top of the first, and reached for his cane. "Well, I'll leave you to keep Kristin company while she eats. I want to go home and share this cake with my own bride of sixty-one years. A pleasure to meet you, young man."

Luke smothered a groan.

He was going to have to make more small talk after all.

"Don't worry . . . I eat fast." Amusement glinted in Kristin's irises as Stan headed toward the exit.

Whoops.

She'd picked up on his dismay.

"No need to hurry." He did his best to contain the rush of warmth to his cheeks. "I'm not staying long, but I don't have to leave yet. Shouldn't you be at a head table somewhere, though?"

"If there *was* a head table, yes. But Colin and Trish opted to keep everything simple and low-key since it was a second wedding."

"Colin's been married before?"

"No. Trish has. Her first husband was killed in a car accident a few years ago."

Ah.

That could explain why the bride had forgone the traditional white gown.

"I didn't know that. Like I said, I'm new in town."

"Hey, Kristin!"

A guy with a sprig of flowers in the lapel of his dark suit wove through the crowd toward them.

"That's the best man, Rick Jordan." She leaned closer as she shared that tidbit, and a whiff of some pleasing floral fragrance tickled his nose. "Hey, Rick." She lifted her hand in greeting and made the introductions.

"Sorry to drag you away"—the best man gave him a visual frisk as he responded to Kristin—"but Colin wants a Treehouse Gang picture."

Treehouse Gang?

Luke sent her a quizzical look, which she ignored.

"Sure." Kristin popped the last meatball in her mouth, then tipped her head back and washed it down with a long swallow of soda—giving him a perfect view of her slender, graceful throat. "It was nice meeting you." She smiled at him and picked up her tiny purse.

"Likewise."

With that, Rick grabbed her hand and led her away.

As they disappeared into the crowd, Luke released a long, slow breath and fought back a sudden wave of melancholy.

Colin and Trish had just taken vows as husband and wife.

Stan was hurrying home to spend the rest of the evening with his companion of more than six decades.

Kristin might not have been wearing a ring, but she and Rick seemed like a couple. They'd probably boogie the night away once the small dance floor was cleared of the cake.

He was alone.

And joining his coworkers at one of their tables wasn't going to ease his loneliness.

It was time to leave.

Turning his back on the happy crowd, he fled toward the exit. Pushed through the door. Pulled it closed behind him, separating himself from the festive atmosphere inside.

Chest tight, he surveyed the deserted parking lot.

No one but him and Stan had cut out early.

But you had to be in a party mood to enjoy a party, and he was nowhere close to that.

Shoulders drooping, he shoved his hands in his pockets and wandered toward his car.

Maybe his sister was right, and life would get easier eventually.

Maybe the new job and new town were just what he needed.

Maybe one of these nights coming home to an empty apartment wouldn't feel so . . . empty. And depressing.

But if things hadn't improved after three long, lonely years, he was beginning to lose hope they ever would.

2

How strange.

Kristin pulled into her usual parking spot in the alley behind WorldCraft and inspected the older model Focus next to her.

It was the same make and color as Susan's car.

But her clerk never worked on Tuesdays. She should be at her other job, as a receptionist at the health club, today.

Maybe the car wasn't hers, though.

Maybe it was a coincidence.

Fighting back a niggle of disquiet, Kristin locked her Sentra and circled around the back of the other vehicle, peering through the windows. Nothing inside offered a clue about the owner. It was clutter free.

Like Susan always kept her car.

Kristin drew in a calming lungful of the crisp spring air and continued toward the shop. If it *was* Susan's car, there must be a simple explanation. It was possible she'd left something personal inside when she closed last night and had swung by this morning to retrieve it.

At the back door, Kristin tested the knob before inserting the key.

It turned without protest.

So Susan *was* inside.

She pushed through the door, into the stockroom. "Susan?"

No response.

Her pulse picked up.

"Susan? Are you here?"

Of course she was. If the shop was unlocked, the car in the alley had to be hers.

Though why her clerk had left the back door open was a mystery. That was against the house rules.

Gripping the strap of her shoulder purse, Kristin moved through the back room toward the front of the shop.

At the door to the showroom, she hesitated . . . then twisted the knob.

The display area was shadowy, the window shades she always closed at night blocking the morning sun.

She switched on the light.

The place was empty.

But . . . this didn't make sense.

She crossed to the front door and tested the knob.

Locked.

Where on earth was Susan?

Absently, she straightened one of the candles on the monastery display, skimming the room again.

Was it possible the other woman was in the restroom in back and hadn't heard her greeting?

She retraced her steps across the shop, halting as a dark-brown, dime-sized spot on the floor registered.

As she bent to examine it, another one caught her eye, closer to the display counter that held the register.

That one was smeared.

They kind of looked like . . . dried blood.

Her breath hitched.

Had there been an accident?

Was Susan hurt?

Swallowing past her fear, she edged to the counter and eased behind it.

Oh, God!

No!

She clapped a hand over her mouth and scuttled back, stomach heaving, gaze riveted on the crumpled form behind the counter.

And the pool of congealed blood beneath it.

Gasping for air, she fumbled for the phone on the counter and tried to wrap her mind around the scene in front of her.

It wouldn't compute.

But she did know two things.

Susan was worse than hurt.

And it wasn't an accident.

. . . . .

Murder hadn't been on his agenda for this Tuesday morning.

Sipping an Americano with two extra shots of espresso, Luke pulled in behind one of the patrol cars blocking off the street in the charming, picture-perfect Kirkwood business district.

But today there was nothing Norman Rockwellish about the garish yellow police tape marking the crime scene . . . the shocked faces of customers and shopkeepers who were clustered in small groups on the sidewalk across the street, watching the drama unfold . . . or the camera crews from several area TV stations jockeying for position as reporters thrust microphones in front of anyone who would talk to them.

No wonder the Kirkwood PD had called in County to take the lead on this.

Coffee in hand, Luke slid out of his Taurus and hustled toward the cordoned-off area.

"Where's the responding officer?" He displayed his badge to the uniformed patrolman guarding the perimeter, signed the crime scene log, and ducked under the tape.

"Over by the door." The man motioned toward a woman who was talking into her radio.

"Thanks."

As Luke approached her, she ended her conversation and turned to him. "Detective Carter?"

"Yes." He read her name tag. "What do we have, Officer D'Amico?"

"Homicide for sure." She pulled out a notebook and gave him a quick briefing.

"Is the shop owner around?"

"Yes. We asked her to stick close until you arrived. The guy who runs the insurance office two doors down offered her a place to wait away from the crowds. She's kind of shaken up."

"Murder isn't pretty. I assume you alerted the ME's office?"

"They're on the way."

"Thanks." He started toward the crime scene to do a quick walk-through. Stopped. "What's the name of the owner?"

The woman consulted her notes again. "Kristin Dane."

A shock wave ripped through him.

The woman he'd shared a table with at Colin's wedding owned the murder scene?

"Is she blonde . . . thirtyish . . . slender?"

"Yes." The woman's eyebrows rose. "You know her?"

"We met on Saturday at a wedding. Small world. Thanks for the info."

He continued toward the building, trying to digest the officer's bombshell—and to psyche himself up for another encounter with the woman whose face had flashed across his mind more times in the three days since they'd met than he cared to admit.

At the door, he skimmed the "Member Fair Trade Association" sticker on the window.

Hmm.

Kristin Dane owned a shop devoted to selling products made by workers in developing countries who were fairly compensated and trying to build sustainable businesses.

Admirable.

After slipping inside, he did a quick circuit. The place wasn't large, but the variety of merchandise was. Woven scarves, jewelry, pottery, baskets, purses, clothing, napkin rings, vases, wall hangings, rugs, soap, wind chimes, wooden boxes, greeting cards . . . and more . . . filled the shelves.

Each of the displays was colorful and eye-catching, featuring an information card with photos that personalized the hand-made goods. The items were from all over the world—Africa, Asia, Central America, South America. Meticulous care had been taken to present the products in the most flattering and heart-tugging light.

He stopped at a prominent display of candles from Syria near the front door as he completed his tour. According to the sign, all profits from the pricey item went to a monastery in that war-torn country that provided humanitarian aid to anyone in need.

Impressive.

As was the woman who ran this shop.

A lot of people *talked* about helping those in need. Kristin Dane was doing it.

He gave the space one more slow, practiced perusal, then poked his head into an orderly storeroom in the rear.

Near as he could tell, nothing was disturbed back here or in the aisles in front where the merchandise was displayed.

All of the action during the assault must have taken place behind the counter.

He crossed to it and positioned himself for a clear view of the body.

The woman appeared to be lying where she'd fallen, blood pooled under her upper body. Given the amount of it, plus the spatter pattern, the assailant had cut her carotid artery. Meaning she'd bled out in minutes.

But why would someone kill a clerk in a store like this? There couldn't be that much cash in the till.

Could the perpetrator have had a personal motive?

Kristin might be able to offer some—

"Keep away from the body."

Luke jerked toward the door as Hank, one of the County's Crime Scene Unit techs, pushed through.

"I didn't touch anything."

"You're breathing, aren't you?"

Sheesh.

Each time they ran into each other, the man lived up to his cantankerous reputation. Yet everyone at County respected his every-i-dotted, every-t-crossed professionalism. The unkempt gray hair and razor-sharp tongue might be off-putting, but as Colin had warned him early on, smart detectives humored Hank.

"I was just taking a quick look around. But I'm leaving now. I'll ask one of the officers to alert me after you're finished."

"Hmph." He brushed past, surveyed the body, and set his case down. As he pulled on a pair of latex gloves, he arched an eyebrow over his shoulder.

Luke hightailed it to the door.

In his haste to escape, he almost mowed down Lacey Stevens from the medical examiner's office.

"Whoa!" She latched on to his arm to steady herself. "What's your hurry?"

"I've been ousted."

"Ah. Let me guess. That's Hank's van." She motioned toward the Crime Scene Unit vehicle at the curb, two doors down.

"Yep."

"That figures. How's his mood today?"

"Let's just say he won't win the Mr. Congeniality award. Not that he gives a hoot."

She snickered. "You pegged him fast."

"I was coached—or should I say warned?"

The wind ruffled the tight, gray-streaked ebony curls that framed her latte-hued face. "I like warned better. As in handle with care. But he's the best."

"I know. Will you email me your findings?" He hooked a thumb toward the shop.

"Soon as I have anything to report."

He moved aside and held the door open for her.

"Shut the door!" Hank barked out the command, his voice muffled.

"I'll be in touch." Lacey rolled her eyes and slipped inside.

After ditching his empty cup in a waste can at the curb, Luke continued down the sidewalk toward the insurance office where Kristin was waiting.

"Sir . . ." A reporter from one of the TV stations thrust a microphone in his face as soon as he emerged from behind the crime-scene tape. "Can you give us an update on—"

"Sorry. No comment." He kept walking.

"Are there any leads on—"

"No comment." He picked up his pace.

The reporter trailed after him for several more steps before giving up.

He continued a few more feet . . . stopped on the pretense of taking a phone call . . . then slipped into the insurance office.

A woman seated at a desk jumped to her feet as he entered, clenching her hands in front of her. "May I help you?"

"Detective Luke Carter." He flashed his badge. "I understand the owner of WorldCraft is waiting for me here."

"Yes." Relief smoothed some of the tension from her features. "This has been a very upsetting morning. I can't believe anything like this would happen here." She pulled a key from the desk and opened a door that led to the back. "She's in the conference room on the right."

"Thanks." He walked down the short hall, glancing into a large, unoccupied office on his left as he passed.

At the door to the conference room, he paused. A man with light brown hair was sitting at a rectangular table. He was angled toward Kristin, his back to the door.

Her eyes widened when she caught sight of him, and the man in the suit shot to his feet. He pivoted, posture taut.

"Are you with the police?"

The mid-thirtyish guy kept himself between Kristin and the new arrival, in a clearly protective gesture.

How many male admirers did this woman have, anyway?

A weird little spurt of annoyance juiced Luke's adrenaline.

He didn't even try to figure it out.

Instead, he pulled out his badge and ID and introduced himself.

The man gave the ID a more thorough scrutiny than most people did. At last he extended his hand. "Ryan Doud. I assume you want to speak with Kristin alone."

"Yes."

He refocused on the blonde, and his tone changed from businesslike to warm. "Would you like some more coffee?"

"No, I have plenty. Thanks, Ryan."

"I'll be in my office if you need me." With a dip of his head, he withdrew, closing the door behind him.

"Ms. Dane."

"Detective. It never occurred to me you'd be working this case."

"Luck of the draw. I was available when the call for assistance came in from Kirkwood PD." He took the seat Doud had occupied and pulled out his notebook. "You okay?"

"Yes."

That was a lie.

She was a faded facsimile of the woman he'd met Saturday night.

Her complexion had lost all its color, her eyes were glazed, her shoulders slumped, and based on the rippling java in her cup, she was shaking.

Badly.

"Tough morning."

"Yes."

The word quivered, and he had a sudden urge to cover her hand with his and assure her everything would be fine.

Pressing his lips together, he held on tight to his notebook instead. What was going on? This had *never* happened to him during an investigation.

He needed to get a grip and do his job. For all he knew, Kristin Dane could be involved in this murder—even if his gut said otherwise. "I'd like to hear your version of this morning's events." He extracted a pen.

"I already gave a statement to an officer."

"I know. She briefed me. I'd like to hear it again. Some people recall more on a second telling." Or trip themselves up if they had anything to hide.

"Okay." She set the cup down, linked her fingers on the table, and repeated what she'd told D'Amico, including the fact that she hadn't been in the shop since early afternoon on Saturday, when she'd left to get ready for the wedding, but that she'd spoken with the victim by phone at about noon yesterday.

"I'd like to ask you a few questions."

"I assumed you would."

"Tell me about Susan Collier."

A flicker of distress echoed in her irises, and her knuckles whitened. "I hired her a year ago to work with me part-time. My business is growing, and I needed another set of hands. She has a second part-time job as a receptionist at a health club."

He jotted down the name of the facility she named.

"Is she married?"

"Was. It was a bad situation. Her husband was abusive. They separated two years ago, and she filed for divorce soon after."

"Did she ever mention being afraid of her ex-husband?"

"She didn't talk much about him, but based on the few comments she made, I think she did have some initial concerns for her safety. After he moved to Denver a few months ago to take a new job, those seemed to dissipate."

"Do you know his first name?"

"Les. Do you think he might have . . . that he could have done this?"

"Acrimonious divorces can lead to some bad scenes. We'll see if he has an alibi."

"If Susan's husband isn't involved in this . . . what could the motive possibly be?"

"That's the question we'll be trying to answer. Do you keep much cash on the premises?"

"No. Never more than two or three hundred dollars. Most people pay with plastic. And none of my merchandise is that valuable. Nothing I stock is worth stealing—or killing for." Her eyes misted. "I can't understand why someone would do this."

Neither could he—assuming the ex was clean.

Druggies desperate for a fix could—and did—kill for far less than two hundred bucks . . . but this neighborhood wasn't where that kind of crime usually happened.

"After the medical examiner and CSU tech finish at your

shop, you can see if anything is missing . . . in case robbery *was* a motive."

"When might that be?"

"The ME's office will be done within an hour. CSU could be a while. The guy working the scene is methodical. Are there security cameras on the premises?"

"No."

"I'll see if any of the nearby businesses have one. If they do, it's possible we'll find an image that's helpful. I'll also need a list of customers who bought items in the shop yesterday. Can you provide that?"

"Yes . . . for anyone who paid by credit card or check. I can't help you with cash customers. And we get a fair number of browsers who don't buy anything."

"Understood." He cleared his throat. His next question was standard in this situation, but for whatever reason it was difficult to ask today. "Can you give me a rundown on where you were yesterday?"

A beat passed as she scrutinized him. "You mean . . . like an alibi?"

"We have to cover all the bases."

"Right. I get that." She took a deep breath. "I was at a seminar all day, and afterward I went to dinner with some of the other people who attended. I left the restaurant about nine. I have their business cards if you'd like me to text you their contact information."

"That would be helpful." He continued to write as she provided the location of the seminar and the name of the restaurant. "Did the victim have any children or next of kin we need to notify?"

"She has a sister in Chicago. That's the only relative she ever mentioned—and I don't think they were close. She did give me her sister's cell number in case there was ever an emergency, though." Kristin scrolled through her contacts and recited the information.

"We'll see that she's informed ASAP." He closed his notebook. "It could be several hours before we finish in the shop. There's no need for you to hang around. I can call you as soon as it's clear to come back and we can do a walk-through together. In the meantime, we'll talk with some of the neighboring businesses, see if they noticed anyone or anything suspicious. I'll walk you to your car." He stood.

"Thanks. I'm parked in the b-back."

She rose as he opened the conference room door, splaying her fingers on the table when she swayed.

Driving might not be the best idea.

"Is there a friend you could call who would give you a ride home?"

"I'm fine. I wouldn't want to bother anyone in the middle of the . . ."

Ryan materialized at Luke's elbow. "I'd be glad to run you home, Kristin. It's not that far, and I don't have any appointments until this afternoon."

"I don't want to impose."

"I'm happy to do it."

Luke studied the man. He must be more than a business neighbor if he knew where Kristin lived.

For some reason, that didn't sit well.

Yet he couldn't fault the man's manners—and he'd prefer Kristin not drive. She was still too shaky.

Too bad he couldn't offer to chauffeur her himself.

But there was work to be done here.

Lots of it.

"It's not a bad idea." Luke kept his tone conversational, masking his illogical annoyance at the other man's offer. "I can pick you up later, once we're ready for you at the shop."

She hesitated, but only for an instant—telling Luke she was smart enough to recognize her own limitations.

"Thanks. I appreciate that."

"I'll walk out with you in case any media types are lurking around in the back." He stepped aside to let Kristin pass, narrowing his eyes as Ryan took her arm and guided her toward the rear door, leaving him to fall in behind.

Luck was on their side. No one was in the alley, and the two of them were able to escape without attracting attention.

Luke waited until the car pulled out onto the street at the end of the alley before turning away.

He had people to interview, calls to make, reinforcements to bring in to help canvass the area.

But much as he thrived on the challenges of his job—and despite the fact he'd met Kristin only three days ago—for some odd reason he'd rather be taking her home right now than investigating this murder.

3

How was she ever going to return to the shop she'd poured her heart into for five years without picturing Susan's body behind the counter?

Fingers wrapped around her mug, Kristin took a sip of her tepid tea and slid onto a stool at the kitchen island. Played with a piece of lettuce poking out of the turkey sandwich she'd made after her stomach reminded her it was closer to dinnertime than the lunch hour. Shoved the plate aside.

She needed to eat, but the day's events were twisting her insides into knots—as was the thought of returning to the shop.

Rising again, she resumed the restless pacing that had filled her day. When did the police expect her to do the walk-through Detective Carter had mentioned, anyway? It was already four forty-five. Going in daylight would be bad enough. But returning at night, even with all the lights on, even with the detective by her side?

Ugh.

And why hadn't he called to give her an update? He came across as a buttoned-up kind of guy. Efficient, professional, focused.

Maybe another hot case had called him away.

Or he might have decided to call it a night and head home to the wife—and perhaps family—the wedding band on his left hand indicated he had.

Yeah, yeah, she'd noticed the ring on Saturday night . . . after those dark green eyes, with their hint of sadness, had sucked her in. Not to mention the tall, toned physique, brown hair that looked like it would be oh-so-soft to touch, strong jaw, deep voice with a hint of . . .

A musical chime echoed through the condo and she jerked, sloshing the pale liquid in her mug.

Who would be at her door at this hour of the afternoon?

Heart hammering, she set the mug on the counter. Had one of the reporters who'd called the condo decided to track her down in person?

Rubbing her icy hands together, she tiptoed to the door and peeked through the skylight.

The man on her doorstep wasn't a reporter after all.

It was Rick.

Relief surging through her, she pulled the door open. "What are you doing here?"

"What do you think I'm doing here? And hello to you too." He walked in, juggling a large Panera bag in one hand and a tray with two drinks in the other. He set everything on the table in her foyer, closed her front door, and pulled her into a hug. "I'd have come right after you called if I wasn't in the middle of a slight emergency at the camp. How are you holding up?"

Tears pricked her eyelids, and she gave him a squeeze. "I've had better days."

"I bet."

He didn't release her until she edged back. Even then, he grasped her upper arms and kept her close while he gave her a critical appraisal. "You haven't eaten anything since breakfast, have you?"

"I made a sandwich. What kind of emergency did you have?"

"You're evading my question. Made and eaten are two different things. Which means you haven't had any food. I brought dinner."

She looked at the man who was closer to her than any brother could ever be, and her vision blurred. What would she have done without him and Colin for the past twenty-plus years? Her parents might say they loved her, but her friends were the ones who'd always been there for her.

"I didn't expect you to drive all the way in. I only called so you wouldn't hear about this on the news."

"I don't live *that* far out. And you'd have been in big trouble if I *did* hear about it on the news. Remember—all for one and one for—"

Her bell chimed again.

She cringed. "I hope that's not a reporter." She swiveled around and peeked through the peephole again.

Detective Carter stood on the other side.

Huh.

She hadn't expected him to show up without calling first.

"You want me to handle this?" Rick draped a protective arm around her shoulders.

"No need. It's the case detective. You met him at the wedding on Saturday. I'm supposed to go back to the shop and do a walk-through, see if I notice anything missing or out of the ordinary."

"Not until you eat." He tightened his grip.

She twisted the knob and pulled the door open.

The detective looked from her to Rick. Recognition dawned in his eyes, and he gave the other man a brief nod before his gaze flicked to the arm around her shoulders and returned to her face.

"Sorry to interrupt. I was passing this way and decided to stop by with an update rather than call."

His words sounded a bit stiff. Like he was miffed. Or more likely just tired. The man had no doubt had a long day.

"Would you like to come in?" Kristin backed up.

"Not necessary. The CSU tech needed longer than expected, and we were busy with interviews this afternoon. Rather than go back tonight, why don't I pick you up in the morning? Unless you have another ride?" He glanced at Rick.

"No. Rick lives too far out. I don't expect him to come back into town in the morning to be my chauffeur."

His expression shifted subtly. Kristin couldn't quite identify the emotion, but it almost seemed like . . . relief?

No. That was absurd.

"I'll come by at eight o'clock, if that's not too early."

"That's fine. I'm an early riser. Thanks for stopping in."

He dipped his chin, turned on his heel, and retreated down the curving walk that led from her condo to the parking lot.

"Not the most sociable guy." Rick reached around her and closed the door.

"I suppose dealing with murder and mayhem every day can do that to a man."

"I guess. He wasn't too happy to see me here, either."

"Why would he care about that?" Kristin followed as he picked up their dinner and carried it toward the café table in her kitchen. "And how did you come to such an off-the-wall conclusion, anyway?"

"It's a guy thing."

"Oh, please."

"It is. Ask Colin."

"He'd side with you. He always does about that kind of stuff. Besides, he's not available."

"You should call and let him know what's going on."

"Are you nuts? He's on his honeymoon!"

"You want me to call?" He paused beside the counter to examine her uneaten turkey sandwich, shook his head, and continued to the table with their dinner.

"No! I do not want you to interrupt his honeymoon. Promise me you won't."

"He'll be mad when he finds out you kept him in the dark."

"I'll deal with it. Promise."

"Fine." He sat and motioned to the chair on the other side of the table. "I'm hungry. Let's eat."

She covered the sandwich with some plastic wrap and joined him. He bowed his head while she said a blessing, then dived in.

"You weren't kidding about being hungry." She took a sip of soda.

"I missed lunch."

"Because of your emergency?"

"Yeah." He tapped the box containing her sandwich, waited until she opened it and took a bite, then spent the next fifteen minutes regaling her with a hilarious story about the antics of one of the kids who'd come out for a day camp and promptly wedged himself between two trees.

"As a last resort, we lubricated the trees with a ton of vegetable shortening. It worked, but his clothes were a total loss and he had to stand under a hot shower for thirty minutes to get all the grease off. Pardon the pun, but he was not a happy camper."

By the time he finished, Kristin had eaten most of her sandwich and all of her chips. He'd even managed to elicit a few chuckles.

"You missed your calling, you know. You should have been a stand-up comic."

"I'd rather make people I care about laugh. So . . ." He closed his empty box and grew more serious. "Now that you have some food in your stomach, do you want to talk about what happened today?"

"There isn't much to talk about." She repeated the story she'd told twice already. "I don't know what's been happening since the police whisked me out of the shop."

He covered her fingers with his. "I'm sorry."

That was all he said—but those two words held a world of compassion.

"Me too. Especially for Susan." Her voice hitched, and she took another drink of soda.

"Did the police speculate on a motive?"

"They're going to check out her ex, but I don't think that will amount to anything. He's in Denver."

"What else could it be?"

"I haven't a clue."

He gathered up their empty containers, creases denting his brow. "Are you comfortable staying here by yourself tonight?"

She shot him a startled look. "Why wouldn't I be?"

"I don't know. It just seems odd that your shop was targeted. The jewelry store down the street would have yielded a much bigger payoff."

"Assuming robbery was the motive."

"That's what I mean."

She digested that for a moment. "Are you suggesting this was somehow personal to me?"

"I'm speculating, not suggesting."

"But Susan is . . . she's the one who died."

"She wasn't supposed to be there Monday afternoon, though—right?"

Kristin crumpled her napkin into a hard ball, her dinner congealing in her stomach. "Are you trying to scare me?"

"No. Trying to come up with some theories about what's going on."

"I don't have any enemies."

"I know. Your detective has his work cut out for him." He swirled the ice in his cup. "Did he say anything to you about being careful?"

"No."

The tautness in his features relaxed a hair. "That makes me feel better."

"Why?"

"Because he likes you—and if there was any reason to be concerned about your safety, I think he would have suggested you be cautious."

She choked on her sip of soda. "Wait a minute. Back up. What do you mean, he likes me?"

"You heard me. He likes you."

"That's crazy. He's married."

"How do you know?"

"He's wearing a ring."

"Ah-ha. You checked. And you always claim women are above that."

"It's a distinctive ring. Hard to miss." True—but not the reason she'd noticed. A confession she had no intention of sharing with Rick, despite his best-bud status.

"Married or not, he likes you."

"How in the world did you arrive at that preposterous conclusion?"

"It's all in the eyes." He tapped the side of one of his baby blues. "They warm up when he looks at you."

"I think your lemonade was spiked."

"Nope. I noticed it at the wedding, and again tonight."

"Oh, come on." She didn't attempt to hide her skepticism. "You've spent all of . . . what? Two minutes in the man's company? You're reading far more into whatever you're seeing than is there."

"Think so?" He stood and deposited the trash from their dinner in her waste can.

"Yeah."

"Then why did he seem relieved to hear I wasn't spending the night with you?"

Maybe she hadn't imagined the detective's reaction, if Rick had picked up on it too.

"You're being ridiculous."

"Nope. I'd bet you on it, but I don't want to take your money."

She stood too. "I'm done with this discussion."

"You're blushing, you know."

"I am not." Yes, she was. Her cheeks were hot.

"If you say so." He grinned and strolled toward the door. She followed.

When he turned back to her, though, his demeanor was again serious. "Call if you want to talk. Or if you decide you'd rather not be here alone tonight."

"I'll be fine, Rick. But I appreciate the thought—and the dinner."

"Anytime. Call me tomorrow?"

"Yes."

After another hug, he followed the same curving path to his car that Detective Carter had taken.

She waited until he pulled away with a wave out his window, then shut and locked the door.

Truth be told, she wouldn't have minded some company tonight. But Rick led a busy life, and he had a long drive home.

Besides, much as she loved him, she'd prefer a different kind of company this evening.

Like a tall, handsome detective—who was *not* named Colin.

Too bad her detective buddy wasn't around, though, so she could ask a few questions about his new colleague.

Not that it mattered, of course.

A man who wore a wedding ring was either married or sending a "not available" signal.

In other words, he was off-limits.

Which was one more downer on this mother-of-all-downers day.

4

Luke pulled into a parking spot in front of Kristin's condo, straightened his tie, and checked the clock on the dash.

Eight o'clock on the dot.

Unless he'd misread her, Kristin was waiting for him. She struck him as the reliable type—among her other appealing attributes . . . some of which had kept him awake last night until the wee hours as images of her flashed across the dark ceiling in his bedroom.

Especially after her alibi checked out and he'd crossed her off his list of potential suspects.

Clenching his jaw, he shifted in the seat and resisted the urge to loosen his tie.

How could a virtual stranger have such a potent effect on him after three years of immunity to the opposite sex?

Perhaps meeting her at a wedding, with all the emotions that sort of event stirred up, was the reason she'd stuck in his mind.

But that didn't explain why he'd gone out of his way last night to deliver a case update in person instead of calling her.

No, that decision had been prompted by a whole different motive . . . and dancing around the truth wasn't going to change it.

He'd wanted to see Kristin Dane for one reason and one reason only.

He was attracted to her.

And that felt wrong, wrong, wrong.

Jenny might be gone, but no one could ever take her place in his heart.

He wouldn't let them.

In any case, whatever the explanation for why she'd caught his fancy, Kristin was a temporary occupant in his life. After this case was over, he'd have no reason to see her again.

A notion that did *not* give him the comfort he'd hoped for.

In his peripheral vision he caught a movement, and he twisted his head toward her front door.

Kristin had emerged from her condo and was locking her door.

Yep. She'd been watching for him.

Quashing the unsettling thoughts that were undermining the tight grip he usually kept on his emotions, he got out of his car.

She was already halfway down the walk before he finished circling the hood.

"I saw your car. When you didn't ring the bell, I figured you might be waiting for me to come out or were on the phone. I decided to save you a trip." Her long legs ate up the distance between them.

"I appreciate that." He leaned past her to open the passenger door, again inhaling the pleasing floral fragrance that was distinctively hers.

"Is there any news?"

"If you mean do we have a suspect, no. I'll fill you in on the rest during the drive."

She tucked herself into the seat in one smooth, lithe motion, and he shut the door.

As he took his place behind the wheel, he gave her a discreet perusal. Her skinny-leg jeans, soft wool sweater, and leather flats were more laid-back than the striking best-woman number and bow-bedecked heels she'd worn Saturday—or the skirt and soft top she'd had on yesterday—but the casual attire didn't cause the slightest dip in her appeal meter.

Unfortunately.

"I accessed the shop records on my laptop last night." She dug through her large shoulder bag and retrieved a single sheet of paper. "I pulled up the credit card transactions from Monday, if you still need them."

"I do. Thanks." He searched her face as she handed him the list.

She hadn't slept well.

It didn't take a detective to deduce that the faint purple shadows under her lower lashes, the tiny lines at the outer corners of her eyes, and the slight pallor she'd tried to disguise with makeup were all signs of a restless night.

Kind of like the one he'd had.

For very different reasons.

"Do you mind if we hit a Starbucks drive-through? I could use some caffeine." He pocketed the list and put the car in gear. It wouldn't kill him to have another cup of coffee this morning if she needed some caffeine.

"I've already had more than my daily limit. But I wouldn't object to some hot chocolate. A comfort beverage would hit the spot."

Before I have to revisit the murder scene.

She didn't need to say it for him to hear the rest of her unspoken message.

"One hot chocolate coming up. What time did you begin ingesting caffeine this morning?" He kept the question conversational as he pulled out of the parking spot.

"Early."

So not only had she had a restless night, she'd also been up at dawn.

"Finding a murder victim is traumatic—especially if you know the person. It's not easy to sleep after an experience like that."

"No." She played with the clasp on her purse. "You know, much as I love my shop, I keep wondering how I can go back there and do business as usual. I keep seeing all that blood . . ." Her voice trailed off.

"It can be removed. I brought along the names of a few cleanup and mitigation services the Crime Scene Unit has on file."

"Can they mitigate memories too?"

At her soft, rhetorical question, he squeezed the wheel.

If there were firms that could work that miracle, he'd have hired one long ago.

"No. But time will—or so I'm told." His voice roughened, and he felt her glance over at him. Better redirect the conversation. "Let me bring you up to speed on what we've learned. The ME has estimated time of death in the 5:00–7:00 p.m. range Monday night."

"Around closing." Her brow pleated. "I wonder if that means someone was waiting around for her to lock up for the night."

"It could. And it wasn't her ex. The Denver police tracked him down. He was on a plane returning from a business trip at the time of death."

"Did my neighbors see anything?"

"No—and none of the ones in close proximity have security cameras."

"So there are no leads and no motive."

"Yet. But we're working on finding both."

"Was there any money in the register?"

"Yes—and the victim's purse and wallet didn't appear to be touched."

"So robbery wasn't the reason behind this."

"That would be a reasonable conclusion." He swung into a Starbucks, and she fell silent while he placed the order and drove to the window to retrieve their drinks.

When she reached for her purse, he shook his head. "I'll get this."

"I can pay for my own."

"It was my idea." He handed the woman in the window his gold card and passed Kristin the hot chocolate.

Once clear of the drive-through, he looked over at his passenger. She was staring out the front window, expression pensive, furrows denting her brow.

She was dreading the next half hour—and he couldn't blame her.

As if sensing his scrutiny, she turned toward him. "Sorry. I'm not much company this morning."

"I didn't expect you to be."

She played with the lid on her drink. "It's just . . . I'm confused about everything that's happened. Why was my shop targeted? Why kill someone for no apparent reason? Who could have done this? For what purpose?" She sighed. "The questions keep coming."

"Most cases start off with more questions than answers. It's like putting together a puzzle."

"But you have to have pieces to work with to do that."

"They're there. It's our job to find them. The walk-through might give us a few. You know the shop better than anyone. If anything is missing or out of place, you'll spot it. Tell me about WorldCraft." Maybe talking about the work that appeared to be her passion would help her relax a little.

"I opened it five years ago. The idea for it came to me while I was in the Peace Corps."

"You were in the Peace Corps?" His basic background check hadn't revealed that nugget.

"Yes. I double-majored in business and public policy in college, but since I wasn't certain what to do with those degrees after I graduated, I joined the Peace Corps and went to Ethiopia for two years."

"Ethiopia." And he'd thought relocating from Virginia to St. Louis was a major move. "That must have been a culture shock."

"Yes . . . but it was also one of my best decisions. My stint there made me realize how important it is to foster community economic development that's fair to workers. By the time I came home, I knew what I wanted to do with my life." She sipped her drink.

"WorldCraft."

"That was my ultimate goal—but I needed some hands-on retail experience first, so I worked a few years for an import company. After I saved enough money and learned how to run a business, I opened my own shop." She swiped at a speck of whipped cream clinging to the sip spout of her drink. "It may not make a huge difference in the big scheme of things, but it's my little contribution to the world."

"It's bigger than most people make."

Way bigger.

The character he'd noticed in Kristin's face the night they'd met was clearly more than skin deep.

He swung into the alley behind her shop, and the tension in the car shot up.

So much for trying to take the edge off the walk-through.

But he'd do everything he could to lessen the trauma as much as possible for her.

The police tape had been removed from the premises, and the media was nowhere in sight.

That helped.

"Sit tight. I'll get your door." He set the brake and slid out of the car.

She waited as he'd asked—and even after he opened the door, she remained in her seat.

"We'll do this as fast as we can."

"Okay." She inhaled, grasped the edge of the doorframe, and pulled herself out of the car.

He took her arm as they walked toward the rear entrance of the shop. "What I need you to do is eyeball the shop—the merchandise, your desk, the stockroom—for anything that's out of place or missing. We'll start in the back." He halted at the door. "Let me know when you're ready."

▪ ▪ ▪ ▪ ▪

Ready?

Kristin squeezed the shop key until her fingers began to grow numb.

Was he joking?

How could anyone ever be ready to revisit a murder scene?

But as she'd learned long ago, there was no sense delaying the inevitable.

"Okay. Let's do this." She leaned forward to insert the key—and promptly dropped it.

Not surprising, given the tremors in her fingers.

"Let me." Detective Carter scooped up the key and slid it into the lock.

Instead of stepping back to let her precede him, he entered, felt around for a switch, and turned on the lights. After a quick sweep of the room, he angled back to her and held out the key.

She slid it into her purse and joined him, taking a visual inventory of the stockroom.

Back here at least, everything seemed normal.

On the surface, anyway.

"Go ahead and poke around. Take your time." His tone was

conversational, his posture relaxed, as if he was attempting to put her at ease.

Nice try—but not going to happen on this visit.

She did a methodical circuit of the room, inspecting all the shelves, then riffled through the drawers in her desk.

Closing the last one, she faced him. "As far as I can see, everything back here is exactly the way I left it on Saturday."

"Let's move up front."

He took the lead again, opening the door between the two sections of the store and flipping on the light. "Give me a minute."

Without waiting for a response, he slipped through the door, shutting it behind him.

As far as she was concerned, he could take an hour.

All too soon, though, he was back. "Do a circuit through the aisles. I'll wait for you by the cash register."

The very spot she didn't want to visit.

She forced herself to walk through the door, ignoring the right side of the shop, and did as he asked, examining the displays, stretching out the process as long as she could.

But at last, she could delay no longer.

Steeling herself, she walked toward him.

Luke had positioned himself to block her view of the register area as much as possible—but once she drew close . . . once the blood spatters on the wall behind him came into sight . . . her stomach heaved.

He took a step forward and grasped her arms. "Keep breathing."

She did her best to follow his instruction, focusing on the broad chest inches away that filled her field of vision.

As soon as she was certain she wasn't going to lose the bagel she'd choked down for breakfast, she nodded. "I'm fine."

He waited another few moments before releasing her arms. "Anything out of place or missing in the store?"

"No."

"Take a quick look at the items in the display case. As far as we can see, it's undisturbed—but you're the only one who can confirm that."

One fast skim of the glass case was all she needed. She knew every item in her store and every item in inventory by heart.

"Nothing is missing or moved." Through the glass case she could see the floor where Susan had fallen. It was covered now with a tarp that was draped partway up the wall, hiding much of the gore.

Standard operating practice by the CSU—or a thoughtful gesture on the part of the case detective?

It shouldn't matter.

But it did.

"Did you do that?" She motioned toward the tarp, averting her gaze.

"It wasn't a sight you needed to see again. As far as I'm concerned, we're finished here." He indicated the stockroom. "Shall we?"

He might be willing to dismiss his kind deed, but she wasn't.

"Thank you."

"No problem." He extracted a sheet of paper from his pocket and handed it to her. "Those are the mitigation companies I mentioned in the car."

"Thanks." She tucked the paper in her purse and pulled out the small "reopening soon" sign she'd printed off last night at home, along with a roll of tape. "Give me a minute to put this in the window."

He waited while she raised the shades to secure the sign. After finishing that task, she paused at the table of candles from the monastery to straighten a few.

"I noticed the high price point on those." Luke joined her. "Do you sell many?"

"Yes. People don't mind opening their wallets when they know all proceeds will go to humanitarian aid."

"How did you connect with such a remote place?"

"Brother Michael came and spoke at our church about three years ago." She pointed out the smiling monk in the group photo taken at the monastery. "He was traveling around the country while he was back in the US visiting family, soliciting donations."

"He's American?"

"Yes. The monastery has drawn people from all over the world. The US, Europe, South America. It's a small group, but they do wonderful work. Brother Michael was an amazing man."

"Was?"

Of course he'd pick up on the past tense. She'd wager not much got past this man.

"He died several weeks ago." She told him the sad tale. "It's kind of ironic. I was always afraid he would end up being a victim of violence—yet violence ended up striking closer to home." She flicked a quick glance toward the register area again and suppressed a shiver.

"Unfortunately, it's part of the world we live in. Nowhere is 100 percent safe. Ready to go?"

"More than." She hurried toward the back room, keeping her face forward.

He didn't speak again until they exited into the sunlight and she locked the door.

"We notified the victim's sister, and she's making arrangements to have the body transported to Chicago for burial after it's released from the ME's office."

"Did you get an address?" She dropped the key in her purse as they walked toward her car. "I'd like to send her a note."

"Yes. I can email it to you if you'd like."

"Thanks."

"You're free to begin cleanup and open the shop as soon as you want to. We're finished here—but I may be in touch as the investigation progresses should we need any additional information." He pulled out a card and handed it to her. "If anything else comes up, or you want to speak to me for any reason, call my cell. I answer day or night."

"Not a nine-to-five job." She stopped beside her car and fingered the card.

"Nowhere near. But I knew what to expect when I signed on."

"You sound like Colin. He always says if you're not willing to be available 24/7 for the cause of justice, you don't belong in law enforcement."

"That's true." Luke propped a hip against the hood of her car. If he was in a hurry to leave or had other places to go, he gave no indication of it.

But she shouldn't detain him. He had work to do, and delaying him just because she found his presence comforting was selfish.

"Well . . ." She unlocked her car. "I'll get working on the mitigation."

He hesitated . . . then pushed off from the hood. "Once I have some definite news about the case, I'll give you a call."

"Thanks."

He pulled the door open for her, and she took her place behind the wheel. A second later, he closed it.

Luke remained where he was while she backed out of her parking spot, drove down the alley, and pulled onto the street.

After she turned the corner, however, she lost sight of him.

And that was for the best.

Men who wore wedding rings were off-limits. Period.

Besides, despite Rick's take, the man had no interest in her even if he did happen to be available. After all, he hadn't wanted to linger at the reception once Stan deserted them, had he? And Detective Luke Carter appeared to be integrity personified. He might be kind and empathetic with people who'd discovered a dead body, but that was business. There was nothing personal about it.

End of story.

Someday, if it was meant to be, she'd meet an available man who would win her heart.

In the meantime, though, she needed to forget about the tall, handsome police investigator who'd awakened longings in her that were best kept under wraps until the right man came along.

· · · · ·

The vibrating phone was not a good sign.

Pulse leaping, Darrak pulled out his cell.

Caller ID was blocked.

Meaning Amir was still trying to contact him from his latest burner phone.

He muttered a curse and began to sweat.

If he continued to ignore the calls, Amir would get suspicious. Better to talk to him and play dumb. Act like everything was cool. Because it would be. Soon.

Whatever it took.

Hunkering down in his car, he kept one eye on the house across the street, pressed the talk button, and said hello.

"Why haven't you been answering your phone?" Amir's barked-out question took the place of a greeting. "I've been trying to reach you since yesterday."

"I haven't been in a position to talk."

"Why?"

"Too many people around whenever you called. And I didn't have a signal last night."

Silence.

Beads of sweat popped out on his forehead as the seconds ticked by.

"There was trouble at the shop you visited."

Darrak exhaled. Amir must have believed the excuse he'd just given for not taking his calls.

"What kind of trouble? Everything was fine when I was there yesterday."

"What time was that?"

"Mid-morning." He wished. If he'd gotten there when he intended instead of waiting until late afternoon, he wouldn't be in this mess.

"You had nothing to do with the murder?"

"What murder?" A drop of sweat trickled down Darrak's temple, and he swiped it away with his sleeve.

Several beats ticked by before Amir responded. "Don't lie to me, Darrak."

"I'm not lying."

"I hope not. I despise liars."

"I have no reason to lie."

"Then you secured the merchandise?"

"Yes."

"I have delivery instructions for you."

Darrak pulled out a pen and piece of paper. "Ready."

He wrote as Amir gave him the directions, hoping he could read his own shaky writing later. There could be no more missteps.

"Is everything clear?" Hostility continued to score Amir's words.

"Yes."

"After I have confirmation of delivery, I will see that you are reimbursed for your expenses."

The line went dead.

Darrak let out a slow breath and pressed the end button.

He should never have taken this job.

Yes, it was important to the cause. And yes, he'd been honored to be tapped by someone of Amir's standing to assist.

But he'd also been warned that the man didn't tolerate mistakes.

And this whole assignment had gone wrong from the beginning.

He surveyed the house again, sweat soaking through his shirt. He still had a chance to fix this. Compared to what he'd had to do at the shop, this should be a piece of cake—as long as he timed it right. As long as he waited until the house was empty. As long as . . .

A car began to back down the driveway, and he slumped lower behind the wheel, pulling his baseball cap down over his forehead and adjusting his dark glasses.

This might be his window.

As the car rolled past him, he studied the woman behind the wheel.

Yes!

She matched the photo he'd found online.

If all went well, he should be finished with this in less than half an hour and could make Amir's delivery with no delay.

As soon as the car rounded the corner at the end of the street, he gave the neighborhood one more thorough inspection. No one was tending a garden or walking a dog.

Excellent.

He retrieved the hard hat from the back seat and slipped on the jacket that could pass for a utility serviceman's uniform.

Clipboard in hand, he slid out of the car and hurried toward the side of the house. He shouldn't have to contend with a dog or an alarm system. His reconnaissance over the past thirty-six hours suggested the woman didn't have either.

So if all went as he expected, he'd get in, do what he had to do, and get out—leaving behind no evidence of the task he'd come to complete . . . or its connection to the murder at WorldCraft.

5

Done.

From the stockroom door, Kristin gave the WorldCraft checkout counter one final slow scan.

The mitigation firm had done a stellar job—and in less than twenty-four hours after she'd called them too. But as the technician had warned her, the walls needed to be repainted, and a section of the flooring would have to be replaced. She'd need a new display cabinet too.

Some stains didn't come out.

Yet the carpenter who'd left ten minutes ago had assured her he could have all the necessary work done by end of day Friday—including relocating the display cabinet and register farther down the wall so she wouldn't have to linger in the spot where Susan had died.

Now that she'd moved the merchandise out of his way, she could go home and—

Rap, rap, rap.

She jerked toward the front door.

Why would anyone knock with a closed sign in the window?

Skirting a display table, she crossed back to the front of the shop and peeked around the shade.

Brow smoothing, she unlocked the door and smiled at her neighbor. "Hi, Ryan."

"Hi. I just got back from a meeting and noticed your car in the alley. I tried knocking on the rear door, but you didn't answer."

"Sorry. I've been up front. I didn't hear you." She gestured toward the interior. "I'm going to have the carpenter reposition the display case while he's here doing repairs, and I needed to clear the area of merchandise."

"I would have been happy to lend a hand."

"I appreciate that—but it didn't take long, and nothing was very heavy."

"So how are you doing?" Concern softened his features.

"Hanging in."

"I guess that's about the best you can hope for in a situation like this." He shook his head. "I never expected anything like this to happen in Kirkwood."

"That makes two of us."

"Do the police have any leads?"

"Not that I've heard. It wasn't Susan's ex, though. His alibi is solid."

"It's unsettling to think whoever did this is still on the loose."

"I know."

"Well . . . if I can do anything at all to help in the next few days or after you open again, let me know."

"I will. Thank you."

He twisted his wrist to display the face of his watch. "Could I interest you in a cup of coffee? I have half an hour before my next meeting."

She shifted her weight. Sociable as Ryan was, she did *not* want to encourage any personal interest . . . not that he had any. He might pop into the shop on a regular basis, but if he hadn't asked her out on a real date in the almost three years they'd been neighbors, she was probably safe.

"I appreciate the offer, but I have a long list of chores to take care of today."

"Understood. When are you reopening?"

"Saturday, I hope."

"I'll see you then. Take care."

As he strolled back to his office, she locked the door and retraced her steps through the shop to the back exit.

Stepping into the sunlight, she took a deep breath to clear the antiseptic-laced air from her lungs. Hopefully the new-paint smell would help disguise the odor permeating the shop. She could always prop the front door open on Saturday too, and burn some aromatic candles.

In time, WorldCraft would smell normal again.

But would it ever *feel* normal again?

Hard to say.

Sighing, she got into the Sentra, started the engine, and drove down the alley. She did need to run some errands, but there was no hurry. She had an open day and a half to take care of the mundane business of grocery shopping, getting an oil change, running to the post office . . . all the chores she typically crammed into her schedule during her limited leisure hours.

Maybe slowing her usual pace would help her chill.

Keeping one hand on the wheel, she flipped on the radio with the other. A bit of mellow music couldn't hurt, either.

She surfed until she found some soft jazz, and in the five minutes it took to drive to her favorite sandwich shop, the music had worked its magic.

The popular place was packed at the noon hour, and she surveyed the small in-store dining area while she waited. Every table was taken.

Oh, well. She'd eaten in her car before, and the weather was warm today—

An image of a woman flashed on the TV screen high on the wall in the dining alcove, and she froze.

Was that . . . Elaine Peterson?

A moment later the woman's name scrolled across the bottom of the screen, confirming her identity.

Why was one of her regular customers on the noon news?

The volume was low, but based on the footage of police cars blocking a suburban street and small clusters of people on nearby lawns, something bad had happened.

Relinquishing her place in line, Kristin hurried over to the screen so she could hear the announcer.

". . . discovered after a friend called the police when the victim didn't keep a breakfast engagement. Authorities aren't speculating about a motive, but the death has been classified a homicide. We'll keep you apprised of new developments as they occur. In other news . . ."

Kristin tuned out the announcer and stared at the screen.

She'd just thought about Elaine on Tuesday night, after she printed out the list of customers who'd made purchases in the shop on Monday.

Because Elaine had been among them.

What a bizarre coincidence.

Or . . . was it?

Could the deaths be related?

No.

Impossible.

Susan and Elaine weren't well acquainted. Her part-time clerk hadn't often been in the shop during Elaine's visits.

Yet the back-to-back murders felt like more than a fluke.

Her stomach tightened, and she squeezed the strap of her purse.

What would Luke Carter make of this strange development? Should she alert him to the connection?

Kristin hesitated for only a second. Then, with one final glance at the growing line in front of the order counter, she pulled out her phone and left the store.

There might not be any correlation between the two deaths—but better to let an expert weigh in on that.

And pray that no one else associated with her place of business met an untimely end.

. . . . .

Kristin Dane was calling him.

As Luke read the name on the screen of his cell, his mouth flexed up.

"You need to take that—or can it wait?"

At the impatient question from Cole Taylor, he flattened his lips. "Case related."

His colleague narrowed his eyes. "Then why were you smiling?"

The man was living up to his ace-detective reputation.

"Not important. I'll be with you in a minute."

"Fine."

He turned his back on the other man—and the crime scene they were examining—and gave his full attention to the woman on the other end of the line.

"Ms. Dane. How can I help you?"

"I have some information that might or might not be relevant to Susan's murder. I thought I'd let you make that call."

"Okay. I'm listening."

By the time she finished, every instinct in his body was on red alert.

Yes, it was possible the two murders were unrelated.

But true coincidences were rare—especially if they occurred this close together.

"Are you able to determine what Elaine Peterson bought at the store on Monday?"

"Yes. She used a credit card, and those sales receipts list the items purchased. As soon as I get home, I can call hers up on my computer. Is that important?"

"I don't know—but at this stage, I'm not discounting anything." A police radio crackled to life behind him.

"You sound busy."

"As a matter of fact, I'm at the Peterson crime scene now."

"Are you working that case too?"

"Assisting, not taking the lead. I just arrived—and I'll be here for a while."

"I'll be home within twenty minutes. Expect to hear from me in less than half an hour."

"In the meantime, I'll poke around here, see if I can find anything that raises a red flag in connection with the other homicide. Do you know if the two victims were acquainted?"

"Only through their interactions at the shop—and I doubt they met there more than twice." Kristin exhaled. "I know the timing is odd, but I can't imagine how the two deaths could be related."

"I can't either—but I've seen stranger links in this job." Cole shot him a can-we-get-on-with-this look, and Luke rejoined the man. "I'll wait to hear from you about the receipt." He slid the phone back on his belt.

"Are you sure that was case related?" Cole's razor-sharp gaze drilled into him.

"Yes. Why?"

"It seemed kind of . . . personal."

He'd better work on his poker face if his colleague was picking up on his interest in Kristin.

"I have no idea what you're talking about. But that call may have some bearing on this case. You want to hear about it?"

"Yeah."

Cole listened in silence while Luke brought him up to speed on Kristin's news.

"She's going to call me after she finds the receipt." As he finished, the parallel creases denting the other man's brow deepened.

"While you wait to hear back from her, let's nose around. Why don't you take the upper level, and I'll go through the first floor?"

"You got it."

Luke ascended the stairs and began a methodical sweep of the three bedrooms in the spacious Cape Cod house.

He found two things of interest in rapid succession.

First, an open jewelry box in what appeared to be the master bedroom, the contents in disarray—as if someone had pawed through them and perhaps taken some items.

A CSU tech had obviously noticed it too, since the box had been dusted for prints.

The other item was a small brown shopping bag on the dresser, like the kind Starbucks used. He almost missed the significance as he gave it a passing glance on the way to the closet.

But he jolted to a stop when the WorldCraft logo on the side angled away from him registered.

He backed up and opened the bag wider with his latex-gloved fingers.

Inside was a woven scarf and two small, tissue-swaddled packets.

Luke pulled out the bundles and gently unwrapped them. A necklace and bracelet.

He peered into the bag.

Two cards featuring a photo of the candle-making monks from Syria and information about their ministry lay at the very bottom.

Apparently, the items in the bag had been of no interest to

the person who'd murdered Elaine Peterson. As Kristin had told him, nothing she sold at the shop was worth stealing—or killing for.

So how could there be a connection between the two crimes?

Yet the fact that this woman had been in the shop the day Susan was killed, then turned up dead herself less than seventy-two hours later, wasn't sitting right.

"You find anything?" Cole entered the room.

"Yeah." He motioned to the jewelry box on the dresser. "Someone's gone through that. I expect there are items missing. And I found this." He tapped the bag. "These are the items she bought at WorldCraft. You have anything?"

"Her purse was in the kitchen. The wallet was on the counter, empty of cash and plastic."

"Sounds like robbery."

"Yeah—and the pieces fit. One of the neighbors knew she was meeting a friend for breakfast this morning and saw her leave about eight o'clock. But she came back a few minutes later. The neighbor speculates she must have forgotten something. It's possible she walked in on the thief, and he panicked and killed her."

"How?" Luke should have asked that sooner.

"Cut her throat. Carotid artery."

He stopped breathing.

"What?" Cole homed in on his reaction.

"That's how Susan Collier died."

Cole's mouth settled into a grim line. "Not the most common method of killing."

"No." He'd seen plenty of stab wounds during his career, but only a handful of throat-cuttings.

"Taylor—you up there?" Hank's query echoed in the stairwell.

"I thought he was gone." Luke arched an eyebrow at his colleague.

"No. He's done in here, which is why we're wandering freely. He went out to poke around on the patio."

"Hey! I hear you talking! You want an update or not?" Now Hank sounded annoyed.

"Yes. On the way." Cole headed toward the hall.

Luke followed him down the stairs to find Hank waiting at the bottom.

"You discover some helpful evidence?" Cole eased around the tech, who surrendered a mere inch or two.

"Would I have called you if I didn't?"

Luke squeezed past the man as well.

"You working this one too?" Hank folded his arms.

"Assisting."

"Don't let them dump a bunch of work on you because you're new. I know how these boys operate." He scowled at Cole.

Cole scowled right back.

When neither conceded the staring match, Luke stepped in. "So what do you have?"

Giving the other detective one last stern appraisal, Hank turned to him. "Drops of blood."

"Drops of blood?" Cole looked at the man as if he'd lost his mind. "How is that helpful? There's blood all over the kitchen."

"I didn't find them in the kitchen. I found them on the patio. There's a short trail."

Luke did the math at warp speed. "You think it's the killer's?"

"Gold star to the new kid on the block."

"Hey . . . I thought the same thing," Cole groused.

"He said it first." Hank smirked at the other detective. "My theory is that our killer was injured during the confrontation and left us a calling card."

"It's not going to help unless his DNA is in the database," Cole pointed out.

"You might get lucky. Stay off the patio until I'm finished."

With that, Hank stalked toward the rear of the house.

Cole watched him go, shaking his head. "How'd you manage to get in his good graces?"

"No idea. He was all over *me* at the crime scene on Tuesday." His phone began to vibrate, and he pulled it out.

Kristin.

"Detective Carter?" She sounded winded.

"Yes." He held up a finger to Cole and angled away.

"I'm home. I found the receipt." She rattled off the items Elaine Peterson had bought.

Everything matched—except for two candles from the monastery.

"I found information cards about the monks in the bag, but no candles." He focused on the wall in front of him, trying to make sense of that.

"Elaine liked to buy them as gifts. She said it was two good deeds in one fell swoop—supporting the monks and shopping for birthday gifts at the same time. She might have given them away already."

"But the information cards were still in there. Two of them. One for each candle. Did she usually take those to include with her gifts?"

"Yeah. She did." Kristin sounded as puzzled as he felt. "Why would the killer steal the candles? They wouldn't have any black-market value. Is anything else missing?"

"Yes. Until you called, we'd been playing with robbery as a motive."

"That seems logical. Maybe she forgot to include the cards when she gave the candles away."

"Maybe." Behind him, Cole cleared his throat. "I need to run. I'll keep you apprised as developments occur. And listen . . . until we know what's going on, use a little extra caution."

They said their good-byes, and he swiveled back to find Cole watching him, his expression speculative.

"What?"

"That was friendly."

"Professional."

"And friendly. I've watched you work cases. You're always cool, clinical, no-nonsense."

"That's how I am on this case."

"Not even close."

"What's that supposed to mean?"

"How old is this woman who owns WorldCraft?"

"What difference does that make?" Heat crept up his neck.

"None to me—now. But I worked a crime once that involved a beautiful woman who knocked my socks off. I sounded like you did whenever I dealt with her."

"Is there a point to this story?"

"Yep. I married her." Cole grinned. "So a word to the wise. If you don't intend to follow up, watch your tone of voice or you'll send the lady the wrong signals."

He strolled toward the kitchen.

Luke gave him a sixty-second head start. He needed a full minute to collect his wits—and come up with an action plan.

His new colleagues might know he was a widower, thanks to the rampant grapevine at headquarters, but the last thing he needed was for them to think he was smitten with a woman who was involved in one of his cases.

It was juvenile, unprofessional, and inappropriate.

Not to mention disturbing.

He wasn't in the market for a relationship.

Yet if he was honest . . . if he evaluated Cole's comment objectively . . . his colleague was correct. The tone he'd used with Kristin was a dozen—or two—degrees warmer than the one he used for anyone else he'd ever dealt with during a case. And his cautionary warning at the end hadn't been SOP either.

Lesson learned.

Going forward, he'd quash any impulse to treat her differently. He would be polite and cordial—but all business. Nothing more. He could . . . and would . . . control his behavior on the job.

Even if he couldn't control the starring role she'd begun to play in his dreams.

6

Yusef Bishara set the brake on his car, surveyed the municipal park, and kneaded the knot in his stomach.

He couldn't keep doing this. The stress was killing him.

But what choice did he have? He was in too deep now . . . and if he balked, he had no doubt Amir would carry out his threat.

His own life he would sacrifice in a heartbeat to rid himself of this terrible burden. But not the life of . . .

Yusef tensed as a man sauntered into his field of vision, supersized disposable cup in hand, newspaper tucked under his arm. The twentysomething guy turned toward him. Facing the windshield, he lit a cigarette, blew a puff of smoke, then strolled down the jogging path that wound through the park.

His contact was here.

Yusef took a steadying breath. He wasn't cut out for subterfuge—especially since he was certain it aided and abetted those who were committing atrocities.

But he had no other option.

He waited for five minutes in his car, as instructed. Then, dodging the runners, bicyclists, and walkers who already populated the park at this early hour on Saturday, he walked toward the third bench along the path, where the man was now sitting.

He shoved his trembling fingers into the pockets of his jeans. In his casual attire, he could be one of the lucky people who were here for a relaxing morning of recreation.

If only.

As he approached the bench, the dark-haired man adjusted his sunglasses and laid the folded newspaper beside him. He pulled out his cell, put it to his ear, and walked a few feet away, leaving the coffee cup behind.

Yusef sat on the other side of the bench.

The man continued to talk on the phone, gradually increasing the distance between them, keeping an eye on the activity in the park.

He looked back once, when he was halfway to the parking lot and there was a momentary lull in activity near the bench.

Yusef's cue.

He reached for the newspaper and moved the cup beside him.

The man pivoted away, cell to ear, and continued toward the asphalt lot.

After the path turned, Yusef lost sight of him.

Ten minutes later, per his instructions, Yusef tucked the bulky newspaper under his arm and picked up the heavy cup that contained cargo much more precious than soda or coffee.

He walked back to his car, put the newspaper on the seat beside him, and gently settled the cup into the holder.

The courier was nowhere to be seen.

As usual.

These rendezvous were always the same. A parade of different faces, hidden behind dark glasses. A busy park. No conversation.

And what came next would be the same too. After two years, he was clear on his role.

Only the seller's name and PO box number changed.

He started the engine and pulled out of the park.

Officially, he might be off work today.

But what he did on weekdays was a piece of cake compared to the task on his plate for this weekend.

. . . . .

The bell over the shop door jingled, and Kristin glanced up from the display she was arranging.

"Can I tempt you with some coffee?" Ryan stuck his head in the door and hefted a cup from Kaldi's.

"Sure. That's a step up from my house brew—and a little more caffeine can't hurt." She smiled and crossed the store to join him.

"Any customers yet?" He entered and handed her the cup.

"No. The first hour on Saturday is always quiet. Too quiet, today. I'm glad you stopped by." She took a sip of the coffee. He'd added some sugar, as usual, but the touch of sweetness couldn't mask the bitter flavor that lingered on her tongue from Monday's tragedy.

"I'm glad the place is back to normal." He gave it a quick skim. "And I like where you put the display case and cash register."

"I couldn't leave them where they were. I spend too much time behind that counter."

"Understandable. Speaking of that . . . any updates from the police?"

"No. I haven't talked to the case detective for two days—and *I* initiated the call on Thursday."

His eyebrows rose. "How come?"

"I saw on the news that one of my customers was killed that morning—and she was in the shop on Monday."

His forehead puckered. "You think the killings are related?"

"I don't know what to think. All I know is two people who

had a connection with my shop were murdered within seventy-two hours of each other. I'm more than a little spooked by the whole thing."

"Did the customer live around here?"

"Not far. Sunset Hills."

"Maybe it's coincidence."

"Maybe. But it doesn't . . ."

The bell over the door jangled again, and two women entered.

"I'll get out of your hair and let you attend to your customers." Ryan touched her arm. "If you need anything, don't be shy about asking."

"I won't. Thank you for being such a considerate neighbor."

She took another sip of her coffee as he circled the women and left the shop, then set the cup on the counter and summoned up a smile.

Today was going to be hard—but she'd get through it. And every day to come would be a little easier.

Still . . . until the police figured out the who and why behind the two tragic deaths, it was going to be difficult to shake the feeling that some sinister plot was in the works—and that she was somehow smack in the middle of it.

Especially after Luke Carter's warning to be careful.

- - - - -

"It's about time you showed your face around here."

Before Luke could respond to his sister's wry greeting, the twins barreled through the front door and launched themselves at his legs with squeals of delight.

Chuckling, he bent down and hoisted the three-year-olds, one under each arm. "Where are Mike and Mark? I was hoping to see my nephews on this visit." He strolled into the foyer, maintaining an innocent expression as he inspected the living room to the right.

Giggles erupted.

"We're here, Unc Luke." Mike began to squirm.

"I think I hear someone." Luke pretended to listen.

"Look under your arm." Mark giggled again.

Luke dipped his chin and faked surprise. "What in the world? Did you put them there while I wasn't paying attention, Sis?"

"I'm not lifting anything these days." Becca patted her growing girth.

"Well, I can't imagine how these two motion machines got under there." Luke set them on their feet.

"You picked us up." Mark grinned at him.

"I did?"

"Uh-huh."

"And here I thought it was magic." He tousled the youngster's hair and winked.

"Wanna play?" Mike gave a hopeful tug on his other hand.

"Later. I'm going to feed your uncle a decent breakfast." Becca stepped forward.

"I already . . ."

She held up a hand. "You can eat junk all week, but if you come to visit here on Saturday morning, you get a real breakfast. End of discussion. Boys, go watch cartoons while your uncle eats. You can wrestle with him after breakfast."

"Okay." Mark commandeered Mike's arm and pulled him toward the family room.

"Well-behaved little guys." Luke followed his sister to the kitchen.

"Ha. Try living with them 24/7 and you'll sing a different tune."

"Where's Neal?" He slid onto a stool at the kitchen island.

"He had a release this weekend. And during our dating days, he claimed IT was a nine-to-five job." She snorted.

"Most career jobs these days aren't for clock-punchers." He helped himself to some grapes from a bowl of fruit.

"Neal doesn't keep your hours, though. Pancakes and bacon sound good?"

"You don't have to feed me, Becca."

"I like to cook." She pulled a bowl from the fridge. "And the batter's already made. I was hoping you'd show."

"I said I'd be here."

"Yeah . . . but you bailed on our last two get-togethers."

"Case related. How's the little princess doing?" He gestured toward her tummy.

"Ultrasound was fine. She's an active one, I can tell you that. I have a feeling she'll have no difficulty holding her own with two older brothers." Becca laid some strips of bacon on a grooved microwaveable plate. "You never did give me a report on that wedding you attended last weekend."

The comment was casual.

Her fake nonchalance wasn't.

His sister was totally transparent.

"The food was amazing." Discussing his feelings about the wedding . . . or the woman he'd met there . . . wasn't on his agenda this morning.

Becca spooned some batter onto the griddle. Based on the faint dents creasing her brow, she was trying to come up with a different angle of attack.

He waited her out.

"So . . . did you stay long?"

"No."

"Why not?"

"Why would I?"

"You know why."

"Becca . . ." He injected a faint warning note into his voice.

Huffing, she finished with the batter and faced him. "Look, I care about you, okay? I hate that you have no love or laughter in your life."

"The twins supply plenty of both."

"That's not what I meant, and you know it."

Yeah, he did.

Apparently she wasn't going to let this go unless he gave her a tad more to chew on.

"The truth is, I didn't know anyone at the wedding except work colleagues—and they're all married."

"You could have introduced yourself to a few people. Made an effort." She aimed the spatula at him accusingly. "I bet you found a dark corner and hid out there."

Too close to the truth.

"I met some new people."

"Yeah?" She lifted the edge of one pancake with the spatula, then gave him her full attention. "Who?"

"A very likeable man. Neighbor of the bride. He watched her grow up."

"An older guy?"

"Yep."

"Anyone else?"

"He introduced me to the woman who was sharing his table."

She folded her arms. "I'm talking about younger people."

He plucked another grape from the bowl and popped it into his mouth. "It was an adult event. No kids present."

"You're being purposely obtuse." She tipped her head and studied him. "Why? What aren't you telling me?"

"You want to hear more about the food? The crab cakes were—"

"How old was the woman the man introduced you to?"

He stifled a groan.

Leave it to Becca to cut through the clutter and ferret out the one nugget he didn't want to discuss.

The wrong person in this family had become a detective.

"Why are you so . . ." He sniffed. "The pancakes are burning."

She whirled around, snatched up the spatula, and flipped the slightly charred flapjacks.

"Have you talked to Dad lately?" That wasn't his favorite topic, either—but it was safer than discussing the wedding . . . if she latched on to it.

"Yesterday." She pulled some eating utensils from a drawer and set them in front of him. "He asked about you."

"I'll give him a call soon."

"How long has it been since you two talked?"

"I don't keep a log of our conversations."

"That means too long. Dad evaded the question too."

"I'm busy with the new job. And now that he's remarried, it's not like he's sitting around waiting for my calls. I'm sure Lauren keeps him entertained."

She pulled the bacon out of the microwave and put it on a plate. "You're still mad about him remarrying, aren't you?"

"No."

"Liar."

"It's the truth. I was never mad. More like . . . surprised—and confused. He and Mom were married for thirty-six years. I thought they were in love. But eighteen months after she dies, he gets married again?"

"He's only sixty, Luke. God willing, he has decades left—and he didn't want to spend them alone. Loving someone else doesn't take anything away from the relationship he and Mom shared. Her place is secure in his heart. We all have an infinite capacity to love. To find room for someone new."

All of a sudden, he had a feeling she wasn't talking about their dad anymore.

He took a banana he didn't want out of the fruit bowl and slowly peeled it while Becca dished up the rest of his breakfast. She'd been broaching the subject of his moratorium on dating with increasing frequency, and he was no more inclined to talk about it today than he'd been in the past.

What was there to discuss?

Eight years ago, he'd promised to love and honor Jenny all the days of his life—the same vow his father had taken on *his* wedding day. As far as he was concerned, that promise precluded another trip to the altar.

Yet his dad had reentered the dating game at warp speed and taken that same vow with a new woman.

He'd never understood that.

But . . . was it possible Becca's opinion had some merit?

Could you keep your first vows and also find someone new?

Could he love and honor Jenny all the days of his life even if he fell in love again?

Maybe.

Funny how he was more receptive to that notion now than he'd been in previous conversations with his sister.

Or was it?

Perhaps crossing paths with a woman who sold fair trade goods had laid the groundwork for it.

"Want to tell me about her?" Becca climbed onto the stool next to him.

He yanked himself back to the conversation. "What are you talking about?"

"The woman at the wedding, whose age you seem reluctant to share."

Man, Becca could stick to a subject like gum to a shoe.

"She didn't tell me how old she is, and I didn't think it was polite to ask." But the answer had been in the standard background check he'd run on her after the murder. Kristin was thirty-four.

"An educated guess would suffice. You're a detective. You deal with descriptions every day."

She wasn't letting him off the hook.

"Fine. Thirtysomething."

"Married?"

"We didn't discuss it."

"Was she wearing a ring?"

"No." To pretend he hadn't scoped out her hand would be stupid. Becca knew guys noticed details like that. He'd been the one to clue her in to the ring-check routine years ago.

"Pretty?"

"Yeah." He stuffed a huge bite of pancake into his mouth.

"You should call her."

He ignored that while he chewed the cooked dough until it became mush.

Becca waited in silence.

He forced himself to swallow the soggy wad, took a swig of coffee, and stabbed another bite.

"Hey." She seized his hand as he tried to lift the fork. "Not so fast, bro. We're having a discussion here."

"I'm trying to eat before my food gets cold."

"You need to ramp up your social life. It's been three years. You know Jenny wouldn't want you to spend the rest of your life moping around."

"I'm not moping."

"You could have fooled me. What's wrong with going out on a few casual dates?"

He pulled his arm free and stuck the pancake in his mouth.

"You"—she leaned into his face—"are impossible."

"'Toons are over, Mommy!" Mike raced into the kitchen, Mark on his heels. "You wanna go outside and play, Unc Luke?"

"Next on my schedule. Give me another minute to eat this wonderful breakfast your mom cooked for me." He crunched into a strip of bacon.

"Flattery will get you nowhere." Becca slid off the stool and circled back around the island. "Do me one favor. Call Dad."

"I'll touch base with him next week."

"And find a nice woman to date."

"That's two favors."

"The second one is more for you than me. Track down that woman who caught your eye at the wedding."

How in creation had Becca picked up on his interest in Kristin?

"Aren't you jumping to conclusions? I've hardly said a word about her."

"I noticed—and that's significant."

"How so?"

"If you hadn't cared about her one way or the other, you wouldn't mind talking about her."

He regarded his sister over the rim of his mug. "That must be some kind of convoluted female logic."

"Are you planning to deny my deduction, Mr. I-Never-Tell-A-Lie Detective?"

"Come on, Unc Luke." Mark pulled on his arm.

"My subjects await." He swiped a napkin across his lips and stood.

"I knew it. You *did* like this woman." Becca gave him a smug look.

"If you must know—yes. She was charming. She was also very chummy with the best man. I think they're involved."

"Oh." Becca's face fell . . . but brightened a moment later. "Well, at least you noticed her. That means there's hope for you . . . even if she isn't the one."

He didn't respond. Instead, he let the twins lead him out to the backyard, where he indulged in little-boy fun for the next hour.

But all the while, he was having big-boy thoughts about Kristin Dane—and pondering two questions.

How involved was she with Colin's best man . . . and her friendly business neighbor two doors down?

And should he step out of his self-imposed isolation and put his investigative skills to work to find out?

. . . . .

Darrak was a living, breathing cluster bomb.

But not for much longer.

Amir exhaled. Part luck, part strategy, part divine intervention— whatever the reason the tip had fallen into his lap, he was grateful.

And he'd done his homework.

He replayed the news story about Elaine Peterson's death. Did the same with the Susan Collier coverage. As far as he could tell, there was no proof Darrak had played a role in either of the murders. If the police had any suspicions, they were keeping them close to their vest. And if they had any grounds to arrest the man, he'd be in jail. At this stage, it didn't appear they had any suspects.

However . . . if anyone dug into his background, circumstantial evidence would point toward him as the culprit.

And if the police somehow managed to identify Darrak as a suspect and brought him in for questioning, the man might crack. He didn't know a lot—but he knew enough to cause problems.

Amir rose from his computer and stormed across the room.

That wasn't a risk he could take.

Loose cannons had to be neutralized.

Why the man had killed the two women, Amir could only speculate. But logic suggested the Peterson woman might have bought the merchandise before Darrak arrived to retrieve it. He could have killed the clerk to get the purchase information and tracked down Peterson.

Bad choices all around.

And bad choices had to be punished.

After retrieving the burner phone that was about to become history, he tapped in a number.

As soon as the man who answered verified Amir's identity, the discussion moved to business. Within ten minutes, the plans were complete.

Amir pressed the end button, then punched in Darrak's number.

Unlike his futile attempts to contact the man last Tuesday and Wednesday, this one succeeded after two rings.

"Yes?"

The man's wary greeting was further proof he was up to his neck in the two murders. Why else would he be nervous about this call?

As he had on Thursday morning, Amir got straight to business. "The package you dropped off has been retrieved and delivered. Your part in this operation is finished. Let me give you instructions on where to collect your reimbursement." He recited the notes he'd jotted during his first call. "Any questions?"

"No. I was honored to be of service to the cause." The man sounded relieved their association was winding down.

No more relieved than he was.

And he'd be even happier in thirty-six hours, when far more than their association came to an end.

7

Luke adjusted his tie, flexed his shoulders to straighten his jacket, and tried to tame the anticipatory smile tugging at his lips as he opened the door to WorldCraft.

Seeing Kristin Dane on a Monday morning was an excellent way to launch the workweek.

She looked up when he entered, and her eyebrows rose. Not unexpected. In her place, he'd be taken aback by an in-person response to a voicemail instead of a return call . . . but he hadn't been able to pass up an excuse to see her.

And do a little digging that was more personal than professional.

He ambled over to the monastery display while she finished with a customer. The missing candles at Elaine Peterson's house were a puzzle . . . but as Cole had pointed out, it was a stretch to think they might be relevant to the case. And since other items from the house had also been taken, robbery was sticking as the motive.

For now, anyway.

As soon as the customer left the shop, Kristin came over to him. "Hi. I didn't expect to see you today."

"You said you had some information that might be helpful."

"Yes . . . but I'm not certain it was worth a special trip."

Yeah, it was.

But not in the way she meant.

"I was in the general vicinity. It was no problem to swing by. What's up?"

"Well . . . given how slow it's been this morning, I decided to review my inventory records. I found an aberration that's kind of freaky."

"Related to the two deaths?"

"I don't know. I'll let you decide." She motioned toward a table with a coffeemaker and disposable cups. "As long as you're here, would you like a cup? I brew a pot every morning for the customers, but I end up drinking most of it. There's plenty left today, though. Ryan from the insurance office down the street brought me some higher-end joe this morning."

A visit from her too-friendly neighbor wasn't great news . . . but he kept his expression impassive. "Thanks. I could use some caffeine."

"I'll get it for . . ."

He touched her arm. "I can manage. I've been making my own coffee for years."

Her gaze flicked down to his wedding ring for a nanosecond. "Your wife isn't a coffee drinker?"

"She used to be." He walked over to the table and picked up the pot. "I lost her three years ago."

"Oh." Her eyes widened . . . then softened. "I'm so sorry."

"Thanks." He poured his coffee, surprised at the steadiness in his fingers. Usually they shook when he talked about Jenny's death. "She was the picture of health, and very athletic. An avid runner. But she had an undiagnosed congenital heart defect. During a half marathon, she collapsed. The official name of the condition is hypertrophic cardiomyopathy, but in layman's terms, it was a fatal cardiac arrhythmia."

That was more detail than Kristin needed—or probably wanted—to know.

He turned away to add a splash of cream he didn't want.

I thought you were going to do some digging into her *love life, not spill your guts about your own, Carter.*

Yeah, yeah.

That had been the plan.

But after her story about Ryan Doud's coffee run, he'd followed the urge to veer off track and clarify his own marital status.

A recalibration of his game plan was in order.

Taking a sip from the cup, he swiveled back to her. "Sorry. I shouldn't have dumped all that on you. Mondays can be depressing enough." He tried for a light touch.

"Mondays have never bothered me. I always think of a new week as a fresh start. And I'm glad you told me." She took a step closer—as if she wanted to reach out to him. Stopped. Backed up again and clasped her hands in front of her. "I-I can't imagine dealing with that kind of loss."

"They say it will get easier." He took another sip of his brew and moved the discussion to the official reason for this visit. "So explain this aberration you found."

For an instant, her face went blank . . . but she quickly shifted gears. "Right." She retreated to the register, putting the counter between them. "In general, I review sales and inventory at the end of each month, but as I said, it was quiet here this morning. To keep myself busy, I decided to scroll through the records." She tapped the register. "I discovered that during the first week of this month, six of the candles from the new shipment were sold."

"And that raised a red flag?" He joined her at the counter.

"Yes. Because of the . . . of what happened here . . . the shop wasn't open much after Saturday, when the candles arrived.

On average, I sell a couple a week, except for a sales spike at Christmas."

"So six candles in two days is unusual."

"Yes—and it was only a day and a half. I was here until noon on Saturday, and we hadn't put the candles out yet. In fact, all six sold on Monday."

Definitely odd.

"Have you sold any since you reopened?"

"No. And there's more. After I realized how many had been purchased right after being put on display, I got curious. I knew there was always a small surge in sales after I restocked, but I attributed it to my marketing efforts and their front-and-center location. I never paid much attention to overall patterns, though. Just monthly sales."

"And now you've found a trend."

"Yes. I went back to the first shipment of candles three years ago and scrutinized each subsequent delivery. In the beginning, I sold two or three candles the first few days I restocked the display. Two years ago, that changed to between five and seven. That number's remained constant."

"So someone came in after each shipment and bought four or five candles at once?"

"No. I would have remembered that. No one ever buys more than two or three."

"Curious." Luke set his coffee on the counter and walked over to the monastery display. Picked up a candle. Inspected it from every angle.

It looked, felt, and smelled like what it appeared to be.

"I went through the same exercise." Kristin came to stand beside him, close enough for her faint floral scent to invade his space. "I didn't notice anything about it that would prompt two murders."

"I don't, either—but I want our people to examine it."

"Help yourself. Anything to get to the bottom of this mystery. Let me wrap it up for you."

He followed her back to the counter. "I'll have our people get on this immediately, but in the meantime, I'd like you to keep track of anyone else who buys one of these."

"What if they pay cash?" She rolled the candle in bubble wrap and taped the plastic closed.

"Let's hope that doesn't happen until we have a chance to examine this. If someone does pay cash, though, see if you can get a name, and jot down a description. A license plate would be even better. But in all honesty, I have a hunch none of that may matter."

"What do you mean?" She put the candle in a small shopping bag, like the one in Elaine Peterson's bedroom.

"I'm playing with a theory—but I want to run it by a few people before I get too carried away."

She slid the bag toward him across the counter. "Care to share?"

"Not yet. It's a bit . . . off the wall."

"Now you have me intrigued."

"You'll be among the first to know if the powers that be think it's worth pursuing." He picked up the bag.

Hesitated.

There was no reason to linger—yet he hadn't accomplished one of his goals for this visit.

But he couldn't ask her outright if she was involved with the Rick guy from the wedding. Or Ryan down the street. He needed a more subtle approach to ferret out that information.

While the one he had in mind wasn't perfect, it should give him his answer.

"I'll repeat what I said last week. Until we get this sorted out, be more careful than usual."

Her complexion lost a few shades of color. "You think I'm in danger?"

"I don't know what to think—but caution is never misplaced."

Stay cool, Carter. Maintain a professional manner. Make the next question sound businesslike. "I got the impression you live alone."

"Yes."

"Any friends or . . . significant other . . . you can rely on in a pinch?"

"I have some close friends. No significant other."

Some of the tension in his shoulders eased.

The door was open to pursue a social relationship with this woman . . . if he chose to do so at some point.

The bell jingled, and two women entered the shop, a toddler in tow.

His cue to exit.

"If you have any reason for concern, Ms. Dane, call me. Day or night. Don't take any chances."

Her attention zipped from the shoppers back to him. "Would you mind . . . could you call me Kristin? I'm not into formalities."

"Sure. And I'm fine with Luke. We may be working this case for a while, and first names are easier. I'll talk to you soon."

Bag in hand, he wove around the displays and pushed through the door—only to discover that dark gray clouds had obliterated the blue sky while he'd been inside.

Didn't matter.

His heart felt sunnier than it had for three long years.

Thanks to Kristin.

So the instant this investigation was over, he was going to seriously consider taking his sister's advice about reentering the dating scene.

If the lovely owner of WorldCraft was interested.

■ ■ ■ ■ ■

Ding-dong.

Still stirring the vermicelli noodles for her Tuesday night dinner, Kristin checked her watch.

Who would come calling unannounced at six thirty?

Unless . . . might Luke be making another unscheduled stop to give her a case update on his way home?

Pulse revving, she set the wooden spoon on the counter, fluffed her hair in the mirror on the wall of her small foyer, and peeked through the peephole.

Drat.

It wasn't Luke.

But what in heaven's name was Colin doing on her porch? Hadn't he arrived home from his honeymoon less than two hours ago?

She flipped the lock and pulled the door open.

Before she could say a word, he barreled in, planted his fists on his hips, and glared at her. "Why didn't you call me?"

"Hello to you too." She pushed the door shut. "How was the honeymoon?"

"Don't change the subject."

"I was going to call you tonight. What did you do, go straight from the airport to the office?"

"No. I called in after we got home. Sarge gave me the new-case highlights—or should I say lowlights? Why didn't you call me?"

"You were on your honeymoon."

"I could have taken a few minutes to listen to your story. Does Rick know?"

"Of course. It was all over the news."

"Then he should have called me if you wouldn't."

"I made him promise not to." A sputtering noise sounded from the kitchen, and with a soft exclamation, she dashed toward the back of the condo. "My noodles are overflowing."

He followed on her heels, waiting while she removed the pot from the stove and dumped the vermicelli in a colander.

"Why did you make him promise not to call me?"

"Come on, Colin." She faced him. "You were on your honeymoon, and there was nothing you could do from there. Nor did I expect you to. One of your colleagues is handling the case. He seems very competent."

"I know. Carter. I already talked to him. My beef isn't work-related. It's personal." He moved closer and grasped her upper arms, twin grooves denting his forehead. "You and I and Rick are friends. More than friends. And we promised to always be there for each other. For crying out loud . . . your shop was the scene of a murder! You found the body! How could you not call me?"

"I didn't want to intrude. You deserved a carefree honeymoon." In hindsight, though, she could see his point. She'd feel the same if the situation was reversed. "But I guess I should have called."

"No guessing about it." He took a deep breath. Let it out slowly. Gentled his voice. "So how are you doing?"

"Okay." The word hitched, and she swallowed. It was far easier to maintain her composure while he was yelling at her than when he got all brotherly and solicitous.

"Right." Without further conversation, he pulled her into a hug and held her tight.

She clung to him and closed her eyes, tears leaking out of the corners.

Thank you, God, for the two guys you sent into my life all those years ago when I desperately needed friends.

He didn't pull back until she wriggled out of his grasp and swiped at the moisture on her cheeks.

"I appreciate you coming by, Colin. More than I can say. But I'm fine. Go home to your new wife. I bet she wasn't happy about you running out minutes after you walked in the door."

"She's had me all to herself for nine days. And she knows our history. She sent me with her blessing."

That sounded like Trish.

"You picked a good one."

"Tell me about it." A slow smile lifted the corners of his mouth.

"I assume the honeymoon was . . . memorable?"

"Very—but too short. I wish she could have extended her spring break by more than two days."

"At least you have that trip to Italy to look forward to this summer, after school ends. Two honeymoons is a pretty sweet deal, if you ask me."

"Yeah." His smile broadened.

"So go spend your last free evening with your wife." She took his hand and towed him toward the door.

"You want to join us for dinner?"

"Are you kidding me? Trish gets high marks for tolerance . . . but let's not push it. Enjoy your last twelve hours together before you go your separate ways tomorrow. Real life will—"

Ding-dong.

Kristin halted.

Another caller?

"Are you expecting someone?" Colin frowned at the door and tightened his grip on her hand.

"No. But I wasn't expecting you, either. Let me see who—"

"I'll check." He nudged her aside and commandeered the peephole. Cocked his head. "Now that's interesting."

"Who is it?"

He angled back to her. "Carter."

"Oh." A rush of pleasure warmed her cheeks. "Maybe he, uh, has news."

"What's wrong with his phone?"

"I don't know."

The bell rang again.

Kristin elbowed Colin aside and turned the knob—but she

could feel him hovering behind her shoulder while she pulled open the door.

"Hi, Luke."

"Luke?" Colin's soft comment close to her ear guaranteed only she could hear his one-word reaction—or the inflection that suggested he had a bunch of questions.

Kristin ignored him.

"Hi." The detective glanced from her to Colin and back again. "I was passing by and thought I'd give you an update on the case. Colin." He acknowledged the other man with a dip of his head. "But since you have company, I can—"

"Colin was just leaving." She moved back, making room for him to pass by. "I'm sure Trish is waiting for him. He can get up to speed on all things law enforcement related tomorrow—after he's back on duty." She telegraphed a strong go-home signal to her buddy.

After a brief hesitation, he took her cue. "Fine. Call me if you need anything. Anytime. Got it?"

"Got it. Thanks."

He gave her one more quick hug, edged past the man on her doorstep, and headed for his car.

"I should have called before I came." The bag from World-Craft dangled from Luke's fingers.

"No need. My evenings are typically quiet. I didn't expect a visit from Colin. Come in." She motioned toward the foyer.

He entered, extending the bag as she shut the door. "Your candle—along with a check from the department. There's a nick out of it where the lab took a sample. It's too damaged to sell."

"You didn't have to reimburse me. The cost of one candle is a small price to pay for some answers."

"We have a budget for this kind of expense. Unfortunately, the investment didn't pay off. It is what it seems to be—a candle."

No big surprise . . . but disappointing nonetheless.

"So the candles have nothing to do with the murders?"

"They don't appear to . . . but I'm still playing with a theory." He sniffed the spicy aroma wafting through the condo. "Am I interrupting your dinner?"

"No. It's cooking. You're smelling a new batch of spaghetti sauce."

And she had plenty of noodles too.

She caught her lower lip between her teeth.

Would it be too pushy to ask the man to stay for dinner? After all, he'd only told her about his deceased wife yesterday—and he continued to wear his ring. Wasn't that a no-trespassing signal?

On the other hand, what did she have to lose by inviting him? Worse case, he'd decline and she'd eat dinner alone.

But she'd have a solitary meal anyway if she *didn't* ask him to stay.

Just do it, Kristin. Don't overthink everything.

Curling her fingers at her sides, she took the plunge.

"I'd love to hear your theory, if you have a few minutes. And I have plenty of pasta. Would you like to join me for dinner?"

8

It took a moment for Kristin's invitation to sink in—and for Luke's lungs to refill.

The most he'd hoped for with this impromptu stop was a few minutes in her company.

Instead . . . she'd asked him to share her dinner.

He could almost hear Becca yelling "go for it" from the sidelines.

As the seconds ticked by, Kristin gave him an uncertain smile. "I didn't mean to put you on the spot. I'm sure you're busy, and—"

"No." He blurted out the denial before he could second-guess himself—or she could retract the invitation. "I was, uh, heading home, with a stop along the way for some fast food. Spaghetti sounds much better. I only get homemade meals these days at my sister's."

Too much information, Carter. Stop babbling.

He closed his mouth.

The tension in her features eased. "Come on out to the kitchen while I cook some more noodles." She led him to the back of the condo, where a spacious bay window offered a view of wooded common ground.

"I like your place."

"Thanks." She set the shopping bag on a small island and continued toward the stove. "I rented an apartment after I opened WorldCraft until I saved enough for a decent down payment. I bought this condo eight months ago. Now tell me your theory."

"Why don't you put me to work while I do that? I'm not much of a cook, but I set a mean table and excel at cleanup."

"I'll take you up on the table setting. You'll find plates, cutlery, glasses, and napkins in those cabinets and drawers." She waved a hand to her right and stirred the spicy-smelling sauce. "We can talk about cleanup later."

He had no trouble locating all the items she'd ticked off. "As I told you yesterday, my theory is a little off the wall."

"My life has been off the wall for the past week. I think I can handle anything you throw at me."

"Okay. Try this on for size. What if someone isn't after the candles themselves, but what's in them?"

She frowned at him as he began setting the small table in the bay window. "I thought you said your people confirmed they were just candles?"

"The candle I took with me is just a candle. I even had the ME x-ray it. Nothing inside. But maybe only a few of the candles in each shipment contain some sort of contraband."

"Like what?"

"I haven't a clue."

"It would have to be awfully small." She slid some vermicelli noodles in the boiling water.

"True."

"And the candles are from a monastery. There's no way Brother Michael—or any of the monks—would be involved in anything illegal."

"I'm not suggesting they are . . . but others may have access to the candles. Do you know how the production process works?"

"It's a small-scale operation." She pulled a bag of salad greens from the fridge. "Brother Michael said the monks do most of the work, with help from a few volunteers."

"So other people are involved."

"Yes . . . but I'm certain the abbot vets anyone who works in the monastery."

"In a place like Syria, that can't be easy to do."

"Are you suggesting there might be a . . . plant?"

"I'm not ruling it out." He filled some glasses with ice and water at her fridge.

"Can I be honest?" She sent him an apologetic glance. "It feels like a stretch."

The same assessment Cole and Sarge had offered.

"I can't argue with that. But I worked a smuggling case once in Richmond with a similar setup. What you discovered about the sales pattern also fits with the notion of someone—or more likely a couple of someones, since no single customer bought four or five candles—coming to retrieve certain candles as soon as they arrive here."

"But they all look alike."

"Have you examined each one closely?"

"No."

"It's possible the ones to be retrieved are marked somehow. And if Elaine Peterson bought two of those candles before the intended customer got to your shop, it would connect the two murders. That person needed sales information from your clerk, and the candles from Elaine."

Kristin transferred noodles from a colander to a plate and slid them into the microwave. "That's an intriguing notion. Very cloak-and-daggerish. But how could we ever prove it?"

"With the next shipment."

"That won't be for months. I typically order twenty-five candles every quarter. Ordering sooner would be out of pattern and might make whoever is involved in the scheme suspicious—assuming there *is* a scheme."

"Unless you have a legitimate reason to need candles sooner."

"Such as?"

"An unusually large purchase that's depleted your stock?"

Kristin caught her lower lip between her teeth, shook the greens into a bowl, and pulled two bottles of dressing from the door of the refrigerator. "That could work—but the candles still won't arrive for weeks. What happens in the meantime?"

"I keep my ear to the ground and continue to troll for leads. The colleague who's working the Peterson case and I will stay in close touch throughout. If there's another link beyond World-Craft, we'll find it."

Kristin drained the second batch of noodles, dished up the sauce, and carried their plates to the table. "Have a seat while I get the salad."

He moved to the bay window but stood by his chair until she joined him.

"Impressive manners." She sat and slid the bowl of greens toward him.

"My mom gets credit for that." He took his seat and helped himself to some salad.

"Give her my compliments."

"I wish I could. She passed away a few months after my wife died."

"Oh, wow." Her eyes softened, and her almost tangible sympathy seeped into his soul. "That had to be incredibly hard. I'm so sorry."

"Thanks." His voice hoarsened, and he fumbled for his water glass.

To his relief, she let the subject drop.

"Do you mind if I say a blessing?"

"Not at all. That's how I was raised." Even if he wasn't always as diligent about prayer as he should be.

She kept it short and simple, then dived into her meal.

For a couple of minutes they both focused on their food, but once the edge was off his hunger, Luke broached the subject that had piqued his curiosity at the wedding reception. She hadn't answered his silent query that night, but she might be more forthcoming now that they were sharing a cozy meal in her condo.

"May I ask you a question?"

"Sure. I guess." She added more parmesan to her pasta, her tone a bit wary.

"At the wedding, your friend Rick mentioned that Colin wanted a photo of the Treehouse Gang. Interesting name. Does it also have an interesting history?"

"Yes." Her lips curved up.

"Based on your expression, I'm deducing that history stirs up pleasant memories."

"Of the Treehouse Gang, yes. The childhoods of the members—not so much."

"Including yours?"

"Yes." She wound some noodles around her fork. "I'll give you the condensed version. Colin's family fell apart after his little brother died in a hit-and-run accident. Rick grew up in foster care after his mother was killed in a domestic violence incident. As you might expect, both of them had a ton of issues. They met in middle school and clicked."

"How do you fit in?"

"I didn't, at first. I transferred to their school after they met, when my parents moved into a different district. I was a year younger than them, but in the same class—and the shyest eleven-year-old you can imagine."

He didn't try to hide his skepticism. "Hard to believe, considering how personable, poised, and articulate you are now."

"Thank you for that—but believe it. I was a mess as a kid."

"Any particular reason why?"

"Oh yeah." She picked up the parmesan again and sprinkled more of it on her already cheese-heavy dinner. "Unlike Colin and Rick, I had an intact family. But I was an unplanned addition to my parents' world. My arrival was not their most pleasant surprise."

"Are you saying they didn't treat you well?" Luke stopped eating.

"No. They just had no space in their busy schedules for a child. My dad's a business executive and my mom's an attorney. Their plates were—and are—full. Time has always been at a premium for them, and there was barely enough of it to cover career demands. Neither of them ever got home from work until seven or seven thirty."

"So you were on your own a lot?"

"I had nannies." She lifted one shoulder and took another bite of pasta.

Her matter-of-fact response suggested she'd long ago accepted the lot life had dealt her.

But nannies weren't the same as loving parents. Like the kind he'd had. No matter how diligent they were about caring for their charge, it was a job.

"I'm sorry your mom and dad weren't there for you, Kristin."

There was an infinitesimal hesitation in her chewing, so tiny he'd have missed it if he wasn't watching her closely.

"I coped. And it wasn't like I was deprived. They gave me expensive clothes, paid big bucks for ballet and piano and riding lessons, sent me to high-end summer camps. I had no material wants."

He concentrated on his pasta, unsure how to respond. Being

critical of her parents could backfire—but hadn't they realized time was the most precious gift a parent could give a child? That putting their daughter at the bottom of their priority list could badly undermine her self-esteem?

"I know what you're thinking."

At Kristin's quiet comment, he attempted a smile. "Are you a psychic?"

"No—but I watched people during my shy years, and I learned to read nuances. You're right that material things don't compensate for a day-to-day loving relationship with your parents. It's hard when they aren't around much—and if they miss important events in your life, like National Honor Society inductions or recitals or awards presentations. Or they're out of town on your birthday."

Kristin had stopped eating . . . and the sadness in her eyes told Luke he'd been wrong in his earlier assessment.

She might think she'd put her unhappy childhood memories to rest, but she hadn't. Deep inside, they still hurt.

Fighting the urge to take her hand, he wadded up the napkin in his lap. "I wish you'd had a better home life." Like the one he'd had, where he and Becca had been the center of their parents' world. "It was their loss as much as yours, you know."

"Yeah." She swallowed and twirled some more noodles. "Anyway, to compensate, I read a lot, studied constantly, and aced my classes. On the academic front, I was a star. But I had big self-esteem issues and no confidence—until I met Colin and Rick."

"They befriended you?"

"Yes." Her demeanor brightened, and she began eating again. "They saw me sitting alone in the cafeteria every day and started joining me. They told me later they felt sorry for me. Can you imagine two twelve-year-old boys being that sensitive?"

"To be honest . . . no. I doubt I would have been tuned in to someone else's misery at that age."

"I'm not certain I buy that." She regarded him for a moment before she continued. "In any case, we bonded. With two such staunch friends, my anemic self-esteem got a huge boost. Enough that I let them badger me into trying out for a school play. I got the part . . . and a lot of parts after that. Theater was an amazing ego builder."

Kristin with an audience in the palm of her hands.

Now that fit the image of the self-confident woman he'd met at the wedding.

"Are you still involved in acting?"

"Not on stage—but I direct a children's show every summer at my church . . . and drag the guys along to help backstage. I figured if theater helped me, it might do the same for other kids."

A woman who gave back in multiple ways.

Nice.

"So how did you three become the Treehouse Gang?"

"Oh, right. Back to your original question. Among the many gifts my parents gave me was a deluxe treehouse. I think that may have been the real reason the boys adopted me." Her mouth quirked. "Although in fairness, they didn't find out about that until after they rescued me from my solitary lunches."

"And you've stayed tight all these years."

"Very. We're like family. We meet every other Saturday for breakfast—and barge into each other's lives on a regular basis . . . like Colin did tonight."

He smiled as he gathered the remnants of lettuce on his plate into a pile. "Did you have a secret code, or an oath you all signed in blood?"

"No blood involved, thank you very much. Although the boys probably would have gone for that." She rolled her eyes, then grew more serious. "But we did take a pledge to do our part to make the world a better place when we grew up."

Heavy stuff for a bunch of kids.

"It appears you and Colin followed through on that."

"So did Rick. He was in the military for a while, and now he runs a camp in the country for foster kids."

"Three for three. I'm impressed."

"It *is* amazing how we all turned out, given our backgrounds."

He scooped up the last of his salad. "Do you have much contact with your parents these days?"

"We're in touch every few weeks. It's not like we're at odds or anything. They just have their life, and I have mine. Plus, they've lived in Boston for more than a decade, so distance is an issue. What about you? Is your dad nearby?"

He clenched his fingers around the napkin again. "No. He moved to South Carolina a year ago. But my sister is in St. Louis. That's one of the reasons I relocated here from Virginia in January."

"Virginia isn't as far from South Carolina as St. Louis is. Did you get to see your dad more often while you were there?"

"No." A wave of guilt washed over him, and he gave his last few noodles more attention than they deserved.

"I think I touched a nerve." Kristin laid her fork down.

He tried for a smile. "Are you playing psychic on me again?"

"No. This is called empathy. I have no idea what's on your mind, but I sense . . . conflict?"

"You have excellent instincts." He thumbed a speck of sauce off the rim of his empty plate and exhaled. Why dance around the truth? "I've done a pretty abysmal job keeping in touch with my dad for the past year."

"Sounds like there might be a story there." Her tone was cautious. As if she was afraid he was going to bolt if she got too nosy.

For some odd reason, though, he didn't mind her queries.

Stranger yet, talking about his messy personal life felt . . . safe . . . with her.

"We're not estranged, if that's what you're wondering." Not officially, anyway. "Dad remarried last year and retired. They decided to relocate to South Carolina. His new wife is from that area, and he'd always wanted to live by the ocean. It was a no-brainer for them."

"Do you like his new wife?"

"She's fine. She's just not . . . Mom. And I was surprised Dad replaced her after only eighteen months."

The admission he'd voiced to no one but Becca was out before he could stop it.

"Mmm." Kristin chased a mushroom around her plate, faint furrows creasing her brow. "I'm not certain *replace* is the best word. Maybe he *added* her to his life. I've always believed the heart can expand to accommodate an endless amount of love—and that the more we have, the more blessed we are."

"You sound like my sister."

A dimple appeared in her cheek. "I have a feeling I'd like her."

"I have a feeling it would be mutual." He caught her gaze. Held it. "For the record, I'm beginning to come around to her way of thinking."

Her complexion pinkened as the electricity zipping between them spiked toward the danger range.

With an abrupt move, she broke eye contact and vaulted to her feet. There was a slight tremble in her fingers as she picked up his plate.

"Would you, uh, like some coffee? I wish I could offer you one of my killer brownies for dessert, but all I have is packaged cookies."

He hesitated. There was no reason to rush back to his silent, impersonal apartment.

Yet he'd already spent considerably more time in Kristin's company tonight than he'd planned, and overstaying his welcome wouldn't be wise. Better to leave her wanting more than wishing he'd leave.

"Thank you, but I need to run. I have a few items on my to-do list for tonight. Let me help with the cleanup before I go."

"Not necessary. I'll have everything in the dishwasher in five minutes. Guests shouldn't have to deal with dirty plates and silverware on their first visit."

First visit.

That sounded promising.

And the second visit couldn't happen soon enough for him. Despite some of the heavy topics they'd discussed during the past hour, this had been his happiest evening in years.

"Are you certain?" He rose.

"Yes. I'll walk you out."

He followed her to the foyer, waiting as she pulled the door open.

"Thanks again for dinner." He passed her, stopping on the threshold.

Her color was still on the high side. "It was my pleasure. I'll place another order with the monastery tomorrow and let you know as soon as I get a confirmation."

He had to forcibly shift back into work mode. "That would be great." *Say good-bye, Carter.* "I enjoyed the food tonight— and the company." *I didn't hear a good-bye in there.*

"Me too."

As she wrapped her fingers around the edge of the door, the glow from the porch light warmed her skin. Deepened the gray-blue of her irises. Spotlighted her lips.

Her very tempting lips.

She drew an unsteady breath and watched him, a pulse throbbing in the hollow of her throat. She looked oh-so-appealing— and receptive to . . .

Get out of here before you make a mistake you'll live to regret, Carter! Now!

Right.

He stumbled back a step. "Well . . . see you around."

With that, he escaped to his car as fast as he could without breaking into a jog.

Not once did he look back.

He didn't dare.

If Kristin was still standing there, issuing that silent, subliminal invitation for a kiss, he might succumb.

And that wouldn't be wise.

She might be unencumbered with romantic baggage, but he had plenty weighing him down. Yes, he was coming around to Becca's viewpoint . . . but he wasn't there yet. The ring remained on his finger.

Besides, Kristin was part of a case. An innocent party, but connected. And mixing personal and professional life was never smart.

He took his place behind the wheel, started the engine, and drove away.

Only as he turned the corner did he allow himself one fast peek in the rearview mirror.

She hadn't moved. The slim, inviting silhouette continued to beckon from the open doorway.

It took every ounce of his willpower to maintain pressure on the gas pedal and watch her recede in the distance.

But at least she'd hinted that the door to another get-together was open.

And when the right time came, he intended to walk through it.

9

Finally.

Kristin clicked on the email from the abbot. It had taken two days for the man to respond—but in fairness, he had no clue about the urgency of her latest order. And based on what she'd gleaned about life at the monastery from Brother Michael, the monks marched to the beat of a much slower drummer.

She skimmed the text.

Excellent.

Her order was being processed and would ship on Monday.

Added bonus? She had a legitimate excuse to call Luke.

Smiling, she picked up the phone from the WorldCraft counter and tapped in his number.

Three rings in, he answered in a clipped tone.

Drat.

His brusque manner didn't bode well for a long conversation.

"Luke, it's Kristin. Are you tied up?"

"Oh. Sorry. No. I'm in the middle of typing a report, and boring work requires all my powers of concentration. I'm glad to have an excuse to take a break. What's up?"

"I heard from the monastery." She relayed her news. "Best

case, the candles will arrive mid-May. Worst case, mid-June. Expedited shipping would get them here faster, but I've never used it. Too expensive."

"Let's not change anything that might raise a red flag. We'll just have to wait—even if that taxes our patience. Or mine, anyway."

"Not one of your strongest virtues?"

"Not when it comes to solving crimes. But my sister claims I have exceptional patience with her three-year-old twins."

Another check mark in his pro column.

"Anything new on the case?"

"No. The leads have been few and far between—and are dwindling fast. I'm continuing to work it hard, though." A squeak came over the line, as if he'd leaned back in his chair. "So how are you doing? I know how disturbing this has been for—" Someone spoke in the background, and he cut off his comment. After a muffled exchange, Luke came back to her, his manner more brisk and businesslike. "I need to run. We'll discuss next steps after the items arrive."

Did that mean there would be no communication between them for several weeks?

Her spirits nosedived.

"I'll give you a call as soon as I have the next shipment." Her attempt to sound cheerful was lame, at best.

"Okay." His earlier warmth had vanished.

"Well . . ." She tried for perky again. "Talk to you soon."

"If anything breaks, I'll be in touch." After a perfunctory good-bye, the line went dead.

Kristin removed the phone from her ear and weighed it in her hand. Had Luke just been tapped for a hot new case—or was there another reason for the abrupt change in his manner?

She hadn't a clue.

But as she set the phone back on the counter, she was certain of one thing.

If Luke *didn't* call until the candles arrived, it was going to be a very long spring.

. . . . .

Cole's timing stunk.

Cell glued to his ear, Luke kept tabs on the pacing man in his peripheral vision.

How much of the phone conversation had his colleague heard—and had Cole picked up the personal tone that had snuck into his voice as he'd talked with Kristin?

Only one way to find out.

Bracing, he slid the phone back onto his belt.

"It's about time." Cole marched over to him in the small, two-person office.

"What's with you?"

"I have news."

"About what?"

"The Elaine Peterson case." He slapped a crime scene photo onto the desk, of a male body in the early stages of decomposition. "That blood we found at her place, on the patio?"

"You mean the blood Hank found."

"Whatever. The ME found the same blood under her fingernails. It was this guy's. We got a hit in the DNA database."

Luke leaned closer to the photo. There were abrasions on his face that could be claw marks from Elaine's fingernails. "Who is he?"

"No idea. We ran the prints through NGI. Nothing."

If the FBI's automated fingerprint system didn't provide a match, it wasn't to be found.

"He looks Middle Eastern."

"Agreed."

"What happened to him?"

"Bullet to the back of the head, execution style. He was

buried in a shallow grave in the woods in unincorporated St. Louis County. A jogger's dog found him. According to the police report, the dog went ballistic. By the time his owner got him under control, the mutt had dug down far enough to expose a hand."

"My kind of dog." Luke picked up a pen and turned it end-to-end on the desk. "I wonder if this guy might be on a terrorist watch list. I've got a contact at the FBI field office here I could call."

Cole frowned. "Why would you want to involve the Feds? I mean, we're only speculating, right? As far as we know, there's no link here to terrorism."

"The missing candles are from Syria."

"Circumstantial. I still say that whole connection is a stretch."

"Maybe—but two innocent people are dead . . . along with this guy, in what could be payback for a botched job. I think it's an angle worth exploring."

"If you go to the FBI, they're going to cut us out of the loop to protect any classified information that might surface." His colleague planted his palms on the desk and leaned into his face. "We'll lose control of these cases. Is that what you want?"

"No—but that won't necessarily happen."

"Yes, it will. We'll be marginalized. I know how those guys work." He straightened up. "They're turf freaks."

"And we're not?"

Cole's eyes narrowed. "Fine. I concede your point. But the fact remains, if you pull the FBI into this, we're hosed."

No, they weren't.

Luke shifted in his seat as he debated how to play this. Sarge and the higher-ups at County knew his background, but there'd been no opportunity to bring it up to his colleagues without sounding like he was full of himself. Nor had there been a reason to broach the subject. Who'd have guessed there'd be any use in his new job for such a credential?

Now that there was, he'd have to come clean with Cole.

"You're right . . . in general, the Feds would cut us out. But back in Richmond, I was on the FBI's Joint Terrorism Task Force. My top-secret clearance is valid for another four and a half years. They'll talk to me—and share what they find."

Cole arched an eyebrow and gave him an appraising sweep. "Impressive."

"The Bureau needed a body, and I was available." He shrugged. "It's no big deal—except it will be helpful in this case. I assume you have some other shots of this guy?"

"Yeah. You know Hank. Mr. Thorough."

"More angles will help. If the guy's not identifiable by any of the usual markers, he might be in a terrorist photo and name database."

"Assuming he *is* a terrorist. Just because he looks Middle Eastern doesn't mean he had any link to Syria or those candles."

"True—but it can't hurt to ask. If nothing else, I think you've got the guy who killed Elaine Peterson."

"I'm with you there." He strolled over to the door. "So will you let me know if your intuition about this pans out? Or at least share as much as you can with someone who doesn't have top-secret clearance?"

"Yeah. And listen . . . no need to spread that around, okay? There's not much chance I'll ever have to use it again in this job."

"If that's what you want." He tipped his head. "You must have been involved in some heavy-duty investigations in Virginia."

"Not as many as you might think. Most of my work there was standard detective fare."

"Right." Cole gave him a skeptical look and twisted his wrist. "I'm done for the week. Kelly and I have plans tonight. Unless you want to keep your FBI friend late on a Friday, you might want to call it a day too. See you next week."

As Cole disappeared out the door, Luke leaned back in his chair. It *was* after five—and much as he'd like to connect with Nick Bradley today, the man had a wife and at least one kid waiting at home for him, near as he could recall based on the scuttlebutt he'd picked up from mutual colleagues.

This could wait until Monday—even if he didn't want it to.

In the meantime . . . a long, empty weekend stretched ahead. Unlike Cole, who probably had a date night—or two—planned with his wife, his social calendar was empty.

He could stop in at Becca's and play with the boys, though. That was always fun.

Except odds were high she'd bring up his nonexistent social life again, and that wasn't a subject he wanted to discuss with her.

Yet.

That left just one item on his weekend agenda—and it didn't come anywhere close to being fun.

Apologies never were.

But he owed his dad a big one. Hearing about Kristin's parents—and the less-than-ideal family situations of her friends—and listening to her and Becca's take on love this week had been eye-opening.

Luke shut down his computer . . . sighed . . . and stood. Snubbing his father for seeking companionship and love had been wrong—especially when he was on the verge of doing the same thing.

Funny how fast your perspective could change.

Thanks to Kristin.

Becca might have been hammering away at him for months, but it had taken the lovely shop owner to move his sister's message from the realm of theory to reality. To help him understand what had motivated his dad.

And to help him grasp the truth—that while he'd never stop loving Jenny, his heart might have room for someone new.

He flipped off the light, exited . . . and tried to psyche himself up for the difficult conversation with his father.

Because it was never easy to eat crow.

■ ■ ■ ■ ■

Tightening her grip on her umbrella, Kristin raced through the pouring rain from her car to the Treehouse Gang's favorite breakfast spot.

Mercy.

Someone ought to be building an ark.

She pushed through the door, shook off her umbrella, and shoved her damp hair off her forehead.

Thank goodness she wasn't meeting a date in this bedraggled state.

Like . . . Luke, for example.

As if there would ever be any danger of that.

But a girl could dream, couldn't she?

"Your friends are already here, Kristin." Carmen breezed by with a laden tray. "I'm surprised to see you all on Sunday instead of Saturday."

"This worked better for us this week. We'll be back to our routine for the next get-together."

After depositing her umbrella in the stand near the door, she wound through the restaurant, toward their usual table in the far corner. Colin's choice. He claimed all law enforcement types liked to keep their back to the wall in a spot that gave them a clear line of sight while in public places.

Luke was probably the same way.

Oh, for pity's sake, Kristin! Put the man out of your mind!

If only.

Rick spotted her and waved.

"Sorry I'm a few minutes late." She slid into the empty chair. "The traffic was awful. Thanks for changing days this week. Without backup at the shop, Saturday was impossible."

"No problem. Let's order." Rick searched the room for Carmen. "A little hungry, are we?"

"Always. I had to order that to tide me over until you arrived." He motioned toward a half-eaten bagel.

"I thought Trish might join us." Kristin brushed some drops of water off her sweater, eying Colin.

"Nope. She says marriage isn't an excuse to neglect my friends, and she doesn't want to barge in."

"Here's to Trish—even though she's always welcome." Rick hefted his glass of water and changed the subject. "So Colin says the detective who stopped by the night I was at your place came again this week."

She stifled a groan.

He sure hadn't wasted any time sharing that piece of news.

"Uh-huh." Kristin pretended to read the menu she'd memorized long ago.

"Why?"

"Case update."

"Did he stay for dinner?" Colin leaned forward.

"Why would you ask that?" Despite her yeoman effort to control the warmth creeping across her cheeks, the blush refused to be suppressed.

"You were right. He stayed." Rick snickered and nudged Colin.

"Aren't we going to order?" Kristin waved at Carmen. The woman must have picked up her "save me" vibes, because she bustled over.

Thank you, Lord, for the female sisterhood.

Carmen jotted down their selections, and the instant she departed, Kristin introduced a new subject.

"So tell us about Hawaii. Is it as beautiful as it seems to be in pictures?"

"Yep—but I'd rather hear about your cozy dinner."

Drat.

Her buds were having none of her diversion tactics.

"I bet Luke was impressed. You make terrific spaghetti." Colin watched her with that detective look of his, as if he was trying to see into her brain.

Not happening.

But short of lying, neither could she deny she'd invited the man to stay.

Maybe if she admitted the truth, they could move on.

"Okay. Since you two seem excessively interested in my spaghetti dinner, I'll give you the scoop, such as it is. Luke is the lead detective on my case. He went out of his way to provide an update. Since I'd just made a whole batch of sauce and it was dinnertime, I invited him to stay. He accepted. End of story."

"Or the beginning." Rick broke off a piece of the bagel and popped it into his mouth.

"What's that supposed to mean?"

"You wouldn't ask a repair guy who happened to be there at dinnertime to stay, would you?"

She smoothed a crease from her napkin. "That's different."

"How?" Colin rested his elbows on the table and linked his fingers, still watching her.

"What is this, the third degree? You're not on duty today, you know."

"Touchy, touchy." Rick finished off the bagel.

"Telling, telling," Colin corrected. "But in case you happen to be interested, everything I've heard about the new man in your life is positive."

"He's not the new man in my life."

"Whatever you say. Although you *are* on a first-name basis.

In any case, for what it's worth, *Detective Carter* is one of the good guys."

"How do you know? He told me you two haven't worked much together."

"I ran some background on him after I found him on your doorstep Tuesday."

"What!" Her jaw dropped.

"Hey . . . I didn't dig deep. No more than basic intel."

"You checked out a guy I'm interested in?" She continued to gape at him.

"Ah-ha! Now the truth comes out." Rick grinned.

Shoot.

She'd walked straight into that one.

Ignoring Rick, she focused on Colin. "What possessed you to do that?"

"Rick and I wouldn't want you to date someone who isn't trustworthy."

"We're not dating."

"Yet."

She huffed out a breath. Much as she loved these two, they could be annoying. And overbearing. And nosy.

"I'm through with this discussion." She leaned down to extract a folder from her tote bag, taking longer than necessary, hoping her face would cool a few degrees.

It didn't.

When she straightened up, they were both smirking at her.

Hmph.

They might be grinning now, but she was about to get the last laugh.

"I wanted to talk to you about this year's children's show." She opened the folder . . . and they both cringed.

The exact reaction she'd expected.

And after all the grief they'd given her about Luke, she was going to rope them in now for a significant behind-the-scenes commitment.

"What are you doing this summer?" Colin gave her a wary look.

"*Alice in Wonderland.*"

"Oh joy." He rolled his eyes.

"The sets will be colorful." Rick cast a hopeful glance toward the door to the kitchen, but their order was nowhere in sight.

"That's the spirit. Can I count on you to lead the scenery team again?"

"I guess."

"Such overwhelming enthusiasm." She made a face at him, then transferred her attention to Colin. "Lights and sound for you?"

"Don't I get a year off for good behavior?"

"I'll consider that . . . after I see some good behavior."

"Ha-ha."

"Is that a yes?"

"Yeah, yeah. Sign me up. Trish says she'll help too."

"Excellent. The first meeting is in three weeks. I'll text you the date and time. In the meantime, here's some general information." She gave each of them a set of stapled pages.

"Hey—I think our food is coming." Rick cleared the spot in front of him as Carmen headed their direction with a heaping tray.

Kristin slid the empty folder back inside her tote while the waitress served their food, and the conversation moved on to other topics.

Thank you, Lord!

As usual, the next hour was filled with the laughter and camaraderie she always looked forward to at these breakfasts.

Yet as their meal wound down and they went their separate ways, she didn't feel as upbeat and carefree as usual.

For a reason she had no difficulty identifying.

The whole time she'd been enjoying herself with Rick and Colin, she'd kept thinking that while breakfast with her buds always gave her day a boost, a *perfect* day would also have included dinner with a certain handsome detective.

Who was *not* named Colin.

But that wasn't going to happen anytime soon. Based on Friday's phone conversation, she might not hear from him for weeks.

A possibility that did nothing to brighten up the gray, gloomy day—or take away the chill from the cold rain that smacked her in the face as she left the restaurant.

After a dash to her car, she flipped on her wipers and pulled out of the parking lot. If she stepped on the gas, she could make it to the late service at church.

Not a bad idea.

And while she spent an hour or two in the house of God, she could also pray that when she and Luke did reconnect, the interest Colin and Rick had tricked her into admitting wouldn't turn out to be one-sided.

10

"That's an interesting theory." Nick Bradley rested his fore-arms on the FBI interview room table and linked his fingers, his impassive expression offering no clue about his reaction to the story Luke had told him.

A poker face came in handy in this line of work, and Nick was a master at it.

Luke folded his own hands on the polished surface. After their phone conversation earlier, the Bureau would have double-checked his credentials and clearances before Nick called him back to schedule this late-Monday-morning meeting. In their place, he'd have done the same—especially after he'd used the T-word.

Any mention of terrorists would set off alarm bells with the FBI.

But Nick could be in the same skeptical camp as Sarge and Cole, now that he'd heard the full story.

Best to get his take straight up.

"You won't hurt my feelings if you tell me you think I'm off base. My boss and the colleague who's handling the Peterson homicide both consider my theory a stretch, at best."

"I've heard stranger stories in this job." Nick opened the file folder Luke had brought and examined the photos of the Middle Eastern man again. "One of them involved my wife— before she was my wife—and a Raggedy Ann doll. She was sitting where you are the day she told it to me."

"Sounds intriguing." Curious that Nick would share such a tidbit. Back in their Richmond days, he'd played his personal cards close to the vest.

But life—and love—could change people.

"I'll have to tell you about it sometime. In terms of your theory—I think it's worth investigating. We'll see if our facial recognition software can pick up a match in the terrorism databases. That would lend credence to your hypothesis . . . but it won't help us figure out what's hidden in the candles. We'll have to wait until the next shipment arrives to get that answer."

The same conclusion he'd come to.

It was going to be a long few weeks.

"I've asked the shop owner to alert us as soon as she has them in hand."

"How confident are you she's an innocent party in this whole scheme?"

"Very. Her alibi was solid. I also ran a background check." Standard protocol in a situation like this.

Nick flashed him a grin. "So did we, after your call. I assumed you dotted all the i's and crossed the t's, but given the high stakes, it doesn't hurt to double up on a few details." He closed the folder. "Instruct her to keep this whole situation under wraps—including the arrival of the candles. We'll need a window to evaluate them and put together a strategy if we do find anything inside."

"I'm confident she'll be discreet, but I'll reemphasize that."

Nick had handed him a perfect—and legitimate—reason to see Kristin again.

The agent rose. "I'll be in touch as soon as we've run these images through our software. Thanks for bringing along a flash drive."

"If you need any more information in the meantime, let me know." Luke stood too.

"Your report was thorough—as was the backup." He tapped the file folder. "It's been a while since our paths crossed in Virginia. How are you liking St. Louis?"

"It's fine. I was ready for a change of scene."

"I can understand that. I'm sorry about your wife."

The man was as thorough about intel now as he'd been during their association in Virginia, when the joint task force had helped foil a terrorist plot involving a diplomat's daughter.

"Thanks." His phone began to vibrate, and he shook Nick's hand as he pulled out the cell. "Incoming call. I'll be waiting to hear from you." He pushed through the door of the interview room into the lobby, scanning the screen on his phone.

Becca.

Hmm.

She didn't usually call during a workday.

He pressed talk and put the phone to his ear, exiting the building in downtown St. Louis. Yesterday's rain had cleared, and the sun was peeking through the clouds, coaxing the winter-weary vegetation back to life.

Good.

He was tired of cold and gray.

"Hi, Sis. What's up?"

"You tell me. Dad just called. He said you rang him last night and left a message, and you haven't returned his two follow-up voicemails. He's worried something's wrong."

"Nothing's wrong."

"I didn't think so . . . but if a call from you is so out-of-pattern he panicked, I thought I better ring you myself. Why didn't you get back to him?"

"I've had a busy morning—and I wasn't in a position to talk."

True . . . but he'd also been procrastinating. That was why he'd put off the difficult call to the last possible minute last night, finally placing it only because he'd promised Becca a week ago he would.

But even as he'd tapped in his dad's number, he'd had no idea how to broach the subject he wanted to talk about. The roll to voicemail had been a welcome reprieve.

One that had now ended.

"You took *my* call."

"You caught me leaving a meeting." He picked up his pace.

"Perfect. Then you have a minute to talk to Dad too."

"Quit pushing, Becca."

"He was really worried, Luke."

Wonderful.

Another helping of guilt to add to the boatload he already carried.

"I'll call him in a few minutes, okay? After I have some privacy."

"Fine. I'm hanging up." The line went dead.

Luke continued to his Taurus and slid behind the wheel, weighing the phone in his hand. It didn't get much more private than here, locked in his car.

Might as well get this over with.

Pulse quickening, he scrolled through his directory to the number and placed the call.

His father picked up on the first ring. "Luke?"

"Yeah. Hi, Dad."

"I got your message last night. I've been trying to reach you. Is everything all right?"

The anxiety ragging the edges of his father's question tugged at Luke's conscience.

"Fine. Busy—but that's not unusual."

"You'd tell me if there was a problem, wouldn't you?"

"Of course."

"You're not just saying that to keep me from worrying, are you?"

"No."

"Okay." His dad expelled a breath. "Sorry. I didn't mean to overreact . . . but I know that job of yours can be dangerous."

"Most of my days are routine."

"I have a feeling your version of routine and mine are at opposite ends of the spectrum. But I know you love your work."

"It fits me." A few beats ticked by while Luke scrambled to come up with the words to launch his apology.

"Well . . . I don't want to keep you." His dad broke the lengthening silence. "I know your days are packed, but it's been a treat to hear your voice. I . . . I miss seeing you—and talking with you."

Suck it up and get this done, Carter.

Right.

Bracing, he sent a silent plea for courage toward the expansive canvas of blue sky doming this spring day—and took the plunge. "The gaps in communication have been my fault, Dad. I'm sorry I haven't been in touch more often." He squeezed the cell. Swallowed. "It was a blow when you remarried, and it's taken me a while to come to grips with that."

"I had a feeling that's what's been on your mind. And it's okay, Son. I understand. You thought I was being disloyal to your mom."

Typical Dad. Always loving and forgiving.

Luke's throat tightened. "I was wrong to be upset."

"Don't beat yourself up about it. In your place, I suspect I'd have reacted the same way. To tell you the truth, I struggled with the situation myself after I met Lauren. I never planned to fall in love again, and it threw me."

"How did you deal with that?" There might be a lesson here for him as well.

"I backed off at first—but after I talked to my pastor, I got more comfortable with the notion. He's a young fellow, not long out of seminary, and wise beyond his years. He offered several insights that stuck with me."

"Like what?" He'd take any guidance he could get.

"That not everyone gets a second chance at love. That it's a gift—and refusing to accept it is like throwing that gift back in the Almighty's face."

"That's one way to look at it, I guess."

"I'm convinced it's the best way. He also reminded me that loving Lauren didn't mean I loved your mom any less. Just like loving you and your sister and my grandkids doesn't diminish my love for her. Every love is different and unique, and none of them can take the place of another."

Another valid point.

"Seems like he offered some sound counsel."

"As I said, he's a smart man. So I talked about it with Lauren. Turns out she was having similar doubts, for the same reasons. But after we discussed it, we agreed he was right and embraced the gift. I'm glad we did . . . and I hope someday my example might encourage you to do the same. You're too young to spend the rest of your life alone, Luke."

"So Becca has been telling me for months."

"Uh-oh. Persistence can be her middle name. How are you withstanding the onslaught?"

At his father's wry comment, Luke's lips twitched. "She's a force to be reckoned with once she sets her mind on a goal."

"No kidding. Remember in high school, when she decided to learn to play the violin?"

"How could I forget? She made that thing screech like a banshee."

His father chuckled. "Between you and me, I took to wearing cotton balls in my ears. But she stuck with it."

"Only because she was determined to get that kid who played in the school orchestra to notice her."

"It worked. He ended up asking her to the senior prom."

"And she never picked up the violin again—thank the Lord."

"She wasn't half bad by the time she quit, though. And she achieved her goal. Meaning if Becca has you in her sights . . . watch out."

"I'm already on high alert." No need to mention that his sister's mission to spice up his social life was succeeding . . . with an assist from Kristin—and now his dad. There would be plenty of opportunity to bring up the woman who'd been dominating his thoughts if they ended up clicking after this case ended.

"So . . . any chance you might be able to get away for a long weekend and pay Lauren and me a visit?"

"I wish I could, but I'm too new to have any vacation days."

"Maybe over Memorial Day?"

"I might be able to swing that. Or . . . why don't you two come out here? We could have a family get-together. I have a guest room in my apartment." The bed was buried under boxes he hadn't yet unpacked—but that was easy to fix.

"I'll ask Lauren. It would be wonderful to see you. In the meantime, you'll stay in touch—by more than email?"

"Yes. That's a promise."

He exhaled. "I can't tell you what a burden that lifts from my shoulders. I hate conflict and hurt feelings in a family. It's so much better when everyone gets along. As George Bernard Shaw said, 'A happy family is but an earlier heaven.'"

"I like that."

"Your mom did too. She's the one who shared it with me. I'm glad you and I are back on track."

"Me too. Take care, Dad—and give Lauren my best."

"Will do. Talk to you soon, Son."

Luke tapped *end*, slid the cell back onto his belt, cracked his window, and filled his lungs with the fresh spring air.

The call he'd dreaded was over—and the turbulent father-son waters had been smoothed out.

Whatever else he accomplished this week, nothing was going to top that.

But the visit he was going to pay Kristin before this day ended would be the icing on the cake.

■ ■ ■ ■ ■

Done.

Kristin hung up the phone and smiled.

Giving someone happy news was an upbeat way to end a Monday.

The bell over the WorldCraft door jingled, and she rose from her desk in the back room. Someone was cutting it very close to closing.

But she never turned a customer away.

She pushed through to the front . . . and stopped as Luke angled toward her.

Yes!

This was an even better way to end a Monday.

"You look happy." He strolled over to her.

"Um . . . yes, I am. I just hired a new part-time clerk." At least she had a legitimate excuse for her smile beyond her pleasure at seeing her favorite detective.

"That was fast."

"I called the career counselor who recommended Susan." The mention of her former clerk dimmed her pleasure a few watts, and the corners of her mouth drooped. "She runs an agency that helps women who've been out of the workforce for a while get a new start. She sent over a candidate, and we clicked. Alexa's first shift is Wednesday."

"That should take some of the pressure off."

"Yes. Much as I love this place, being here all day with no break does get tiring. To what do I owe this unexpected visit?"

"I have news."

"I like the sound of that." She glanced at her watch. "Let me lock up first. I'm only a few minutes away from closing, and I don't want us to be interrupted." She crossed to the door, flipped the locks, lowered the blinds, and motioned to the back corner, where two chairs were positioned near a half-open door. "We can sit by the dressing room."

He followed her over.

She tried not to giggle as he folded himself into one of the petite chairs usually occupied by a female waiting for a friend to try on an article of clothing.

"I can tell you're making a valiant attempt to restrain your mirth." He stretched one long leg out in front of him. "And while I admit I feel a bit like Miss Muffet, I've squeezed into kiddie chairs at my sister's to play with my nephews. This is roomy by comparison."

"Would you rather sit on the stool behind the counter?"

"Where would you sit?"

"I could stand."

"So could I . . . while you sit. Or we could stay here. I can handle this for a few minutes. You'll find I'm a very adaptable guy." He gave her an engaging grin.

"I can see that." As well as a host of other admirable attributes. "Let's stay here. I don't want any more delays hearing your news."

"Let me start by telling you about a body that was found on Tuesday."

She listened as he recounted the DNA match to the blood on

the patio at Elaine Peterson's, his visit to the FBI this morning—
and the call he'd received less than an hour ago from the agent
he'd met with.

"You mean the facial recognition software found a match
on the terrorist watch list?" A tiny shiver of fear rippled
through her.

"Yes. We have the guy's last known address—here in St. Louis.
We're going to be delving into his recent activity . . . discreetly
. . . while we wait for the candles."

"I'm still having a hard time connecting the monks with
anything underhanded. All of them have devoted their lives to
prayer and humanitarian aid."

"In other words—they're providing perfect cover for a terrorist plot. Who would suspect monks?"

Stomach churning, she gripped her hands together in her lap.
"Brother Michael would have been devastated. All the monks
will be."

"It's not their fault. And if this plays out the way we hope,
it will come to an end soon."

"So what do we do for now?"

"Wait for the next shipment." He shifted in the small chair.
"In the meantime, please keep everything we've discussed confidential. Don't tell anyone about the candles, the connection we
suspect with the monastery, or when the next shipment might
arrive. I've given you more information than normal protocol
would allow because your cooperation will be necessary going
forward."

"Other than Colin and Rick, there's no one I'd talk to about
this anyway."

"I'd prefer you not discuss it with them, either."

"Even Colin?" She hiked up an eyebrow.

"Yes."

"He's in your department."

"This is being kept under wraps internally too. Terrorism is the FBI's purview. Information is shared only on a need-to-know basis."

"Then why are you in the loop? You're not FBI."

He shifted on the small chair. "I have top-secret clearance from a previous assignment in Richmond."

She waited a few seconds, hoping he'd offer more.

He didn't.

Fine. She wouldn't put him on the spot by asking. "What happens if we find out there *is* contraband inside some of the candles?"

"Depends on what it is. The FBI will pick up the next shipment from you as soon as it arrives and x-ray every candle. If they find anything, we'll formulate a plan to track down the brains behind the operation."

Kristin rubbed her temple, which was beginning to throb. "I feel like I'm in the middle of a high-stakes suspense novel."

"I wish this *was* a piece of fiction rather than real-life drama."

"You don't think I'm in any danger, do you?" She curled her fingers into a ball. "I don't want to sound like a wimp—I mean, I dealt with some rocky situations in Ethiopia—but terrorism freaks me out. Those people don't operate by rules that make sense in my world."

He touched the back of her hand, his fingers warm against her chilly skin. "No. If this turns out to be terrorism related, I'm guessing you're being used as a convenient conduit. Like the monks are. At this point, as far as the people involved are aware, the system is working and you're oblivious. We want them to keep believing that. My goal is to get to the bottom of this mystery . . . and keep you safe in the process. Will you trust me to do my best to do that?"

She considered the detective sitting across from her. A man she'd known for barely two weeks.

Yet despite their short acquaintance, she *did* trust him. As much as she trusted her best buds.

Amazing.

And telling, as Colin might comment if he was privy to her thoughts.

"Yes."

"Thank you." He rose. "Until the new candles arrive, we'll be in a holding pattern."

She followed him to the front of the store. "Does that mean I won't be hearing from you until then?"

"I'll stay in touch." He stopped at the door and turned to her. "But much as I'd like to see you, this is an active case. And I never mix business and pleasure—despite the temptation." His last sentence was infused with warmth.

As for that banked fire in his eyes . . .

Whew.

If she'd had any doubts about his interest, they evaporated under the heat of his smoldering gaze.

"I understand . . . and I'll be looking forward to this mystery being solved so life can get back to normal."

"Better than normal, I hope." His voice held a throaty . . . intimate . . . note.

O-kay.

She needed to go stand in front of the air conditioner—except it was too early in the season to be on.

Not that her body had gotten that message.

"I hope so too." She sounded as breathless as if she'd just blasted across the finish line in a fifty-meter sprint.

"Good to know. Take care . . . and call me if anything comes up that concerns you."

"I will."

He flipped the lock and slipped out into the late afternoon sunshine.

Kristin peeked around the shades, keeping him in sight as long as possible.

But all too soon he disappeared.

For now.

She locked the door and straightened the candles on the monastery display, another shiver rippling through her.

The police and FBI might be all over this case, but she couldn't shake the anxiety that had dogged her since the day Susan was killed. And it continued to swell as the pile of puzzle pieces grew.

A remote monastery in the Middle East.

Murders of innocent people.

Mysterious candles.

A dead terrorist.

How did they all connect?

That was the question everyone wanted answered—but the shipment that might provide the solution was weeks away.

Kristin flipped off the storeroom light and let herself out the back door—scrutinizing the alley in both directions first.

Overkill, perhaps.

But she intended to heed Luke's advice about being cautious.

The mastermind behind this scheme might not realize law enforcement was suspicious . . . but every instinct Kristin possessed told her that if that person discovered they were on to him, the situation could deteriorate fast.

And if that happened, she might suddenly find herself in the eye of a deadly storm.

11

His six Kristinless weeks were finally over.

Hallelujah!

"You look happy. What's up?"

As Colin spoke from his office doorway, Luke exited voicemail, set his phone on his desk, and erased his smile. "News on a case."

"Which one?"

"Nothing you're involved in."

Colin narrowed his eyes and walked in.

Great.

"Is this related to what happened at WorldCraft? Kristin gives me the same kind of blow-off answer whenever I ask her what's going on too."

"I can't discuss her case."

"Because the FBI's involved. I get that. I'm not asking you to discuss it. I'm just asking if that call means things are heating up again."

Luke rocked back in his chair. As far as he could tell, Colin was as solid as they came.

But he couldn't take any chances.

"Depends on how you define heating up."

Colin muttered some unintelligible word and folded his arms.

"Look . . . I don't want to know any state secrets, okay? But I don't want Kristin in the middle of some explosive situation without protection. We have a long history, and we watch each other's backs."

"I know some of the history."

"Is that right?" He strolled over and settled his hip on the corner of the desk. "Dinner conversation over spaghetti, maybe?"

So Colin—and probably Rick—knew about the memorable evening he and Kristin had shared an eon ago.

At least it felt like ancient history after the endless weeks they'd been apart.

"Is that what Kristin told you?"

"She didn't have to. I figured it out." Colin's laser gaze locked on his. "She likes you, in case you haven't picked that up."

"The feeling is mutual."

"I don't want her to get hurt."

"I don't, either."

"I'm not just talking about physically, with this case."

"Me, neither."

Colin sized him up. "She's a very special person. The best."

"I agree. And after this case is over, I plan to get to know her a lot better." No reason to keep that under wraps. Colin—and Rick—would find out soon anyway.

Several silent seconds ticked by while his fellow detective studied him. He couldn't fault Colin for his concern. From what Kristin had told him, he and Rick thought of her as a sister.

But he wasn't about to be intimidated, either.

After a few moments, one side of Colin's mouth hitched up. "You know Rick and I will be watching you, right?"

"I assumed as much. Does Kristin know that?"

"She'll suspect—and she won't like it."

"That sounds like her." His own lips twitched.

"As long as we understand each other."

"Let me clarify. If I do anything you don't like, you'll send a hit man after me. Does that about sum it up?"

"Close." Colin grinned. "I'm glad we're on the same page. Good luck with whatever's breaking."

"Thanks. I hope it helps us wrap this up—soon."

He waited until Colin retreated down the hall, then picked up his phone again. Two calls to make . . . including a return one to Kristin to set up the reunion he'd been anticipating for six long weeks.

·····

The knock on the back door came at exactly three o'clock—as Luke had promised.

Kristin sized up the two customers browsing through the shop. Neither appeared on the verge of checking out or leaving.

"Ladies . . . I have a few chores to take care of in the stockroom. If you need any assistance or find an item you'd like to purchase, just knock on the door."

They nodded in acknowledgment and went back to perusing the items on display.

Kristin left the showroom, closed the door that separated it from the storage area, and finger-combed her hair as she hurried toward the rear door.

The two men she'd expected were waiting for her on the other side.

Luke, in his standard work attire of jacket and tie, was every bit as handsome as she remembered from six weeks ago . . . and the lean, sandy-haired man in the dark suit who stood beside him epitomized the stereotypical clean-cut FBI agent.

"Come in." She ushered them through the door and closed it behind her.

"Do you have customers up front?" Luke smiled at her, setting off a flutter in her stomach.

"Yes . . . but they can knock if they need me."

He did the introductions, and she returned Agent Bradley's firm shake.

"Is the box back here?" The man got straight to business.

"Yes." She led them over to a worktable beside her desk, where the travel-weary carton rested.

"It's big." Luke eyeballed it.

"They always add a bunch of packing material to keep the candles from breaking."

"It arrived this morning?" The FBI agent pulled a folded-up plastic trash bag from his pocket.

"Yes. About ten."

"And it's been here ever since?"

"Yes."

"Does anyone else have access to this room?"

"No."

He shook the bag open. "We'll return the candles as soon as possible."

"Does the box always arrive that dinged up?" Luke gave it another scan.

"Yes. But I've never had a broken candle."

Agent Bradley handed the bag to Luke, picked up the box, and worked the plastic around it.

A knock sounded on the door to the storeroom.

"Go ahead and deal with that. I'll get these back to the office." The agent hefted the box into his arms.

She glanced at Luke.

"I'll let Nick out and stay for a few minutes." He followed the agent to the exit and opened the door for him.

"Okay." Better than okay. After all these weeks apart, with only a few fast phone calls from him to sustain her, she wanted more than five minutes in his company.

Another knock sounded.

"Kristin?"

"That's Ryan." She sighed. Of all times for her neighbor to show up.

"Go deal with him. I'll wait."

She hurried to the door as Luke disappeared behind a shelving unit, pasting on a pleasant expression before she opened it.

"Hi, Ryan." She slipped into the shop, clicking the door shut behind her. Both of the customers were still busy inspecting merchandise. "What's up?"

"Is everything all right?"

"Of course. Why?"

"As I pulled into the lot, I saw two guys going in your back door."

Bad timing.

She straightened a silk scarf on the display beside her as she formulated a response. "Just some leftover police business. They had a few more questions."

"Oh. Any suspects?"

"They're pretty close-mouthed about the case. If they ever do solve this, we'll probably hear about it on the news."

"True." One of the customers walked toward the checkout counter, a glass paperweight in her hand. "I'll let you get back to work. Glad there wasn't a problem. I'm still spooked after what happened here."

"I hear you—and I appreciate your concern."

"Neighbors should watch out for each other." He fell back as she moved toward the counter. "Talk to you soon."

Kristin finished the transaction as fast as she could, and the second customer left empty-handed on the heels of the one who'd made a purchase.

Perfect.

She should have no interruptions while she spoke with Luke.

Back in the storeroom, she closed the door behind her. "Come out, come out, wherever you are."

"*The Wizard of Oz.*" He emerged from behind the shelving unit. "I loved that movie as a kid. It had everything—adventure, fantasy, witches, flying monkeys, a wizard with magical powers."

"I hated the monkeys. They gave me nightmares."

"Becca always said the same thing. Another indication you two would get along well." He stopped in front of her. Inches away. Close enough for her to feel the heat of his body and catch a faint whiff of his spicy aftershave. "It's nice to see you again."

Keep it light, Kristin. Let him set the pace. Don't read more into a husky comment than might be intended.

"Mutual, I'm sure."

"*White Christmas.*"

"You're good at this game." She clasped her hands in front of her to keep them from straying his direction. "But I'm surprised you know that one. It's about as far from *The Wizard of Oz* as you can get."

"Mom made us all watch it together every Christmas. We can recite every line and sing every song. It was a family tradition."

"I like the notion of family traditions."

"We're going to relaunch that one this Christmas. Becca's planning to host. We all decided that at a family barbecue at her house on Sunday. Dad and his wife came up for the Memorial Day weekend."

"And you attended?" Apparently the past six weeks had been productive for him on the personal front, if not with the case.

"Uh-huh. We've mended our fences. Or I should say, I saw the light and apologized."

"I'm glad, Luke."

"So am I." He propped his left elbow on a shelf filled with merchandise for restocking, his ring finger on full display.

It was empty.

Her pulse took an uptick.

It appeared he'd made his peace with a *lot* of issues during the weeks they were apart.

"So, uh, where do we go from here?" She dragged her gaze away from his finger.

"You mean with the case?" Humor glinted in his jade irises. "Because I could answer that a couple of different ways—depending."

Was he flirting with her?

"On what?"

"On how your pal Ryan fits into your life. He hangs around here an awful lot."

"He's nothing more than a friendly neighbor. Never has been, never will be."

"That's what I hoped you'd say. I was afraid your relationship with him might have heated up while we were waiting for the candles to arrive."

"No." Her answer came out in a croak.

If Luke noticed her lapse in composure, he let it pass.

"Then back to your question. In terms of the case, we wait to hear from Nick. They'll x-ray the candles tomorrow morning, so we'll have an answer to the burning question—pardon the pun—within twenty-four hours. If my theory holds, we'll regroup and decide on next steps, depending on what's inside. If it crashes and burns . . . we've waited six weeks for a big disappointment, and we'll be back to square one."

"Meaning if the murders and that dead terrorist aren't connected, someone has gotten away with killing Susan—for reasons we might never discover." A sobering possibility that put a damper on her romantic fantasies.

"No." His jaw hardened. "I'm not giving up on her case if my theory falls through. I'll continue to troll for leads, and I'll revisit all the evidence. I don't intend to stop working it until there's nothing left to work. Victims deserve justice."

That sounded like the man who'd dominated her thoughts since the day they'd met.

"I'm relieved—but not surprised—to hear you say that. You strike me as a man of integrity."

"Always. I take promises . . . and vows . . . seriously. Including this one." He lifted his left hand and wiggled his bare ring finger. "You noticed the ring is missing."

"Yes." No sense pretending otherwise after staring at the empty spot.

"It's taken three years, but I've finally come around to Becca's way of thinking. And my dad's. And yours. I'll always love Jenny—but that doesn't mean I can't find room in my heart for someone else . . . if the right someone comes along. I'm now open to that possibility. Or I will be, once this case wraps up."

She searched his face. "Is that your way of saying you plan to ask me out after this mess is resolved?"

He gave her a beguiling smile. "Yes. I'd like us to get to know each other apart from this case—and I'm hoping you feel the same."

"Yes." *Yes, yes, yes, yes, yes!*

"That's the best news I've had in weeks. Months. Maybe years."

If he was willing to lay his cards on the table, why not do the same?

"Can I be honest?" She sidled a hair closer. "I wish we didn't have to wait."

His irises darkened. "Don't tempt me." He lifted his hand and traced the curve of her jaw with a gentle finger.

Her breath hitched . . . and her nerve endings began to buzz. Without any conscious decision to do so, she swayed toward him.

He hesitated . . . then slowly leaned down.

Her eyelids drifted closed, and . . .

Jangle, jangle, jangle.

Oh, for pity's sake!

Her eyes jerked open to find Luke's lips hovering a whisper away from hers.

Two incidents of bad timing back to back.

What were the odds?

"Saved by the bell." Luke straightened up, his lighthearted comment at odds with the hoarseness in his voice. "I told myself I wasn't going to do that, and I have a fair amount of self-discipline—but you manage to undermine it. That was a close call."

Not close enough, as far as she was concerned.

Like three inches too short.

"I guess this gives us something to look forward to." That was one positive spin on the interruption, anyway.

"Count on it. Now I'll get out of here and let you go back to work."

"I can think of things I'd rather do."

"Hold that thought." He winked and eased back. "I'll slip out the way I came in. I'd rather no one notice I was here."

She started to turn toward the front. Stopped. Swiveled back.

"Darn. I meant to tell you sooner, but I got a little . . . distracted. Someone did notice. Ryan. That's why he stopped by."

"What did he say?" Luke was instantly back in detective mode.

"He said he saw two guys coming in my back door as he pulled into the alley and wanted to confirm there was no trouble."

"What did you tell him?"

"That you were here on some follow-up police business."

"Did he seem to buy that?"

"Yes."

"Okay. I'm not too worried about our visit today. We both parked on a side street, so our cars weren't in the lot to raise any suspicions."

"Why would your cars raise eyebrows? Lots of people park back there. Didn't you say we were under the radar at this point?"

"We are—as far as we know. But now that the candles are here and we're moving toward what could be an aggressive investigation, we're taking extra precautions. We definitely want WorldCraft to appear to be doing business as usual. I'll be more alert as I leave."

"Will I hear from you soon?"

"The minute I have any news from the FBI." He crossed to the back door, cracked it, gave the alley a sweep, and slipped through.

The bell in front jingled again—either the customer leaving already or a new one coming.

She needed to get back to work.

But with the investigation—along with a budding romance—shifting into high gear, she doubted anything in her life was going to be business as usual for the foreseeable future.

12

We have a hit. Can u meet me at our office
ASAP?

Luke skimmed the text message from Nick, pivoted back toward his car in the police headquarters parking lot, and broke into a jog, thumbs working.

On my way.

Once behind the wheel, he sped toward downtown St. Louis.

Nick and another agent were waiting for him after he passed through the magnetometer and the receptionist behind the bulletproof glass window buzzed the door open.

"My colleague, Mark Sanders—who also heads our SWAT team." Nick motioned to the man beside him.

Luke shook hands with the agent, processing his inclusion in their meeting.

If Nick wanted the SWAT team leader up-to-speed on the case, the analysis of the candles must have revealed something very hot.

Nick started down the hall. "We've commandeered a conference room. Let me show you what we have."

He followed the two men through a beehive of cubicles and into a room that held a long table lined with chairs.

Nick closed the door behind them. "We've had a busy—and productive—morning. One that validates your theory."

"So the candles did contain contraband."

"Of a very unique nature." Nick motioned toward the carton they'd picked up from WorldCraft yesterday, sitting on the far end of the table. "There are twenty-one candles in there that are nothing but candles. Those"—he indicated four lined up on the table in front of them—"contained what I believe, based on some googling and a discussion with our Art Crime Team agent, to be valuable and highly illegal items. Take a look." He lifted a cloth that was spread on a small section of the table.

Luke stepped closer and leaned down to examine the objects resting on a square of felt. The gold earrings and necklace he could identify. The three carved tubes, ranging in length from one to three inches? He had no clue what they were.

But all of the items appeared to be old.

"What are those?" He indicated the tubes.

"We think they're cylinder seals. The ancient equivalent of a notary's stamp."

"I take it they're valuable."

"That's what my initial research suggests. I've got a call in to the expert on Middle Eastern antiquities at the art museum to validate that."

Luke dug into his memory, calling up some articles he'd read about the atrocities being committed against ancient sites in the Middle East. "Are you thinking these might be looted artifacts? The kind ISIS has been selling on the black market to fund its terrorist activities?"

"Yes. But before we go too far down that road, I want an expert to weigh in. Are you available to sit in on my meeting with him?"

"Yes." He'd clear whatever was necessary from his schedule to *make* himself available.

"I'm hoping to get in there today. If I don't hear back from him within the hour, I'll place another call. Have a seat and let's talk about how this might play out."

Luke pulled out a chair, and Nick took the one beside him. Mark leaned a shoulder against the wall a few feet away.

"I assume those four candles were marked in some way?" Luke motioned toward the ones in front of him.

"Yes." Nick picked up a small, clear plastic sleeve containing a paper disk. "Every candle has one of these stickers on the bottom. They're printed in Arabic, and each has an illustration of a cross. The crosses on most of the labels have no line above or below them." He passed over the plastic sleeve.

Luke examined the cross on the label. "There's a line over this cross."

"Yes. Two of the crosses have lines at the top; two at the bottom. These were the labels on the four candles containing contraband."

Luke quickly fit the pieces together. "Are you thinking ISIS is sending looted artifacts here in the candles, selling them through some established network to less-than-scrupulous galleries or private collectors, and using the profits to fund US cells?"

One side of Nick's mouth hiked up. "Why aren't you working for us?"

"I like where I am—but thanks for the compliment."

"To answer your question . . . yes. That's our speculation. And here's how they hid the merchandise." He picked up one of the four candles sitting on the table and tipped the top away from them.

The center of the candle had been hollowed out from the bottom.

"Clever."

"Very. All they had to do was insert the items, put in a wax plug, and replace the doctored label. However . . . there's no hard evidence to support our theory that ISIS is involved. As we've discussed, the terrorist-watch-list victim your people found in that shallow grave led nowhere. The few suspicious activities that put him on the list happened more than two years ago."

"Given his presence at Elaine Peterson's house, though—and the missing candles—it's logical to assume he could have been tapped to retrieve a couple of them. Except Elaine beat him to the shop . . . so he had to track them down."

"That's our assumption."

"And Kristin—Ms. Dane, the shop owner—said no one has ever bought more than two candles. More than one person must be retrieving the marked candles."

"Duly noted. Now let's talk strategy. Assuming our expert verifies the authenticity and value of the items we found, how willing do you think Ms. Dane will be to work with us?"

Luke's antennas went up. "Define 'work with us.'"

"We want to put some cameras in her shop to get visuals of the people who buy these candles. We'd also like to place a mic near the checkout counter. We'll want her to alert us with a specific code word when the marked candles are purchased. Our agents stationed within watching distance of the shop can then follow the buyers."

"I'm confident she'd cooperate—but I'm not crazy about putting a civilian in a position like that." The plan didn't sound dangerous . . . but setups like this could go wrong in a thousand different ways.

And he didn't want Kristin in the line of fire.

"If it was a larger shop, we could have one of our undercover people play the part of a clerk. But she only has one part-time employee. A new face could raise suspicions."

He couldn't argue with that.

"Are you concerned she'll get nervous and tip off the courier?" Mark joined the conversation for the first time.

"No. She's steady—and she's done some nonprofessional theater work."

"That's helpful." Nick leaned back in his chair. "And our people will be close by. Based on past patterns, the candles are retrieved within a day or two of arrival. Surveillance at the shop won't last long."

"You're not expecting the people who pick up the candles to lead you directly to the person running the show, are you?"

"No. I assume they'll leave them at a drop location. We'll follow whoever picks them up there as well. I would anticipate a minimum of two layers between the minions and the brains of this operation. Perhaps more."

"What about the person who's infiltrated the monastery?"

"At some point we'll need to alert the monks about the breach. We have less influence there . . . but we do have CIA operatives in that area who can help."

Luke looked back at the hollowed-out candle . . . and suddenly Kristin's story about Brother Michael's tragic death took on an ominous cast.

"You remember the monk I told you about, who died in the candle-making workshop at the monastery?"

"You're wondering if it wasn't an accident after all."

So they were on the same page.

"He died at night. No witnesses. He might have come upon someone doing that." He motioned toward the hollowed-out candle.

"The same thought crossed my mind. When our CIA operative talks with the abbot, he'll mention that possibility. It might make the monks more willing to cooperate with our people in outing the man if they suspect he killed one of their own. However, our first priority is to get the US situation under control. The last thing we need here is more funding for terrorist cells."

"I hear you."

"We can approach Ms. Dane about her involvement—or you can lay the groundwork after we meet with our expert at the art museum." Nick rested his elbows on the arms of the chair and steepled his fingers. "It might be best if you take the lead on this with her. You seem to have developed a . . . rapport."

Was his interest that obvious?

"I can do that." He kept his expression as neutral as possible. But it didn't fool Nick.

"I've been in your shoes. Remember the Raggedy Ann doll case? Mark's been there too. He met his wife during a case. But hang tight until we get this resolved."

Luke glanced at the agent leaning against the wall, who gave him a flicker of a smile. He hadn't participated much in their discussion—but he'd obviously been paying attention.

"I keep my work and social life separate." Even if he'd come close to mingling the two yesterday.

"Smart move. I'll call you as soon as we have an appointment with our contact at the art museum. We can reconvene there." Nick stood. "I'll walk you out."

Luke shook hands with Mark and followed Nick to the security door that led to the lobby.

"Thanks for keeping me in the loop." He extended his hand to Nick as well.

"You have excellent creds—and a connection to one of the key players." The man gave him a firm shake.

"I'm not expecting there will be any danger to Ms. Dane . . . are you?" Luke locked onto Nick's gaze, watching the man closely, as he retained his grip on his hand.

"No. Her part in this is small, and in the early stages of the transfer of artifacts. She should be out of the picture before any complications might arise." Nick didn't so much as blink.

As far as Luke could see, the agent was leveling with him. And his response made sense. There was no reason for this to get dangerous until they were closing in on the person calling the shots—well past Kristin's role.

He released Nick's hand. "I'll wait for your call."

"It could be soon."

"The sooner the better." For reasons both personal and professional.

He pushed through the door to the lobby and headed toward the exit.

Outside, the sun was bright, the sky cloudless, the temperature climbing to unseasonable heights for the first day of June.

And the heat was ratcheting up on this case too.

If the expert they would soon consult concurred with Nick's assessment about the artifacts, the FBI would quickly implement a takedown plan. There wouldn't be much time lapse between retrieval and disposal of the items. Hanging on to contraband was dangerous, and the leader would want to minimize the risk as much as possible.

However . . . he could be directing the operation from a distance, insulated to avoid detection. No one in the chain might know his identity. This had been going on for two years, and there'd been no slipups. The man in charge—and he assumed it was a man, given terrorist views of women—was well hidden.

But no one had been on his trail, either. Now that law enforcement was involved, every angle of this operation would be scrutinized. If the piece of scum who was aiding and abetting vile acts of terrorism had any vulnerabilities, they'd find them.

And they'd do everything in their power to bring him down.

. . . . .

The man from the FBI had called again.

Heart pounding, Yusef picked up the message that was front and center on his desk and lowered himself into his chair.

He had to return the call. Now. The art museum trustee meeting that had occupied his morning was over. He had no more excuse to delay.

"You're back."

Yusef lifted his head. His administrative assistant stood on the threshold of his office, glasses propped in her graying hair . . . as usual. Demeanor solemn . . . as usual. Penny took her job as seriously as he took his.

"Yes. The meeting was long."

"I see you found the second message. It sounded urgent."

"I was just getting ready to return the call. Go have some lunch. Your work can wait until you return."

"You never go to lunch anymore."

He tried for a smile, but his lips barely moved. "I eat a big breakfast." True at one time—but not in the past two years. Not since constant worry had robbed him of his appetite . . . and joy . . . and the peace he'd once found in this land of freedom where he was no longer free. "Go. I will be here the rest of the afternoon."

"Can I bring you a sandwich?"

"No. Thank you." With the message from the FBI staring at him, the mere thought of food turned his stomach.

"I'll be back in half an hour."

"There is no need to rush. Enjoy your lunch."

"Call if you need me." She motioned toward the messages on his desk, curiosity sparking in her eyes. "I wonder what they want?"

"I have no idea."

But that was a lie.

He was pretty certain he knew exactly what they wanted.

The timing of this call was too coincidental, coming on the heels of Amir's alert that a new shipment would soon arrive.

But how had the authorities tracked him down?

Had he made some sort of slip?

And if he had, what did that mean for Touma?

Another wave of crushing panic swept over him.

"Dr. Bishara . . ." Penny took a step toward him, twin furrows creasing her brow. "Are you all right?"

"Yes. Fine." He tried to fill his lungs with air. "Tired after that long meeting, though. Go have your lunch."

After a brief hesitation, she retreated through the door, pulling it closed behind her.

As it clicked shut, he sank back in his chair, wrestled his emotions into submission, and forced the left side of his brain to engage.

If the FBI knew about Amir's operation . . . and if they had proof of his own part in it . . . they wouldn't call. They'd swoop in and arrest him.

So maybe this was a fishing expedition.

And if so, maybe he could deflect their suspicion.

It might be best to play this as cool as he could, see what they had to say before jumping to conclusions. Speculation was fruitless. He was a man of facts—and he had too few in this situation to draw any conclusions.

Instead of letting fear cloud his thinking, he needed to see what this agent had to say, analyze what he learned . . . then do what was best for Touma.

Expelling a shaky breath, he sat upright . . . put the phone to his ear . . . and punched in the number for the FBI.

. . . . .

As her phone trilled from the depths of her purse, Kristin dashed across the kitchen, dumped the sacks of groceries onto the counter, and burrowed through her shoulder bag.

This could be the news she'd been waiting weeks to hear.

At last her fingers closed over the cell. It was almost four o'clock, and Luke had promised yesterday to call her as soon as he heard from the FBI.

Please let this be him!

She yanked the phone out and skimmed the screen.

Froze.

It wasn't Luke.

The number *was* familiar, however—though it didn't appear on her screen often.

And never in the middle of the afternoon on a workday.

She put the phone to her ear. "Hi, Dad. This is a surprise."

"Sorry to bother you while you're working." His voice sounded strained.

Uh-oh.

Bad vibes began wafting over the line.

"No problem." She swallowed and took a steadying breath. "My assistant is covering the shop this afternoon. Is everything okay?"

"No. I . . . I'm at the hospital. There's been an accident."

Kristin's stomach bottomed out. "Are you hurt? What about Mom?"

"I'm fine. Your mom is . . . it was a car accident. We were going to a luncheon . . . a business function she had. I was meeting her there." His sentences were choppy, as if he was having difficulty breathing. "I spotted her ahead of me . . . half a block away. Another driver . . . he . . . he ran the light and crossed the intersection as she was driving through."

Dear God!

Kristin gripped the edge of the counter and braced. "Is she . . . is she . . ."

"No! But her arm is broken, and she . . . she has head injuries. She's been unconscious since the accident."

Which would have been . . . what? She forced her brain into

gear. Her dad had said a luncheon. It was an hour later on the East Coast. This had happened . . . almost six hours ago?

And he'd waited until now to contact her?

"Why didn't you call me sooner?" The question came out half accusation, half miffed.

"I was trying to get an update from the doctor." Her father sounded puzzled by her tone. "I didn't want to interrupt your day until I had some news."

"The accident was news enough."

"I'm sorry . . . it's been busy here. And there wasn't anything you could do. It didn't occur to me you'd be upset about the delay."

No, of course not.

Thoughts of her had always been at the bottom of his priority list.

Typical Dad.

Get over it, Kristin. This is just how it is with them. How it's always been. How it will always be.

She forced herself to quash the hurt that bubbled up. "What did the doctors say?"

"It's a traumatic brain injury. Her skull isn't fractured, but they said the sudden jar from the collision caused serious bruising and tore some blood vessels, which resulted in bleeding. They said there could be other damage too, but that can be difficult to detect with brain scans. We won't know the full extent of her injuries until she wakes up."

Bleeding in the brain.

That was the message seared in Kristin's mind.

Her hands started to shake, and she felt behind her for a stool. Sank onto it. "This is bad, isn't it?"

"It could be—and it will get worse if her brain swells." His words rasped, and he cleared his throat. "She's in the neuro ICU, so she's being monitored closely."

"Do you have any kind of prognosis?"

"Not yet—but the longer she remains unconscious, the less optimistic it is."

Call waiting beeped, and she checked the screen.

Luke's number.

"Kristin? Are you there?"

"Yes." She refocused on her dad. "I'll fly out."

"You have obligations there."

Yes, she did. More, at the moment, than he realized.

She massaged her forehead. She probably should have shared the harrowing events of two months ago with her parents . . . but her mom had been in the middle of a huge legal case and her dad overseas much of April.

Plus, they never asked much about her life, other than the generic "anything new" question they always threw in during their brief and infrequent conversations.

Had she talked to them at all in April?

Not that she could recall.

"Kristin?"

"Yes. I'm . . . I'm thinking. Let me see what I can work out."

"I understand if you can't get away. Your mom would too. We know your business is by and large a one-person show. Arranging time off must be difficult."

The practical sentiment sounded like her dad . . . but had she detected a slight hint of yearning? Like he might actually want her to come? Perhaps even *need* her?

Or was that wishful thinking?

The latter, Kristin. You've let yourself go down that path in the past, and you've always been disappointed.

Right.

However—her family had never before faced a disaster of this magnitude, either.

No matter their history, she couldn't leave her dad in the lurch.

"Let me make a few calls, Dad. I'll get back to you as soon

as I know my plans. But if anything . . . if there's any change in Mom's condition . . . will you call me right away?"

"Yes—and I'm sorry to inconvenience you like this."

"Being there for your family isn't an inconvenience." Or it shouldn't be. "And this wasn't anything you had any control over."

"That's not quite true. I should have picked your mom up. She asked me to, but I . . . I was tied up in a meeting." His voice broke.

Kristin closed her eyes. Never once had her dad—or mom— suggested it was a mistake to give business the highest priority. Work always came first. Period.

Too bad it had taken a life-threatening event to shake that conviction.

Now her father almost seemed to be seeking comfort and reassurance—the very things that had been in short supply during her growing-up years, until Colin and Rick had filled that gap.

But why not do for her dad what he and her mom had never done for her?

"It wasn't your fault, Dad."

"This wouldn't have happened if she'd been in my car."

"You don't know that. *Your* car could have been the one crossing the intersection."

"Unlikely."

"But possible. We need to accept where we are, move on from here, and pray—a lot."

"I'm a little rusty at prayer outside of church."

Her parents must still be shoehorning Sunday services into their schedules so they could cross the Almighty off their to-do list for the week.

Thank heaven Rick and Colin had helped her find a deeper, more sustaining faith than the one in which she was raised.

"God doesn't expect eloquence, just earnestness."

"I suppose I could give it a try."

"It couldn't hurt. I'll call you back later tonight, as soon as I have my schedule worked out."

"That's fine. I'll be at the ICU, and the phone doesn't always work in there. If you can't reach me, leave a message and I'll get back to you. Talk to you soon."

The line went dead.

No "Good-bye." No "I love you." No "Hang in, we'll get through this together."

Again . . . typical Dad.

Pressure building in her throat, she blinked to clear her vision, gave herself a minute to regain her composure, and pressed Luke's number.

After three rings, it rolled to voicemail.

That figured.

She scrolled through her texts and found one from him.

Have news. Will call later.

Since he wasn't answering his phone, all she could do was wait.

Moving on autopilot, she put away the perishable groceries while her mind grappled with her dilemma. Despite the little voice in her head urging her to do what any good daughter would do and jump on the next plane for Boston, she couldn't finalize any travel plans until she talked to Luke. If his theory had proven correct and the candles had some connection to a terrorist operation, she—and her shop—might be key to whatever plan law enforcement was concocting. It wasn't as if her parents needed her, after all.

They never had.

Yet as she picked up a melting box of her favorite mint chocolate chip ice cream and blinked away the mist obscuring her vision, she faced the truth.

Maybe she still needed them.

13

Nick Bradley was waiting for him by the door to the art museum, briefcase in hand.

"Have you been here long?" Luke picked up his pace as he approached, ignoring the sudden vibration of his phone against his hip. He wasn't late . . . but he suspected the FBI agent had beaten him by a fair margin.

"I always arrive early. It's been helpful on a number of occasions. Let's go."

Luke followed him through the door, and a few minutes later they were being ushered into a book-lined office.

A gray-haired man who appeared to be in his early to mid-sixties rose from behind the desk as they entered. "Good afternoon, gentlemen. Yusef Bishara."

"Special Agent Nick Bradley." Nick reached across the desk to take the hand the man extended and passed him a business card. "This is Detective Luke Carter from St. Louis County."

Luke shook the man's hand and shared a card too.

"Please . . . let us make ourselves comfortable." Motioning toward a small conference table on the side of the room, Dr.

Bishara emerged from behind his desk and joined them there. "May I offer you some coffee or water?"

"I'm fine." Nick looked his way, and Luke shook his head.

"Then please tell me how may I help you?" He took a seat at the table.

"We're working on a case that appears to involve artifacts from the Middle East. Since you're an expert in that field, we're hoping you can authenticate the items and perhaps give us some idea of their history and value."

"I would be pleased to do my best."

Nick retrieved five small boxes from his briefcase and set them on the table. One by one, he lifted the lids to reveal the carved tubes, the necklace, and the earrings.

Dr. Bishara leaned forward and examined each item in silence, hands folded on the polished wood in front of him. Then he stood. "A moment, please."

He crossed back to his desk, rummaged through a drawer, and returned with a jeweler's loupe and a pair of gloves. After retaking his seat, he donned the gloves, picked up one of the cylinders, and examined it from every angle. He repeated the process with the other two cylinders, but left the jewelry in the boxes as he studied it.

At last he leaned back and set the loupe down.

"What do you think, Dr. Bishara?" Luke pulled a small notebook from his pocket.

"You must understand I am not an authority on every object that comes out of the Middle East, though that region is my specialty. My primary interest is statuary and decorative objects."

"But you have broad knowledge of artifacts from that part of the world, correct?"

"Yes."

"Whatever you can tell us about these items will be helpful." Luke clicked his pen into the ready position.

"The necklace and earrings appear to be authentic. Based on style, they could be fourth to first century BC. Further examination would be warranted to verify that. Did all of these pieces come from the same place?"

"Their origin is unknown." Nick indicated the carved cylinders. "What about those?"

"Do you know what they are?"

"Cylinder seals?"

"Ah." The man offered a smile that seemed strained. "You've done your homework."

"Only enough to make an educated guess. We hoped you could tell us more."

"I will give you a topline, as my students used to call it during my university days. These types of seals were in use from about 3500 to 300 BC. One of their main functions was administrative—comparable to a notarized signature today. They could also be used to indicate ownership of an object."

"How did they work?" Luke surveyed the three cylinders again.

"They were rolled over damp clay. You'll notice the carving is intaglio—that is, the design is cut into the stone, so when it is rolled across a soft surface, the design is raised, not indented. The seals also functioned as amulets to protect the owner from harm. The hole running through the center allowed them to be strung and worn around the neck."

"Can you identify their country of origin?" Nick asked.

Dr. Bishara picked up one of the seals that had a blue hue and examined the carvings again. "The general style and motifs suggest Syria, as does the use of lapis lazuli for the cylinder. That particular semiprecious stone was popular in that region."

"Do you believe they're authentic?" Luke finished jotting a note.

"Based on a very preliminary examination, yes. The hole

running through the seals was always drilled from each end and did not often meet precisely in the center. That is true of these examples. Also, because seals were in daily use, you would expect to find some wear, most often around the edges of the drill hole. Again, these seals show such wear. In addition, I see traces of a chisel and the fine lines of a file. All of these characteristics suggest the pieces are genuine."

"What are they worth?" Now that they had confirmation on authenticity, Nick was cutting to the chase.

"It would depend on provenance—that is, the verified and documented history of the object. Without that, it is difficult to know whether an artifact was removed from its resting place a hundred years ago or a few weeks ago. These days, given the large number of artifacts being looted from the Middle East, most museums in the US won't buy objects that left their country of origin after 1970 unless they have proof of legal exportation."

"Why 1970?" Luke asked.

"That is when the Unesco conventions on antiquities were put in place. They prohibit trade in illicitly exported cultural artifacts."

"Which leaves the black market." Luke doodled a dollar sign in the margin of his notebook.

"Correct."

"Can you give us a ballpark estimate on the value of these items on the black market?" Nick motioned toward the objects on the table.

A few beads of sweat popped out above the man's upper lip. Curious.

"The black market is not my area of expertise."

"I'm not suggesting it is." Nick's expression remained neutral, but unless Luke was reading him wrong, his colleague had noted the man's sudden discomfiture too.

"No. Of course not." Bishara waved a hand in dismissal.

"But for archeologists and those who value antiquities, that is a sore subject. As for value, I can tell you only what I have read in the journals and heard spoken of at conferences."

"That's fine."

"The two pieces of jewelry together could sell in the legitimate market for upwards of $20,000."

Not the kind of number Luke had expected, given all the effort that had gone into this operation.

Based on the quick look Nick shot him, the agent had the same thought.

The real money had to be in the seals.

Bishara's next comment confirmed that. "The cylinder seals are another story. They are far rarer than scarabs, for example, which are about the same size. In the legitimate market, at auction, a seal in excellent condition—and with provenance—has brought in as much as $250,000. On the black market, the figure would be much lower, but if the right buyer was found you could see numbers in the $25,000 or more range."

So if four or five seals were sent to Kristin's shop every quarter, the contraband operation was bringing in about half a million dollars each year.

It wasn't a huge sum in the big scheme of things—but it could fund a number of US terrorist cells . . . and with minimal effort, now that the system was in place.

"This has been very helpful." Nick began closing up the boxes.

"May I ask if you are investigating a local black market operation?" Bishara discreetly thumbed off the sweat above his lip.

"All I can say is we're working on a situation that involves artifacts like these. I'm not at liberty to discuss an ongoing investigation." Nick slid the boxes back into his briefcase and stood. "Detective Carter and I appreciate your assistance. It's been invaluable."

Luke rose, as did Bishara.

"If I can be of any other assistance, please do not hesitate to call upon me." He extracted a card for each of them from his pocket.

"Thank you." Nick took the card and held out his hand.

After a couple of seconds, the man took it.

Luke leaned forward to shake hands as well.

Bishara's palms were sweaty.

Also curious.

Once in the corridor outside the man's office, Nick checked his watch. "Let's find a spot outside to regroup for a few minutes before we go our separate ways."

Luke remained silent until they emerged onto a sidewalk that led to the parking lot. "Why don't we claim that shade?" He indicated a nearby tree.

"Works for me."

As soon as they were under the shelter of the branches, Nick turned to him. "Interesting meeting."

"Very. On a number of fronts."

"Such as?"

"We got confirmation that the artifacts are genuine, along with an estimate of value. But Bishara's reaction to our black market questions raised a red flag for me."

"Likewise. What's your take on why that discussion might make him uneasy?"

"Giving him the benefit of the doubt . . . a visit from an FBI agent and police detective could unnerve anyone. Also, it's obvious he has a passion for antiquities, and the widespread looting in Syria could be upsetting to someone who's spent his entire life studying them, as he noted."

"True." Nick shifted the briefcase from one hand to the other. "But absent benefit of the doubt—guilt or fear can also cause nervousness."

"Guilt or fear about what?"

"I don't know—but my gut tells me it bears investigation. Why don't we each run some background on him and compare notes? Would two o'clock tomorrow work for you?"

"Yes. In the meantime . . . what about those?" Luke nodded toward the briefcase.

"We'll keep them under wraps. Other than Bishara and Ms. Dane, no one outside of law enforcement knows we have the artifacts in our possession. That buys us a few days to do any necessary research and get all our people in place for surveillance and a takedown."

"Okay. I'll see you tomorrow." No need to verify the location of their meeting. If the FBI got involved, gatherings were always on their turf.

With a lift of his hand, Nick left the shade and headed toward his car.

Luke veered the other direction.

Pulling out his cell, he picked up his pace and scrolled through his missed calls—Kristin's among them.

Finger poised over her number, he hesitated. He'd promised her an update today.

But there were better ways to deliver one than via phone.

▪ ▪ ▪ ▪ ▪

The meeting had not gone well.

Fingers clenched at his sides, Yusef watched from the window of his office as the FBI agent and detective emerged from the shadows of the building and returned to their respective cars.

He fumbled for his handkerchief and mopped his brow.

They'd picked up on his nervousness.

The sweaty lip, the clammy palms. There had been nothing he could do to prevent that physiological reaction to danger after they mentioned black market antiquities sales.

But he'd known the instant they'd set the seals and jewelry on the table that they'd intercepted Amir's shipment.

And Amir had no clue they were on to him, based on that heads-up message the man had sent him a few days ago to prepare for another rendezvous and sale.

The two agents disappeared from view, and he slowly turned away from the window.

What to do now?

He wandered back to his desk and sat, surveying the familiar surroundings that had been his life for the past nine years.

A life that would have been perfect if only Touma had listened to him.

But pragmatic arguments were impotent in the face of idealism. He'd been young once too—and deaf to practical counsel.

And now it was too late for practicalities.

Now it was a matter of survival.

From the bottom drawer of his desk, he withdrew the photograph of the smiling young man who had brightened his world for thirty-four years.

No one could have been blessed with a better son.

No one.

Touma was brave, selfless, caring, committed, passionate— and willing to sacrifice everything for the principles in which he believed.

And he had done just that.

Only his life had been spared . . . but at a steep price.

One Touma himself would never have paid.

But how could a father not do everything in his power to protect the son he cherished?

Yusef placed the photo gently back in the drawer, where it had been for the past two years. Seeing it every day was too painful a reminder of their separation. Penny had noticed it was gone from his credenza, of course, but with her usual discretion, she'd never pressed him after he'd given her the it's-a-long-story brush-off.

He closed the drawer, picked up the two business cards the law enforcement men had left, and set them side by side on his desk.

Learning to pay attention to nuances would be part of their training. The fact they'd noticed his nervousness shouldn't be a surprise.

The question was, would they follow up by running background on him?

And if they did, would they find anything incriminating?

He tapped one of the cards.

Unlikely.

He'd covered his tracks.

However . . . if they decided to put a tail on him, he was doomed. They'd follow him to the next pickup site, wherever that might be—and watch him walk away with illegal artifacts stuffed into yet another super-sized coffee cup.

Maybe the very artifacts they'd laid on the table today.

But if he refused to participate, Amir would follow through on his threat—and Touma would die.

He set his elbows on the desk and dropped his head into his hands.

Oh, God, what am I to do?

He waited, but no answer boomed from the heavens. Nor did a voice whisper in the recesses of his heart.

It never did.

The response to his countless pleas for guidance had been resounding silence. If the Lord was sending him messages, they weren't getting through.

Yet who else could he turn to for assistance?

Only God could help him at this point.

He lifted his head and looked out the window, at the clear blue sky spanning the heavens. All he could do was pray again tonight—and hope when morning dawned, the path before him would be clear.

If it wasn't . . . he was in serious trouble.

Because now that the FBI and police were onto Amir's scheme, they'd launch an aggressive investigation.

Fast.

And he needed to be ready to counter it with a plan of his own.

14

As Luke straightened his tie and leaned forward to press Kristin's bell, her front door swung open.

He yanked his hand back and stared at Colin.

"I saw you coming up the walk as I passed by the window. Did Kristin call you?" His colleague frowned at him.

"She *returned* my call—but I was heading into a meeting and it rolled to voicemail." A muted conversation between a man and a woman was taking place somewhere in the recesses of the condo. "Is Rick here too?"

"Yeah."

An alert began to beep in his mind.

"What's wrong?"

"Colin, who are you . . ." Kristin's voice trailed off as she came into view, Rick behind her. "Luke! I didn't expect to see you today." *But I'm glad you're here.*

She didn't have to say those words for him to hear the unspoken message her tone and expression conveyed.

Based on her pallor, trembling fingers, and the subtle glaze in her red-rimmed eyes that was typical of fading shock, trauma had apparently tainted her life *again*.

Shouldering past Colin, he strode across the foyer and took her cold hand. "What's going on?"

She gripped his fingers like she'd never let go. "My dad called. My mom . . . she's . . . there was a car accident. She's in a c-coma."

His gut clenched.

Could this woman ever catch a break?

Ignoring her two buddies—and all the rules he'd set for himself about keeping his distance until the candle situation was resolved—he wrapped his arms around her, cradling her head with one hand and stroking her back with the other.

She held on tight, burying her face against his chest.

Out of the corner of his eye, he saw Rick skirt past them and move toward the door. A muffled rumble of voices followed, but he couldn't pick up the gist of the conversation.

Didn't matter.

Whether her buddies liked his presence or not . . . whether they thought he was butting in or not . . . he was staying.

"Uh . . . Kristin?" That from Rick.

Swiping at the moisture on her cheeks, she eased back and peeked around him. "Yes?"

"As long as you have company, Colin and I are going to take off."

She looked up at him, and Luke's throat tightened at the silent appeal in her eyes. "Are you staying for a while?"

That hadn't been his plan—but no way was he leaving her alone to deal with this new crisis. "Yes."

"I appreciate you guys coming over so fast." She crossed to Colin and Rick and gave each of them a fierce hug. "You're the best."

"I think we have some competition on that front." Colin sized him up over Kristin's shoulder as he returned her embrace.

"A person can never have too many friends." Her reply came out muffled but clear.

"You still want me to pick you up tomorrow morning, if the trip is a go?" Colin transferred his attention back to her.

"If it's not too much trouble."

"Never."

"I'll call you later to confirm. I need to talk to Luke first."

"Understood." Colin directed his next comment to him. "See you at the office."

Luke nodded.

Rick offered a mock salute and followed Colin out the door.

"Sorry you walked in on my meltdown." Kristin closed the door and pivoted toward him. "That doesn't happen often."

"After all you've had to deal with in the past two months, I'd say you were overdue."

"No." Her chin rose a notch. "It's self-indulgent to cry—and it doesn't fix problems. When bad things happen, you have to pick yourself up and carry on."

That was true.

But she didn't have to carry on alone through this latest ordeal. Not with Colin and Rick—and now him—in her corner.

"How can I help?"

The flicker of a smile dispelled a tiny bit of the distress from her face. "Your presence has already done that. I'm surprised to see you, though."

"A detour here wasn't on my original agenda, but I'm glad I came."

"Me too."

Nice to know.

"Sorry about chasing your friends away." Sort of. Her buddies deserved a lot of credit for dropping everything to come and offer their support—but he much preferred having her to himself.

"They have places to go. I interrupted their day as it was."

"I don't think friends mind those kinds of interruptions." He held out his hand. "Want to tell me the whole story?"

In answer, she closed the space between them and linked her fingers with his. "Why don't we sit on the patio? I'd rather be in the sunlight."

"Fine by me."

"You want a soda? I have some in the fridge."

"Maybe later." He led her toward the patio doors, slid one open, and guided her toward a cushioned chair under a striped umbrella. He claimed the one next to her, angling it to better see her. "When did all this happen?"

"Noonish, East Coast time. Dad called about two hours ago. He said he waited because he didn't want to disrupt my day and he hadn't talked to the doctor yet."

The hurt in her voice was almost palpable—confirming what he'd concluded the night she'd told him about her growing-up years.

She might think she'd made her peace with the status quo, but deep inside she still yearned for a closer relationship with her parents.

"What do you know so far?"

He listened without interrupting as she recounted the conversation she'd had with her father.

"Bottom line, I didn't commit to anything. I wanted to talk to you first, see if your theory about the candles panned out and whether you need me for anything."

"My theory did turn out to be sound." He brought her up to speed on all that had transpired since he and Nick picked up the candles yesterday from WorldCraft. "Nick and I are meeting early tomorrow afternoon, after we both do some additional research, to work out specifics. Everything will move full speed ahead as soon as you put the candles on display. We expect your part in this will be over fast."

"So going East now isn't the best idea." She chewed on her lower lip.

"It's the best idea for you and your parents. How long do you plan to stay?"

"Through the weekend, unless my mom . . ." She swallowed. "Unless there's a change in her condition."

"Let me grab that soda you offered, and while I'm in there I'll call Nick, get his take on this. Would you like one?" He rose.

"No thanks."

"Sit tight for a few minutes, okay?"

"Sure. I have a couple of calls to make, anyway." She pulled her cell out of her pocket.

He gave her shoulder an encouraging squeeze and retreated to the condo.

Inside, he retrieved a soda from her fridge and tapped in Nick's cell number.

The agent answered on the first ring.

In the space of a few sentences, Luke briefed him on Kristin's situation and her tentative travel plans.

"I don't think a weekend trip should be a concern, but I wanted you to weigh in." He sipped his soda, watching her out the window as she talked on her own phone. If necessary, he'd press Nick to find a way to accommodate her. Kristin needed to be with her parents.

"It's not the best timing, but if she only intends to stay through the weekend, it won't affect our operation. We need a few days to get all the pieces in place on our end."

The tautness in his shoulders eased. "That's what I figured. I'll let her know—and I'll see you tomorrow."

"I've got the conference room booked. By the way, I've already begun running background on Bishara. Comparing notes should be productive."

Right. He had some digging to do before their meeting too.

But he could worry about that later.

At the moment, Kristin was his top priority.

After ending the call, he rejoined her on the patio. "Nick agrees that a weekend trip is fine." He retook his seat.

Relief smoothed some of the strain from her features. "Good. Alexa's willing to cover for me at the shop for the next three days, and I have airline reservations on hold. But I didn't want to pull the trigger until you cleared the travel."

"When's your flight?"

"Six in the morning tomorrow, with a return on Sunday night at eight."

"Is Colin taking you to the airport?" That must be what their parting exchange had been about.

"Yes."

"I'm also available."

"I appreciate that . . . but imposing on an old friend is one thing. You and I are just getting acquainted—and it would require a very early wake-up call. I don't want to infringe on your sleep."

He took another swig of his soda. She was already playing havoc with his shut-eye—but this might not be the appropriate time to share that.

"I don't mind . . . but if you want to stick with Colin, why don't you let me pick you up on Sunday? Unless Rick has volunteered for chauffeur duty that night?"

"We didn't get that far in our discussion. I know he would have—but since you offered first, I accept. I can email you flight information after I confirm the reservation."

"That works." He finished the soda. "Is there anything else I can do for you tonight?"

"No. I need to pack and finalize my arrangements, and I'm going to turn in early. That three thirty wake-up call is going to roll around much too fast. Even if I manage to get to bed by nine, I'll be short of my usual eight hours."

His cue to leave.

"I won't hold you up, then." He stood.

She rose more slowly. "You don't have to go yet."

He hesitated, temptation warring with his nobler virtues. He'd like nothing better than to spend the rest of the evening here—but if he did, he'd be cutting into Kristin's sleep and she'd be a basket case by tomorrow.

Nobility won—by a hair.

"You need to rest up for that early flight, but I'll tell you what . . . why don't you call me later and give me the flight information by phone? And if you need to talk to me while you're gone—or want to hear a friendly voice—call my cell. Night or day."

"Thanks." She shoved her fingers into the pockets of her jeans, letting a few beats pass before she continued. "I'll, uh, walk you out."

He followed her to the door, waiting as she twisted the knob and pulled it open.

When she turned, his pulse stumbled. The strength, independence, and confidence he'd come to associate with her were gone. Tonight, this woman who'd started a humanitarian business, donated a portion of her life to the Peace Corps—and who was fast making inroads on his heart—seemed lost and vulnerable.

"I wish I could do more to help, Kristin."

"Prayer would be much appreciated." She gripped the edge of the door.

"Already in progress—for your mom *and* for you."

"Thank you." Her irises began to shimmer, and her knuckles whitened. "A visit with my parents is awkward under the best circumstances, given our history. My mom tries to keep the conversational ball in play, but my dad's not a big talker. I can't imagine what the next few days will be like."

He could.

Uncomfortable, difficult, and stressful—at the very least.

"Call me if you need to vent, okay? But sometimes in crisis situations like this, relationships change. People rethink priorities, reevaluate their lives. I don't want to give you false hope, but it's possible."

She offered him a sad, resigned smile. "I wish that was true—but you haven't met my parents."

No great loss, based on everything she'd shared.

He moved toward the threshold, and she backed up to give him room to exit.

Instead of leaving, however, he stopped in front of her. "I greeted you with a hug. I'd like to say good-bye with one too. Any objections?"

Wordlessly she shook her head.

Wrapping his arms around her, he pulled her close. This might be pushing the bounds of professionalism—but her mother was in a coma, her shop was in the thick of a terrorist plot, and her father wasn't likely to provide much moral support during her visit. She needed to know he was there for her in spirit if not in body during the days ahead.

Short of a kiss . . . a definite no-no at this stage . . . a hug was the best he could offer.

Kristin didn't say anything, just rested her forehead against the curve of his neck, splayed her hands on his chest, and sighed a soft, endearing whisper of warmth against his skin.

He closed his eyes and dipped his chin, inhaling her sweet, fresh fragrance.

She felt so right in his arms. Like she belonged there—for always.

And he didn't want to let her go.

But as the minutes ticked by and she made no attempt to end the embrace, he forced himself to take the initiative—before escalating temptation overpowered his good intentions and he did something he might regret. "I should leave." The words scratched past his throat as he gently extricated himself.

"I-I guess so." She tugged her hands from his chest and clasped them in front of her.

"Call me later."

"I will." Her irises began to glisten again.

Get out, Carter, or you're going to cave.

Backing up, he felt for the frame . . . hung on for a few seconds until his legs steadied . . . then walked out the door.

Half a minute later, safely behind the wheel of his Taurus, he looked back. Kristin was standing in the doorway, as she'd been on his previous visit.

Making it even harder for him to drive away.

But she needed sleep—and he had research to do. The latter could wait until tomorrow . . . yet with every nerve ending in his body tingling, it would be senseless to go home. He might as well return to the office and stay until he was so tired he'd have no trouble falling asleep whenever he *did* collapse into bed.

There was just one little problem with that plan.

If he stayed at his desk until the potent buzz from their embrace dissipated, he might be there until dawn peeked over the horizon.

15

As the first streaks of light illuminated the Thursday morning sky, Yusef gave up on sleep. At best he'd clocked three hours of fitful slumber during the night—and he wasn't likely to get any more.

Pushing back the covers, he swung his feet to the floor, scrubbed his hands down his face, and sat on the side of the bed. He was as tired as if he'd pulled an all-nighter on a dig, as he used to do in the old days when the team was on the cusp of an important discovery.

At least that tiredness had produced results.

Not so today.

He was as directionless now as he'd been last night, the hoped-for divine guidance as elusive as ever.

Rising, he took a moment to steady himself on the bedpost, then padded over to the window. From his eighth-floor Central West End condo, a tiny section of the museum roof, high on Art Hill, was visible. At a brisk pace, he could walk the just-over-two-mile route to work in thirty minutes. It was excellent exercise on a warm day.

But despite the cloudless sky on this June morning, he barely had the energy to trudge to his car—let alone trek to the museum.

He wandered into the compact kitchen and started the coffeemaker. What he wouldn't give for a few sips of the thick, strong, heavily sugared brew of his homeland—but after all these years in St. Louis, he'd grown accustomed to the weak, watery American-style coffee.

Considering his turbulent state of mind this morning, however, a cup of soothing zhourat tea would be much better. The wildflower/herb blend always calmed his stomach.

Too bad he didn't have any on hand.

He dropped a piece of bread in the toaster, sat at the kitchen counter, and stared at his cell phone in the charger.

Soon, Amir would call. Their conversation, as always, would be brief. A time, a place. Nothing more. He knew the stomach-churning routine by rote.

And after he had the materials in hand, he would begin the process of finding buyers, using his standard spiel to get big bucks for the items.

Or as big as was possible with clandestine transactions.

The toast popped up, but he grimaced at the singed bread, sick to his stomach. Sick at heart. Sick of the lies and deception that plagued his days.

You want this to end, Yusef. So end it.

He stiffened as the words echoed in his mind, clear as if they'd been spoken aloud.

Could that be the direction he'd been praying for—or was it his subconscious speaking?

No matter. There was no big revelation here. Of course he wanted the whole horrible charade to end. That proactive directive at the end, telling him to take matters into his own hands, might be new—but it was impossible to follow.

He couldn't end this mess without risking Touma's life.

Are you certain of that?

He frowned at the annoying follow-up question.

Yes. He was certain. If there'd been a way to escape his plight without endangering Touma, he'd have done so long ago. Nothing had changed.

Or . . . had it?

His brain began to hum as the seed of a bold idea sent down a few tentative roots.

Was it possible the nerve-racking visit from law enforcement hadn't been a threat but an opportunity?

Pulse pounding, Yusef rose and began to pace, the audacious idea blooming as fast as a flower in time-lapse photography, the pieces falling into place with dizzying speed.

It might actually work.

But there was risk.

Big risk.

Yet there was also risk in what he was doing for Amir—and it would increase as the FBI investigation intensified. If Amir suspected his scheme was under scrutiny, he might fold his tent and disappear.

And if that happened, he would have no more use for a museum curator—or his son.

Touma's life would be worth nothing to him.

Hands quivering, Yusef picked up his coffee and took a sip of the caffeine-laced beverage. He couldn't dally if he wanted to implement his idea. Once the FBI agent and that detective dived into the case, his bargaining power would diminish.

But whether law enforcement accepted or refused his offer, there would be serious consequences.

For him.

He squeezed his eyes shut, fighting back a choking fear. If he took this step, he would be deprived of the work he loved . . . and could spend the rest of his days behind bars.

The mere thought turned his stomach.

Yet such a sacrifice would be bearable if it guaranteed his son's safety.

The problem was, he couldn't be certain it would. In fact, the plan might backfire and put Touma in worse jeopardy.

If he did nothing, however, Amir's operation would fall apart and Touma would surely die.

The coffee sloshed over the rim of the mug, the hot liquid searing his fingers. The same way it had the day the first photo arrived from Syria, two long years ago, when the nightmare had begun.

Mug cradled in both hands, he trudged back to the kitchen and set it on the counter. His nerves were already too jittery. He didn't need to agitate them further with more stimulant.

Bypassing the charred bread in the toaster, he returned to his bedroom to dress for his workday and continue his morning routine as if everything was normal.

Except nothing about this day was routine . . . or normal.

And before it ended, his life could change forever—if he found the courage to follow through on the daring proposition that might give his son a fighting chance to survive.

∎ ∎ ∎ ∎ ∎

Clenching the handle of her overnight bag as the elevator whisked her to the Massachusetts General neuro ICU, Kristin leaned against the wall, a wave of weariness sweeping over her.

It had been thoughtful of her father to send a car service to meet her at the airport . . . but she wasn't going to read anything personal into it. That was the sort of courtesy he extended to professional colleagues every day. Standard operating procedure in the business world.

Nevertheless, the gesture had been welcome.

But after rising at three thirty with only a few hours of fitful sleep to sustain her, jolting through an obstacle course of air pockets for twelve hundred miles, and arriving in the middle of a deluge that could rival the great flood, a comforting hug from her father would be even more welcome.

Like the kind Luke had given her yesterday.

The door whooshed open—dispelling that fantasy.

Her dad wasn't there.

Tamping down her disappointment, she stepped out. He might have said during their brief conversation on her ride from the airport that he'd wait for her by the elevator . . . but how many times had her parents promised to do their best to be there for some important event in her life, only to have a work priority infringe?

Shoulders drooping, she set her bag down and fluffed her rain-dampened hair.

Wait for her dad to show up . . . go in search of her mother's room . . . or call Luke?

No contest.

Hearing Luke's voice would shore up her spirits and give her the boost she needed to deal with whatever lay ahead.

She rummaged through her purse until her fingers closed over her cell, and . . .

"Kristin!"

She released her hold on the phone and lifted her head.

Did a double take.

Could the man striding toward her in the wrinkled shirt, with a stubbled chin and disheveled gray hair, be her father?

Impossible.

John Dane was always impeccably dressed and groomed—and his hair was more brown than gray.

As he drew closer, the disconnect became more pronounced. Deep crevices were etched around his mouth, parallel grooves scored his forehead, and dark crescents hung beneath his lower lashes.

"I'm glad you're here." He touched her arm for a nanosecond, then bent and picked up her bag. "I'll take you back to see your mom."

She released the air trapped in her lungs.

Not much of a reunion for a father and daughter who hadn't seen each other since she'd flown up for her mom's sixtieth birthday bash three years ago.

But Dad had never been the demonstrative type.

She fell in beside him, searching for words to fill the silence as they walked down the hushed corridor. He'd already given her an update on her mom's condition during their phone conversation less than fifteen minutes ago, leaving little to say about that topic.

"Have you, uh, been here since Mom was admitted?" Lame . . . but it was all that came to mind.

"Yes. I cleared my agenda for the rest of the week. I had my assistant bring me my laptop first thing this morning, so I can take care of any urgent business from here. I don't want to leave in case she wakes up."

"Has there been any indication that might happen soon?"

"No—but it's possible. I've been reading up on brain injuries." He detoured into a waiting room and walked over to a couch that held a crumpled pillow and blanket. "I managed to clock a few hours of sleep here last night when I wasn't sitting with your mom." He set her bag beside the couch and rejoined her. "I'll take you to the ICU. It's just down the hall."

He accompanied her to the entrance, then handed her off to the nurse and backed away.

"Aren't you coming in?" A wave of panic crashed over Kristin.

"I thought you might like a few minutes alone with your mom. I'll be in the waiting room."

Without giving her a chance to respond, he retreated down the hall—leaving her to face this alone.

What else was new?

Drawing a quivering breath, she straightened her shoulders. Fine. She could do this. So what if he hadn't pulled her into a hug the instant she got off the elevator . . . or given her a kiss on the cheek . . . or offered words of comfort . . . or taken her hand and walked with her through this door into the scary place beyond?

Touchy-feely had never been her dad's forté.

She ought to be used to it.

But Colin would have stayed by her side, if he was here. And Rick.

And Luke.

Definitely Luke.

"Have you ever been in a neuro ICU?" The nurse flicked a disapproving glance at her father's retreating back.

"No."

"Don't be alarmed by all the monitoring equipment and unfamiliar sounds. Everything you'll see is standard procedure for traumatic brain injury patients."

"Okay. Thanks."

The woman led her through a set of double doors.

As they approached her mom's bed, the nurse spoke over her shoulder. "Feel free to stay as long as you like. And I'd encourage you to talk to her. Patients in comas might not be able to respond, but they can often hear voices."

With that, she motioned Kristin forward and retreated.

Kristin took two steps toward the bed . . . got her first unobstructed view of her mom . . . and froze.

Merciful heaven!

She groped for something . . . anything . . . to hang on to, settling for an unused IV stand that was none too sturdy.

If she'd been shocked by her dad's disheveled state, her mom's appearance was like a punch in the stomach.

In all the years they'd shared the same roof, Kristin had rarely seen her mother look less than perfect. Alison Dane was the epitome of a high-powered attorney—expertly coiffed hair, designer-label clothes, flawless makeup. Even in her limited free time, clad in casual attire, she oozed elegance.

The woman in this hospital bed—wearing a standard-issue hospital gown, face makeup free, hair a mess, polished fingernails broken and chipped—bore only the faintest resemblance to her mother.

But . . . it was her.

And she was alive.

That was all that mattered at the moment.

Filling her lungs, Kristin edged closer to the bed and touched the back of her mom's uninjured hand.

Now what?

The nurse had said coma patients could often hear voices . . . but what was there to say? Their mother-daughter conversations usually revolved around work or current events, topics inappropriate in the present setting.

That left personal subjects.

And they'd never discussed many of those.

Best to keep it simple.

"Hi, Mom. It's Kristin. I flew in this morning. You're getting excellent care here at Massachusetts General, and Dad's on top of the situation, as usual. You don't need to worry about anything. He and I will be close by, waiting for you to wake up. So, um, I'll be back later to see you again."

If her mother had heard her, she gave no indication of it.

Kristin started to turn away.

Hesitated.

Could her comments have been any more stilted?

If she were the one in the coma, would those bland, unemotional reassurances lift *her* spirits?

Not a fraction of an inch.

She needed to do better.

Maybe her mother hadn't been a strong maternal role model
. . . and maybe they hadn't been all that close . . . but given her
present condition, it might help her to hear the words that had
only been spoken on rare occasion in the Dane household.

Gripping the rail on the side of the bed, Kristin bent down
and kissed her mother's cool forehead.

"I love you, Mom. I always have. Please come back to us."
Her voice hoarsened, and as she straightened up, the room
around her began to swim.

Blinking to clear her vision, she choked back a sob. She and
her parents might not have the closest relationship, but she
wasn't ready to say good-bye to either of them.

Yet as she left the ICU and walked down the hall to rejoin her
father, she knew her mom was in very real—and immediate—
danger of losing her life.

Worst of all, there was nothing she could do to help her
recover.

Except pray.

■ ■ ■ ■ ■

"Yusef Bishara has an interesting history." Motioning for
Luke to take a seat at the same conference table they'd used
during their last meeting at the FBI offices, Nick pulled out a
chair for himself.

"I agree." Luke sat and laid the folder of background material he'd amassed on the table.

"So let's compare notes." Nick opened the file in front of him.
"I'll give you my topline. Bishara is a Syrian native and spent all
of his life there until he immigrated to the United States nine
years ago. He earned his PhD in archeology at Damascus University, taught there for two decades, then became the director

of two different museums in the country. His wife died ten years ago, and he has one son, Touma, who didn't emigrate with his father. As far as I can tell, the son is still in Syria."

"That matches what I found. I was curious why he left, so I scoured some of the articles written about him after he took the job here, hoping to find some answers."

"Good idea. I didn't get that detailed."

He wouldn't have, either—but what else had there been to do in the middle of the night with thoughts of Kristin keeping sleep at bay?

"I didn't find much, but in one article he cited safety concerns."

"Not surprising, given the volatile environment over there. I compiled quite a bit of general information"—Nick indicated his file—"but nothing suspicious. Did you uncover any red flags?"

"No. Following the initial flurry of articles after he took the job at the museum, he's maintained a low profile. And he seems to have kept his nose clean. I didn't find even a parking ticket."

"I know. He pays his bills on time, shows up for work, is a member of some professional organizations. The man's led a full and busy life, but if he's hiding anything of a questionable nature, we'll have to dig deeper to—" Nick pulled his phone off his belt. "Huh. I think this is Bishara's number."

Luke hiked up an eyebrow as Nick put the phone to his ear, greeted the caller . . . and nodded. "Good afternoon, Dr. Bishara . . . No, I'm free to talk . . . Yes, we'd be happy to. When did you have in mind? . . . Nine o'clock tomorrow morning in your office?" Nick looked over at him.

Luke gave a thumbs-up.

"That works. Detective Carter will come with me . . . We'll see you then." Nick set the cell on the table. "Bishara said that after giving our meeting yesterday further thought, he has some additional information that may be useful to us."

"Which he didn't want to share by phone." Some sixth sense began to prickle along Luke's nerve endings. Like it had in the man's office yesterday, after Bishara had grown uncomfortable with their black market questions.

"Right." Nick tapped his pen against the table. "I was going to discuss plans for next week, but in light of this development, it might be better to wait until we hear what he has to say."

"I agree."

"Sorry to bring you down here for such a short meeting."

"No problem. I'd rather proceed with more information than less."

"Let's hope whatever he has is useful. Shall we meet at his office again?"

"Fine with me."

Nick rose. "I'll walk you out."

After shaking the agent's hand and exiting the building, Luke picked up his pace as he headed toward his car. The double homicide that had come in this morning meant all hands on deck for the rest of the day . . . and possibly into the night.

But come nine o'clock tomorrow morning, he'd be back in Bishara's office.

And by the end of their meeting, they might be a whole lot closer to shutting down a terrorist operation that had been functioning right under law enforcement's nose for far too long.

16

Purse slung over her shoulder, tote bag dangling from her arm, and juggling two venti coffees and a breakfast sandwich from the Starbucks she'd noticed on the drive to her parents' condo last night, Kristin peeked into the waiting room on the ICU floor.

It was empty early on this Friday morning except for her dad, who was stretched out on the couch, forearm resting on his forehead, eyes closed.

Before this day ended, he needed to go home, take a shower, and get a few hours of sleep in a real bed. She could stand vigil here while he was gone—an offer he'd refused last night, but one she intended to push hard today.

She crossed the room and stopped a few feet from the couch. "Dad?"

No response.

She set his coffee and sandwich on an end table. Maybe it was better to let him sleep. She could always nuke his . . .

His eyes fluttered open, and he squinted at her. "Kristin?" He peered at his watch and swung his feet to the floor. "You're back early. Didn't you sleep well?"

"I'm always restless in a strange bed—but I had a much better sleep than you did. That couch can't be comfortable."

"It's an improvement over most of the planes I've slept on during overseas flights. Any news on your mom?"

"I just got here." She handed him a coffee and the sandwich. "I'll run down and talk to someone at the ICU while you have this."

"You didn't need to bring me breakfast."

"I was there anyway, getting some food for myself. I'll be back in a few minutes."

Leaving him to eat, she ducked in to see her mom, had a quick exchange with a nurse, and returned to the waiting room.

Her father looked up as she entered, the empty bag crumpled on the table, the coffee already half gone. "Any change?"

"No."

The fleeting flicker of hope that had sparked in his eyes died. "We're closing in on forty-eight hours. She should be awake by now. This is going on too long."

That was true. Based on the googling she'd done, every hour that passed without any signs of returning awareness was bad news.

"She could wake up anytime." The platitude sounded hollow even to her ears, so she didn't dwell on it. "The nurse said the doctor would be here soon to give us an update."

"Okay. I'm going to freshen up. Is that the gear I asked you to bring?" He indicated the tote bag.

"Yes. Toiletries, change of clothes, cell phone charger."

"Thanks." He picked up the bag and the coffee. "I'll be back as fast as I can. If the doctor shows up, knock on the men's room door."

With that, he left her to her coffee.

As it turned out, the two men converged on the waiting room from opposite directions ten minutes later.

Her father introduced her to the neurosurgeon, who motioned them to some chairs and sat facing them, his demeanor serious.

Kristin's stomach clenched, and the egg-white breakfast sandwich she'd downed congealed into a hard lump.

"You don't have good news, do you." Her father's comment was more statement than question, mirroring her own reaction.

"Not the best." The doctor rested his elbows on the arms of his chair and linked his fingers. "We're seeing some swelling. That's not unusual in this type of injury, but if the pressure inside the skull increases too much, it can restrict blood flow."

"And the brain needs the oxygen the blood carries." Her father's already pasty skin lost a few more shades of color.

"Yes. Swelling also prevents other fluids from leaving the brain. In severe cases, we remove part of the skull to relieve the pressure—but I want to try a less aggressive procedure first. It involves cutting a small hole in the skull and inserting a drain tube."

Kristin pressed a hand to her stomach, willing her breakfast to stay put. Cutting a hole in someone's skull sounded pretty aggressive to her.

"There's no other option?" Based on the strain in her father's voice, the two of them were tracking the same direction for once.

"The tube is the fastest way to deal with the problem. If we wait, and the swelling gets out of control, we risk brain injury. That complicates recovery after a patient comes out of a coma."

"So you *are* expecting her to recover?" Kristin didn't care if she sounded desperate for reassurance.

"Anything is possible." The man's tone was measured—and cautious. "But she's in a deep coma, and those are hard to predict. What we do know is that every day it persists makes the recovery more difficult and less comprehensive. Are we in agreement to insert the tube?"

"Yes." Her father didn't hesitate, but his answer held none of its usual decisiveness.

"We'll get her prepped." The doctor rose. "After this procedure is over and she's stable, I would suggest you go home for a few hours and get some food and rest. We can call you if there are any changes. Your wife—and mother—will need you more after she regains consciousness than she does now." He turned and disappeared out the door.

Thirty seconds of numb silence crawled by.

At last her father rubbed his bleary eyes and expelled a shaky breath. "I can't believe how much a world can change in the space of forty-eight hours."

She could . . . ever since terrorism had put her—and WorldCraft—in the middle of a deadly plot two months ago.

But he didn't know about that—and this wasn't the time to tell him.

"It makes you appreciate ordinary days, that's for sure." She swirled the dregs of her coffee.

"How long are you staying?" The hint of anxiety in his question suggested her presence meant more to him than she'd expected.

"I booked a return flight for late Sunday afternoon. I can change it if I have to."

"You have someone covering the shop while you're gone?"

"Yes. Through tomorrow."

"Your mom wouldn't want you to neglect your work to sit in a hospital."

"That's what you're doing." She hadn't even seen him check email yesterday. That had to be a first.

"I'm her husband."

"I'm her daughter."

His Adam's apple bobbed, and his eyes grew moist. "She'd be touched by the effort you've made to be with her. *I'm* touched."

Pressure built in her throat at his out-of-character comment. "This is what daughters do."

He kneaded the bridge of his nose. "To tell you the truth . . . I'm not certain we deserve that kind of devotion."

"Dad, I—"

He held up a hand. "Let me finish. In between snatches of sleep, a remark your mom made last month as we were driving home from the wedding of a friend's son came back to me. She said we kind of missed the boat on the family thing." He stared at his shoes. "We didn't dwell on it, but last night it kept looping through my mind. I think she was right—and I regret that."

In the silence that followed, Luke's comment the night she'd told him about her relationship with her parents replayed in *her* mind.

It was their loss as much as yours.

How sad that it had taken this long for her parents to recognize the truth of that sentiment.

And there was no going back.

"We can't rewind the clock, Dad. But maybe—"

"Mr. Dane?" A nurse appeared in the doorway of the waiting room.

"Yes?" He vaulted to his feet.

"We're getting ready to prep your wife for her procedure, but if you and your daughter would like to spend five minutes with her, I can take you back."

"Yes, we would." He started toward the door.

Kristin fell in behind him. Too bad the woman hadn't waited a few more minutes to summon them instead of interrupting the first meaningful conversation she'd ever had with her father.

But perhaps they could return to that discussion before her flight on Sunday afternoon. While they could never recapture the lost years or create the kind of family she'd craved as a child, maybe she and her parents could find a way to bridge the gap and build a closer relationship going forward.

If her mom recovered.

. . . . .

This time, Luke arrived at the art museum first.

As he waited in the shade of the tree where they'd talked after their last visit, he pulled out his cell. Kristin had texted him, as promised, after she'd landed in Boston—but there had been no communication from her since.

It wouldn't hurt to let her know she was in his thoughts . . . especially if her father wasn't offering much moral support.

He put his thumbs to work.

Less than half a minute later, as he was finishing up his message, Nick arrived.

"I see you beat me this time." The FBI agent flashed him a quick grin.

"I learn fast." He slipped his phone into its holster.

"I figured that out in Richmond during our previous terrorist case. Ready to hear what our antiquities expert has to say?"

"More than."

"Let's do this."

They entered the museum and wove through the corridors to Bishara's office, where the same administrative assistant who'd shown them in on their last visit did the honors again.

The man rose as they entered—and Luke had to work hard to keep his expression impassive.

Their Middle East antiquities expert looked as if he'd been on an all-night bender, eyes bloodshot, hands shaky.

As he motioned for them to take a seat at the table where they'd met during their first visit, Luke exchanged a quick glance with Nick.

The other man arched an eyebrow.

They were on the same page.

"May I offer you coffee or water?" The curator's voice wasn't quite steady as he extended the courtesy.

"I'm fine." Nick took the same seat he'd occupied two days ago.

"Me too." Luke sat as well.

Bishara paused a moment, fingers splayed on the table, then eased himself into his chair, as if every movement was painful. "I appreciate you both coming back today."

"We're always willing to listen to information that might help us with a case." Nick folded his hands loosely on the table.

But while his posture was relaxed, his eyes were sharp and watchful. Luke could sense the electricity pinging below the surface.

It matched the energy thrumming through his own veins.

"What I have to say to you . . . it is a rather long story."

"We're in no hurry." To emphasize that point, Luke settled back in his chair.

"Then I will begin . . . at the beginning. When I was growing up in a small town in Syria, my friends and I played in the shadow of ancient monuments. They were literally in our backyard. We took them for granted, without a thought to their antiquity—or historic value." Bishara unscrewed the cap on the bottle of water he'd pre-set in his place.

"But that changed, or you wouldn't be doing what you do today." Nick continued to watch the man, gaze incisive, tone conversational.

"Yes. One day, an archeological team came to excavate some ruins on the outskirts of our town. I was fascinated by the work, and by the stories the man who was leading the dig told. His passion for preserving the links that artifacts and architecture provide to our past was contagious. He lit a fire in me that summer which has never been extinguished. I vowed always to do my part to protect this irreplaceable heritage." The man took a long drink of water.

"Your teaching career, supervisory work on a number of digs, and high-level positions at two museums in your country would suggest you kept that vow."

The tiny smile Bishara offered Nick was tinged with resignation. "You have done your research—as I assumed you would after you observed that I was uncomfortable during our discussion about the black market a few days ago."

The man was on the ball if he'd picked up their veiled reactions.

"Why were you uneasy?" Luke asked. As long as Bishara had brought it up, why pretend they hadn't noticed?

"I will get to that—but first I must give you more background." He wiped a stray drop of water off the table. "Did your research reveal that I have a son?"

"Yes. Touma. And a wife who died ten years ago," Nick said.

"Correct. Did you know Touma is also an archeologist?"

"No." Luke frowned. Odd that this piece of information hadn't surfaced in his reading—but he'd focused more on Bishara's career than his personal life.

"Touma is the reason I asked you to come here today."

Not what he'd expected to hear.

Based on the momentary hike in Nick's eyebrows, the revelation had also blindsided him.

Before either of them could ask a question, Bishara picked up his story.

"When I left my country nine years ago to take this job, it was with a heavy heart. But Syria was in turmoil, and terrorism was growing. While al-Qaeda was the dominant extremist group, ISIS was in the wings. A rebellion was brewing, and I feared conditions would deteriorate."

"As they did," Nick said.

"Yes. I pleaded with Touma to come to the United States

with me, but he was finishing his studies and refused to leave. I tried again to convince him after he received his PhD, but instead he took a job with a museum—to preserve and protect our heritage, as he told me. His dedication filled me with both pride and shame. He cared enough to stay. I did not." Bishara took another long swallow of water.

Luke was beginning to get a glimmer of where this might be leading. "From what I've gathered based on reports in the media, being an archeologist in Syria isn't the safest profession. The manager of the museum in Palmyra was publicly beheaded three years ago."

The man's name escaped him, but the brutal act against an eighty-two-year-old who'd dedicated his life to antiquities had kicked him in the gut.

"Khaled al-Asaad. He was a treasured colleague and friend." Grief twisted Bishara's features. "They killed him because he would not reveal where valuable artifacts had been hidden for safekeeping. He had spent his life protecting and preserving them, and he did not want them destroyed or sold on the black market. Many others who have undertaken this dangerous defensive work have suffered too."

Luke deferred to Nick in case he wanted to join the conversation, but the other man sat back, giving him the floor.

It appeared the extensive reading he'd done on this topic during the sleepless hours Wednesday night after he'd left Kristin hadn't been wasted after all.

"Is your son among them?"

The man's breath hitched. "Yes."

"Tell us what happened."

Bishara wrapped his fingers around the almost-empty bottle of water. "He and his colleagues received word that a group of ISIS fighters, armed with machine guns, was on its way to their museum on a loot-and-destroy mission. No one fled. Instead, they rounded up trucks and loaded as many items as they could. They had just finished when the jihadists arrived and opened fire. Two of the museum staff members were wounded."

"Including your son?"

"No. He was spared that, at least. They managed to get the wounded into the trucks and took off. The injured staff members were dropped at the office of a doctor who was sympathetic to their cause, and the rest of the staff dispersed the items to safe places and went into hiding."

Luke leaned forward. "Is your son still underground?"

"No. He was discovered by ISIS after he ventured out to take food to one of the wounded men's family."

"How long ago?"

"A little more than two years."

The magic number.

Luke glanced at Nick. His narrowed eyes suggested he'd linked the timing of the WorldCraft monastery candles operation with Bishara's story too.

"What happened then?" Luke could guess what was coming next.

"They knew he was related to me . . . and the powers-that-be within the organization decided I could be useful to them."

Bingo.

"They threatened you."

"No. They threatened Touma. They said unless I cooperated, he would be killed."

"Cooperated with what?"

"A scheme to raise money for ISIS cells in the US by selling looted artifacts. That has never been spelled out to me, you understand. Only my role has been explained. But I know what is going on." The plastic water bottle crinkled under the pressure of his fingers, and his face contorted. "I had no choice. If I did not do as I was told, Touma would die."

"Why are you telling us this now?" Nick rejoined the conversation.

"The items you asked me to evaluate—those are the exact type of artifacts that are passed on to me to sell. I have seen many cylinder seals and quite a few pieces of jewelry. I'm assuming you somehow intercepted a shipment. It would only be a matter of time until you discovered my role. I hoped, by coming forward and offering to assist you, we could reach an agreement."

"What sort of agreement?"

"If I cooperate fully—provide all of the information I have and follow every instruction you give me so this operation can be shut down and the person running it brought to justice—I ask that you attempt to rescue my son from his captors and bring him safely to the US."

Luke looked at Nick. That wasn't a deal he could make—nor could an FBI agent broker such an agreement without consulting higher-ups.

But it would be useful to have Bishara on their side. They could do this without him, but his cooperation would help the investigation.

"Do you know the identity of the leader here in the States?" Nick asked.

"No. I only know the name he uses in our phone conversations. But I know the names of the people who buy the artifacts—and I have their contact information." He leaned forward. "It would behoove you to have someone working on your behalf from the inside."

A few beats of silence passed.

"What is your exact role?" Nick asked.

"The items are passed on to me at a drop location, along with forged provenance. I get in touch with legitimate potential buyers known to me or contact buyers from a list that is provided."

"Under what name?"

"My own."

Nick's eyebrows peaked. "Isn't that risky?"

"Everything I am doing is a risk. But using my own name was a condition of the job. It gives the operation a veneer of respectability."

"What do you say to these buyers?" Luke asked.

"The spiel is always the same—a seller has contacted me, the museum isn't interested in buying the items, I want them to find a home where they will be appreciated. I am able to negotiate a significantly higher price than the items would get on the black market because of my credentials. The buyers send a cashier's check to a PO box I pass on to them from my contact, and I send the items to the buyers."

"You aren't concerned one of these buyers will get suspicious and talk to law enforcement?"

"It is possible—but I always ask that the transaction be kept confidential, explaining that I'll be inundated with calls from buyers if word gets out I'm helping to place items for sellers. The legitimate collectors and dealers I know are grateful I offer them the items first, and the buyers provided by my contact are practiced at under-the-table transactions and very discreet." He leaned forward. "You haven't yet responded to my proposal."

"Rescuing your son would be difficult given the volatility in Syria." Nick steepled his fingers. "Do you know where he's being held?"

"No—but your CIA excels at finding that kind of information . . . and your special forces soldiers are trained to extract hostages under hostile conditions."

"How can you be certain he's still alive?"

Bishara pulled out his cell phone, tapped the screen a few times, and angled the device toward them. "Before every deal, I ask for proof of that. This came two weeks ago by email."

Luke leaned closer to the screen, as did Nick. A skinny, thirtyish man, with shaggy hair and a beard, was holding a copy of a current newspaper.

"A shot like that could be doctored." Luke hated to burst the curator's bubble, but Photoshop could work magic.

"I realize that. But every pose is different, as is every background. And I know my son. I have watched him grow progressively thinner and more haunted. That cannot be faked in Photoshop."

"Forward the message to me. I'll have our computer forensics people try to trace the source—but I'm not holding my breath." Nick leaned back. "What do you want in exchange for your cooperation?"

"As I already said, my son. Alive. Here."

"I mean for yourself."

"Nothing."

Surprising.

In a situation like this, most people asked for immunity from legal prosecution.

"You understand you could be facing a prison sentence for your part in this operation, whatever your motivation." Luke watched the man.

He didn't flinch. "Yes. It is worth the sacrifice to secure my son's freedom."

"We'll need to discuss your proposal with some higher-level people," Nick said.

"I assumed as much. But if the artifacts you showed me are from the most recent shipment, suspicion will be aroused if too much time elapses before they enter the system."

"We're aware of that." Nick pushed back his chair and stood. "We'll be in touch as soon as we have some direction."

Luke rose too. "You'll be available by cell?"

"Always." Bishara levered himself to his feet. "And you

HIDDEN PERIL

do not need to worry, gentlemen. I am going nowhere . . . nor will I share our discussion with anyone. I want as much as you to bring this man down. Touma is all I have, and his fate rests in this monster's hands." His voice rasped, and he dipped his chin.

"We'll let ourselves out." Luke inclined his head toward the door, and Nick circled around the table to follow him out.

Neither spoke until they were in the hall.

"Do you have time for a short detour to the café?" Nick scanned his missed calls.

"Yes." Luke did the same. Nothing from Kristin—but Sarge needed him for some more work on the homicide ASAP.

Once they had coffee in hand, they claimed a secluded corner in the café.

"You must have put in some long hours getting up to speed on the artifact situation in Syria." Nick gave the café patrons a practiced sweep before shifting his attention back to him.

"It's a compelling subject—and there's plenty of material out there. What's happening in that part of the world to ancient treasures is a travesty . . . and people like Bishara's son are risking their lives to stop the plunder and destruction. They're the Syrian version of World War II's monuments men—but with far less resources at their disposal."

"Impressive."

"Yes—and given his background, it has to be killing Bishara to help the enemy instead of his colleagues."

"I agree he's a man caught between a rock and a hard place. But even though he's doing this to keep his son alive, willfully aiding and abetting terrorists carries stiff penalties." Nick took a swig of his coffee.

"Curious that he didn't ask for any consideration for himself in exchange for assisting us."

"It would appear his sole concern is for his son."

Luke swirled the coffee in his cup. "How much can our people do to help Touma?"

"Depends on how many resources are allocated, how long it might take to locate him, and how heavily guarded he is."

"We don't have the luxury of time."

"I know."

"So what's the plan?"

"I'll get with my boss as soon as I return and see how high he wants to take this. As soon as I have some direction, I'll give you a call. Is Ms. Dane still planning to return on Sunday?"

"Last I heard."

"With this latest development, we might need a few extra days to get everything in place—but I'm hoping we're ready to go by midweek. Will you alert her to that?"

"Yes."

Nick drained his cup and stood. "I need to get moving on this."

"And I need to pitch in with a double homicide." Luke rose too.

"Sounds like both of our workweeks are ending with a full plate."

True.

But as they parted in the parking lot, Luke suspected their lives were going to be a whole lot busier *next* week.

And a whole lot more dangerous.

17

The weekend was gone . . . and she and her dad had never returned to the interrupted conversation about their lack of family life.

Heaving a sigh, Kristin set her overnight bag down in the foyer of her parents' condo as her father descended the stairs from the upper level.

Other than the gray hair, he looked more like the man she remembered from her last trip to Boston. Some of the lines of strain in his face had diminished, and he was back to his usual attire of crisp shirt and knife-crease slacks. Taking shifts to stand vigil over her mom had been smart . . . even if that had meant she'd spent too many solitary hours pacing the hospital hall.

"Heading back to the ICU?" She checked her watch. The car her dad had ordered to take her to the airport should be here any minute.

"Soon. I'm glad I came home for a quick shower, though . . . and to say good-bye. It's the first time since the accident no one's been there with your mom—but the nurse said it was safe to leave for a couple of hours."

Sadly, it was. The deep coma showed no signs of relinquishing its grip.

"I wish there'd been an improvement while I was here."

"I do too. But at least the drain relieved the pressure in her skull. That's one worry we can put to rest."

"You'll let me know if there's any change?"

"Of course. Are you going back to the shop tomorrow?"

"Yes."

"I envy you that." His expression grew wistful. "We take routine days for granted, but they're a blessing—one we only recognize in hindsight. I'd give anything to be returning to a normal workweek too."

So would she.

But there wasn't much chance her week would be anything close to normal.

Tell him about what happened at WorldCraft, Kristin. Keeping that kind of news from your parents isn't going to help build a closer rapport after this crisis is over.

She shoved her hands into the pockets of her jeans and curled her fingers into a tight ball. "To tell you the truth . . . I don't think my week will be routine."

He stopped adjusting his cuff link and squinted at her. "What do you mean?"

For once, her dad had listened to her with more than half an ear—and picked up the undercurrents.

"It's kind of a long story. Let me try to give you the executive summary version." She flashed him a stiff smile and launched into her tale, glossing over the details of her current involvement.

As she wrapped up, some of the color that had crept back into his face over the past two days evaporated.

"Good heavens, Kristin! We had no idea you were in the middle of such a horrendous situation. Why didn't you tell us?"

She shrugged. "Mom had a big case . . . and you were traveling. I didn't want to bother you."

"Bother us." He flinched, and a muscle twitched in his cheek. "Your mom was right. We've blown the whole family thing."

"I got through it. Colin and Rick came around more than usual."

And Luke.

But she wasn't ready to share that.

"I'm glad they were there for you—and I'm sorry we weren't."

So was she . . . but voicing that would only heap guilt on her dad, and he was already under severe stress. Yet she didn't want to lie with a perfunctory "it's okay" comment.

A horn honked outside.

Perfect timing.

"My ride's here." She picked up her overnight bag.

"Kristin." He crossed to her, and his Adam's apple bobbed. "I want you to know that despite our shortcomings as parents, you've been . . . I think you turned out to be a fine woman. Your mom and I are both proud of you."

Pressure built behind her eyes as the encouragement she'd longed to hear as a child finally arrived.

Funny how Luke had read the situation better than she, predicting that trauma might prompt her parents to rethink priorities.

"Thank you for that. It means a lot." The horn tooted again. "I need to go."

"I know. Have a safe trip." He hesitated, then leaned over and gave her a one-armed hug.

It was awkward.

But it was a beginning.

"Take care of yourself, Dad."

"I will." He opened the door for her.

She walked through, her heart lighter than it had been three days ago when she'd stepped off the elevator into an empty corridor. No, her father hadn't said the coveted L-word. And maybe, after her mom recovered, everything would return to the status quo.

Yet deep inside, she sensed she and her dad had blazed a new path this weekend.

Wishful thinking?

Perhaps.

For now, though, she would cling to that dream.

Because with everything else going on in her life, she needed a healthy dose of hope to sustain her.

·····

Kristin had had a long, stressful weekend.

Even from a distance, buffeted by the crowd surging out of the gate area on Sunday night at Lambert Airport, Luke could sense her fatigue. The weary sag of her shoulders said it all.

And as she drew close, the shadows under her lower lashes and the faint lines etched at their corner confirmed his first impression.

Yet she summoned up a smile of greeting as she approached him. "I hope you weren't waiting long. Our gate wasn't ready and we had to sit on the tarmac for a few minutes."

"I had plenty to keep me busy." He lifted his cell, then slipped it into his pocket and leaned down for her bag.

"I can carry this."

"My mother taught me better manners than that." With his face inches from hers, he had to call up every ounce of his willpower to keep from giving her a proper welcome home.

One that involved lips.

As she gazed at him, a pulse began to throb in the hollow of her throat.

"You want to let go?" He arched an eyebrow.

"W-what?"

"The bag." He gave a slight tug and hiked up one side of his mouth.

"Oh. Right." She released her grip, soft color stealing over her cheeks.

"Let's collect the rest of your luggage and get you home. I'm sure you've had a long day . . . and a long weekend."

"There's no luggage to collect. That's it." She indicated the overnight bag.

"Seriously?" He examined the small bag. Despite Jenny's many stellar attributes, she had not been a minimalist packer. His wife had always taken two crammed suitcases on every trip they made, no matter how long they planned to be gone.

"Uh-huh. I spent two years in the Peace Corps, remember? I learned to cope with a bare-bones existence and travel light."

"I'm impressed."

"My dad was too. Whenever they go on a trip, Mom takes a bag this size just for toiletries and makeup. My makeup, on the other hand, would fit in one ziplock bag—another of the so-called necessities I learned to live without in Ethiopia."

"You don't need much to look beautiful, anyway." The words tumbled out of his mouth faster than he could catch them.

Her color deepened. "Thank you."

"You're welcome." He winked at her, and as he started toward the exit to the garage, she fell in beside him. "How was everything today?"

"The same. Thank you for the texts. It helped to know I had some moral support back here."

"I bet Colin and Rick were in touch too."

"Yes. I felt like I had a whole cheering section in St. Louis."

"Even so, the past few days can't have been easy."

"No. But my dad and I actually bonded a little. It gave me hope our relationship might improve in the future. It's just sad it took such a traumatic event to nudge that door open."

"I'm glad *some* good came out of the accident. I'm over there." He motioned toward his car.

She faltered. "Where?"

"The dark gray Accord."

"I thought you drove a Taurus?"

"That's my work vehicle." He popped the trunk, stowed her bag, and held her door while she slid inside.

Thirty seconds later, he settled behind the wheel. "Are you hungry? We could stop somewhere and get some food if you like."

"To be honest, all I want to do is go home and fall into my own bed. Yogurt and cereal will be plenty." She angled toward him. "Tell me about the case. Your texts and phone messages didn't mention it much. Does that mean there's nothing new to report?"

"No. A lot's been happening—but I didn't see any reason to complicate your life while you were dealing with the situation in Boston." He glanced over at her. "You certain you want an update tonight? I could fill you in tomorrow, after you get a decent night's sleep."

"I'll rest better knowing what you've discovered."

Maybe not.

But Kristin wasn't the kind of woman who put off dealing with hard stuff.

"Okay. I'll give you a quick recap."

By the time he finished telling her about the meetings with Bishara and answering all her questions, the quick recap had turned into a twenty-minute briefing and they were pulling into her condo development.

As he parked the car, she leaned back in her seat. "That poor man. Having a son held hostage and being forced to undermine the heritage you've spent your life protecting. He must be a basket case." She studied him. "Are you going to agree to his proposal and try to free his son?"

"That decision had to be made much higher up the food chain than me or Nick—but yes, we are. Nick called to let me know an hour ago. Several high-ranking people had to weigh in on this, and it's been a scramble over the weekend to get all the ducks in a row. But the consensus is that Bishara's help is valuable enough for CIA operatives in Syria to attempt to locate his son and line up some special ops forces to stage a rescue after he's found."

"How long will all that take?"

"Possibly too long. As Bishara noted, since he's been alerted to expect another pickup soon, the brain behind this knows the candles should be arriving any day. You said transit can take as long as eight weeks. That gives us, at most, ten days to play with. We'd rather not push it beyond that and raise suspicions about the delay."

Her forehead puckered. "Can they find the son that fast?"

"I don't know—but we can be working the early stages of our plan here while our overseas operatives are doing their thing. Ideally, we'll be closing in on the head honcho after the son is located and our special ops forces are getting into position to snatch him. We can't pull him out until we have our guy here or the leader will vanish."

"The timing could be tricky."

"That's an understatement."

"So how can I help?"

"The first priority is access to the shop to install some cameras and sound equipment. Preferably during off hours. Nick's people will pose as electricians in case anyone notices their presence."

"I don't open until ten, so any morning would work. I can come early to let them in."

"Nick's targeting Tuesday."

"That's fine. Let me know what time and I'll be there. Then what?"

"He'll give us the date to put the candles on display. After they're out, agents will be stationed in a van nearby, monitoring the audio and video. As soon as the marked candles are purchased, you'll alert them by using a code word, and they'll follow the person they see on the monitor. After all the candles are retrieved, your part will be over."

"It seems like a simple job."

"It should be."

She cocked her head. "That doesn't sound too definitive."

No, it didn't—for good reason.

There was risk for anyone connected to this operation, even if their involvement was peripheral.

"These are evil people, Kristin. Their focus should shift to other parties after the candles leave the store—but I can't make any guarantees. Sometimes innocent people end up in danger."

"Like Susan." She swallowed. "And Elaine Peterson."

"Yes." He needed to share their suspicions about the death of a man she'd met and admired. He reached for her hand, gentling his voice. "And very likely Brother Michael."

Her eyes widened as she absorbed the implication. "You think he . . . that he walked in on some shady activity in the workshop the night he died and was . . . killed?"

"I think it's a reasonable scenario—but it's too late to get a definitive answer. If the monks had called a doctor, he or she might have realized the head wound was too serious to have been caused by a fall. But I'm certain they saw no point in that. He was already dead, and they had no reason to suspect foul play."

"Brother Michael . . . murdered. I can't believe it." Shock echoed through her whispered words. "Do the monks know?"

"Not yet. The CIA will deliver the news this week. Hopefully they'll cooperate with our investigation."

"I'm sure they will. They're all heartsick about the destruction taking place around them. They'll be devastated to discover they're harboring a terrorist." She exhaled. "I knew these people were evil, but after what they did to Brother Michael . . . and Susan . . . and Elaine . . . now it's personal. I'll do anything I can to help bring these monsters down."

"Cuing the agents when the candles are purchased will be a huge help." He watched her as he continued. "Do you have any concerns you might get nervous and tip off the persons picking up the items?"

She caught her lower lip between her teeth as she considered his question. "I don't think so . . . but I've never been involved in anything like this."

"Your theater background should help."

"True—except no one in the audiences I played to was a terrorist."

"Nick and I discussed putting an agent in WorldCraft as a clerk . . . but a new face could arouse suspicion."

"Yes, it could—and I don't want to take that chance." Her jaw firmed, and he saw the conviction he'd been waiting for spark to life in her irises. "I can do this."

"I have no doubt of that. Let me walk you to your door."

She waited as he retrieved her bag from the trunk, easing closer to him after he took her arm for the short walk up the path. As if she'd missed him while she was in Boston and was glad to be in his presence again.

He could relate.

On the tiny porch, she fished out her key, opened the door, and took her bag. "Thank you for picking me up."

"Thank you for letting me. Was Rick miffed?"

"I think he was relieved, to be honest. It's a long drive from the camp to the airport, and this is his busy season. Besides . . . between the two of us . . . I prefer you as a chauffeur."

"Glad to hear it. And I'm available anytime. I also work

cheap." Without second-guessing himself, he leaned down and brushed his lips across her forehead. "Bill paid."

She looked up at him—and the longing in her eyes sent his pulse skittering. "What about the tip?"

He groaned. "You're killing me here, you know."

"Sorry." She gave him a sheepish grin and backed up. "I know you have professional rules. Chalk my lapse up to stress and fatigue. I'll have my emotions under control by tomorrow, after a solid night's sleep."

"Hold the thought, though—for down the road. Go on in tonight instead of waiting to wave good-bye. I know you're tired."

She hesitated, but in the end she did as he asked, gently shutting the door behind her and leaving him alone on the porch.

Better.

If she wasn't within touching distance, he was safe from temptation.

Still, as he returned to his car, a pleasant tingle of anticipation raced through him. If all went well, in a couple of weeks this case would wrap up and he could leave her at the door with more than a simple kiss on the forehead.

But dozens of pieces had to fall into place between now and then—and the tiny margin for error in an investigation like this was sobering.

One misstep . . . one glitch in timing . . . one slip in communication . . . could lead to disaster.

Meaning unless this operation went like clockwork, more innocent people could die.

18

"We'll be done in about ten minutes, Ms. Dane." The FBI tech agent, dressed in jeans and a tool belt for his electrician role, looked up from below the checkout counter as Kristin passed.

"No hurry. I'm not scheduled to open for another hour."

She checked on the other agent. He was adjusting one of the cameras concealed inside a colorful wall hanging a few feet away.

All of the devices they'd installed were tiny—and none were visible to the naked eye.

Juggling the newly arrived box of batik cushion covers from Zimbabwe, she started toward a display table in the center of the store . . . but pulled up short when a knock sounded on the front door.

Both agents froze for an instant, then went into action. The one on the ladder descended and stashed it in the back room, while the other came out from behind the counter, toolbox in hand.

"Any idea who that might be?"

"No."

"We'll be in the back. If someone noticed our presence, the story is you're having some new outlets installed in the storeroom."

He followed his colleague and closed the door between the two parts of the shop.

Heart hammering, Kristin set the box of cushion covers on the floor, crossed to the door, and peeked out around the shade.

Oh.

Exhaling, she flipped the lock on the door. "Hi, Ryan."

"Good morning. Sorry to disturb you . . . but I could tell the lights were on inside and I wanted to make sure everything was okay. You're not usually here this early."

"I, uh, needed to have a couple of outlets put in the back room. The electricians had me first on their list this morning."

"Ah. That explains it. I didn't mean to overreact, but I'm still spooked after everything that happened a few weeks ago."

"So am I. I appreciate your concern." She forced up the corners of her stiff lips.

He tipped his head and scrutinized her. "You certain there's no problem? You seem kind of . . . tense."

So much for her acting ability.

"Just tired."

"I bet." Sympathy softened his features. "I popped in on Saturday, and Alexa told me about your mother's accident—and your trip to Boston. I would have stopped by yesterday to see how she was doing, but I had meetings that kept me out of the office. Any updates?"

"Nothing's changed. She hasn't shown any sign of regaining consciousness."

"I'm sorry. You've had a tough few weeks."

And the next one wasn't going to be any less stressful.

"The shop keeps me busy, though. That helps."

"I hear you. Work can be all consuming sometimes." He flicked a glance at the fingers she'd curled around the edge of the door.

She loosened her white-knuckle grip. "I like being busy."

"Running an almost one-person business is a guarantee of that, as we both know." He gave the interior a sweep over her shoulder. "The shop looks great, by the way. I noticed while I was in on Saturday that you've rearranged some of the displays."

"It's important to mix things up every few weeks, keep it fresh, or regular customers get bored."

He chuckled. "I guess that's why I'm in insurance instead of retail. Well . . . back to the salt mines." With a lift of his hand, he continued down the sidewalk to his office.

After watching him walk away, Kristin closed and locked the door.

This wasn't good.

If a knock from a friendly neighbor could send her pulse skyrocketing, what would happen when the bad guys showed up to retrieve the hollowed-out candles?

She needed to get a grip on her emotions.

Fast.

She'd assured Luke she could handle her small part in this operation without tipping anyone off, and she did *not* want to let him—or the innocent victims—down.

Thank heaven she'd had this trial run with someone who was on her side instead of a terrorist. Next time she'd be more prepared.

She crossed to the back room and cracked the door. "All clear."

The two agents dropped their pretense of working on an outlet and rose.

"Who was it?"

"My neighbor. He noticed the lights were on earlier than usual and was checking on me. We're all a bit on edge after everything that happened here in April."

"Got it." They both returned to their tasks in the showroom, and Kristin trailed after them.

"Do I need to activate all this once you guys are ready to roll?" She waved a hand to encompass the cameras and mics they'd installed.

"No. We control the equipment from our surveillance van. Your main job is to say the code word to alert our people."

"I don't have that yet."

"I believe Agent Bradley will provide it as soon as they're ready for you to display the merchandise. Give us a few minutes to test this, and we'll be out of your hair."

She wandered back to the pillow covers, sorting through them while the two agents communicated by phone with someone who verified the cameras and mics were working.

Within ten minutes, they'd packed up their tools and were gone.

Now all she had to do was wait—and hope the people who were going to retrieve the candles showed up fast after they were on display.

Preferably on a day Alexa wasn't working.

But her clerk had said she could be flexible in her schedule over the next two weeks in light of the situation in Boston—so if Luke gave her sufficient notice, she'd rearrange the hours to ensure she was on duty for the first two days after the candles were put out.

Assuming the people running the operation didn't want to risk another regular customer buying them again—as Elaine had—that would be long enough. The candles would be purchased, ending her role in this drama.

And removing her once and for all from the reach of terrorism's deadly tentacles.

.　.　.　.　.

"They found Bishara's son."

As Nick passed on the news, Luke angled away from the

crime scene he'd been working and adjusted the cell against his ear, a surge of adrenaline jacking up his pulse. "That's welcome news on a Friday morning."

"And none too soon."

True. They were closing in on the eight-week mark since the candles had been shipped. With or without a location for Touma, in another few days they'd have had to roll or risk raising suspicion at this end.

"What's next?"

"Special ops has been notified. A rescue mission is in the planning stage. The location doesn't appear to be all that secure, so the extraction shouldn't be difficult. For now, the ball shifts back to our court. We need to be close to our guy before they move."

"Understood. When do you want the merchandise to be put on display?"

"Tuesday morning. Will you pass that on . . . along with the code word we discussed earlier this week?"

"Yes. I'll take care of it today." A perfect excuse to see Kristin . . . and a perfect end to his workweek.

"I've alerted Bishara about the new development too."

"I'm sure he was relieved."

"That would be an understatement. He's already passed over all the contact information he has for buyers, as well as the PO box numbers he's been given in the past for funds transfer. Those are all over the country. If you have some time, we could use more manpower on this. There's a ton of information to track down in a very condensed timeframe."

"I'm at a crime scene now—but I can clear my schedule for the rest of the day and swing over there next." After a brief detour to WorldCraft. "Any luck tracing the source of the email with the photo of Bishara's son?"

"No. It appears to have gone through a number of remailers. We've got a trap on Bishara's cell, though. I assume his contact—who goes by the name of Amir—is using a burner phone and will keep the call short, then ditch the cell. But at least we'll be able to get a rough idea of his location. I'm hoping he's in town. That would simplify our job."

Nothing about this was simple . . . but keeping the takedown local would be less messy. All the players who were fully briefed would be on hand.

"Sounds like this is picking up speed. I'll be there in less than an hour."

He ended the call and turned to find Colin frowning at him.

"What's picking up speed?"

"Another case."

"Does that mean you're bailing on me with this one?" He waved a hand toward the crime scene.

"After I clear it with Sarge."

Colin squinted at him. "Is this Kristin's case?"

"Yeah." Now that he had a better handle on her relationship with her childhood buddies, he couldn't fault the man's concern.

"If you need help on anything that doesn't require top-secret clearance, let me know."

Kristin must have passed on that nugget to her buddies . . . unless Cole had let it slip.

"I will."

"Watch her back."

"That's my plan."

Colin stared at him long and hard for several beats. Finally he gave a clipped nod and walked away.

Kristin was fortunate to have such staunch friends—as he told her thirty minutes later after he entered WorldCraft and the bell over the front door summoned her from the back.

"Yeah. Colin and Rick mean the world to me." She smiled up at him. "But I'm always open to new friends."

"Count me in that category—and aiming for more."

"Promises, promises." She shot him a teasing grin, then grew more serious. "I missed seeing you this week—but I appreciated your texts."

"We've been slammed with cases. And I didn't have any news to report, anyway . . . until now." He filled her in on his call with Nick.

"I'm glad they found Bishara's son—and I'm glad this is winding down." She swallowed. "So Tuesday's the day."

"Yes." He scanned the deserted shop and dropped his voice. "The word is *dangerous*. Work it into the conversation, maybe in reference to the conditions in Syria."

"No problem. I often talk about the situation over there to customers who buy the candles."

"Are they in the back?"

"Yes. The pseudo electricians brought them and showed me what to look for on the bottom label."

"You won't have any trouble checking that unobtrusively?"

"No. I always wrap anything breakable in bubble wrap, and while I'm doing that it will be easy to turn the candles over." She smoothed her palms down her slacks. "Will you keep me updated after the candles are gone?"

"As much as I can. And now I need to run. Nick asked me to come by and help research some of the information Bishara provided."

"You want a cup of coffee to go?" She gestured to the pot she always made for customers.

"Yes. Thanks." He followed her over. "How's everything in Boston?"

"No change." She poured his coffee. "My dad's getting discouraged. We both are. Nine days is a long time to be in a coma." The last word hitched as she put a lid on a disposable cup and handed it to him.

"You can go back out there after the candles are purchased if you want to."

"I may do that—but I'll decide after this is over. Let's get through the next few days first."

"Okay." He gave her fingers a squeeze. "Hang in. And if you need to hear a friendly voice beside Colin's or Rick's, I'm only a phone call away."

"I know . . . but I've been trying not to sabotage your keep-it-professional policy."

"I'm beginning to regret making that rule."

"Don't. It's a smart one—and I respect you for it. We'll have plenty of opportunity to be together after this is resolved."

She gazed up at him . . . and for a moment he got lost in her eyes. They were the most amazing color—like the beckoning horizon where sky meets sea, calling him to a voyage brimming with possibilities.

As that thought flitted through his mind, his mouth twitched. For a guy Becca had once called utterly unpoetic, that wasn't half bad.

"Luke?" Kristin studied him. "What are you thinking?"

"That I'm going to bend my rule a little." Without waiting for a response, he bent down and pressed his lips to her temple.

Lingered.

Until her shuddering breath whispered against his ear and nudged him back to his senses.

"I'm out of here—for now." He retreated until he was beyond touching range. "But expect to find me on your doorstep the instant this is over."

"I'll hold you to that. The sooner the better."

He resisted the urge to loosen his collar as an appealing dimple dented her cheek.

She wasn't the only one counting down the hours on this investigation.

But after lifting a hand in farewell at the door, he deliberately switched gears. For the next few days, his focus needed to be on dismantling a terrorist organization that funded ISIS cells in the US—and finding the man who was controlling the players like a chess master manipulating his game pieces.

Because unless they got the top man, he'd disappear into the shadows, recruit new minions, and create another scheme to carry out his mission.

That wasn't an acceptable outcome.

They needed the brain behind this . . . and neither he—nor Nick and his people at the FBI—would rest until Amir was caught.

Preferably before anyone else got hurt . . . or killed.

■ ■ ■ ■ ■

Kristin smoothed a hand over the cloth covering the round table near the shop entrance, adjusted the placard with the photo of the monks and their story, and backed a few feet away to survey the results of her last chore on this Saturday afternoon.

The table was well-positioned to draw the attention of anyone entering . . . but it needed more visual interest.

She surveyed the shop, homing in on a display of colorful, woven table runners.

Perfect.

After retrieving one, she draped it across the round table.

Much better.

All was in readiness for her to set out the candles on Tuesday morning—and since Alexa had agreed to work Thursday and Friday afternoons next week instead of Wednesday and Friday, the candles should be gone before she was back on duty . . . assuming everything happened as fast as Luke expected.

Kristin twisted her wrist to display the face of her watch. Almost closing time. But there was no hurry to lock up. She had nothing on her evening agenda. No rehearsals yet for *Alice in Wonderland*, no bookwork for the shop, no chores at the condo . . . no date.

Based on Luke's parting remarks yesterday, however, her Saturday nights should be far more lively as soon as—

Her phone vibrated, and she pulled it out of her pocket, her smile fading as the name on the screen registered.

Uh-oh.

Her father had stayed in touch with texts and emails for the past few days, but he'd only called once.

Please, God, let this not be bad news.

Finger trembling, she pushed the talk button. "Hi, Dad. Is everything okay?"

"Yes." A hint of excitement crackled over the line. "Better than okay. Your mom is showing signs of regaining consciousness."

Kristin rested a hand on the empty candle display beside her and took a deep breath. *Thank you, God.* "That's fabulous news! Tell me what happened."

"She's making sounds and showing some reaction to pain and to touch. She hasn't opened her eyes yet, but she's moving around a little. The doctors are very hopeful. This is a huge step forward."

"I wish I was there."

"So do I—but I know you have a full plate . . . and this is a waiting game for now. If all goes well, we should see more and more awareness returning. But it could be a long, slow process."

"I still wish I was there."

"Maybe you can come back in a week or two. Your part in the situation you told me about should be finished soon, right?"

"That's what I'm counting on."

"Why don't you plan a trip then? It would probably be better if you came after your mom was more communicative, anyway."

"I suppose that makes sense, but I . . ."

The bell above the door jingled, and Ryan entered.

He hesitated and nodded toward the phone, but she motioned him in.

"Did someone come into the shop?" Her father's query pulled her back to their conversation.

"Yes, but I can talk."

"I think we're caught up—and I'm on my way in to see your mom. I'll call you again tomorrow with an update."

"Thanks, Dad. Take care."

"Will do. Talk to you soon."

She slid the phone back into her pocket and exhaled as Ryan joined her.

"I hope that wasn't bad news."

"No. The opposite. Mom appears to be coming out of the coma. I just wish the timing was better. With everything going on here, I don't know how soon I can get back out there."

"Is there some sort of problem with the shop?"

Whoops.

"Um . . . not really. But the business doesn't run itself, and I'm still playing catch-up from being gone last week. After asking Alexa to work extra during my last trip, I don't want to impose on her again."

"I got the impression from talking to her last Saturday that she'd be happy to have more hours. I expect there's always plenty to do in a shop . . . like fill up empty displays." He smiled and tapped the table beside them.

"Displays are easy." She waved a hand in dismissal. "This one will be full again by Tuesday. Keeping up with inventory and the books, however—not to mention evaluating potential vendors and communicating with existing ones—is time consuming."

"Can't you do most of that from your laptop?"

"Some. I may head East next weekend, depending on how fast Mom improves."

"Seems reasonable. In the meantime, why don't you let me treat you to dinner at Panera to celebrate the news about your mom?"

Kristin tried to mask her dismay.

Of all days for Ryan to decide to ask her out.

Nice as he was, there was only one man who interested her . . . and she'd rather spend the evening with a good book than go on a date she knew would lead nowhere.

"I appreciate the thought, Ryan . . . but I'm actually in the mood for a quiet night of chilling with a book."

"Another time, maybe."

She was saved from having to answer by the arrival of a last-minute customer who poked her head in the door.

"Sorry to show up so near closing, but I need a hostess gift for tonight. If I shop fast, can you give me five minutes?"

"Of course. Let me help you find something."

"I'll talk to you next week." Ryan offered her an amiable grin and let himself out.

Ten minutes later, after locking the door behind a satisfied customer, Kristin closed the front window shades, flipped off the lights, and exited out the back door, into the alley.

She hadn't lied to Ryan. Her evening plans did include reading. She was only halfway through the critically acclaimed suspense novel she'd picked up in the airport while waiting for her flight to Boston.

But it was hard to immerse yourself in a fictional tale, no matter how exciting, when your life was beginning to feel like a bestselling thriller.

As she'd learned from this ordeal, however, she much preferred her suspense between the covers of a book.

And once this was over, she was going to focus on romance in her reading . . . and in her life . . . for the foreseeable future.

19

"Delicious meal, Sis. Thanks for the invite." Luke sat back in his chair on Becca's patio. "Beats what I cook for Sunday dinner, that's for sure."

She snorted. "Last I heard, your culinary repertoire consisted of Cheerios and Ragu spaghetti sauce."

"They're nutritious."

"You can't live on cereal and pasta. There are other food groups, you know."

"Then keep inviting me on Sunday." He raised his glass in salute and took a sip of his iced tea.

"You're always welcome. If you'd like to come more often, all you have to do is—"

"No! I want Unc Luke to put me to bed!" Mike barreled through the patio doors with Mark on his heels, a frazzled-looking Neal in hot pursuit.

"Sorry." Neal shot Becca a contrite glance. "I thought I had them corralled. Come on, guys. I'll tell you a story."

"Unc Luke tells better stories. They have guns in them." Mark eluded Neal's lunge with a practiced dodge and raced over to Luke's chair. "Will you tell us a story, please?"

He tousled the boy's hair as Mike flanked his chair on the other side and added his plea. "I think I'm outnumbered."

"Neal." Becca arched an eyebrow at her husband and sent him one of those coded husband/wife signals he and Jenny had often used in front of other people.

"I'm trying, okay? I have a master's in IT, not child psych—or martial arts." He moved in on the twins. "Come on, guys. Don't get me in trouble with your mom."

"Please, Unc Luke." Mike tugged on his hand.

"I'll let you watch a few minutes of *Finding Nemo* on my phone if you come right now." Neal held up his cell.

"Bribery is not in the child-rearing manual." Becca narrowed her eyes.

"Fine. You want to try?"

Luke started to rise. "I can run up with them. I don't mind—"

"Sit." At Becca's field-marshal tone, Luke sank back into his seat. "Boys, it's time for bed." She gave the two hooligans a stern scrutiny. "Go with your dad. Now. If I hear one more word, our field trip to the Magic House next week isn't happening."

The twins regarded each other across Luke's legs . . . and meekly traipsed back into the house.

"You're good at that." Luke grinned at his sister as the trio disappeared inside. "But you *have* had years of practice. You were bossy when we were growing up too."

"Ha-ha." She jabbed him in the arm.

"I wasn't kidding."

"I know." She made a face at him and broke off a piece of the brownie on the plate in front of her.

"Fitting another bite in there might be a challenge." He surveyed her rounded tummy. "When's the little princess due again?"

"Two weeks. And I can always find room for chocolate." She

popped the morsel into her mouth. "So you've been telling my boys bedtime stories with guns in them?"

"Hey—I'm a detective, remember? But only the bad guys get shot."

"Great." She rolled her eyes.

"My stories are much tamer than those animated films kids watch now . . . like *Finding Nemo*. Doesn't the mother fish get eaten by a barracuda at the very beginning? That's pretty traumatic for a three-year-old, if you ask me."

"Fine. I'm not going to argue the point. I'd rather talk about baseball. Neal managed to snag four corporate tickets for the Cardinals game next week. You want to go?"

"I might. Who's using the fourth ticket?"

"Well . . ." Becca broke off another hunk of brownie. "There's a new member in my book club, and we had a long chat after the last get-together. Lovely person. She took a PR job at Webster University about five months ago and doesn't know many people in town outside of work. I think you'd like her."

Ah-ha.

Now he understood why she'd relegated the tucking-in duties to Neal. She'd wanted to get him alone so she could put on her matchmaker hat and pair him up with some female.

Not happening.

"I'll pass."

"Oh, come on, Luke. It's not a lifetime commitment. It's a baseball game with your sister and brother-in-law, for pity's sake."

"It's a blind date."

"Partly. But I promise, you'll like her. I've never tried to set you up with anyone before, have I?"

"No."

"Well . . . there you go. This is special. I wouldn't be pushing unless I thought this had real potential."

"For what?"

She gave him a get-real look. "To relaunch your social life."

"My social life doesn't need relaunching."

"Ha!"

"It doesn't. Trust me."

Her eyes thinned at his definitive tone. "Is there a message in there—or are you just in denial?"

"My social life is about to pick up dramatically."

"Why?"

No reason to play coy at this point. She'd find out about Kristin soon enough if everything went as he hoped it would. "I met someone."

"Really?" Excitement sparked in her eyes, and she leaned toward him as much as her girth allowed. "Tell me everything. Who is she, where did you meet her, how did you—"

"Whoa!" He held up his hand. "One question at a time."

"Fine. Who is she?"

"The woman from the wedding."

Becca peered at him. "I thought you said she was involved with the best man?"

"I was wrong."

"How did you find her again?"

"Coincidence. She has a connection to a case I'm working."

A flicker of alarm darkened his sister's irises. "What kind of case? You only deal with crimes against persons . . . like homicide. Is she in some kind of trouble?"

"I can't give you any details. It's an open case. But her involvement is peripheral."

"So she's not in any danger or anything, right?"

"She shouldn't be." But if that was true, why couldn't he shake the uneasiness that continued to dog him?

Becca didn't give him a chance to dwell on that question as she continued her inquisition.

"When do I get to meet her?"

"We haven't even been out on a date yet."

"Why not?"

"Professional conflict."

"Then how do you know she's interested?"

He gave her a slow smile. "She's interested."

"Yeah?" She studied him. "Okay. I'll take your word for that. And I repeat . . . when do I get to meet her?"

"Let's not immerse her in the family too fast or we might scare her off." Not likely. Kristin would love Becca and Neal and the twins . . . but he wanted her to himself for a while first.

"Fine—but you have a standing invitation to bring her to dinner as soon as you're ready to let her meet the family."

"I'll keep that in mind."

"So what are the odds of that?"

"Of what?"

"That it will progress to meet-the-family stage?"

He took a sip of his iced tea as he pondered that question.

Becca wasn't asking about the probability of him bringing a date to a family dinner.

She was asking about the probability that Kristin might be *joining* their family at some point.

He hadn't let himself think that far ahead . . . but all at once he realized his heart was way ahead of his mind.

Because Kristin had already staked a claim there.

"Honestly? I think the odds are high."

"Hallelujah! That's the best news I've heard in weeks. You need someone to—"

She stopped abruptly as a drop of rain flicked against his nose. He lifted his head. The dark clouds that had been snuffing out the blue sky section by section all evening had finally finished the job.

"Guess that's our cue to move inside." Becca heaved herself to her feet and picked up her plate and glass.

Luke followed her in. "I need to get going anyway. I've got a busy few days ahead."

"I hope you'll be indoors." She cringed as a flash of lightning slashed through the sky, accompanied by a house-shaking boom of thunder.

"I should be."

"Glad to hear it. This kind of weather is predicted through midweek, and being in the middle of an electrical storm is dangerous."

So was being in the middle of a plan like the one they were about to launch.

He didn't have any worries about his own safety—but Touma Bishara's life hung in the balance.

And other innocent parties could die during this takedown too. With three casualties already, Luke wasn't taking anything for granted.

That's why come Tuesday morning, he'd be sitting in the FBI van close to WorldCraft—not only because he wanted in on this operation, but because he wanted to be near Kristin.

Just in case.

■ ■ ■ ■ ■

Something felt off.

Amir paced the length of his living room. Turned. Paced back.

Why had this shipment of candles taken longer than usual to arrive?

Why was that detective continuing to visit WorldCraft—as recently as Friday?

Why was the empty candle display about to be refilled on the heels of law enforcement's last visit?

Was the timing coincidence . . . or connected?

Impossible to know.

And unknowns were unnerving.

A rumble of thunder reverberated through the house, and he crossed to the window. Eased the curtain aside. Sheets of rain were slamming against the pavement.

The weather was as stormy as his emotions.

He let the drape fall back into place and resumed pacing.

Perhaps he was overreacting, letting the unsettled weather feed his anxiety.

But perhaps not.

And he wasn't going to begin taking chances now.

Meaning there would be extra precautions with this retrieval.

The two people he'd lined up came with impeccable references from trusted associates with proven loyalty to the cause . . . and they were skilled at avoiding detection.

Nevertheless, a well-trained tracker might be able to follow them.

The deception he'd worked out—and the layer of retrieval he'd added—should increase his security, however.

As should the other safeguards he would put in place. Like using burner phones only once . . . and in remote locations.

Still, if law enforcement was paying attention to the latest candle shipment, it would be better to have some inside information.

And the best place to get it might be from the woman who had been an unwitting partner in his whole operation—and who might now be cooperating with the cops.

Kristin Dane.

■ ■ ■ ■ ■

This was the day.

Kristin maneuvered her Sentra down the narrow alley behind WorldCraft . . . swung into her usual parking spot . . . and took a deep breath.

She needed to stay calm, cool, and collected. Pull out every acting skill she'd ever learned and give the performance of her life for this limited engagement.

And she would.

Her role might be small, but it was critical to the master plan to shut down a terrorist operation and find justice for three innocent deaths.

Straightening her shoulders, she collected her purse and tote bag, opened her umbrella, and hustled toward the back door.

"Morning, Kristin. Perfect timing."

She swiveled toward the adjacent businesses. Ryan lifted a hand in greeting as he hurried from the back door of his office toward his car, dodging raindrops.

"Why is my timing perfect?"

He opened the passenger side door and pulled out his briefcase. "I stopped at McArthur's on my way in. I've got client meetings this morning and wanted a few baked goods on hand. One of them is your favorite—a caramel pecan stollen." He grinned at her and shut his door. "Your shop doesn't open for half an hour—and we never did get to celebrate the news about your mom. Want to share a piece with a cup of coffee?"

She hesitated as he bolted back toward his office. The rich confection *was* her favorite . . . and she *was* early . . . and she *did* feel bad about giving him the brush-off on Saturday.

What could it hurt to share a piece of coffee cake for five minutes?

Besides, though tension had chased away her appetite earlier and she'd skipped breakfast, the growl in her stomach reminded her she owed it some food.

"I can spare a few minutes."

"I won't be offended if you eat and run." He waited on the threshold to hold the door open for her.

Once she was inside, he motioned toward his office. "There's an umbrella stand in there. You can leave your bags beside it. I'll put the goodies out."

She continued to his office, deposited all her paraphernalia, and joined him in the conference room. The stollen, a box of Danish, and a white bag were on the table.

He poured her coffee, handed it over, and pulled out his phone, frowning at the screen.

"Go ahead and help yourself while I take this." He picked up his coffee and walked toward the door. "I'll be back in two minutes. There are napkins and plates in the bag."

As he exited the room, Kristin wandered over to the table, opened the box with the stollen, and took a sniff of the rich caramel aroma.

Maybe her day was destined to be stressful, but at least it was beginning on a pleasant note.

After pulling out a plate, napkin, and fork, she cut a slice of the stollen and sat at the conference table to enjoy the un-expected treat.

Five minutes later, her cake reduced to a few lingering crumbs and her coffee cup almost empty, she ventured into the hall. Ryan's door was closed.

She hesitated.

Interrupting his call would be rude . . . but she needed her things and she couldn't hang around forever.

Five more minutes wouldn't hurt, though. Ryan would surely remember she was waiting and open his door soon.

Coffee refill in hand, she prowled around the conference room and pilfered a few more loose crumbs from the cake.

Just when she'd decided she'd have to tap on his door, he reappeared. "Sorry about that. The call was from the CEO of a big account I've been wooing. I didn't want to cut him off. Did you have some cake?"

"Yes, but I need to get to the shop."

"Of course. I didn't mean to delay you. Let me get your things." He returned to his office and retrieved her purse, tote, and damp umbrella. "I hope you have a quiet and uneventful week. Might I even suggest boring?"

If only.

"Boring sounds welcome after the turmoil of the past couple of months. Thanks again for the coffee cake."

"If there's any left after my meetings, I'll bring you another piece later."

"Unless your clients are on a diet, I have a feeling you'll be down to crumbs. McArthur's is hard to resist. Talk to you soon."

He opened the back door for her, and she dashed through the rain to WorldCraft.

After depositing her purse and tote in the back, she quickly tackled her first priority of the day—setting out the candles on the display. Then she opened the shades, booted up the cash register, brewed her usual pot of coffee . . . and waited.

And waited.

And waited.

Every time a customer entered, her pulse skipped a beat—but no one did more than glance at the candle display all morning.

By noon, she was getting fidgety . . . and her stomach was growling again.

The one customer in the store was in no hurry to settle on a purchase, but as soon as Kristin finally rang her up, she retreated to the storeroom and pulled the turkey sandwich she'd made for lunch out of the small fridge, along with a soft drink.

As she popped the tab, the bell over the front door jingled again.

Her hand jerked, and a geyser of soda spurted out, coating her fingers.

Good grief.

No more coffee for her today.

She didn't need to be any more jittery than she already was.

Wiping her hands with a paper towel, she crossed to the door that led to the shop and opened it.

Froze.

A woman who appeared to be Middle Eastern was examining the table of woven scarves.

This could be it, Kristin. Put those acting skills to work.

"Welcome to WorldCraft." She propped up the corners of her mouth and returned to the counter. "If I can help you find anything or answer any questions, let me know."

"Thank you." The woman flashed her a quick smile and continued to browse, selecting a pair of earrings before wending her way to the monastery display, where she began to examine the candles.

Kristin busied herself rearranging the jewelry displayed under the glass case in front of her, trying to keep her lungs supplied with air.

In. Out. In. Out. Keep it even.

At last the woman picked up one of the candles and came to the checkout counter.

"You've selected some excellent items." Kristin maintained a pleasant expression as she pulled a piece of bubble wrap from the roll under the counter and laid the candle on its side.

"Thanks. You have quite a variety of merchandise. That"— she motioned toward the candle—"will make a great gift. In fact . . . I think I'll buy another one to keep in reserve." She wandered back to the display.

As Kristin taped the bubble wrap in place, she tipped the candle and scanned the label.

Marked.

The second one the woman added was also marked.

Luke had been right.

Whoever was running this show wasn't waiting to retrieve the candles this go-round.

While she found a small box for the earrings and rang up the purchases, she gave the woman a bit of history about the candles. "And as you may have noticed on the sign, all proceeds from these sales go to humanitarian aid in Syria." She slipped the second candle in the bag as she concluded.

"It sounds like a worthy cause." The woman counted out the cash for her purchase.

"Yes. The monks do commendable work in a very dangerous environment. I'm glad to be able to help them out in a small way." She handed over the bag, hanging on to her amiable tone even as the atrocities this lovely young woman was helping perpetuate turned her stomach. "Enjoy the rest of your day."

"Thank you."

The customer left the shop, the bell tinkling behind her.

Kristin leaned back against the wall . . . inhaled . . . exhaled.

One down, one to go.

But during the endless afternoon that followed, no one came to get the other two marked candles.

They remained unclaimed when she closed at five.

The second pickup must be scheduled for tomorrow.

That meant another restless night lay ahead. However . . . if the next transaction went as smoothly as today's, by this time tomorrow she would be out of the spotlight and home free.

After all, once the candles were retrieved, why would the terrorists have any further interest in her?

20

"That's a wrap." Nick rose as Kristin flipped off the lights in WorldCraft and the view on the monitor in the FBI van dimmed.

Luke unfolded his long frame too, and stretched. Wedged into a cramped seat in the back of the crammed-with-equipment vehicle had not been a fun way to spend his Tuesday.

"It's not a wrap for *all* of us." The agent at the console shot them both a wry grin.

"Sorry. We need to keep eyes on this in case someone decides to go out of pattern and pay an off-hours visit to retrieve the last two candles." Stooping, Nick headed toward the back of the van.

"It's not like this is the end of our day, either, you know." Luke rotated the kinks out of his neck. If he *was* clocking out, he'd swing by Kristin's condo, share a cup of coffee, and commend her on her excellent acting job. "We'll be burning the midnight oil at the office."

"I assumed as much. At least I get to hand this off in an hour." The agent at the console went back to watching the screen.

Nick cracked the back door . . . surveyed the area . . . then opened it all the way. "Clear."

Not surprising.

The white utility van was nondescript, and they were in a parking lot a block away from Kristin's shop. In addition, their casual attire of jeans and T-shirts were more workmanlike than law enforcement. Why would anyone pay attention to them?

"You getting hungry?" Luke followed him out.

"Yeah. Let's grab some grub on the way back." Nick took the lead toward his car at the other end of the lot. "What'll it be—burgers or burritos?"

"Burgers."

"You got it."

Half an hour later, after chowing down their fast-food dinner and barreling east on I-64, they were back in the FBI conference room they'd claimed as an operations center for the duration.

Mark Sanders, who'd taken on the role of their office point person, slipped in moments after they entered. "You guys ready for an update?"

"Yes." Nick sat on a corner of the table.

Luke remained standing. If he didn't sit again for a week it would be too soon. The inactivity of surveillance gigs was the worst part of the job.

Next to paperwork.

"We managed to follow the subject who retrieved the candles, but she led our people on a very circuitous route, with two stops along the way."

"Did she spot them?" Luke asked.

"They don't think so."

"Then why the meandering course?"

"It's possible all couriers have been told to dry clean themselves."

True. The guy running this operation was smart. Instructing his minions to take precautionary measures in case they were under surveillance would fit his MO.

Mark moved to a laptop, woke it up, and keyed in a few strokes. "Here's where she left the items." A photo of a community rec center appeared on the screen. "And here's a shot of her stashing the items in the locker area of the fitness center inside. One of our people followed her in."

Another image appeared on the screen, but hard as Luke peered at it, he couldn't make out much detail. Best he could tell, the woman was holding a box of energy bars. "How do you know the items are in that?"

"She didn't drop anything off at any of her other stops—and even though she visited this gym, she wasn't interested in exercise. All she did was leave the box."

"Unless the box was a decoy, and she still has the items."

"True—and possible. That's why we're still watching her . . . and will continue surveillance until this case wraps."

"You told us earlier the plates on the car were muddied." Nick claimed one of the bottles of water sitting on the table. "I assume that slowed down the intel work."

"A little. After we followed her home, we did some research on the address. Once we identified the occupants, we were able to dig deeper. She's from Iran and is married to a Syrian native. Neither is on a terrorism watch list."

"They are now." Nick took a swig of the water.

"Anyone retrieve the items from the rec center?" Luke asked.

"Not yet." Mark folded his arms. "It's possible there's only one drop spot, and whoever retrieves the rest of the candles will put their items in the same place. Assuming, as you noted, that this woman actually left the items."

Nick rotated the water bottle in his fingers. "Do we have any leads on the PO boxes where past buyers have sent payments?"

"No. All of them have been closed. All were registered to different names. All the names were bogus. We tried to run background on the first dozen. There wasn't any."

"Naturally." Luke propped a hip on the table.

"What did your research on the buyers produce?" Mark snagged a water too.

When Nick deferred to him, Luke responded. "They're all over the country, like the PO boxes. The ones on Bishara's personal list seem aboveboard and appear to be taking his word the items are legit. The ones on the list provided by Amir, not so much. None of them have been charged with illegal dealings, but most are on local law enforcement's radar."

"Bishara doesn't have the PO boxes yet for this drop, does he?" Mark twisted the cap off his water.

"No." Nick jumped back in. "It should be coming any day, now that the candles are being retrieved. What's the latest on Bishara's son?"

Mark tapped the computer keys again, and the screen shifted to a photo of a dilapidated walled stone structure. "He's being held here—not far from the town where he lived. There are never more than one or two armed guards on-site. It shouldn't be difficult to pull him out, and the special forces guys can be in position on short notice. They're already—"

"Hold on a sec." Nick scanned the screen of the cell he'd just pulled off his belt. "This is a Washington area code." He put the phone to his ear. "Bradley . . . No problem. I'm in the office. I can call you back on a secure landline. Stand by." He returned the cell to his belt. "Adam Lange from the CIA. One of their operatives visited the abbot at the monastery today, and he wants to brief us."

"It appears we're not the only ones putting in long hours tonight." Luke claimed a chair.

"Goes with the job—as I always remind my wife on nights like this." Nick flashed him a grin, picked up a phone on the credenza, and punched in a number. "Adam? I'm going to put you on speaker so two of my colleagues can listen in." He pushed a button and set the receiver down. "I have Special Agent Mark Sanders and St. Louis County Detective Luke Carter with me."

"Good evening, gentlemen. I won't keep you long, but I wanted to bring you up to speed on our visit to the monastery. One of our operations officers visited Abbot Gagnan today. The man was shocked by the story and very cooperative."

"Does he have any idea who the plant might be?" Luke asked.

"No—but he supplied our officer with the names of everyone who has worked on the candle operation in recent years. Most are monks, but a few others have assisted. Two men have been helping for an extended period, living on-site. They're the most likely candidates for the middle-of-the-night assumed murder. One of the men is a local townsperson who lost his entire family in a jihadist attack, the other a refugee who came for aid and ended up staying."

"What are their names?" Nick pulled a blank pad of paper toward him from the center of the table.

The man rattled them off.

Nick arched an eyebrow. "Could you spell those, please?"

The CIA officer complied, and Nick jotted down the letters as Lange continued. "We've already done some preliminary investigation, since we have boots on the ground there. The first man is well-known in the town, his family has lived there for generations, and he hates the jihadists."

"He sounds clean."

"Agreed. The second man, Khalil, is much more suspect. He appeared out of nowhere, and our people haven't yet found any background on him. We've got some of our foreign agents making discreet inquiries, but my money's on him."

"We'll do some research from our end too, but I'm guessing you're on the right track. Thanks for your help."

"Happy to assist. If we find anything else of interest, I'll let you know."

As Nick ended the call, Luke leaned back in his chair. "Let's hope nothing the CIA did—or is doing—tips off the guy at the monastery."

"They're decent at being discreet." Nick doodled a box on the paper in front of him, brow creasing. "Even if this Khalil is our guy, though, there may not be much we can do other than alert the monks after we wrap the case up here and hope local law enforcement will arrest him."

Silence fell in the room, and Luke figured his FBI counterparts had come to the same discouraging conclusion he had.

With everything else the local authorities were dealing with in Syria, a scheme to send a few artifacts overseas wouldn't get much attention—and without exhuming Brother Michael's body and doing an autopsy, it would be impossible to prove a murder had been committed.

The chances of the latter happening were about as miniscule as a peaceful resolution to terrorism in the Middle East.

"I don't suppose extradition is a realistic option." Luke wished he was wrong—but was pretty certain he wasn't.

"No." Mark finished his bottle of water in several long gulps. "It's a federal crime when US citizens are killed abroad in terrorism-related incidents—and the victim *was* from Florida. The FBI could open an investigation, but we'd need the approval of the Syrian government . . . such as it is . . . as well as their willingness to transfer the suspect to the US to stand trial. Not going to happen in this case. And our government won't authorize a grab for a guy who's committed one murder when dozens of people are often killed in a single incident."

That was the longest speech Mark had made since Luke had met him—and the ring of authority in his voice was unmistakable.

He might be the leader of the St. Louis FBI SWAT team now, but his expert assessment of an international issue suggested the man had much broader experience.

Nick confirmed that—and then some—with his next comment. "Sounds like your HRT experience speaking."

HRT?

As in Hostage Rescue Team?

Whoa!

If Mark had been a member of the nation's primary civilian counterterrorism asset, he'd seen some serious action.

No wonder Nick had tapped him to be part of this case. With his experience in that elite FBI unit, he had way more to offer than SWAT expertise.

"I learned a few things on the team that come in handy on occasion." Mark set his empty bottle on the table. "I wish we could bring the inside guy to justice . . . but that's out of our control. On the plus side, his monastery gig will be over after we give the monks the high sign to alert local authorities. For now, we need to concentrate on the US-based operation. Let's talk about next steps."

And that was what they did for the next four hours.

Yet as they parted in the parking lot at eleven, Luke knew the two FBI agents shared his frustration.

As far as they could see, based on current information, there was no direct link to the man known as Amir.

The PO boxes in other cities had been rented by different individuals who'd used bogus IDs. Even if the FBI was able to locate those folks, it was unlikely they knew Amir's real identity . . . or his location.

None of the buyers of the items had direct contact with Amir.

The couriers who picked up the candles at WorldCraft could and would be kept under surveillance . . . but again, they might have nothing more than phone contact with the man.

Bishara did talk to Amir . . . and the museum curator's phone was set up to trap the expected call . . . but he had no clue about the man's identity, either. The best they would be able to determine from the trap was the general location of the cell. They'd get agents to the area as fast as possible—but Amir wasn't going to hang around waiting for them.

Surveillance would continue on the locker room at the rec center, and they'd follow the person who retrieved the packages . . . follow Bishara to his next pickup . . . and follow the man who dropped off the items for the museum curator to peddle.

Yet there was a very real possibility no one in the organization knew who Amir was or how to find him.

Bottom line?

They needed to smoke the man out.

But how?

Luke dashed through the rain toward his car, flinching as a slash of lightning strobed across the black sky, a crack of thunder booming on its heels.

The weather continued to be as unsettled as this case.

While they needed a plan to draw Amir into the open, after wrestling unsuccessfully with that challenge for hours, sleeping on it had seemed the best option.

Luke smothered the yawn that snuck up on him as he hit the auto lock on his car. After putting in sixteen straight hours, his brain was turning to mush.

About all he could muster up energy for tonight was dialing Kristin's number.

But it was too late for that. Given the situation in Boston, she didn't need the kind of adrenaline-spiking, late-night call that often signaled an emergency.

He'd have to wait until tomorrow to talk with her—preferably after the last two candles were retrieved and she was no longer in the line of fire.

That couldn't come soon enough for him.

Even better would be the day they marked this case closed.

And as he drove home through the pummeling downpour,

he prayed that someone working this case would have a brain-storm overnight that would help them nail the kingpin and end the flow of money to terrorist cells bent on creating chaos on American soil.

■ ■ ■ ■ ■

The second candle retriever was a surprise.

At first, Kristin didn't pay much attention to the blonde, blue-eyed woman who came in half an hour after the shop opened on Wednesday. But when the new customer wandered over to the monastery display, picked up two candles, and carried them and a batik scarf to the checkout counter, Kristin's antennas went up.

"Did you find everything you needed?" As she rang up the purchase, she smiled at the woman who appeared to be in her early twenties.

"Yes. You have some cool stuff." She opened her purse. "I'll be paying cash today."

The alert beeping in Kristin's mind intensified.

This woman might not look like a stereotypical Middle East-ern terrorist, but she was following the same pattern as yester-day's retriever.

Unless . . .

Could she be an innocent customer who was simply buy-ing some candles, as Elaine had, soon after they were put on display? Maybe these two weren't marked.

Time to find out.

While the woman counted out her money, Kristin pulled some bubble wrap off the roll. Turned one of the candles on its side, bottom facing her as she encased it in the protective material.

It was marked.

She repeated the procedure with the other candle.

Also marked.

Her pulse picked up.

This was bizarre.

Why would a woman who didn't appear to have any Middle Eastern ancestry aid terrorists intent on destroying the West?

"Isn't that the right amount?"

Kristin blinked. Refocused. "Yes." She took the bills and change, put them in the cash drawer, and slid the purchases into a small bag. "Thank you for supporting the work of the monks."

The woman gave her a confused look.

"The candles." Kristin motioned toward the bag. "All proceeds benefit their humanitarian work in Syria."

"Oh. Yeah. Glad to help." She reached for the bag.

"I admire their courage for persevering under such dangerous conditions, don't you?"

"Uh-huh. Thanks." She edged away, pivoted, and hurried toward the exit.

Kristin waited until she disappeared from view outside the window, then eased onto the stool behind the counter.

Why in the world would a young woman like that be involved with terrorists?

It didn't compute.

The phone in her pocket began to vibrate, and after glancing at the screen, she smiled and put it to her ear. "Hi, Luke."

"Hi. Sorry I haven't been in touch more. We've been putting in some long hours."

"I bet. Did you watch what just happened in here?"

"Yes. Nick's people are on her."

"She wasn't what I expected."

"We were surprised too. I'll be curious to see how she's connected. Great job for the past two days, by the way."

"Thanks. All I can say is I'll be glad to leave clandestine work to the experts in the future. Are you close by?"

"Yes . . . but busy." His voice dropped . . . and deepened. "I'm hoping that will end soon, and we can move on to the other activities we've discussed."

"The social ones?"

"Yes."

"I like that idea." She leaned her head back against the wall as the sound of muffled conversation came over the line. "I take it there are people nearby listening in?"

"Correct. It's a bit crowded in here."

"Too bad. It would be a welcome change to converse about a topic that doesn't relate to terrorism."

"We'll get there. How's your mom?"

"Continuing to wake up. I spoke to Dad last night. She's not talking yet, but her eyes are open and he says she's beginning to show signs of awareness. She even squeezed his hand when he asked her to."

"Glad to hear it. Let me know if there are any more positive developments."

"I will. Good luck."

"We'll take as much of that as we can get. Talk to you soon."

The line went dead.

After a moment, Kristin pressed the off button and let out a long, slow breath. Luke and the FBI might still be neck-deep in this investigation, but her part was officially over.

Which meant that for the first time in weeks, she could go to bed tonight secure in the knowledge that no more pulse-pounding, thriller-novel episodes were lurking in the shadows, waiting to disrupt her life.

21

"I'll hold until she gets to her car." Nick angled his cell away from his mouth and spoke to the agent at the console in the surveillance van. "Continue monitoring until further notice. I want all contingencies covered on the off chance we have another Elaine Peterson situation."

As the man nodded, Luke ended his call to Kristin and slid his phone back onto his belt. He'd have preferred to extend their conversation—but not in front of an audience.

"Everything okay with Ms. Dane?" Nick tossed the question over his shoulder.

"Yes. She was glad to take a bow and move off stage."

"I don't blame her." Nick spoke again into his cell. "Glad to hear it . . . Yeah, that works. Let me know what you find out and keep us apprised. I'm also available to tag team this, since we're done here . . . got it." He ended the call.

"Was the plate covered with mud again?"

"No."

"That makes it easier."

"We were due for a break." Nick rose. "You want to discuss

next steps over a breakfast sandwich at McArthur's? The bowl of cereal I had this morning is long gone."

"Sure. My bagel feels like ancient history too."

Fifteen minutes later, seated in a corner of the busy bakery that offered a clear view of the entrance and dining room, Nick added some Tabasco to an egg, cheese, and bacon concoction that was stuffed with chili sauce and pickled jalapenos.

Luke's tongue burned just looking at the thing.

"What?" Nick continued dousing the sandwich with Tabasco.

"I'm trying to decide whether I should put the fire department on standby."

"Very funny." He set the bottle back on the table. "I happen to like hot and spicy."

"I do too—within reason. What you're doing is way outside those boundaries."

"And that"—he indicated Luke's standard ham-and-egg selection—"is boring."

"Nothing at McArthur's is boring."

"I'll concede that point." He picked up a stray jalapeno and popped it in his mouth. "Neither is this case."

"Agreed." He surveyed the dining room. The only other occupant at this mid-morning hour was an older man reading the daily paper while he enjoyed a sweet roll and coffee. Nevertheless, Luke lowered his voice. "To be honest, I'm not liking where we are."

"I'm not either. After our brains tanked last night, I was hoping one of us would come up with a plan by this morning to flush out our subject."

"I wonder if Mark had any ideas."

"Negative. I talked to him earlier. Our guy has insulated himself well. Getting to him is going to be a serious challenge."

No kidding.

Barring a serious slip on his end or a brilliant idea on theirs about how to draw him into the open, they were at a stalemate.

"So all we can do after today is sit around and wait for him to contact Bishara." Luke forked a piece of egg that had escaped from his sandwich.

"Yes—but that may not help much, either. Unless we happen to have people nearby, he'll be long gone before we can move in. I don't want to start hauling in the peripheral players until we've exhausted every other—" He pulled out his phone, checked the screen, and put it to his ear. "Bradley . . . Yes . . . Got it. I'm on the way." He ended the call. "You up for some surveillance work?"

"Yes."

Nick finished his sandwich in two huge bites and washed it down with a gulp of coffee. "Today's retriever appears to be following a similar winding path and making stops. There's a whole contingent of agents assigned to this, but they could use us in the rotation."

"Let's go." He wadded up his napkin.

As they stood, a familiar man with light brown hair came into the bakery. He glanced their way . . . did a double take . . . hesitated . . . then walked toward them.

"Do you know him?" Nick spoke quietly, his gaze glued to the approaching man.

"He has an insurance office two doors from WorldCraft. I met him the day Kristin discovered her clerk's body."

"I'm going to stay here and make a call while you talk to him."

Luke met the man halfway across the dining area.

"Detective Carter, right?" Doud stopped in front of him, flicking Nick a quick look.

"Yes. Good morning, Mr. Doud."

"I'm flattered you remembered my name. In your line of work, you must meet dozens of people a week. A colleague from County?" He inclined his head toward Nick.

"No. Different branch of law enforcement."

"Ah. Are you working a case together?"

"Comparing notes over breakfast."

"It can't hurt to have extra brainpower on challenging cases—like the murder at WorldCraft. What a terrible tragedy. And poor Kristin. I can't imagine what a shock it must have been to discover the body." He shook his head, twin grooves denting his brow. "I haven't heard any updates recently. I hope you're continuing to work on it."

"It's an ongoing investigation." Luke pulled out his keys, hoping the guy took the hint.

He did.

"Glad to hear it. I'll let you be on your way." He retreated toward the counter.

Nick met up with him at the door, but they didn't speak again until they were outside.

"Did he have anything helpful to offer on the WorldCraft murder during the initial investigation?" Nick surveyed the fair-trade goods shop, half a block down on the other side of the street.

"No. He was in Chicago at the time of death established by the ME. His only involvement was giving Kristin a place to hang out away from the media until I got there."

"He sounded concerned about her during your chat. Is he a rival for the lady's affections?" One side of Nick's mouth quirked up.

He could evade the question . . . but there was no reason to pretend he wasn't interested in Kristin. And Nick was astute enough to see through him if he did.

"I thought that might be the case at the beginning. Not anymore. But I'm in a holding pattern until this is over."

"Then let's hope we wrap this up ASAP." Nick picked up his pace.

Luke did too.

But he had a sinking feeling that unless they got a break soon, the mystery of the monastery might forever remain unsolved.

Especially if Amir somehow got wind of the fact they were on to him and simply melted away.

. . . . .

The car came out of nowhere.

Or more likely, he was distracted by his ringing cell phone and not paying attention to the road.

Whatever the case, by the time Yusef spotted the red four-door crossing the intersection, it was too late to do anything but jam his brake to the floor.

It wasn't enough.

Tires screeching, he clipped the front fender of the other vehicle.

Hard.

Gripping the steering wheel, he held on tight as a bone-jarring thud rolled through him, accompanied by the dissonant sounds of crumpling metal and shattering glass.

The noise seemed to go on forever.

When at last the car stopped shuddering and the clamor subsided, he lowered his forehead to the steering wheel.

Could the timing of this car accident be any worse? Didn't he have more than his fair share of worry already?

God, I'm beginning to feel like Job. Could you please—

A rap sounded on his window, and he jerked his head up.

The thirtysomething man on the other side, cell to his ear, frowned at him. "Are you okay?"

Yusef rolled the window down. "Yes. I think so."

The guy held up his index finger and angled away. "I want to report an accident."

Stomach churning, Yusef stayed where he was through the litany of answers the man provided to the 911 operator.

It was fortunate the other driver had placed the call and was supplying details, because he had no idea what had happened. He'd been too busy fumbling for the phone, heart racing, expecting to hear Amir on the other end of the line.

But this pulse-jarring call, like all the others over the past week, hadn't been from the man who controlled his son's fate. Penny's name had flashed on the screen.

Soon, though, the instructions would come . . . and if that detective and FBI agent were as skilled as they appeared to be, they'd find this monster—and Touma would be rescued.

Thank God they'd pinpointed his son's location. Knowing that soldiers were on alert to swoop in and rescue him as soon as they got the word was the one heartening—

"Did you know you ran a red light?" The guy from the other car swung back to him again, furrows still creasing his forehead, mouth tight.

He could understand the man's reaction.

If someone had complicated *his* life by running into him, he'd be mad too.

"No. I'm sorry. I was distracted. Is anyone in your car hurt?"

"It's just me, and I'm fine." He grimaced at his mangled fender. "Unlike my car."

"I'm sorry." He repeated the lame apology—but what else was there to say?

Horns began to honk, adding to the headache forming behind Yusef's eyes, and cars edged past, the occupants gaping at the damaged vehicles. In the background, the faint wail of a police siren added to the cacophony.

What a mess.

"Excuse me." A middle-aged woman waved at the driver of the red car from the sidewalk. "I saw the accident. If you need a witness, I'll be happy to give you my contact information."

"Thanks." The guy jogged over to talk to her.

Yusef almost called him back, told him not to bother. Witnesses weren't necessary. He wasn't going to dispute the man's claim. How could he? He hadn't even *noticed* the light at the intersection.

But summoning the man—or moving from behind the wheel—required too much effort.

However, after the police arrived, he was forced to dredge up the remnants of his energy and get out of his car.

Hard to do, when your stomach was on fire.

The officer squinted at him. "Are you sure you're all right?"

"Yes. Fine." He leaned against the fender.

"Why don't I call the paramedics, have them check you out?"

"No. I am upset. Nothing more."

After giving him another skeptical scan, the officer began filling out the report.

Yusef remained propped against the fender while he and the other driver provided insurance cards, exchanged contact information, and determined his car was drivable. Only then was he able to get behind the wheel again.

As he prepared to pull back into traffic, he glanced in the rearview mirror while he readjusted it. Did a double take.

No wonder the cop had been concerned about him.

His complexion was pasty . . . and his hands were shaking.

He needed to go home and lie down.

Now.

Too bad it was the middle of the workday.

He put the car in gear, waited until there was a clear opening in the traffic, and carefully pulled out, pointing the car back toward the museum. The banking he'd planned to do could wait, and there was no need to stop for lunch. His appetite had vanished.

Besides, he'd better use the noon hour to alert his insurance rep to expect a call about some very expensive repairs.

The man wouldn't be happy about such a large claim—but accidents happened, and he'd paid his premiums like clockwork.

There was one stop he had to make before he placed that call, though. The bottle of antacids in his office was empty, and he needed to tame the gnawing pain in his stomach that had worsened each day following Amir's most recent call.

If all went as he hoped, though . . . if the authorities were able to end this travesty and rescue his son . . . maybe the pain would go away.

And if it didn't—they had doctors in prisons.

. . . . .

The day was over . . . and none too soon.

Kristin flipped off the lights in the back room at WorldCraft, hoisted her purse onto her shoulder, and stepped outside.

Everything had been routine after the last two candles went out the door, but she was beat. A quiet dinner, a phone chat with Rick about the sets for *Alice in Wonderland*, and a restful sleep were her priorities for the remainder of the day.

As she walked toward her car, Ryan exited his office too.

He lifted a hand in greeting. "We must both be punching out at the same time for once."

"I'm ready. I plan to go home, put my feet up, and chill."

"Busy day?" He tested the knob on his door and strolled over.

"Not too bad." She fished her keys out of her purse, keeping her tone conversational. "I'm just a little tired. The trip East was stressful, and I got behind on sleep while I was there. I'm still catching up."

"I hear you. Stress can take a toll—and you do look tired. At least the news from Boston is positive. Now that your mom's opened her eyes, I bet she'll take a quantum leap forward."

Kristin wrinkled her brow. "How did you know about that? I didn't find out until last night, and I haven't seen you all day."

He shrugged. "You mentioned she was rousing from the coma when we spoke on Saturday. I assumed that meant she was becoming more aware of her surroundings—which is difficult to do if your eyes are closed." He smiled.

That was true.

"Good point." She massaged her temple.

He cocked his head. "Are you okay? You seem kind of . . . out of it."

Did she?

Possible.

Between worry over her mom and the terrorist activity at the shop, clocking her usual eight hours of sleep had been difficult. The fatigue and strain could be catching up with her.

"It's been a long couple of weeks."

"You should go home and get some rest." He started to turn away. Pivoted back. "By the way, I ran into that detective today who's working Susan's case. At McArthur's."

Luke had been within shouting distance and she'd missed him?

Drat.

"Did you talk to him?"

"For a minute. He was with another law enforcement guy. I wonder what they were doing there?"

She lifted one shoulder, pulling out the acting skills she'd packed away hours ago. "Having a snack?"

"I thought it might be related to the case and they'd stopped in to see you."

"No. I haven't had an update about Susan for weeks. As far as I know, they don't have any significant new leads."

"That's too bad. No one should be able to get away with a crime like that. The detective did say it was an open case—but if TV crime shows have any basis in reality, it has to be growing cold by now."

"I hope not."

"Me too. Well, have a relaxing evening." With a lift of his hand, he ambled to his car.

Kristin continued to her Sentra, the relief she'd felt after the last candles left the store evaporating.

Must be residual tension. She *had* been under considerable pressure, and her chat with Ryan hadn't been their usual light fare about the weather or the Cardinals' latest baseball win.

Brain injuries and murder weren't the kinds of topics that left one feeling relaxed and carefree.

A few vehicles up, Ryan backed out of his parking spot, waved through the window, and disappeared down the alley.

After lifting her hand in response, she continued toward her car—with zero regrets about leaving her shop behind for the day.

Another unhappy fallout from all that had happened.

Her fingers tightened on the keys in her hand, the sharp edges digging into her palm.

Spending her days in WorldCraft had never been a burden. How could it be, when the work she did made a difference in the lives of people around the globe? Her little shop might not change the world . . . or garner her a Nobel Peace Prize . . . but Mother Teresa had been right. Not everyone was able to do great things, but everyone could do small things with great love.

Now, however, the shop was more a source of heartache than happiness, tainted with death and terrorism.

It was almost as if evil had permeated the soul of the business she'd launched with such noble intentions.

She slid behind the wheel and slowly exhaled.

The whole thing was a nightmare.

But dwelling on the past wasn't going to change it.

All she could do was pray for fortitude and hope the future held more good than bad.

Like a heaping dose of a certain tall, handsome detective who seemed destined to play a major role in her life.

She toyed with the zipper on her purse, battling the temptation to pull out her phone and call him.

Be strong, Kristin. He's busy with the case, probably working ridiculous hours. It would be selfish to intrude on his time, distract him—even if he did say you could call day or night.

True.

Clamping her lips together, she backed out of her parking spot and aimed her car toward home.

Later, however . . . if she still felt uneasy and off-balance . . . she might give him a quick ring.

Because an infusion of the strength and competence he exuded would be the perfect antidote to the sudden, puzzling apprehension she couldn't shake.

22

Okay, so he was breaking his rule about keeping his personal and professional lives separate during a case.

Sort of.

But Kristin's part was finished . . . it had been a long, tiring, discouraging day . . . only an empty apartment was waiting for him . . . and he needed a pick-me-up.

So shoot him for making this quick detour.

Luke pressed Kristin's bell and checked his watch. Nine o'clock wasn't too late to come calling, was it?

Unless she was exhausted from all the trauma and had gone to bed early.

He frowned.

Maybe this hadn't been his best idea after all.

What if she was annoyed to find him on her porch, and—

The knob turned.

Too late for second thoughts.

He opened his mouth to apologize for showing up late—but closed it after her expression of surprise morphed into a welcoming smile.

"Luke! I was just thinking about calling you." She gave the

jeans and casual shirt he'd worn for the surveillance gig a quick, appreciative sweep. "Nice look. Come in."

In view of the warmth in her eyes, there was no need to apologize for this impromptu visit.

Nevertheless, it couldn't hurt.

"Sorry to come by this late without warning, but I was on my way home and couldn't resist a quick side trip." He stepped inside and, with the pad of his thumb, gently traced the arc of the shadowed half circle beneath her lower lashes. "You look tired."

She swallowed. "You're the second one to . . . uh . . . tell me that today."

His touch appeared to distract her.

Encouraging.

"Yeah? Who else got up close and personal enough with you to notice?" He gave her a teasing grin.

"I saw Ryan in the parking lot as I was leaving. You know, the insurance guy with the office two doors from WorldCraft."

His mouth flattened. "I remember him."

"He said he ran into you in McArthur's today."

"Briefly. He seems very interested in your case—and in you."

She tilted her head. "Do I detect a hint of jealousy?"

"That would be misplaced, wouldn't it?"

A dimple dented her cheek. "Clever ploy to get information without answering my question, Mr. Detective—but for the record, yes, it would be misplaced. I have my sights on another man."

"Anyone I know?"

"That would be a safe bet." She waved him further into the condo and closed the door. "Can I offer you a drink?"

"I'd love a soda—but I'm not staying long." He followed her to the kitchen. "Why were you thinking about calling me?"

She motioned him toward the table while she filled two glasses with ice. "I was feeling kind of uneasy, and I knew talking to you would help. But I assumed you'd had a long day and hated to bother you." After pouring two sodas, she joined him.

"Hearing from you is never a bother. Why are you on edge?"

"I don't know." Creases scored her brow.

"Did Doud . . . hold on a sec." He pulled out his cell and scanned the screen. "Nick." He put the phone to his ear. "What's up?"

"I heard from Adam Lange at the CIA. His local agents have found some connections between our guy Khalil in the monastery and ISIS. They're confident he's our man. I assumed you'd want to know."

"Thanks. I wish we were as far along on our end."

"Agreed."

"You certain you don't need me tomorrow?"

"No. We'll keep the locker facility at the rec center under surveillance, but until someone shows up to retrieve the items or we detect a different drop spot, not much will be happening. I'll text you as soon as there's any news. I expect your boss will be glad to get you back."

"So he told me when I touched base with him. I'll wait to hear from you." He slid the phone back on his belt.

"News?" Kristin swiped a bead of condensation off her glass.

"Some. Our people in Syria have established a connection between the inside man at the monastery and ISIS. Closer to home, we're on hold until the items are retrieved." He took a drink of his soda.

"The woman from the shop today didn't provide any leads?"

"Not many. She led us on a tour of several shopping malls and met a guy who appeared to be Middle Eastern at an outdoor café for coffee. After they finished, the two of them hugged—and he left with the WorldCraft bag."

"Do you know who she is?"

"Yes. The FBI ran her plates and did some digging. She's a college student. Best guess, she met this guy somewhere and they're dating. He must have asked her to pick up the candles for him. Her personal history is pristine."

"What about him?"

"Mud-smeared license plate, like yesterday. We tag teamed tailing him. He dropped a package in the same place the other courier did and went home. After we had an address, we ran his background. A Syrian national, here on a visa. No apparent ties to terrorism."

The puckers on Kristin's forehead deepened. "Where is the main guy finding these people?"

"I suspect they're being recommended by trusted connections."

"So did anyone pick up the packages?"

"Not yet."

Kristin swirled the ice in her glass. "He could send another courier to pick those up too. What if he never has any face-to-face contact with anyone?"

"We're beginning to think that's a real possibility."

"Does that mean he might get away with everything?" Some of her color faded.

"I hope not. The one piece of good news is that his operation is dead in the water. As soon as we give the monks the go-ahead, they'll notify local authorities about the inside man who's putting the artifacts in the candles. No matter how they choose to handle it, he'll be gone from the monastery."

"But if the coordinator here gets away, won't he recalibrate and set up shop somewhere else?"

"He's got an elaborate plan in place in St. Louis, and putting all the necessary pieces together again will be a challenge. But yes . . . if we don't nail him on this, he could relaunch in another city."

Distress darkened her irises. "That would be terrible."

"I agree—and we're doing everything we can to keep that from happening."

No need to tell her the odds were against them at this point. She was already stressed out—and he could always admit defeat later if they couldn't crack this.

"I'm glad you came by, Luke." She touched the back of his hand.

The warmth from her fingers seeped into his skin . . . and rocketed straight to his heart.

"Me too—but you need to get some sleep." He finished his soda and forced himself to stand, even though every impulse in his body was prodding him to stay. "Walk me out?"

"Sure."

She started toward the front door, and he fell in beside her . . . their hands inches apart.

His fingers began to tingle.

He flexed them.

Fisted them.

Gave up.

He might have overcome the temptation to stay, but he couldn't resist the urge to take her hand.

Her step faltered as he twined his fingers with hers. "I thought we were hands off—pardon the pun—until this was over?"

"Your part *is* over—and we're winding down on the rest. I think I can bend the rules a little."

"How much is a little?"

The flirty lilt in her voice kicked up his libido and broke the flimsy hold he had on his restraint.

He paused at the door and turned toward her. "Shall I demonstrate?"

Watch out, Carter. You're edging into dangerous territory.

"You know what they say." She gave him a frisky nudge with her shoulder. "Actions speak louder than words."

His heart stumbled.

Oh, man.

Where had Kristin been hiding this new, coquettish side?

No matter.

He liked it.

A lot.

And he was in too deep now to back out.

Very deliberately closing the distance between them, he gave her a slow smile. He knew how to play the flirting game too. "Consider this a preview—but cut me some slack. I'm a little out of practice."

"Trust me." Her tone was more serious now. "You have loads more experience than I do."

He traced the curve of her jaw with a whisper touch, her skin soft beneath his fingertips. "If you've lacked for dates, it had to be by choice."

"When I . . ." Her voice failed, and she cleared her throat. "When I was a teenager, I was too shy to have anything to do with boys—except Colin and Rick. In college, I was too busy studying to have much of a social life. The dating opportunities in Ethiopia were nonexistent. And after I got back here, I was too focused on WorldCraft to have time for . . . this." Her breath hitched as he skimmed his fingers across her lips.

"Do you have time now?"

"I'll make time."

"I like your priorities." He brushed back a stray strand of her hair. "You're incredibly beautiful, you know that?"

"No, I'm not." She shook her head, her inflection matter-of-fact—and definitive. "As my father used to say, I have an interesting face rather than a pretty one."

Funny.

That had been his first impression too, at the wedding reception. In truth, Kristin wasn't beautiful—by Hollywood standards.

She was better.

Instead of being starlet glamorous, or gorgeous in a conventional sense, she had a face you noticed—and remembered.

As far as he was concerned, that was beauty in its own right. "I stand by what I said."

A soft blush spread over her cheeks. "Well . . . to use another old adage, beauty lies in the eye of the beholder—and even if I'm not beautiful, you make me *feel* beautiful."

"Don't sell yourself short. You have the kind of looks that will last. In twenty years, you'll still be the most captivating woman in any room—and still attracting men's attention." He fingered the silky strands of her flattering shag cut and studied her lips.

So generous.

So appealing.

So tantalizing.

Now *his* breath hitched.

And another caution sign began to flash in his mind.

Maybe he should wait until the case was over once and for all before taking this step, as he'd planned to do from the beginning.

That would be safer.

More prudent.

But he'd been playing by sensible rules since this investigation began . . . his patience was wearing thin . . . and the lady was willing.

It would take someone with Superman's powers to resist the temptation standing inches away from him.

And he was no Superman.

Besides, what was the harm in one simple kiss? It would give them a taste of what lay ahead, help sustain them until the specter of terrorism was forever banished from their lives and they could take their relationship to the next level.

"Hey . . ." Kristin touched his jaw, her fingers as warm and gentle as the breeze on this June evening. "If you want to wait, I unders—"

"No." More like *no way*. He was past the point of resisting. "I'm just savoring the moment. The best things in life shouldn't be rushed. And you definitely fall into that category. Colin isn't the only one who thinks you're best woman material."

Her lips curved up. "You have a way with words."

"Thanks. But I think we should move past words and introduce some action, don't you?"

Without waiting for her to respond, he dipped his head to claim the kiss he'd been dreaming about for weeks.

And everything in the universe ceased to exist except the two of them.

Sound stopped.

Worry stopped.

Time stopped.

All because of the woman in his arms.

She gave as much as she took, her arms slipping around his neck, her soft curves molding to his firmer planes as if the two of them had been designed to fit together. Playful yet sensuous, eager yet shy, she held nothing back. What she lacked in experience she made up for in enthusiasm.

It was the most extraordinary kiss he'd ever experienced.

And he didn't want it to end.

Finally, calling up every ounce of his willpower, he forced himself to ease away. "We need to come up for air." He rested his forehead against hers, his words as rough as the stubble that appeared on his chin when a case kept him on the go for forty-eight hours.

"I think my lungs stopped working . . . like . . . five minutes ago." Her whispered comment sounded as shaky as he felt. "If that was a preview, my heart may not be able to take the main attraction."

"You want to bail?" He played with the hair at her nape.

"Are you kidding me?" She grinned up at him. "My heart may give out . . . but what a way to go."

He chuckled and tucked her back against his chest. "I like how you think, Ms. Dane."

"I like how you kiss, Detective Carter."

"We need to do this again soon."

"Name the date."

"Pencil me in for an upscale dinner a week from Saturday. We're going to launch this courtship in style."

She wiggled free again so she could see his face. "You think this will all be over by then?"

"Doesn't matter in terms of our date. After the items are retrieved from the rec center—or wherever they end up being stashed—Bishara should receive instructions to pick them up. Unless we can get our people to the source of that call fast and nail the brains, we'll have to resort to interviewing couriers who may not have a clue to his identity. The investigation could drag on forever, and I doubt I'll be part of an extended probe."

"I hope that doesn't happen. I want a resolution to this."

"I'm with you." He dropped another kiss on her forehead and backed away. "I need to go."

"Will you stay in touch?"

"Every day. Barring a break, I'll be back at County tomorrow—counting the days until a week from Saturday. Wear that dress you wore to Colin's wedding, okay?"

She blinked. "You noticed my dress?"

"Trust me. There wasn't a man in that room who *didn't* notice it."

"Thank you for that ego boost—but I'm surprised *you* did. You seemed . . . distracted . . . that night."

His mood sobered. "It was the first wedding reception I'd attended since Jenny died. I wasn't in a party mood."

"Oh." Sympathy softened her features. "In that case, I'm amazed you remembered me at all."

"I was too . . . which told me you were special."

"I guess we owe Stan Hawkins a debt of gratitude for introducing us. Who'd have imagined he'd end up being a matchmaker?"

Luke smiled as he conjured up an image of the older gent who'd shared a cocktail table with him. "Any man who calls a wife of sixty-one years his bride and hurries home to share a piece of wedding cake with her is a romantic at heart."

"Seriously?" Her own lips bowed. "That is so sweet."

"An example to emulate."

"I'll second that— though at my age, a sixty-first anniversary might be a long shot."

"But fifty's a strong possibility."

"Depends on when I get married."

"I'm thinking sooner rather than later."

"Is that a proposal?" The cute dimple reappeared in her cheek . . . but she held up a hand before he could respond. "Just kidding. It's much too soon to be discussing anniversaries or proposals."

"Is it?"

Her eyes widened. "Well . . . yes. I mean . . . we've only known each other a couple of months. That's way too fast to get serious . . . isn't it?"

Maybe not. With Jenny, he'd known within minutes she was special. It had been the same with Kristin, though he'd refused to admit it until Becca forced his hand.

Conclusion? Unless his instincts were failing him, a proposal would be on his agenda in the not-too-distant future.

But while he, unlike her, wasn't convinced they were moving too fast, it would be better not to push and risk scaring her off.

"Could be. There's no need to rush, anyway." He gave her one more brief good-bye kiss. "We have lots of tomorrows ahead."

And as he walked down the path to his car, the corners of his mouth tipped up.

Because for the first time in a long while, he was looking forward to the days and weeks and years to come.

■ ■ ■ ■ ■

Spewing out a string of expletives vulgar enough to make an X-rated moviegoer cringe, Amir slammed his fist on the table beside his computer.

This was all Darrak's fault.

He muttered another oath and crumpled the empty soda can beside him.

If the man had shown up on schedule to retrieve the candles back in April, Elaine Peterson would never have bought them.

Then he'd made matters worse by killing her *and* Susan—two women with connections to WorldCraft—which had caught the attention not only of the police but the FBI.

Talk about a total screwup.

Offing the man had been eminently satisfying.

But it didn't solve the problem he'd created.

Amir jabbed at the button on the computer and replayed the entire phone conversation that had taken place between the detective and Kristin this morning after the final candle pickup.

Carter had been careful not to say too much over the line—but the call had validated his suspicion that law enforcement was on his scent. The only new piece of information he'd gleaned was the cop's interest in Kristin.

However, the conversation that had just taken place between them in her condo had provided a few more details . . . until they'd walked away and their voices had faded out.

He drummed his fingers on the table. The confirmation that they were watching the rec center locker didn't surprise him—but the stashed items were his. All the provenance had been prepared based on the photographs provided weeks ago, and the merchandise was worth too much to let it slip away. Those artifacts would fund him . . . and many of the cells . . . until he could reestablish a new operation somewhere else.

And if his retrieval plan worked as well as he expected, by tomorrow night they'd be in his hands.

But how had the cops discovered the candles contained artifacts in the first place? All of the items from the last shipment had been retrieved—albeit messily—and sent on to new homes. None had been intercepted by the police.

So what had tipped the authorities off?

He hadn't a clue.

All he knew was that the well-thought-out scheme that had worked flawlessly for two years was finished.

This iteration of it, anyway.

The question was, what to do now?

He rose and began to pace, letting the analytical side of his brain take over.

First, given the insulation he'd built between himself and all of his contacts, his identity should be secure.

Second, the authorities didn't know he'd discovered they were on to him. That bought him some time to think about next steps.

Third, the detective and his cohorts had no idea he had a connection that gave him access to bits and pieces of inside information about their investigation.

Fourth, they were unaware of his capability to tap into private communication, as he had today.

His lips twisted into the semblance of a smile.

The cops weren't the only ones adept at placing bugs.

However . . . none of those advantages changed the fact that he was going to have to cut his losses here, leave behind the comfortable cover he'd created, and start over somewhere else.

He kicked at the leg of the chair as he passed and spat out another curse.

The whole thing sucked. His setup here was sweet.

But his real work had to be the priority, no matter the sacrifices involved.

So he'd retrieve the items, lay low here for a while, then disappear . . . and begin again somewhere else.

First, though, he needed to tie up a few loose ends.

Like Bishara.

He crossed to the window and stared into the darkness.

There wasn't much chance the cops had linked the curator to the scam. Why would they? He'd had no contact with the man since the new shipment arrived, and Bishara had no clue about the connection between the candles and the artifacts.

The man *did* have customer and PO box information from past transactions—but unless some of the cells that had set up the boxes were as sloppy as Darrak had been, they were safe too.

Even if one or two of them were exposed, however, the network—such as it was—was known to him alone. All cells operated in isolation. If one was discovered, it wouldn't hurt the overall mission.

He propped a shoulder against the wall and folded his arms, watching the taillights of a lone car disappear down the street.

His key advantage was that no one . . . no one . . . in the US network knew him as anything other than Amir. Only one person, far away in Syria, was aware of his true identity—and that man would never, ever betray him.

Still, Bishara was no longer of use, and without continued proof his son was alive, he might be desperate enough to risk criminal charges and approach the authorities himself for help.

It would be better if he was gone.

Another item to add to this week's to-do list—but one that could be handled with a simple phone call.

Which brought him to Kristin Dane.

Narrowing his eyes, he closed the blinds with a sharp snap, cutting off his view of the quiet suburban neighborhood.

If she and that detective were getting tight, she could know some useful details about the investigation. Picking her brain might help him avoid future mistakes.

Trouble was, he'd have to reveal his identity to do that.

And then she'd have to die.

That would be unpleasant.

But she *was* the enemy.

All Americans were the enemy.

The words that had launched him on this mission replayed in his mind.

Never forget your purpose. Do not let the American ways pollute your mind. Stay true to the cause. Put it first, above all else.

His jaw hardened.

Kristin Dane was nothing.

If, after weighing the pros and cons of revealing himself to her, he decided it was worth the risk for whatever information she might be able to offer, he wouldn't hesitate to use her.

And kill her when he was finished.

23

At the sudden ring of her landline, Kristin jolted awake.

Rolling toward her nightstand, she peered at the LED display on the clock and tried to convince her eyes to focus.

Was it . . . twelve thirty?!

Heart stumbling, she snatched up the receiver and squinted at caller ID.

Uh-oh.

It was her dad.

God, please don't let this be bad news!

"Dad?" She shoved off the covers and bolted upright, pulse pounding. "What's wrong?"

"Nothing. I'm sorry to scare you. I know it's late, but I had to call." An upbeat lilt spiked his pitch. "Someone wants to say hello." A fumbling noise sounded, and then her mother spoke. "Krishtin?"

She clenched the phone.

Her mother was talking?

"Yes. Yes, I'm here, Mom." She choked out the words.

"I jush wanted . . . to tell you . . . I'm getting awake . . . and I hope you'll . . . come back again."

"I will, Mom. As soon as I can." She blinked to clear her vision. "It's wonderful to hear your voice."

"I . . . heard yours . . . when you were . . . here. I love you . . . too."

Her throat tightened, and a tear slipped past her lower lash.

Apparently the emotional bedside comment she'd almost walked away without offering hadn't been wasted.

After more fumbling noises, her dad came back on the line. "I'm sorry again to wake you, but I thought you'd want to know about this right away."

"I'm glad you called. This is amazing news." Her mom's language might be stumbling . . . halting . . . slurred—but she was coherent.

That was huge.

"The doctors are thrilled. She started mumbling a few words last night, and was up to short sentences within hours. They said progress should be steady going forward. We're discussing therapy tomorrow. I'll call and give you an update after our meeting."

"I'd appreciate that."

"Everything okay there? You finished with your part in that case?"

"Yes—as of yesterday."

"Maybe you can come back out in a week or so."

"I'll make arrangements tomorrow."

"Sounds good. I'll let you get back to sleep. At least you won't have to worry as much about your mom in the days ahead."

That was true.

But as for sleep . . . not happening in the immediate future. She'd been too wired after Luke's impromptu visit to drop off until an hour ago, and now she was wired again.

Might as well put all this adrenaline to productive use and work on the July rehearsal schedule for *Alice in Wonderland* until she was tired enough to fall back to sleep.

After all, Alexa would be at the shop the next two afternoons, leaving her free to slip home for a nap if she needed to. Her clerk was more than capable of handling customers on a normal day.

And there was no reason to think the days ahead would be anything but normal.

■ ■ ■ ■ ■

Amir slowed his car . . . angled into a spot at a twenty-four-hour Waffle House . . . and pulled out the prepaid international burner cell he'd kept in reserve for an emergency.

Tonight qualified.

And this was going to be a difficult call.

The smell of frying bacon wafted across the parking lot despite the late hour, roiling his already queasy stomach.

How was he going to tell the man he admired more than life itself that their carefully constructed plan was in ruins?

But putting off distasteful tasks didn't make them any easier, as that very man had taught him years ago.

Filling his lungs with the humid night air, he tapped in the number.

"MarHaba."

"Al'abb, it is Amir."

"There is a problem?"

It was a logical question in a relationship where phone calls were reserved for critical communication—and his father had never been one to waste words on politeness.

"Yes." He explained the situation, keeping his briefing as concise as possible.

Several beats of silence ticked by after he finished . . . and though thousands of miles separated them, the chill that came over the line sent a shiver through him despite the June heat.

"This is most unfortunate."

"I'm sorry. Darrak was not a reliable courier, and one loose link can break a chain."

"Do not offer excuses!" The rebuke snapped like a whip.

Amir flinched and remained silent. That had been a stupid lapse. Offering justifications or defenses was a sign of weakness.

Another lesson he'd learned from his father.

"I assume this loose link has been dealt with." The curt comment allowed no room for denial.

"Yes."

More silence.

Amir scrubbed the cold beads of sweat off his forehead.

"Very well." The anger in his father's voice had been replaced with his usual tone of businesslike practicality. "We will take care of the issues at our end—but the interruption in funding will present difficulties to those loyal to our cause. I will expect you to come up with another creative way to subsidize our cells."

"I will work toward that end."

"It appears you are well-insulated from detection—but if your identity is discovered and our plans thwarted, you understand what is expected."

It was a statement, not a question.

"Yes."

But he hoped it wouldn't come to that.

Much as he supported the cause, he would rather live for it than die for it at this stage of his life.

"You do not sound decisive." Again, disapproval crackled over the line.

He straightened his shoulders and spoke with more conviction. "I will do what needs to be done."

And he would—if left with no other options.

"Good. You have made me proud all your life. I would also be proud of you should it be necessary for your life to end. Praise to Allah. Death to America."

Amir repeated the phrases . . . and the line went dead.

Squeezing the cell, he swallowed. Hard.

If all went smoothly in the next two days, he could lay low after that while he dreamed up a new plan.

But if it didn't, he needed to be prepared for a more drastic—and final—end to the current scheme.

Meaning he had some high-priority contingency work to do. Fast.

He scanned the parking lot. It was deserted, so he removed the battery from the phone, slipped out of the car, dumped the cell in a trash container, and drove away.

One call down, one to go.

The next conversation would be much easier.

After driving fifteen minutes to a small municipal park, Amir pulled out another burner phone.

Calling Syria at seven thirty in the morning local time was one thing; placing a call to a US number at this hour of the night was another.

But waiting could delay the arrangements.

He wanted this set up tonight—and finished by Friday morning.

Five rings in, a gruff voice answered.

"It's Amir."

"Do you know how late it is?"

"Yes. I wouldn't disturb you unless it was important."

"It better be."

"I have a job for you that needs to be carried out fast."

"How fast?"

"Friday morning."

"I assume it pays well."

"The same rate as the previous job—and there will be no body to dispose of."

"Tell me what needs to be done."

Amir gave him the details.

"There is much more risk with this arrangement."

"At that hour of the morning, it's quiet there. You should have no trouble."

"*Should* is not a guarantee. The amount of money you've offered is too small for the risk."

Exactly what Amir had expected him to say.

"I'll add 25 percent."

"Fifty."

Amir hesitated—not because the price was too high, but to discourage the man from pushing for even more.

"Fine."

"Then we have a deal. You have a photograph of this man?"

"Google him. You'll find his picture on the internet."

"You're certain he'll be at the location you provided?"

"I've studied his habits. It's on his agenda every Friday. Don't leave without finishing the job."

"I never do. I need half the money in my account in advance, like our previous deal."

"Look for it tomorrow. The rest will be there Friday by noon."

Amir ended the call without a good-bye, tossed the phone in a trash receptacle after removing the battery . . . and exhaled.

Everything was in motion.

If Allah smiled on him, by Saturday this would all be over and he could relax.

As for whether to tap into Kristin's knowledge about the case . . . that remained an option. It would be helpful to know what had triggered law enforcement's suspicions.

He could wait and see how everything played out over the next couple of days before making that decision, though.

But if she ended up as collateral damage . . . so be it.

■ ■ ■ ■ ■

"Luke! Hang on."

At the summons, Luke turned to find Colin jogging toward him down the sidewalk in front of County headquarters, Rick a few paces behind.

"What's up?"

"That's what I was going to ask you. I didn't know you were back from the other gig. Is that case over?"

Luke sized up Rick, who'd stopped a few feet back. "No. We're in a waiting mode."

"For what?"

"The next move on the other side."

"Gee, thanks for that enlightening insight." Colin fisted his hands on his hips. "We can't get anything out of Kristin, either. She's as closemouthed as you are."

"We can't say much." In his peripheral vision, he saw Rick fold his arms.

If he didn't know better, he'd be worried that Kristin's friends were about to exert some serious pressure to convince him to talk.

The physical kind.

"Look, we just want to make sure she's not in any . . ." Colin yanked his phone off his belt, glared at the screen, and spoke over his shoulder as he walked a few yards away. "Don't go anywhere."

Luke checked on Rick.

He hadn't said more than a few words in their previous encounters, but his steely gaze and wide-legged stance would intimidate a lesser man.

"Kristin's lucky to have two such staunch defenders." He kept his inflection casual. Alienating friends of the woman he was falling in love with would be stupid.

"We care about her."

"I know."

"And we're not crazy about her being anywhere close to anything related to terrorism."

"Colin made that clear. But her role in this is over. There shouldn't be any danger at this point."

"Terrorists aren't predictable."

Luke considered him. The man's authoritative tone suggested his statement was more than a generic comment.

"Is that your military background speaking?"

A few seconds passed, silent except for a honking horn and a screech of tires.

"What did Kristin tell you about that?"

"Only that you were in the service. I'm guessing you might have done a tour or two in the Middle East."

"That would be a safe bet."

"What branch were you in?"

He hesitated a moment before answering. "Army. Night Stalkers."

Luke blinked.

Rick had been a helicopter pilot with the Army's elite aviation regiment?

The one that flew into hostile territory to insert and extract special ops soldiers—among other hazardous missions?

"That credential would put you in the terrorist-expert category."

"I don't claim to be an expert—but I *have* had some up-close-and-personal experience with extremists. I guarantee they don't operate under any set of rules you or I would recognize. That's why we're still worried about Kristin."

So was he . . . especially after hearing Rick's take.

"I'm in touch with her every day. I'll warn her to be extra cautious until this wraps up."

"We already did that. She blew us off. But you might get better results. She seems . . . taken . . . with you."

"The feeling is mutual." No sense playing games with these guys. They'd find out his intentions as soon as he and Kristin began dating.

"That's what we figured."

"You have a problem with that?"

"No. Colin says you're a straight shooter, and he has decent judgment—most of the time." A spark of amusement flickered in his eyes.

"Where were we?" Colin rejoined them and slid his phone back into its holster.

Luke hitched up one side of his mouth. "You were about to strong-arm me for information on the case."

"I wouldn't go that far. We know you can't share details, but we're concerned about Kristin."

"We covered that topic while you were gone." Rick checked his watch. "You ready for lunch? I've got a long to-do list for this afternoon."

"Yeah." Colin glanced at him. "You want to join us? We're going to Panera."

Luke's own phone started to vibrate, and he pulled it out. Nick.

"I'll have to pass." He hefted the cell. "This may be an update on the case we were discussing."

"Your FBI buddy?"

"Yes."

"Like I've told you . . . if you need any help that doesn't require security credentials, let me know. I can clear it with Sarge."

"Will do. See you around." He put the phone to his ear.

"Count on it." Rick shot him a quick grin and nudged Colin toward the intersection.

"What's up, Nick?" He continued toward the entrance of the headquarters building.

"The packages have been picked up. You want to join the surveillance team?"

"Yes." He switched direction and jogged toward the parking lot. "Where are you?"

"Heading west on I-64. Our subject has left the rec center and is in the Manchester/I-270 area."

"You want me to meet you out there? I'm in Clayton."

"Negative. I'll swing by and pick you up in front of the main door at County. ETA is about five minutes."

The instant the line went dead, Luke pressed Sarge's number.

It seemed he was going to be spending some additional time with the FBI.

But hopefully not for long. If the artifacts were being retrieved, they might be closing in on the end of this drama.

And after his unsettling conversation with Rick about the unpredictability of terrorists, that couldn't happen fast enough to suit him.

24

Something was ringing.

As the noise penetrated her sleep-fogged brain, Kristin groped for the phone on her nightstand and pressed the talk button. "Hello?"

No response.

"Hello?"

The ring sounded again.

Sheesh.

It was the doorbell, not the phone.

She threw back the sheet, swung her feet to the floor, and dashed barefoot down the stairs. Maybe Luke was paying another one of his unexpected visits on this early Thursday evening.

But neither of the familiar faces on the other side of the peephole belonged to the handsome detective.

One of them, however, leaned closer . . . and the bell pealed again.

She twisted the knob and opened the door.

Colin and Rick took a fast inventory.

"Were you in bed?" Colin's eyebrows dipped into a *V*.

"Yes." She combed her fingers through her pillow-flattened shag. "I came home to take a nap this afternoon. Alexa's minding the store. I guess I slept longer than planned. What brings you two here on a weeknight?"

"Ted Drewes." Rick hefted a white bag.

"The world's best frozen custard? In that case . . . come in." She swung the door wide.

They didn't need a second invitation—and they made themselves at home, as usual.

"Why did you need a nap?" Colin headed for the kitchen.

"Restless night."

"More news on your mom?" Rick set the bag on the table and began removing lidded containers, plastic spoons, and napkins.

"Not since I talked to you both this morning." She sat at the table and opened the container Rick slid toward her.

"So why couldn't you sleep?" Colin plunged a spoon into his custard. Cherry, as usual.

No way was she telling these guys about the kiss that had kept her tossing until the wee hours.

"I was thinking about *Alice in Wonderland*." Not a lie. The show *had* crossed her mind during the long, sleepless hours. For a few fleeting moments. "You guys will be at the production meeting on Sunday afternoon, right?" A discussion about their least-favorite summer activity ought to distract them.

"Yeah." Rick dived into his usual caramel.

"Trish has it on our calendar. She actually thinks it will be fun. Maybe she can represent me, now that we're married." Colin gave her a hopeful look.

"Sorry. She's helping with costumes. You're on for lights and sound."

His face fell.

"Aren't you going to eat that?" Rick waved his plastic spoon at her carton. "Or don't you like Oreo anymore?"

"It's still my favorite." Man, the three of them were creatures of habit—in terms of Ted Drewes, anyway.

"You know . . . she probably hasn't had dinner yet if she was sleeping." Colin stopped eating. "You want us to run out and get you a sandwich somewhere? You could put your custard in the freezer until later."

"Nope." She scooped up a spoonful of the creamy concoction. "Ted Drewes will do fine for dinner. So what gives with the impromptu visit? Not that I'm complaining, you understand—but you"—she pointed her spoon at Colin—"have a new bride at home, and you"—she aimed the spoon at Rick—"are in your busy season."

The two men exchanged a look.

"We just thought we'd swing by." Rick continued to shovel in his custard.

"Right." She didn't attempt to hide her skepticism. "Want to try again?"

"Fine." Colin jabbed his spoon into his cup and leaned toward her. "We ran into Luke in Clayton this morning. It sounded like the case was heating up. He ditched County for the FBI again this afternoon."

"Yeah?" She stopped eating. That was news to her.

"You didn't know about this?"

"No. I haven't talked to Luke since last night."

"We wanted to come by and remind you again to be careful." Rick kept eating, but his focus was pinned on her.

"My part's finished."

"The terrorists might not realize that."

"Gee, thanks for that encouraging thought." She attempted a teasing tone but couldn't quite pull it off. If these two had orchestrated a special trip over here to see her, they were genuinely worried. "What do you want me to do? Hibernate in a cave until this is over?"

"You know . . . that's not a bad idea." Rick sat back in his chair. "I have a few on my property that would work. They're on the cold and damp side, but no one would find you there."

He was kidding, of course.

Wasn't he?

"Listen, you guys." She set her spoon down. "I appreciate how much you care. More than I can say. But I can't lock myself away until this is over. Luke said there shouldn't be any . . ."

Her doorbell rang again.

"Are you expecting anyone?" Colin shot to his feet.

So did Rick.

"No."

Before she could protest, they took off for the front door.

This was getting out of hand.

"Hey!" She scurried after them. "I can answer my own—"

"Shhh!" Rick lasered her a warning glare.

Lifting her chin, she folded her arms.

Fine.

Let them answer the door.

The odds that trouble waited on the other side were miniscule . . . but if it made them feel better to go into protective mode, why complain?

Colin peered through the peephole. Exchanged a glance with Rick. Pulled the door open.

"Well, if it isn't Detective Carter. Fancy meeting you here." Colin stepped back and waved him in. "It appears the second shift has arrived."

"What?" Kristin gaped at the three of them. "You guys co-ordinated this?"

"No . . . but great minds must think alike." Rick gave her a one-sided grin.

"Very funny."

"Someone want to let me in on the joke?" Luke entered and scanned the assembled group.

"It's not a joke." She gave her two friends the evil eye.

"No. It's not." Rick looked at her with one of those penetrating stares of his that had probably been a useful asset in his military days. "Remember that."

"We made our pitch about being careful . . . again." Colin called over his shoulder to Luke as he returned to the kitchen to retrieve his and Rick's concretes. "Time for you to provide some backup."

Rick pulled her into a hug. "Watch your back—and listen to what Carter says."

She squeezed him tight. Hard to be annoyed at people who had your best interest at heart. "You guys are the best—even if you do have a tendency to butt in."

"I heard that." Colin handed Rick the remains of his concrete and gave her a one-armed hug. "I prefer to think of it as watching out for each other." He lowered his voice and spoke close to her ear. "Although I think someone is waiting in the wings to take our place."

At the subtle hint of melancholy in his words, pressure built in her throat.

"No worries on that score—guaranteed. Our bond has been tempered by fire and is too strong to break. Now go home and enjoy your evening with Trish."

After one more squeeze, he released her and followed Rick out the door with a "see you at the office" to Luke.

As they started down the walk, Luke shut the door behind them. "I didn't mean to interrupt a Treehouse Gang get-together."

"It was impromptu—and you can interrupt anytime. The guys like you."

"I wasn't so sure about that today."

"What do you mean?"

"Long story. What did Colin's second-shift remark mean?" He strolled over to her.

"Their real agenda for tonight was to warn me to be vigilant. I told them to stop worrying, that my part was over. I think they hoped you'd reinforce their warnings."

"As a matter of fact . . . that's my plan."

Not what she'd expected to hear.

"You want to explain that?"

"Let's sit while I fill you in." He motioned toward the couch. "It's been a long, tiring, and unprofitable day."

"Okay. Would you like a soda while I finish the frozen custard the guys brought for me?"

"No thanks. I've been slugging coffee and soda all day."

"Have you eaten dinner?"

"I did a drive-through on the way over. I'll wait for you in the living room while you get your custard."

After she retrieved the frozen treat, he took her hand and tugged her down on the couch beside him.

"Is there a glitch with the case?" She studied the fine lines beside his eyes, the weariness in their depths.

"Not so much a glitch as a zilch."

"What does that mean?"

"Better finish that or you'll have soup instead of custard." He motioned to her melting concrete.

"I'll eat while you talk." She scraped up some more of the dissolving confection.

"The packages were retrieved from the locker around noon. We followed the guy all day, trading off tails to keep him from getting suspicious. He went to a dozen places. Nick had people on foot who followed him into stores, a restaurant, a bank, the men's room. The daypack he put the packages in never left his shoulder."

"So he still has them?"

"Unless he used some sleight of hand one of the agents missed."

"Could be he's going to pass them on tomorrow . . . or the next day—unless *he's* the main man." She finished her concrete and set the cardboard cup on the coffee table.

"We don't think so. We ran his background. Another Syrian national, here on a visa. We can't find even a remote link to any terrorist group."

"Did Bishara get any instructions yet?"

"No. Nick talked to him yesterday. But he's had a tough week. Apparently he was in a fender bender a couple of days ago, and Nick said he sounded rattled."

"I can imagine. A car accident on top of worrying about his son and dealing with a terrorist—doesn't seem fair for one person to be dumped on that much." She pulled a cushion onto her lap. "So what does all this have to do with me being careful?"

"I ran into Rick and Colin in Clayton today."

"They mentioned that."

"I had a minute alone with Rick. He told me he'd been a Night Stalker."

She raised her eyebrows.

Luke must have impressed him if he'd offered that personal tidbit.

"He doesn't share that with many people."

"Why not?"

"There are a lot of incidents from his military years he'd rather forget."

"I can understand that—especially in light of his dealings with extremists. Because of his experiences, I listened when he reminded me that while we might think the danger is past in your case, terrorists aren't predictable. I can't see why they would have any interest in you, but I second what Rick and Colin said. Use extra caution until this wraps up."

She kneaded the edges of the cushion. "Message received. Tell me what happens next."

"The FBI is continuing to watch the guy who raided the locker. Nick says he's at a rock concert tonight with a woman friend."

"It must be tough to keep track of someone at an event like that."

"There are pros and cons. It's easier to blend into the crowd—but you *can* lose sight of your subject for brief moments. That's why Nick has a full contingent on the job at the venue."

"Do you think the handoff will happen there?"

"It's possible. But if there's no clear indication it has, I'll be back at County tomorrow. They don't need me for routine surveillance." He clapped a hand over his mouth as a yawn snuck up on him. "Sorry. I think I'm going to make this an early night."

Too bad. She wouldn't have minded his company for another hour . . . or two . . . or three. Thanks to all the warnings that had been lobbed at her this evening, odds were high it was going to be another long, restless night.

But asking him to stay would be selfish. He looked exhausted.

"Walk me out?" He stood and held out his hand.

"Sure."

It took far too few steps to reach the door in her small—or cozy, as the realtor had called it—condo.

"I'll call you tomorrow. Will you be at the shop all day?"

"No. Alexa's covering for me in the afternoon. I have some errands to run."

"Stay alert to your surroundings."

"I learned to do that long ago. It was a handy skill to have in the Peace Corps."

"It's a handy skill in any walk of life these days." He looped his hands around her waist. "I hate to leave."

"Maybe we could sweeten up the parting a little."

He grinned. "You know . . . I'm glad you're not the type who likes to play hard to get."

"I don't play games with people I care about." She met his gaze straight on, no trace of levity in her tone.

His expression sobered. "I already figured that out. That's one of the things I lo . . . I admire about you."

He'd almost said the L-word.

A tiny shiver of delight spiraled through her.

"I have other fine qualities too."

"I know—and I plan to explore them all in the coming months. But I've already discovered a few . . . including the fact that you're a world-class kisser. Care to demonstrate that skill again tonight?"

"My pleasure."

He dipped his head, and she rose on tiptoe to meet him.

When he at last backed off, she had to hold onto him until her world steadied.

"You make it very tough to say good night." He clasped her hands, his grip firm yet tender.

"The feeling is mutual. But I'll be here tomorrow . . . and the day after . . . and the day after that. We can pick this up when you're not dead tired."

"I don't feel all that tired anymore." He stroked his thumbs over the back of her hands, giving her a slow smile.

He'd stay if she asked him to.

But that would be selfish, Kristin. Let the man go home and get some rest.

"You'll be tired tomorrow, though, if you hang around. And you need to be at the top of your game on the job—especially with all that's going on."

He exhaled. "I'm glad one of us is maintaining perspective."

"Only with superhuman effort. Save some of your energy for our big date."

"No worries. I'll be fully charged." After one more quick kiss, he walked through the door. "I'll call you tomorrow night . . . or sooner, if there's any news. Lock up while I wait."

"I don't think anyone is hiding in the bushes by my front door."

"Humor me."

"Okay. Be safe." She closed the door, clicked the lock into place, and moved to the sidelight.

Luke was already halfway down the walk to the parking lot.

The man must be super tired.

She, however, was wide awake after her long afternoon nap.

An early night wouldn't hurt her, though. And until she fell asleep, she could cuddle up in bed with that suspense novel she'd never finished during her trip East.

And pray that her three visitors tonight were way off base, and the only danger she'd encounter in the days ahead would be in the pages of her book.

■ ■ ■ ■ ■

The noise was deafening.

How could anyone call this music?

While the powerful bass beat pounded his ears and ricocheted through his body, Amir checked on his courier again, a few rows below him. The man was in the seat designated on the ticket he'd provided, with a date beside him, as planned. Positioning himself for the handoff wouldn't be difficult after the stupid concert ended and the masses were thronging toward the door.

He just had to endure the din—and sacrifice a few decibels of hearing—until the racket was over.

As he'd done every few minutes during the so-called concert, he gave the crowd a casual perusal.

Anyone in the audience could be an FBI agent or detective in undercover mode. They came in all shapes and sizes. Most likely there were more than a few here, hanging around the fringes, since all seating in the venue was assigned. But they couldn't fill the theater with agents, and the handoff had been meticulously choreographed. It would happen in the blink of an eye. So fast and out of sight that the agents who had the courier under surveillance would never notice.

There was no reason to think his plan wouldn't work.

Even if he himself was on law enforcement's radar—and there'd been no red flags to indicate he was—no one would recognize him. In his cargo shorts, black T-shirt with a peace sign on the back, garish temporary tattoo, baseball cap, and fake glasses, he bore no resemblance to the man he'd created for his cover life.

His own mother wouldn't know it was him—if she had any idea what he looked like now. Which she didn't.

The eight-year-old she'd abandoned and the grown man he'd become were two different people in every way.

The reverse was true too. He had nothing except hazy memories of her.

But that was of no consequence.

His father had done an excellent parenting job alone. They hadn't needed her.

He took a sip of the overpriced Bud Light he'd bought from a vendor. Not his first choice of beverage . . . but a necessary prop if he wanted to blend into this crowd.

The band wound down its last set to thunderous applause . . . then launched into an encore after the crowd demanded more.

Amir gritted his teeth.

The bone crushing noise was pure torture.

But he forced up the corners of his lips and boogied to the beat with everyone else until the band mercifully finished for the night and the theater lights came up.

His pulse accelerated.

This was it.

The chances of anyone in law enforcement being super close were next to nothing. They'd had no idea in advance where the courier would be sitting, and he and his date were surrounded by fans who'd bought tickets further in advance, insulating him from the Feds. All part of the plan.

Amir joined the crowd surging down the aisle . . . edged in front of the courier to display the back of his T-shirt and tattoo . . . lowered his hands until they were hidden in the crush of people . . . and felt an aluminum can slide into one as the Bud Light he was holding in the other was plucked from his grasp.

Done.

He continued to shoulder through the crowd, putting distance between himself and the courier, never letting the man see his face.

In the lobby, he veered toward the men's room. The courier would continue to the exit, as instructed, tossing his empty beer can in a trash container along the way.

Once in the men's room, Amir claimed a stall . . . pried open the top of the doctored beer can . . . removed the items inside . . . and tucked them into the pockets of his cargo shorts. Then, flushing the toilet to mask the noise, he crushed the can flat in his hand and slid it into another pocket.

He paused to wash his hands, giving the other two men in the restroom a surreptitious perusal. Both had been there when he arrived. Neither appeared to be interested in him.

Without lingering, he left the theater and struck off for the MetroLink station, maintaining a measured pace, staying within a group of people. He needed to mingle so he didn't stand out as a loner—or someone in a hurry to get away.

But ten minutes later, after chatting up a blonde beside him who was high on either the music or something more potent,

he boarded the light-rail train in the midst of a horde of revel-
ers and claimed an open seat. In thirty seconds, the train was
packed, the aisles lined with concertgoers gripping the overhead
handholds.

The doors closed, and the train pulled away.

Amir let out a slow breath.

Unless he'd miscalculated or missed some sign, no one had
an inkling a switch had been made at the venue. Or that he
was now in possession of artifacts destined to fund his new
operation, whatever . . . and wherever . . . that turned out to be.

He needed to work on those plans—as soon as the last few
pieces of old business were finished.

One of those would be dealt with in less than eight hours in
St. Louis. His father would take care of the rest in Syria.

So he'd go home, get a solid night's sleep—and continue to
play the role that had protected him for the past three years
while he considered whether the inside information Kristin Dane
had might be of value to him.

25

Give it up, Carter.

As that advice echoed in his mind for the third time, Luke heaved a sigh and peered at his watch.

Eleven fifty-three.

And sleep wasn't even a distant speck on the horizon.

He should have stayed at Kristin's condo for another hour or two instead of opting for an early night. All he'd done after going to bed was pummel his pillow, think about her—and try to wrestle a boatload of restless energy into submission.

A full-throttle run would expend some of his tension—but at this late hour, he'd have to settle for a workout session with his weights.

Swinging his feet to the floor, he reached for his phone on the nightstand just as it began to vibrate.

Huh.

Odd hour for a text.

He scanned the screen . . . and his pulse picked up.

Why would Nick contact him this late at night?

He skimmed the brief message.

New activity. Didn't want to disrupt your sleep.
Call in AM when you get this.

Wait seven hours to get an update?

No way.

Since his FBI colleague obviously wasn't sleeping either, Luke called him.

Nick answered on the first ring. "Did I wake you?"

"No. What's going on?"

"We have a problem."

Not welcome news at midnight.

"What happened?"

"Amir knows we're aware of his operation."

Luke tightened his grip on the phone. "How do you know?"

"I had a call ten minutes ago from Lange at the CIA. The abbot at the monastery alerted him that Khalil disappeared overnight. Lange's people in Syria also contacted him. The local agent who's been keeping tabs on Bishara's son is seeing unusual activity at the compound where he's being held. It appears they might be planning to shut down that operation."

His stomach bottomed out. "Is Touma still alive?"

"As of a couple of hours ago. My guess is, not for long. If the US operation is folding, he's no longer of use. Our special ops people are moving into position now to snatch him."

"How could Amir have found out we were on to him?"

"There must be a leak somewhere. Who's privy to the details in your organization?"

"No one. Even Sarge didn't ask for too many particulars."

"How much does Kristin Dane know?"

"More than anyone else, since she's in the middle of this. But she's been discreet. One of her best friends is a colleague of mine, and she's told him next to nothing. I'll double-check with her to make sure she didn't inadvertently pass on any information, though. Could Bishara be the leak?"

"I plan to call him first thing in the morning, but I doubt it. He has too much to lose to risk sabotaging this operation."

Luke stared at the shadows on the wall across from him. "Maybe one of the couriers realized they were being followed, communicated that to Amir . . . and he got spooked."

"Possible—but with all the effort he put into setting up his elaborate arrangement, I doubt he'd shut it down on mere suspicion. I think he knows with absolute certainty that we're closing in."

Luke couldn't argue with Nick's logic—nor squelch the sudden cold chill that rippled through him.

What if Amir also had begun to suspect that Kristin was cooperating with authorities?

Might he go after her?

"I wouldn't worry too much about Ms. Dane." Nick answered his unspoken question. "And no, I'm not a mind reader—but I'd be wondering how concerned I should be if I was in your shoes. Amir will be too busy eluding us to fret about secondary players."

That was probably true—and with any other case, he'd dismiss his concern.

But that was a lot harder to do when your heart was involved.

Nevertheless, he forced himself to shift gears. "Any updates on the courier we trailed yesterday?"

"Negative. He went home after the concert and his place is dark."

"No suspicious activity at the theater?"

"None that we spotted—but the crowd was huge, and during his arrival and departure he was surrounded by a crush of people. Otherwise, he never left his seat."

"Did your people go over the area where he'd been sitting?"

"Yes. Nothing was left behind. We retrieved the beer can he

bought during the concert, which he tossed in a trash can as he left, but it was nothing more than a beer can."

In other words, surveillance at the concert hadn't yielded a single new clue.

"So what's next?"

"I'm heading to the office to watch the covert video our people took of him during the show. One of our guys masquerading as an usher was able to stick pretty close—but I'm not overly optimistic it'll be of much help."

"You want some company?"

"Two sets of eyes are always better . . . but this could be a bust. He might still have the items at his apartment."

"I'm wide awake anyway."

"In that case, you're welcome to join the party. I'll be there in thirty minutes. Call my cell when you arrive and I'll meet you at the door."

"Got it." Pressing the end button, Luke detoured to his closet.

Ninety seconds later, dressed in a shirt and jeans, he grabbed his keys and stepped out of his apartment into the darkness.

Praying they'd spot something . . . anything . . . on the video that would give them a clue to follow.

Because if they didn't . . . if Amir was setting plans in motion in Syria to shut down the operation . . . if he'd managed to retrieve the artifacts from the last shipment . . . there was a high probability he would vanish and launch a new scheme somewhere else.

Leaving the murder of three innocent people in his wake.

Perhaps four, if they didn't get to Touma.

Fast.

. . . . .

God, I feel so lost.

From his seat in the second row of the small Byzantine chapel that had been his spiritual home since coming to St. Louis, Yusef bowed his head, shoulders sagging.

Here, he could worship in public each weekend . . . and in private every Friday morning before going to work . . . without fear—unlike the persecuted Christians in his beloved homeland. Yet today his soul was as parched as the hot, dry winds that swept across the vast, barren desert of eastern Syria.

He'd already asked God to save his son. Pleaded for mercy on his soul for the part he'd played in Amir's diabolical scheme. Thanked the Almighty for the blessings that had graced his life these past nine years in his adopted country.

What else was there to add?

He flipped through the worn book of prayers he'd brought with him to this new land. Skimmed the passages that usually comforted and uplifted. Closed the book.

No words of consolation could vanquish the worry and anguish and despair that consumed his soul.

And that was his fault, not God's. A human weakness, not a divine snub. If he gave his burdens to the Lord, as his faith taught, the Almighty would help him carry the load.

Today, however, summoning up the trust and strength that required was beyond him.

I'm sorry, Lord. Forgive me. I'll try harder this week to get back on track, to overcome my . . .

A door opened softly behind him, and he checked his watch. Seven ten already? He'd stayed longer than usual this morning. Better not linger, or George might stop unlocking the door for him early every Friday. The maintenance man had more to do than sit around waiting to close up again while one congregant finished his half hour of private contemplation and prayer.

Slipping the book into the pocket of his jacket, he rose and turned.

"I'm sorry, George. I lost track of . . ."

The apology died in his throat.

A brawny stranger was standing at the back of the dim cha-pel. The baseball cap pulled low on his forehead cast shadows on his face, masking his features . . . but his eyes were cold.

"Can I help you?"

"Yusef Bishara?"

"Yes."

"Give me your wallet."

His jaw dropped.

"I said, give me your wallet. Now." He pulled a pistol out of his jacket.

Yusef's heart stuttered.

He was being robbed . . . in church?

This was surreal.

"I said now!"

At the man's harsh command, he dug out the billfold.

"Throw it over here."

He tossed it toward the man.

Keeping the gun trained on him, the intruder bent down. Picked up the wallet. Pocketed it.

Lungs locked, Yusef waited for him to lower the gun and disappear out the door.

He didn't.

Instead, he walked a few steps closer . . . the gun never wavering.

That's when Yusef knew.

The man was going to kill him.

His legs began to shake, and he groped for the back of a chair to steady himself.

"You have what you want." He pushed the strained words past the constriction in his throat. "Please . . . there's no reason to hurt me."

"There are thousands—and thousands—of reasons." He

steadied the gun with his other hand and aimed it at Yusef's chest.

Yusef caught his breath, stiffened . . .

The back door opened again, and George stuck his head in. No!

He couldn't let the man who'd patiently waited for him early each Friday morning die too.

The robber swung toward the door.

Move, Yusef! You have only seconds!

But his legs refused to budge.

A gunshot exploded, shattering the serenity of the sacred space despite the silencer attached to the front of the pistol.

Panic clawed at Yusef's windpipe.

Had George been hit?

No way to tell. The robber was blocking his view.

Nevertheless, the shot propelled him into action.

Calling up every ounce of his strength, he barreled toward the man and launched himself at his legs.

A pathetic tackle from a sixty-three-year-old desk jockey wouldn't stop a killer, of course. But it might buy George enough time to get away and run for help—if he wasn't badly wounded.

He made contact just as the intruder spun back. The force of the impact toppled the shooter, and he went down. Hard.

But he never lost his grip on the gun.

Yusef lunged for his wrist and locked onto it with both hands.

The man jerked. Twisted. Kicked.

Calling up his last reserves of energy, Yusef held fast.

They continued to struggle . . . until the intruder suddenly rolled sideways and yanked his arm with what felt like super-human strength.

Only then did Yusef's grip loosen.

The man wrestled his arm down, until the gun was between them.

A second shot exploded—and a monstrous pain erupted in Yusef's stomach.

Another shot shattered the stillness.

Then another.

The room around him began to blur.

The light dimmed

And as searing pain purged everything else from his consciousness . . . as a pool of red formed beside him . . . Yusef sent one last plea heavenward.

Please, Lord, let Touma live!

. . . . .

"Want a refill?" Nick rose and motioned to Luke's empty disposable cup on the conference room table.

"No thanks. I'm already ODed on caffeine."

"Good point. If we ingest any more high octane brew, we'll be too wired to sleep once we go home and crash." Nick sat back down and set his cup aside.

"Unfortunately, I think our departure is imminent. We've scrutinized every video—and triple scrutinized the sections where it's possible, in the crush of the crowd, a handoff occurred. And other than a serious case of eyestrain, we have zip to show for our all-nighter."

"Tell me about it." Disgust laced Nick's comment.

"I assume the courier's tickets were a cash transaction, but are you planning to contact the theater and see if you can get credit card info for the people who bought seats in his immediate vicinity?"

"Yes—but only recent purchases are relevant. The elaborate handoff scenario was likely a last-minute decision, given that Amir just discovered his people are under scrutiny. If the adjacent tickets were purchased more than a few days ago, there can't be any connection."

"True." Plus, the agent playing the role of usher had gotten decent video of the courier during the entire performance. They'd have spotted a handoff if it had happened then. "My money's on the switch being made in the crowd before or after the show."

"Agreed. And we're nowhere with that."

"Except for the pushy guy in the baseball cap, with the tattoo." Luke tapped his empty cup against the top of the table.

"I know he caught your eye, but I think he was simply in a hurry to leave. Traffic getting out of those venues is a bear. Besides, all we have of the guy is a back view. Not much to go on."

"I can't argue with that." Yet he couldn't shake an unsettling feeling of déjà vu about the man.

Feelings, however, weren't going to get them anywhere.

"I guess this is a wrap. You ready to call it a night . . . or should I say morning?" Nick angled his wrist. "It's almost eight o'clock."

"I can't see any reason to hang around. We're spinning our wheels here."

"I'm going to call Bishara, then bail. Assuming he's not our leak, he needs to watch his back."

Yeah, he did.

Too bad law enforcement didn't have the resources to provide personal security in high-risk situations like this.

"Do you want to get an update on Touma from your CIA contact too? I'd think by now that special forces would have moved in." Luke smothered a yawn.

"It wouldn't hurt to give him a call. He did say they were going to wait for an optimal . . ."

"Hold on a sec." Luke pulled his vibrating phone off his belt.

Sarge.

Whoops.

He should have texted or left a voicemail about his all-night plans—and late arrival this morning.

"My boss." He put the phone to his ear while Nick picked up their empty cups and left the room. "Morning, Sarge. I was going to call you."

"Where are you?"

"The FBI office downtown. We pulled an all-nighter."

"You have any juice left?"

"Sure." He took a fortifying breath. "What's going on?"

"A shooting in Afton. They requested our assistance."

"Okay." He wiped a hand down his face and tried to psyche himself up for a busy morning. Strange that Sarge wasn't cutting him some slack after hearing he'd had no sleep. That wasn't the man's usual style. "Are we shorthanded?"

"No, but I thought this one would interest you. We have two people down in what a witness described as an attempted robbery. One of them is Yusef Bishara."

"What!" He vaulted to his feet, all vestiges of fatigue vanishing. Nick reappeared in the conference room doorway, and Luke waved him in. "When? Where?"

"The responding officer can give you details. Bishara was at church." Luke wrote down the name and address as Sarge recited it. "It happened about forty minutes ago."

"How's Bishara?" In his peripheral vision, he saw Nick freeze.

"He has a gunshot wound to the stomach. He's at St. Anthony's, being prepped for surgery as we speak."

"What about the other guy?"

"Dead from two gunshot wounds. The maintenance man at the church interrupted the scene. Turns out he has a concealed carry permit he was prepared to use."

"Good for him. Who's the responding officer?" He scribbled the name as the man reeled it off. "I'm on it."

"I take it we won't be seeing you around the office today."

"Between this case and the FBI situation, I'd say that's a fair conclusion."

"Get some shut-eye when you can."

"I'll try." But it wasn't likely to happen anytime soon.

Nick joined him the instant the call ended. "What's going on with Bishara?"

"He's been shot."

Nick sucked in a breath.

As Luke filled him in, his colleague's demeanor grew more and more grim.

"A robbery in a church that's unlocked each Friday for one specific parishioner." A muscle in Nick's jaw clenched. "What are the odds?"

"Zero. Amir targeted Bishara. The robbery was to cover the real motive. I doubt warning him to watch his back would have helped in this situation."

"Yeah." Nick massaged his temple. "I wonder if the dead guy is Amir?" The moment that speculation left his mouth, he shook his head "Scratch that. Blame it on fatigue. Amir has other people do his dirty work."

"Right."

"The question is, did he want Bishara dead because someone tipped him off that the man was working with us—or because he was tying up loose ends, getting rid of peripheral people, before launching some new scheme?"

Loose ends.

Peripheral people.

Luke's heart skipped a beat.

"Kristin Dane could fall into either of those categories." He tried to keep his tone neutral—and almost succeeded.

Nick's brow puckered. "I can't see how. Bishara was a willing participant. She had no idea about her role in the candle scheme until her clerk was murdered. That might be a stretch."

It might be.

Or not.

And the uncertainty was turning his stomach into a pretzel.

He pulled out his keys—and tried to put the brakes on his accelerating pulse. "You want to go with me to the scene?"

"I'd like to . . . but I also want to talk to Bishara as soon as he's able to communicate. Why don't you handle the scene and I'll call you with an update from St. Anthony's?"

"That works. Did you reach Adam Lange?"

"Yes. No word on Touma yet."

Another piece of bad news.

"I hope we don't lose both of the Bisharas."

"Me too." Nick picked up his own keys from the table. "I'll walk out with you."

They wove through the FBI building, half empty at this early hour, and parted in the parking lot.

But as Luke hit his sirens and lights and took off for the small chapel where Bishara had been shot, he wasn't all that optimistic about the fates of father and son.

Nothing in this case was playing out as they'd hoped.

And while Nick's assessment of the danger to Kristin seemed sound, Rick's comment from yesterday kept echoing in his mind—and jacking up his pulse another notch with every mile he drove.

Terrorists aren't predictable.

26

Bang, bang, bang, bang!

Kristin fumbled the pottery bowl she'd just unpacked, snatching it a millisecond before it crashed to the floor.

Who could be pounding on the back door of WorldCraft an hour before the shop opened?

Clutching the bowl to her chest, she grabbed her cell and cautiously approached the barrier between her and the determined visitor. "Who is it?"

"Colin. Open up."

Colin was here?

She set the bowl down on top of an unopened box and twisted the lock.

He barged past her.

"Come in, won't you?" She sent him a wry look and closed the door.

"Why didn't you answer when I knocked out front?"

"I've been back here, unpacking merchandise." She waved a hand around the storeroom, where the contents of half a dozen boxes from around the world were strewn. "And I didn't hear you with the music playing." She switched off her iPod, muting the soaring notes of *Phantom of the Opera*. "What are you doing here?"

"Have you talked to Luke today?"

"No. Why?" She scanned her phone. No missed voice or text messages.

"He's investigating a robbery that involved a shooting. The name Yusef Bishara mean anything to you?"

"Bishara's been shot?" She grasped the edge of a shelf as the world tipped for a moment. "Is he . . . is he alive?"

"Last I heard, yes."

"Did they catch the shooter?"

"He's dead. The maintenance man interrupted the scene—and he had a gun." Colin folded his arms. "Given that Bishara is a Syrian native and an expert on artifacts . . . and the monastery that supplied your candles is in Syria . . . and Sarge sent Luke to investigate despite the all-nighter he pulled at the FBI office . . . I'm assuming there's a connection to your case."

Luke had spent all night at the FBI office after planning to go home and call it a day?

What else had happened that she didn't know about?

"Kristin?"

She pulled herself back to the conversation. "It's not my case. I'm a bit player in a much larger drama."

"You're connected. That's all that matters."

"Only peripherally."

A muscle in his cheek clenched. "I don't like this."

Neither did she.

But dwelling on her situation wasn't going to change it.

"I feel bad for Bishara." She set her phone on the desk. "He's had some very tough breaks."

"I'm more worried about you—and Luke is too."

She blinked. "How do you know?"

306

"He called me. I couldn't get any details out of him, but the mere fact he reached out tells me this is serious."

Luke had asked one of her best buds to watch out for her in his absence?

Sweet.

But also scary.

If Luke had gone to that much effort to protect her, there was reason to be worried—not that she intended to let Colin know she was scared. He had his own life to live, and a new bride who deserved his full attention. "I'm fine, Colin. No one has any reason to come after me. Bishara was an active participant in the . . . situation. I wasn't."

"But I'm guessing he was cooperating with the authorities—and so are you."

"No one is aware of that . . . *except* the authorities."

"As far as you know." He yanked at his tie to loosen it and began to prowl around the back room. "I'd stick close if I could, but I have my own cases to investigate."

"You don't have to babysit me. I can . . ."

Her phone began to vibrate, and she snatched it up again.

Rick.

She narrowed her eyes at Colin. "Did you tell Rick about this?"

"Of course."

Shooting him a disgruntled glare, she put the phone to her ear. "Hi, Rick. Colin's here. I'm fine. You two need to stop worrying. This is getting blown out of—"

"Good morning to you too."

She snapped her jaw closed.

Rein it in, Kristin. Who's acting over-the-top now?

"Sorry. Good morning."

"Better. I called to let you know I'll have my cell close at hand all day. If you need anything, don't hesitate to call."

At least he wasn't being as high-handed as Colin.

"I appreciate that." Even if he was too far away to be of much help on the off chance she needed assistance.

"And I'm booking your guest room for tonight."

She blinked. "What?"

"I have some errands to run tomorrow in town. I can get an earlier start if I stay at your place. You did offer to put me up anytime I needed a place to lay my head, didn't you?"

"Yes, but—"

"Expect me about nine."

"Rick, this isn't necess—"

"Gotta run. One of the counselors is waving at me. See you tonight."

The line went dead.

Weighing the phone in her hand, she turned back to Colin. "You two worked this out, didn't you?"

"What?" His innocent expression was as plastic as the pink flamingo gag gift he and Rick had propped on her lawn after she moved into her condo.

"You know what."

"I'll take the Fifth." He twisted his wrist and huffed out a breath. "I have to run. Keep your phone handy today. Don't hesitate to use it. I'm closer than Rick—or you could always call Luke. He might manage to get here even faster than me." With a wink and a quick grin, he crossed to the door. "Keep this locked."

"I always do." She followed him to the back of the shop. "And stop worrying. You're all overreacting. Big time."

"For once, I hope you're right and I'm wrong. You can lord it over me later and I won't say a word. Promise."

With that, he slipped outside.

She locked the door behind him, swiveled back to the shop, and squared her shoulders. She was *not* going to let the three men in her life freak her out. Caution was wise; paranoia was dumb. Why would Amir have any interest in her? She'd been no more than a pawn in his game, an unwitting accomplice. She knew nothing about his operation that would interest law enforcement or threaten him with exposure.

Holding on to that reassuring thought, she marched back to the box of pottery and plunged her hands into the packing material. Yelped as she encountered a sharp object. Jerked her hands back out.

Blood was dripping down her index finger.

She yanked some tissues from the box on the desk and dabbed at the jagged cut. One of the bowls must have broken during shipment—a first for this supplier.

Not the most comforting omen . . . if one believed in such nonsense.

Which she didn't.

Retreating to the bathroom to wash the cut, she dismissed that whole superstitious notion.

But perhaps it wouldn't hurt to consider the incident a reminder to use caution in the days ahead.

Because just in case there was any reason for concern, it might be better not to plunge into anything without first making certain no danger was lying in wait—ready to pounce.

▪ ▪ ▪ ▪ ▪

Bishara wasn't dead.

But his hitman was.

Amir wadded up the paper napkin from his takeout coffee and hurled it into the trash can beside his desk.

This was not the best beginning for his Friday.

He leaned closer to the computer, straining to hear the conversation taking place in WorldCraft between Kristin and that detective friend of hers, Colin.

But the voices grew fainter.

They must be walking toward the door.

No problem. Their discussion had been winding down anyway.

It had, however, been replete with warnings from Colin—as if he and his buddies were worried the man behind the artifact scheme might have an interest in her.

Leaning back in his chair, he swiveled toward the window and studied the blue sky.

Funny. He'd more or less written Kristin off. Decided getting any information she might have wouldn't be worth the risk.

However . . . if she was clued in about Bishara—as she obviously was—she might know other details worth taking a chance to discover. Since that smitten detective had been in touch with her more often than mere business demanded, it was likely he'd told her details about the case he'd shared with few others.

And those details might help him in the next iteration of his cell-funding scheme.

Amir drummed his fingers on the desk. He'd have to bide his time, though, in light of this latest turn of events. If his hired gun had followed the plan and confronted Bishara in the parking lot as he left the chapel, robbery would have been a far more convincing motive for the killing. Why on earth had the man gone inside?

Furrowing his brow, he stood and jammed a hand in his pocket, jingling the change.

Given that the Feds were aware of Bishara's connection to him—and the man was cooperating with them—they'd assume the shooting was a contract hit.

But there was no direct line between him and the gunman. He'd tossed the throwaway phone. The money he'd deposited into the man's account had come from an offshore bank with no traceable connection to him.

He should be safe.

Should being the operative word.

The law enforcement guys on his tail, however, were sharp.

One tiny blunder was all it might take to establish a link between him and the artifact scheme.

He hadn't committed any that he knew of.

But if he'd made some incriminating slip that could lead them to him, he'd better duck out of here early and finish the contingency plans he was putting in place at home.

Because if this ended up going south, he didn't intend to be taken quietly.

He would go out with a bang that would ricochet around the world . . . and make his father proud.

. . . . .

Luke paused at the door of the crowded surgical waiting room at St. Anthony's and zeroed in on Nick in the far corner, exactly where his text had said he'd be waiting.

The instant the FBI agent caught sight of him, he rose and joined him in the hall.

"How's Bishara?" Luke moved out of the way as a woman in scrubs hurried past.

"He made it through surgery and is in recovery. The doctor will come here to talk to us. I also heard from Lange. Our people have Touma. They're in a helo heading for the air base at Rmeilan in northeastern Syria."

"Is he okay?" Luke dodged another scrubs-clad staffer.

"I don't think the past two years have been a cakewalk—but he's alive."

"That's one piece of good news."

"What's the story on the shooting?"

"I interviewed the custodian who took out the hit man. When he saw the guy pull into the parking lot at such an early hour, he got suspicious and stuck close. More so after the shooter approached the chapel. He followed him and opened the door on the pseudo-robbery. Despite the fact he almost took a bullet himself, he felt terrible he couldn't get a shot at the guy before Bishara was wounded."

"That's crazy." Nick frowned. "Bishara would be dead if he hadn't had a concealed carry permit he wasn't afraid to use. He's a hero."

"That's what I told him."

"Any ID on the shooter yet?"

"His car was a rental, and the ID he gave Avis appears to be bogus. His prints aren't in the database, either. I'm wondering if we might get a match to some of the random DNA the ME found on the body of the courier who killed Susan Collier and Elaine Peterson."

Nick folded his arms. "It's possible. There's no reason Amir wouldn't use the same hit man."

A fortyish woman in a white coat, a plastic bag in hand, sped past and poked her head into the waiting room. "Bishara?"

"Here." Nick stepped forward.

She swiveled around and gave them both a doubtful perusal. "Are you with the FBI?"

"I am." Nick pulled out his creds. "This is Detective Luke Carter with St. Louis County PD."

Luke displayed his ID as well.

"Sorry. You don't look like the usual law-enforcement types."

Hard to argue with that. The jeans, wrinkled shirts, and day-old stubble didn't fit the spit-and-polish image of either an FBI agent or a County detective.

"We've been on the go for more than twenty-four hours." Luke put his badge away.

One side of her mouth hiked up. "That would explain the bloodshot eyes too. Reminds me of my resident days. Connie Cerutti." She shook hands with both of them. "There's a small private conference room two doors down. Let's do this in there."

She led the way, and they filed in behind her.

After setting the bag on an end table, she motioned to a small grouping of chairs. "I haven't been up for a full day, but after several intense hours in the operating room, I don't mind sitting for a few minutes."

"When can we talk to Dr. Bishara?" Luke dropped into a straight-backed chair while Nick took the one on the other side of the doctor.

"He's awake but groggy—and still in recovery. I understand he has no family in St. Louis."

"Or in the country." Nick leaned forward. "I spoke to his administrative assistant at the museum. She said he mentioned once that his pastor has all of his legal and medical directives. I have a call in to him. How serious is his condition?"

"Normally we only talk with family members or legal representatives about a patient's condition. HIPAA rules—"

"Don't supersede the Patriot Act, which allows the FBI access to medical records as part of a counterterrorism investigation." Nick's tone was polite but resolute.

"Even without that, HIPAA gives law enforcement access in a medical emergency in connection with a crime," Luke added.

"Okay." She threw up her hands. "I won't debate HIPAA with you—and I didn't realize this had any connection to terrorism. That's a new one for me."

"So when can we talk with him?" Nick asked.

"We don't typically let anyone into the recovery room. Patients may be conscious, but they're often not lucid."

"We need access ASAP."

"I'll authorize a quick visit, but you'll be able to have a more coherent discussion in about thirty minutes."

"We'll wait. What's the prognosis?"

"The bullet missed the vital organs and lodged in the stomach. We removed it without complications. But while we were in there, we discovered a tumor, which we biopsied."

Luke frowned. "Tumor as in cancer?"

"It's possible. Has he been having any pain?"

He looked at Nick, who shrugged. "No idea."

"We'll talk to him after he's more conversant." She motioned toward the bag on the table. "Those are the personal items and salvageable clothing that were removed in the ER. We'd like to get some insurance information, but would prefer a family member—or authorized party—go through his things and see if there are any cards in there."

"We can do that." Luke reached for the bag.

"Thanks. I'll ask one of the nurses to come and get you here as soon as he's more awake. If you find an insurance card, you can give it to her." She rose, but as he and Nick began to stand too, she waved them back down. "I appreciate the courtesy, but conserve your strength." Flashing them a grin, she slipped through the door.

"You know . . . I can't condone conspiring with terrorists—but that guy's been through the wringer. A son held hostage, a car accident, a gunshot wound . . . now a tumor." Nick shook his head.

"Yeah." Going more than two dozen hours without sleep was nothing compared to all the stuff that had hit Bishara's fan. "Want me to tackle his personal items?"

"That works. I need to call the office." Nick rose. "Since the whole notion of heading home to crash is down the tubes, I'm going to scrounge up some coffee in the waiting room. My energy is dipping into the danger zone. You want a cup?"

"Either that or a syringe of adrenaline."

"I'll see what I can do."

As Nick exited into the hall, Luke rose too. Stretched. Rotated his neck. Maybe a few push-ups would get his blood flowing.

Too bad he didn't have the energy to drop to the floor let alone engage in any strenuous exercise.

Still standing, he opened the bag the doctor had delivered and poked through the meager contents.

Shoes and socks, belt, a small book with a cross on the front, pocket change, car keys, wallet, glasses in a case, an almost empty pack of Tums, and a pen.

Luke snagged the wallet. That had to be where Bishara kept any cards he carried.

Flipping through the clear sleeves, he skimmed the plastic. Visa . . . Panera . . . Starbucks . . . driver's license . . . United Healthcare. There. That was it.

While he worked his fingers into the protective sheath to slide it out, he glanced at the next card in the lineup. It was stuck between two sleeves, as if it wasn't usually in the wallet.

He read the name.

Did a double take.

Read it again.

Froze.

Ryan Doud, the business neighbor who paid an excessive number of friendly visits to Kristin's shop, was Bishara's insurance agent?

He seized the bag and set off in search of Nick, brain processing at warp speed.

Doud was in a perfect position to keep tabs on new merchandise in Kristin's shop—and given his connection to Bishara, he had to be aware of the man's expertise.

Yet there was little in his appearance to suggest Middle Eastern ancestry . . . or any connection to Syria.

Meaning it was possible all of this was nothing more than coincidence.

But as Luke jogged down the hall, dodging wheelchairs and family groups, his surging adrenaline chasing away every bit of his fatigue, he knew it was more than that.

And he also knew they'd just had their best lead yet in a case that had so far confounded them.

27

"I'm out of here, Alexa." Kristin slipped the strap of her tote over her shoulder. "Don't hesitate to call if you need me."

"I've been here long enough to feel pretty confident about handling anything WorldCraft can throw at me." Her clerk shooed her out. "Go enjoy this sunny Friday afternoon."

"That's my plan . . . in between errands. See you tomorrow."

The bell over the entrance jingled, and Kristin headed for the back room as Alexa greeted the new customer.

Taking a quick visual inventory of the boxes of merchandise waiting to be unpacked tomorrow, she continued to the rear door and let herself out—fighting the temptation to give Luke a call and find out what was going on with Bishara and the case.

But if he'd worked all night, as Colin had said during his unexpected visit this morning, he must be up to his eyeballs in whatever was happening. Not to mention exhausted.

Resist, Kristin. Give the man some space. He'll get in touch as soon as . . .

She stopped and peered at a shiny glint in the patch of grass near where Ryan usually parked his car.

Was that a . . . cell phone?

Switching direction, she crossed to it.

Yep. It was a cell.

She picked it up and turned it over. Based on the gold case, it was Ryan's phone. He'd shown her the new protective cover less than a week ago.

Since his parking spot was empty, he must have dropped it getting into his car.

Better leave this with his office assistant in case he realized it was missing and asked her to look around for it.

Rather than circle around the whole building, she detoured back through WorldCraft.

"Can't stay away, huh?" Alexa arched an eyebrow.

"I found Ryan's phone on the ground in the parking lot. I'm going to drop it at his office before I leave."

Without stopping, she continued out the front door and down the street to his storefront.

According to the woman at the front desk, however, he was gone for the day.

"He said he wasn't feeling well and left about an hour ago. I'd call him at home, but he doesn't have a landline." The woman bit her lip, eying the phone. "He'll be missing that for sure. It's always glued to him."

Kristin hesitated. A side trip to Ryan's house wasn't on her agenda . . . but considering how kind he'd always been to her, it would be the neighborly thing to do.

Stifling a sigh, she conjured up a smile. "I'll tell you what. I'm going to be near his place this afternoon. I'll run it by there."

Relief smoothed the tension from the woman's features. "Are you certain you don't mind? I know he'd be grateful."

"Not a problem. His house isn't that far from here anyway."

"Do you need the exact address or directions?"

"No. I was there in December." At the spark of curiosity in the woman's eyes, Kristin tacked on a caveat before his assistant could jump to the wrong conclusion. "An older woman from my church lives on his street. I always deliver a tin of homemade Christmas cookies to her, so I took some for Ryan too." She walked toward the door. "Enjoy your weekend."

After retracing her steps down the sidewalk, she cut through WorldCraft again.

"I bet he was glad to get his phone back." Alexa continued checking out a customer as she spoke.

"He went home sick, but I'm going to drop it off at his house while I'm out and about this afternoon." She kept moving. "See you tomorrow."

Once she was in her car, she mentally reviewed her stops for the afternoon. It would be easier to swing by Ryan's after she went to the post office and picked up her dry cleaning rather than circle back for those errands. A delay of twenty or thirty minutes shouldn't make much difference.

Besides, no matter when she showed up, Ryan would surely be grateful she'd gone out of her way to be do a good deed.

■ ■ ■ ■ ■

"Excuse me . . . you're waiting to talk with Yusef Bishara, correct?"

As the nurse spoke from the doorway of the small meeting room at the hospital, Luke rose. "Yes."

"He's still in recovery, but his surgeon authorized a fast visit for two people." She scanned the room.

"My colleague had to go outside to make a call. He'll be back momentarily."

"Sorry about the inconvenience. Cell phones don't work in some parts of hospitals."

"I know." He'd been in enough of them in the line of duty

to find that out. "If you could wait for . . ." Nick appeared behind the woman in the doorway. "Never mind. He's back."

She swiveled around, and Luke picked up the bag of Bishara's personal items.

"If you'll follow me." She edged around Nick.

The FBI agent let her get a few yards ahead as Luke joined him. "I've got Mark doing a quick analysis on our person of interest. If even one red flag surfaces, we'll get surveillance on him 24/7 while we dig deeper. Mark agrees the connection between him and two of the players in this case is suspicious."

"Maybe one of those players can shed some light on the situation." Luke motioned toward the door where the nurse had stopped.

She angled toward them. "Letting people back here isn't our usual policy. Please keep this as brief as possible."

"Understood." Nick waited until she opened the door, then followed her in. Luke took up the rear.

When the nurse stopped beside a bed, he almost didn't recognize the museum curator. The man was beyond pale, his eyes were closed, and his chest was barely rising and falling.

"Mr. Bishara." She put a hand on his shoulder. "You have two visitors."

As his eyelids fluttered open, Luke took a position on one side of the bed while Nick flanked it on the other.

"I lived." The man's raspy comment was tinged with incredulity.

"Yes." Nick edged in closer as the nurse retreated. "I have more good news for you. Touma is safe. He was rescued a few hours ago."

Bishara's features contorted, and his eyes began to shimmer. "Thank God. And thank you. I will be . . . forever grateful."

"Mr. Bishara, we have a question for you." Luke leaned down

and dropped his voice. "We found an insurance card in your wallet for an agent by the name of Ryan Doud."

"Yes. I had a . . . car accident. I put it there . . . in case I needed to speak with him . . . again."

"How long has he been your agent?"

"Two years . . . or so."

About when Khalil had appeared at the monastery.

The timing fit.

"Why did you buy your insurance through him?"

"My administrative assistant . . . you met her at the office . . . recommended him, and he . . . offered a reasonable price. Pleasant young man. He always asks about . . . Touma."

A monitor began to beep, and the nurse reappeared. "Are you about finished?"

"Yes. We can talk to him again later."

Bishara groped for Nick's hand. "Thank you for all you have done . . . for Touma."

"I'm glad it worked out for him."

"He will be in the United States . . . soon?"

"As soon as it can be arranged."

"Thank you." He reached for Luke's hand too and gave it a weak squeeze.

The nurse escorted them to the door, and Luke took the man's medical insurance card from his pocket. "The surgeon said you'd need this."

"Not me . . . but the number crunchers will. Let me make a copy and you can keep the original with the patient's personal items."

The instant she walked away, Nick faced him. "Here's my theory. Two years ago the stars aligned for Doud. He already knew Kristin Dane when she began importing candles from the monks in Syria, and he recognized them as a perfect way to send artifacts to the US. When Bishara crossed his path, he found the ideal person to fence the artifacts. Especially after he secured some potent leverage with Touma's abduction."

"I agree with all that—but I'm having difficulty wrapping my mind around the notion of Ryan being Amir. He doesn't fit the mold."

"Another reason why this would work well. Based on appearance, he would raise no suspicion. Hopefully Mark will have some initial information for us as soon as we ditch this place and get a decent connection."

The nurse returned with Bishara's card, and they headed toward the exit.

As they left the building, Nick motioned toward the parking lot. "Let's sit in my car and I'll put Mark on speaker."

Less than sixty seconds later, the other agent was on the line. "Did you talk to Bishara?"

"Yes. The timing of his relationship with Ryan fits our scenario. What have you got?"

"I have several people working this, and we've found some useful info. First, Ryan Doud might pronounce his name Ryan and call himself Ryan, but the legal spelling is R-a-y-a-n. After we discovered that, we made some serious headway. For example—instead of a US birth certificate, he has a CRBA."

Luke raised an eyebrow at Nick, who shrugged.

"You're going to have to spell out that acronym for us, Mark."

"Sorry. Consular Report of Birth Abroad. If an American has a child overseas, he or she can report the birth to the US consulate or embassy. Doud's document was issued in Damascus."

Kristin's neighbor was Syrian?

Strange that he hadn't tried to mask his background by creating a fake ID before launching his scheme.

Then again—if you didn't intend to get caught, using your real identity was less of a hassle.

"What's the story on his parents?" Luke asked.

"His mother was the daughter of two Danish nationals who were in the US for a temporary job assignment when she was born. That gave her automatic citizenship. After the project ended, they returned to Denmark. While she was in college, the daughter met and married a Syrian national named Tayeb during a trip to the Middle East. Rayan was born. Eight years later, the repressive lifestyle became too much for her, and she fled back to Denmark, leaving her son behind."

"How on earth did you find all that so fast?" Luke continued to process the data dump as he asked the question.

"It wasn't hard after we had the right name spelling. The passport led us to the CRBA, which gave us the parents' names. We checked the mother's birth certificate for the names and nationalities of *her* parents. Our overseas attaché in Copenhagen worked overtime to find the rest."

"Did they talk to anyone in the family?"

"Doud's grandmother. She told them the story. The grandfather is dead and the mother remarried. We have a call in to her too."

"Did you find anything on Doud's father?" Luke cracked his door open as the temperature in the car rose.

Taking the hint, Nick started the engine and cranked up the air.

"That's been tougher. We contacted Adam Lange, and they're digging. One nugget that's already surfaced is that he does have ties to ISIS and is on a watch list in Syria."

"It sounds like our case here could be a father/son operation." Nick tapped the steering wheel with his index finger.

"But we don't have any direct links between Doud and his apparent alter ego, Amir, or the artifact operation." Luke frowned. Without some specific incriminating evidence tying the man to everything that had happened, they couldn't arrest him, let alone charge him with a crime.

"Amir, by the way, means 'commander' or 'prince' in Arabic—

perhaps suggesting how he views his role in this operation," Mark said.

"Trouble is, he's still in command if we can't find the link Luke mentioned." Nick expelled a breath. "Okay. Keep digging. We'll be down shortly to hash out next steps. But I want to put some surveillance on Doud. We know he's on to our investigation, and I don't want him to disappear, resurface somewhere with another identity, and create a new scheme."

"I'll get with the SAC as soon as we hang up."

Luke had no doubt the Special Agent in Charge of the St. Louis FBI office would jump all over this, but there were limits on staffing in any organization.

"I can talk to Sarge if we need additional bodies for short-term surveillance."

"We'll keep that as an option. Let's see how this plays out over the next few days. Anything else, Mark?" Nick turned the air down a notch.

"Those are the highlights."

"I'll be back in twenty minutes." He slid the phone onto his belt and shifted sideways. "You willing to continue this marathon?"

"At this stage, sleep can wait. We need to figure out a way to nail this guy."

"Agreed. I'll meet you at the entrance to our secure lot. Just follow me in."

"Thanks." Luke slid out of the car and strode toward his Taurus. After he was on the road, he'd give Kristin a call, bring her up to speed. Now that Doud was front and center in their sights, she needed to be extra cautious.

Because if what they suspected was true, the man's friendly demeanor was a mask for a cold-blooded killer committed to the destruction of America.

. . . . .

Kristin parked in front of Ryan's modest bungalow, set the brake, and picked up his phone from the seat beside her. A quick handoff at the door should suffice, especially if he wasn't feeling well, and she could continue on to the grocery store without losing much time.

After locking her car, she followed the brick path to the front door, past two planters waiting to be filled with summer flowers. The grass was on the long side too.

The insurance business must keep him hopping if he couldn't squeeze in some basic yard work.

She ascended the two steps to the small porch and pressed the bell.

Twenty seconds ticked by.

She tried again.

No response.

Maybe he hadn't come home, after all.

Or—on a beautiful day like this—he might be in the screened porch attached to the back of the house, where he'd told her he liked to spend his free evenings in the summer.

It was worth a quick detour if it saved her a return trip.

She circled around to the rear, into a backyard lined with a tall hedge of arborvitae that hid the space from the view of neighbors.

The screened porch came into sight—and it was empty.

Drat.

Not much of a reward for being a good Samaritan.

She started to turn away.

Paused.

If the screened porch was unlocked, why not try knocking on the back door? It was possible the doorbell wasn't working . . . or the sound didn't carry to all parts of the house . . . or Ryan was sleeping soundly. A hard knock might catch his ear—and eliminate the need to swing back by here later.

She climbed the steps to the porch and twisted the handle on the door.

Yes!

It was open.

Entering the small screened porch, she surveyed the space. The furnishings were sparse and bland—but this *was* a bachelor pad. Ryan apparently fit the bare-bones-decorating stereotype for single guys.

She approached the sliding doors, which were covered by closed vertical blinds. The window adjacent to the porch was also shuttered, though it was cracked a few inches, offering a glimpse inside—along with a whiff of some strong, pungent odor she couldn't identify.

A shadow moved past the window shade.

Huh.

So Ryan was home.

Her theory about the front doorbell must be . . .

A crash sounded inside the house—followed by a string of harsh expletives that burned her ears.

It was Ryan's voice . . . but never in the years they'd been business neighbors had she heard him say a single vulgar word.

O-kay.

This was awkward.

How was she supposed to knock after witnessing that rant? He'd be mortified if he knew she'd overhead him.

It might be better to wait a couple of minutes, then bang the screen door on the porch as if she'd just arrived. That would save them both some embarrassment.

She tiptoed to the threshold and waited.

From her new spot, she had a clear view into a sliver of the kitchen, where Ryan was busy at the small island.

But he wasn't cooking.

She examined the odd assortment of items arrayed on the countertop.

Sections of metal pipes. A bag of what appeared to be small metal balls. Large containers of . . . she squinted, trying to read the labels . . . hydrogen peroxide? Like the chemical used in hair dye?

And what was that white powder in the adjacent container? It looked like laundry detergent . . . or sugar?

She inspected the surrounding countertops, inching closer to see better. Coffee filters, a thermometer, glass bowls, a bag of ice . . .

What the heck was Ryan doing?

Suddenly, as if sensing her presence, he glanced toward the crack in the window.

Their gazes met.

Shock flattened his features for a fleeting second . . . then every muscle in his face tightened and fury flashed in his eyes.

The angry man staring back at her was nothing like the genial Ryan she'd come to know during his visits to WorldCraft.

Kristin stumbled backward, a chill rippling down her spine.

Ryan might be a respected businessman who'd always seemed like a straight arrow, but every instinct in her body screamed "Run!"

Fast.

She pushed through the screen door and clattered down the steps, praying she could reach her car before Ryan was able to unlock the sliding doors and follow her.

Because no matter how he tried to explain whatever he was up to on this so-called sick day, she wasn't going to buy it.

Not after his shock had morphed to rage—hatred, even— once he'd spotted her watching him.

Bypassing the last step, she leaped to the ground . . . raced toward the side of the house . . . flew around the corner.

And came face-to-face with Ryan.

Gasping, she jolted to a stop.

He must have gone out the front door and circled around to intercept her.

The hows and whys of his sudden appearance, however, were her least concern at the moment.

The only thing that mattered was the gun pointed straight at her heart . . . and the words he uttered.

"Make one wrong move and you die."

28

"We have more." Mark looked up from his computer screen as Luke pocketed his keys and followed Nick into the FBI conference room after their pedal-to-the-floor trip from the hospital.

"What?" Nick walked past several other agents also working on laptops at the large conference table.

"Our attaché in Copenhagen talked with Ryan's mother. She hasn't had any contact with her former husband or son in twenty-four years—but Lange's local agents in Syria managed to turn up a fair amount of intel on Tayeb Doud. He has strong ties to ISIS, with particular emphasis on fund-raising efforts for various cells around the world—like the one here that was spearheaded by Ryan."

"So he arranged for Khalil to infiltrate the monastery and also set up Touma's kidnapping?" Luke settled a hip on the edge of the table.

"We can't prove that, but it's a reasonable assumption." Mark swiveled around in his chair. "The one helpful piece of information Ryan's mother provided was her ex-husband's educational background. He received a double degree in accounting and economics at the University of Mosul in Iraq."

"Why is that important?" Nick pulled out an adjacent chair and sat.

"It adds credence to the intel that suggests he's handling finances for terrorist cells—but his affiliation with that university is also significant in light of what's happened there during the past few years."

"ISIS took over in 2014." Luke had no problem calling up the article he'd read less than a month ago on this subject. "They destroyed thousands of books . . . many of them ancient . . . and shut down whole departments—or took control of them. The chemistry lab became a bomb-making training center. Jihadists came from all over to learn how to mix volatile explosives, then went off on missions to other countries."

"Correct." Mark sent him an approving glance.

"Are you saying Ryan learned to make bombs?" Nick leaned forward, posture taut.

"We can't prove that either. But we do know from his passport activity that he came to the US three years ago. Twelve months later, he booked a one-week cruise in Greece, which he took. However . . . he was gone four weeks."

"Leaving three weeks unaccounted for." Luke rubbed his forehead. "And Greece isn't far from Syria."

"Right. He could have paid his father an under-the-radar visit in Raqqa while he was overseas to solidify the plans taking shape here."

"His father lives in Raqqa? The city that was a major ISIS stronghold for years?" Luke clamped his fingers tighter around the edge of the table.

"Yeah. And with Dad's connections to the University of Mosul, it's not a stretch to think he might have sent his son there to take a course that could prove useful if there were any glitches here."

"Where do we stand on surveillance?" Nick asked.

"Getting ready to dispatch agents as we speak."

Luke pivoted toward the speaker—a lean, wiry man with short gray hair, who entered the conference room and held out his hand. "Marty Holtzman, SAC."

"Nice to meet you." Luke rose to return his firm clasp.

"Likewise." He angled to address all of them. "I've assigned two agents 24/7 for now. If our subject starts to play games, I'll beef that up." He shifted back to mark Mark. "Anything new since the last update?"

"No."

"Keep me up to speed."

He swept out as fast as he'd entered, vitality pinging in his wake.

"I could use a little of his energy about now." Luke dropped back onto the table. "Does he get involved in every case?"

"More or less. More in a high-profile one like this. A lot of SACs are political figureheads who spend their days attending meetings, but Marty likes to get hands-on. Comes from being a top field agent in his heyday, I suppose." Nick lifted his hand to cover a yawn.

"Why don't you guys go home and crash for a few hours? I can call you if we find anything hot or if the surveillance gets interesting." Mark linked his fingers over his stomach. "Given that he knows we're on to him, Ryan may lay low while he calculates his next move."

"Or he may have a contingency plan already in place." The twin creases embedded on Nick's forehead deepened. "I don't like the bomb-school scenario that could account for at least part of those missing weeks during his trip to Greece."

"You read my mind." Luke tried to tame the sudden turbulence in his stomach. "His backup strategy to avoid capture might not be pretty."

"That's why we'll be keeping him under surveillance." Mark looked between the two of them. "You guys need to clock some z's. We've got this covered. He makes one wrong move, we'll be all over him. And if that happens, we'll need everybody at 100 percent capacity. Sorry to say, but neither of you are close to that at the moment."

"Thanks a lot." Nick tried to stifle another yawn. Failed.

"I rest my case." Mark steepled his index fingers.

"Fine. We'll get some shut-eye." Nick stood. "I'll check in with you in a few hours."

"And I'll call you if anything breaks—both of you."

"Thanks." Luke rose too, falling in beside Nick as they silently wound through the cubicles to the rear door.

After they parted in the parking lot, Luke pulled out his phone and walked toward his car.

Frowned.

Kristin hadn't returned his call or his text.

That wasn't like her.

She'd said she had several errands to run this afternoon, though. It was possible she hadn't had a chance to respond.

But somehow that didn't feel right.

He slid behind the wheel and dialed her again.

When it rolled to voicemail after three rings, the red alert beeping in the recesses of his mind intensified.

Overreaction due to fatigue—or legitimate concern?

He stuck his key in the ignition and started the engine while he debated that question.

Sixty seconds later, as he followed Nick out of the lot, he still had no answer.

And until he was certain Kristin was okay, it would be useless to go home and try to sleep.

Maybe Alexa knew where she was. Kristin could have mentioned her plans for the afternoon. Or there might have been a rush at WorldCraft and she hadn't been able to get away yet.

It was worth a call.

Half a minute later, Alexa gave him his answer.

"She left about an hour and a half ago, Detective. I know she had a bunch of stops to make, including a swing by Ryan Doud's house to return his cell. She found it in the parking lot after he went home sick."

Kristin was going to Doud's place?

His pulse stuttered.

"Thanks."

Ending the call with a sharp jab of his thumb, he clenched the wheel and forced back the panic nipping at his composure. Ryan might be Amir, but there was no reason to think he had his sights set on Kristin. The cell return might be nothing more than a handoff at the door. It was possible she hadn't even gone there yet.

So before he got too freaked out, he'd try to call her once more.

If she answered, he'd give her the scoop and tell her to walk a wide circle around Doud.

If she didn't . . . his already long day was going to get a whole lot longer.

■ ■ ■ ■ ■

This wasn't part of his plan.

Balling his fingers, Ryan stopped pacing and glared at the shell-shocked woman he'd hustled into his kitchen.

Kristin didn't have a clue what she'd stumbled into—but if she described what she'd seen to those cop friends of hers, they'd have all the grounds they needed for a search warrant and arrest.

That couldn't happen.

"Ryan . . . I don't understand. What's going on? I thought we were friends." Kristin watched his gun as she spoke.

Friends?

What a laugh.

She'd been nothing more than a means to an end.

"Shut up while I think. You've messed up everyth . . ." The cell in her tote began to chirp, and he motioned toward it. "Take that out and toss it to me."

Her hands were shaking as she picked up the bag and began to root through it.

Good.

The more scared she was, the less trouble she'd give him.

Especially since she hadn't connected him to the candle operation and had no idea yet who he was—or what was in store for her.

But she would soon.

Kristin removed the cell and lobbed it to him.

After a one-handed catch, he skimmed the screen.

Detective Luke Carter was calling.

And this wasn't his first attempt to reach her, based on her phone log.

The cell stopped ringing. He switched it off and removed the battery.

"Your friend is persistent—and we don't want him tracking you down. Sit." He waved the gun toward a straight-backed chair in the kitchen.

"Why are you doing this? And what's going on here?" Kristin gestured to the array of materials on the counter in the foul-smelling kitchen.

"You'll find out soon. I said sit."

When she hesitated, he switched the gun to his left hand and lunged toward her, slamming his fist into her jaw.

Her head snapped back, and she swayed.

Before she could regain her balance, he shoved her into the chair, pulled her arms behind her, and bound her wrists together with a length of wire he grabbed from the island.

He circled back in front of her and got in her face. "Why did you come here today?"

She blinked several times, as if she was having difficulty focusing. "You . . . you dropped your cell in the parking lot. I-I was returning it."

He felt in his pocket.

His phone *was* missing.

"It's in the outside compartment of my . . . my tote."

He snatched it up and rummaged through the pouch, lips twisting. "So you came here to do a good deed. Ironic."

"Why is th-that ironic?"

He set his phone on the counter beside hers. "Because now we're both going to pay a very high price."

She gave the materials spread out in the kitchen a sweep. "I don't know what you're doing here, but I'm guessing it's illegal."

He barked out a harsh laugh. "Smart guess."

"But . . . why? You have an established business. A great life. Why would you want to mess it up with . . . this. Is it meth?"

Meth?

He scanned the counters again.

Yeah, he supposed she might think that—if he was as far off law enforcement's radar as he'd assumed. Many of the ingredients were similar.

But meth was child's play compared to this operation.

"No. I'm not into meth."

Yet this material was equally explosive.

And now that Kristin had blundered into the middle of it, he wouldn't be off law enforcement's radar for much longer.

That left him only one option.

334

He was going to have to do what his father expected—go out in a blaze of glorious martyrdom, taking as many infidels with him as possible.

Including the one sitting in his house.

· · · · ·

Kristin watched Ryan stride from the room—and went to work on her wrists. This might be her only opportunity to try and free them.

But whatever binding he'd used cut into her skin with every flex of her fingers.

Gritting her teeth, she kept trying. A little pain in her wrists was better than whatever Ryan had in store for her.

Despite her efforts, though, the ties didn't budge one iota.

"Give it up, Kristin." He spoke from behind her, and she froze. "All you're doing is cutting your wrists on the wire."

He'd bound her wrists with wire?

No wonder it hurt so much.

"Listen, I don't know what you've got going on here, but . . ."

He circled around her, and the words died in her throat as the object in his hands registered.

She'd never seen one in real life, but there had been similar photos in the media. The vest-like garment, with a hole that went over the head, had pockets filled with pipes, all connected by different colored wires. Small metal balls encased in plastic sleeves were secured in rows below the pockets.

It was a suicide vest.

Which had to mean that Ryan was . . . Amir?

She sucked in a breath.

"I see you figured out the connection." His eyes were cold, his tone flat.

"It was you all along? You were running the artifact operation?" Somehow she managed to choke out the questions.

"I had help on the other end, but yes . . . I was in charge here. It was a perfect setup until one of my couriers made a bad mistake."

"The one who killed Susan and Elaine?"

"Yes." His gaze remained icy. "I don't care about the killings. People are expendable. But he left evidence behind that helped the cops connect those deaths to your shop . . . and from there to the candles. *That* was his mistake." He gingerly set the vest on the counter. "I'd hoped I wouldn't need to use one of these. Ever. But thanks to you, now I will."

"Why don't you leave me here and just . . . disappear? You could still get away." She eyed the vest and tried to drag in some air despite the suffocating panic paralyzing her lungs.

"With your detective friend breathing down my neck? It wouldn't surprise me if he's already in search mode. Did you tell anyone you were coming here today?"

She tried to maintain a neutral expression. "No."

He backhanded her.

The stinging blow sent heat radiating throughout her cheek, and her eyes teared.

"You don't lie well, Kristin. Who did you tell?"

She clamped her mouth shut. No way was she mentioning Alexa's name and potentially putting her in danger.

Ryan's features hardened, and a muscle twitched in his jaw. "Fine. It doesn't matter. Your detective will ferret it out sooner or later. In any case, we don't have much time. So let me tell you how this is going to play out."

He moved in close. Close enough for her to see into the murky depths of his dark irises.

And as he explained his plan . . . as his diabolical scheme—and its impact—began to register . . . the familiar features of her genial business neighbor slowly mutated.

Until she found herself looking into the face of hell.

29

Keeping one hand on the wheel, Luke called Nick.

Two rings in the man answered. "What's up?"

"Do you know if your people have Doud in their sights yet?"

"No—but if they don't, they're in the process of scoping out the alley behind his office to see if his car's there."

"It's not." Luke filled him in on the conversation he'd had with Alexa. "And Kristin's not answering her cell."

"Is that significant?"

"Yes. She always answers my calls." Her frenetic trip to Boston had been the sole exception. "One miss, I could live with. Three rolls to voicemail raises a red flag."

"Okay. Let me alert our people that Doud went home in case they're still working the office location."

"In the meantime, I'm going to do a drive-by of his house myself. See if Kristin's car is there. I'm not that far away."

"If you find anything suspicious, call for backup before you make any move."

"That was my plan." His response came out sharper than he intended—but he wasn't a rookie at this. He knew how to rein in his emotions and let the left side of his brain take over in dangerous situations.

Even if this case might put that skill to the test.

"Sorry." If Nick was put out by his attitude, the man's conciliatory tone gave no indication of it. "We all have a tendency to overreact when people we care about are involved. Been there, done that. I'll call you back as soon as I get an update on the surveillance."

"Thanks."

Luke dropped the cell onto the seat beside him, hit his lights and siren, and pressed on the gas. Only when he was within a mile of Ryan's house would he pull back on the emergency maneuvers.

Nick might think they were overkill, anyway.

But his gut said otherwise.

And in all the years he'd been in law enforcement, his gut had rarely lied to him.

Something was going down. He could feel it in his bones.

Even worse, he had a sinking feeling Kristin was in the middle of it.

* * * * *

"You understand what I've told you, correct?"

Kristin tried to speak, but her voice choked as Ryan carefully lifted the bomb-laced vest and approached her. She nodded instead.

"Nevertheless, I'll remind you again. This type of explosive is volatile and unstable. The chemicals are sensitive to heat, shock, and friction. I have the control button, but the more you move, the higher the risk it will detonate on its own. Keep that in mind."

He stopped in front of her and lowered the hole in the vest over her head. As the twenty-plus-pound weight settled over her, the air whooshed out of her lungs.

She was now a walking bomb. One that could blow up at

any moment—either deliberately, with the push of the button at the end of the wire Ryan had shown her, or by mistake if she happened to inhale the wrong way.

And there was no escape.

Even if Luke somehow discovered her predicament, he couldn't help her. Ryan controlled the button, and he could press it before anyone got close.

Based on everything she'd read about suicide bombers, however, he would prefer to detonate it in a crowded place where he could inflict the maximum amount of harm.

"Stand up."

With a fervent plea to the Almighty for protection, she struggled to her feet under the weight.

Ryan disappeared behind her, and a second later a sharp snap freed her wrists from the wire restraints.

"Hold your arms straight out at your sides."

She lifted them, parsing out each breath.

He leaned in close and secured the front and back of the vest, pulling the straps taut under her arms until the deadly garment was snug against her body.

Backing off, he gave her a swift perusal, then picked up a man's sturdy, long-sleeved denim shirt from the counter and held it open behind her. "Slide your arms into this."

After she complied, he stepped in front of her again. "Button the front and the sleeves."

Fingers trembling, she did as he instructed while she tried to jump-start her numb brain.

Think, Kristin! Don't give up, no matter how low the odds you'll survive. Buy yourself some time to come up with a plan. Get him talking.

"Why did you . . . did you arrange to have Dr. Bishara killed?" She grasped at the first thought that came to mind. "He couldn't identify you."

"He was a loose end." Ryan crossed to the laptop on the counter and tapped some keys. "Too bad the maintenance man was armed. But Bishara may not survive anyway."

She fumbled a button. "How do you know about the maintenance man?"

Ryan's lips twisted as he jotted a few notes on a pad of paper beside him. "The cops aren't the only ones who can listen in on conversations."

"You bugged me?" She stared at him. "How?"

"There are apps for everything these days. It's easy to put a tap on a phone—and turn a cell into a microphone. All you need is access to someone's phone for five or ten minutes."

"You never had . . ." Her words trailed off. The day he'd invited her in for coffee cake, she'd left her purse in his office before going to the conference room . . . and he'd disappeared to take a call.

"I see you figured it out." He waved the slip of paper at her with a grim smile. "I'm glad I did some preliminary research on venues. This won't rival 9/11, but it will definitely make a statement." He folded it in half and tucked it in his pocket.

"Why don't you tie me up and leave me behind? You don't need me to do this."

Her desperation-laced plea had no impact on the man she'd once thought of as a friend.

"On the contrary." He picked up his keys from the counter, his face devoid of all emotion. "It could come in handy to have a hostage if anyone tries to stop me."

Hostage.

Her stomach did a flip-flop.

Keep it together, Kristin. Don't panic. Stall.

"What are you p-planning to do?"

"You'll see soon enough. Let's go." He picked up the detonation button at the end of a long cord and motioned for her to precede him out the door, into the attached garage.

"Can't we—"

"I said let's go." He glared at her, impatience flashing in his eyes. "Now."

So much for her delay tactics.

He followed her into the garage, but at the car she hesitated. "If I lean back against the seat, won't I set this off?"

"It's possible. So I'd advise you not to lean back."

Her legs began to shake, and she groped for the car, easing gently inside after he opened the door.

He closed it with a soft click, circled around to the driver's side, and took his place behind the wheel. A few seconds later, the garage door rumbled up behind them, and light spilled into the dark space.

"Brace yourself." He leaned forward to start the engine.

As he backed out of the garage, Kristin angled sideways in her seat, gripping the dash with one hand and splaying the fingers of the other on the seat back, cringing with every bump and sway as he rolled down the driveway and swung onto the street.

"Where are we g-going?"

He didn't respond.

Apparently he was through talking.

And maybe it didn't matter.

She might not know their destination, but she knew what was going to happen after they got there.

Dozens—perhaps hundreds—of people would die.

If Luke and his cohorts had an inkling about what was happening, they might be able to contain some of the damage. Not save *her*, but spare the lives of a multitude of potential victims.

Unfortunately, they had no clue what was unfolding.

Only she was privy to Ryan's plans.

And you can minimize the death and destruction.

As the startling truth echoed in her mind, she froze.

She *did* have some control over this situation.

She was wearing the vest—and because it was volatile, she had a say in when it detonated too.

Meaning she could let Ryan drive this car to wherever he intended to wreak chaos . . . or she could force his hand in a location where just the two of them would be killed.

Her heart began to hammer even harder.

If the vest was as unstable as he'd indicated, all she had to do was fall on the ground . . . or tackle him . . . or lunge for the button in a spot where the fewest people would be injured.

But taking such a heroic leap would require a huge amount of courage.

Perhaps more than she possessed.

Only at the moment of decision would the true depth of her bravery be tested.

In the meantime, all she could do was pray she'd have the mettle to do what needed to be done when the time came.

· · · · ·

Wait!

Luke did a double take as he passed a car at the corner of Doud's street. Kristin was in the passenger seat, perched at an odd angle, half twisted toward the driver.

None other than Doud.

He bit back a word that wasn't pretty as they continued on their way, neither of them paying any attention to his car.

Not that it would have mattered if they did. The dark-tinted windows hid his features.

But he'd had an unobstructed view of them. And though his glimpse of Kristin had been brief, one thing had been clear.

She was pale as death.

Quashing the urge to hit his lights and sirens again and take off after them, he executed a quick U-turn as Doud made a left at the corner. After falling in behind him, he kept several car lengths between them while he punched in Nick's number.

The FBI agent answered at once. "I passed on your message to our agents. They're en route to Doud's house as we speak."

"Too late." Luke accelerated through a yellow light, focusing on Doud's car. "I just got here. He was pulling out of his street as I arrived—and Kristin's in the front seat. Based on her pallor and body language, she's not a willing passenger."

A beat passed, and when Nick spoke again, his tone was grim. "I'll have our guys join the tail. Expect a call from them momentarily. You can keep them apprised of your location until they meet up with you. I'll have the second agent in the car do the same for me so I can join the entourage too."

"Could we get some air support?" It would be disastrous if the ground tail lost Doud.

"Too problematic. It could tip off Doud that he's being followed. I'll also alert Mark to put the SWAT team on standby."

"Let's hope we don't need them."

"Agreed."

But as Luke ended the call and accelerated to keep Doud's car in sight, it was clear they might need a lot more than a SWAT team to stop a man with ISIS connections—and to save a passenger who could very well be a hostage.

■ ■ ■ ■ ■

Was that Luke's Taurus back there?

Kristin squinted out the back window as the black car continued to follow in their wake.

It *looked* like his vehicle.

But that had to be wishful thinking.

Why would Luke appear out of nowhere just when she needed help?

Ryan executed a sharp left, and Kristin's heart lurched as she scrambled to brace herself again.

"It appears your boyfriend might be tailing us." Ryan flicked a glance in the rearview mirror.

So he'd noticed the car too—and the same thought had crossed his mind.

Yet it still made no sense.

"He has no idea where I am."

"Who knew you were planning to stop by my house? And don't lie to me again."

"Your assistant. I tried to return your cell at the office first. And Alexa. That's it."

Ryan's jaw hardened. "Alexa might have told your detective if he phoned the shop looking for you. That could be why he's been trying to call you."

"He wouldn't know where I am now, though."

"Unless he was watching my house." Ryan drummed his fingers on the wheel, twin crevices denting his forehead. "Let's find out."

For the next few minutes, he drove a winding route through the streets, checking the rearview mirror every couple of minutes.

Kristin continued to watch out the back window too, searching for signs of the Taurus.

But the car eventually disappeared.

Along with her misplaced hope.

Fear bubbled up inside her again as her gaze traced the wire that ran from under her shirt to the detonation button draped over Ryan's leg. Even if Luke *had* been following them, there was nothing he could have done to save her. All Ryan had to do was reach down and press the button if anyone got close.

That might not be how he wanted this to end, but if his plans went south, she had no doubt he'd set off the bomb rather than risk capture.

Since the black Taurus was gone, however, Ryan would be free to carry out whatever nefarious plan he'd concocted, without any interference.

Except from her.

She shifted around to scan the route ahead rather than watch the road behind.

Maybe she didn't have the fanatical mind-set of a jihadist who placed no value on his own life, but she cared about other people—and the only way to save them was to ensure the bomb went off in a spot where there would be the fewest possible casualties.

Where that might be, she had no idea. Certainly not here, in the midst of Friday afternoon traffic.

But once they came to a place that would work, she'd have to make a quick decision and go for it full out.

Because she'd have only one chance. If she failed, Ryan wouldn't let her try again.

She eyed the button in Ryan's lap again, a wave of nausea rolling through her.

God, please help me see this through! Give me the courage to do what needs to be done—and to trust that you will be with me to the end.

30

"Do your people still have Doud in view?" Luke repositioned the cell against his ear, maneuvered around a sluggish driver, and accelerated.

"Affirmative. He's moving south." Nick's tone was clipped and businesslike.

"Okay." Relinquishing the tail to the FBI agents had about killed him . . . but the standard protocol of switching follow cars did reduce the risk of being spotted. If he didn't have a personal interest in Doud's passenger, he wouldn't have given it a second thought.

Letting Kristin out of his sight, however, wasn't sitting well.

"Mark's assembled the SWAT unit—and our top sniper team is en route too."

Sniper.

Luke's blood chilled at the thought of Kristin anywhere near a sniper's line of sight.

"What about a negotiator?"

"We have one on standby—but this isn't a negotiation situation. One of the agents in the follow car has a pair of high-powered binoculars trained on the occupants. Doud's in a T-shirt. Ms. Dane's wearing a bulky, oversized long-sleeved shirt."

Oversized clothing plus long sleeves in ninety-two-degree weather.

As he did the math, the wheel grew slippery beneath Luke's palms.

"You think Doud put his bomb-making skills to work and she's wearing the result."

"I think that's a strong possibility. We dispatched some of our people to his house. From the back window they had a view into his kitchen—and what they saw gave us plenty of grounds for an exigent circumstances search."

As Luke listened to Nick describe what they'd found, his stomach knotted. "It sounds like he was making TATP."

"We concur. How much do you know about that?"

"A fair amount. I was on the bomb squad in Richmond for a while. Triacetone triperoxide is a favorite of suicide bombers, so it fits with what we already know about Doud and his background."

"I agree. At least he's driving the car, which suggests we're not dealing with a dead man's switch."

"True." Trying to keep a switch depressed while maneuvering a car through traffic would be tricky. One slip of his finger, the bomb would detonate. "So the question becomes, is there an activation button or is it a wireless trigger?"

"We're going to cover the latter contingency by flooding the airwaves with radio frequencies to jam the signal. Too bad he's not driving a GM car."

"Yeah." It would give them far more control if they could have that company's OnStar technology remotely disable the car at a place of their choosing. "Since that's not an option, what's the plan?"

"I'm going to take over the tail in about half a mile. We've got more agents on the way, but stick close. We may need you back in the rotation until they get here. Cross street coming up."

As Nick read it off, Luke adjusted his course. "I'm a quarter mile back. If you need me, I can catch up fast."

"I'm hoping our people get here first. Doud may know your vehicle. You paid WorldCraft several visits, correct?"

"Yes." He couldn't dispute the possibility the man had taken note of his car.

"If we can keep you out of the rotation . . . hold." A muted voice spoke from Nick's radio, then he was back. "He's on the ramp for I-44 westbound."

West?

"I would have expected him to head east, into the city. There are all kinds of events going on in town on a Friday night—baseball game, concerts, conventions."

"A suicide vest would have a problem getting through security at those venues."

"There's not much security in the peripheral areas, though. Or the large public gathering spots, like Kiener Plaza and Ballpark Village. The Paris bombings were all in public spaces." Luke maneuvered around a slow car.

"But there were several bombers involved in that incident, adding to the impact. Doud is working alone. Given his connections to a top ISIS figure in Syria, I suspect he's picked a target that will make a bigger statement than killing random civilians."

"If he gets that far. The vest could blow all by itself." The words left a rancid taste in his mouth—but dancing around the facts wasn't going to improve Kristin's chance of surviving this.

"I know how sensitive and unstable TATP is—and I'm aware of the danger to everyone involved. Particularly Ms. Dane." A beat passed, and when Nick continued, his voice was shadowed with regret. "There's no good solution to this, Luke. People are going to get hurt."

And some were going to die.

Kristin among them, unless the odds somehow shifted in their favor.

Squeezing the wheel, he tried to keep his inner turmoil under wraps. "All we can do is our best."

"And that's what we'll do. All of us."

Luke swallowed hard and hung a left. "I'm coming up on the I-44 entrance ramp."

"Copy that. I'm in position to relieve the previous tail. Hang tight."

What other choice did he have?

Five minutes later, his cell buzzed again. "He's exiting onto I-270 south."

"Got it. Keep me apprised."

"Will do."

Luke dropped the phone onto his lap, turned on his blinkers for the I-270 exit, and tried to make sense of Doud's route.

Failed.

And driving blind stunk.

How were they supposed to plan a strategy if they didn't know the destination?

As minute after minute ticked by with no update from Nick, Luke's grip on the wheel tightened. They were running out of Missouri exits.

Was the man going to cross the Mississippi into Illinois? And what was on the other side of the river this far south other than cornfields and . . .

His phone buzzed again, and he grabbed it.

"He's exiting onto Telegraph north."

At Nick's grim tone, Luke tensed. "Is that significant?" Being new to a city was a definite disadvantage in a situation like this. Too bad his work hadn't yet taken him this far south.

"There's a banquet center on Telegraph that draws large crowds. Jefferson Barracks is down there too."

He frowned. "The veterans' cemetery?"

"There's also an adjacent park with the same name. They often have special events there."

Park.

Special events.

Luke's brain began clicking.

The department-wide alert that had gone out earlier in the week—it had mentioned Jefferson Barracks. But with all that had been going on, he'd given it no more than a fast skim.

Focus, Carter. Pull it up on your internal screen.

Concentrating, he let it scroll through his mind—and as the content began to register, his pulse stuttered.

"The state VFW convention is having a picnic there today. We were notified earlier in the week that extra officers might be needed to deal with the crowd." He reached deep, calling up as many details as he could remember. "The Mid-America Air Force Band from Scott AFB is performing, and the governor is scheduled to speak. Hundreds of veterans and spouses are attending."

Nick's breath hissed out. "That is very bad news."

A vast understatement.

What better target for an organization that hated America than one comprised of people who'd fought for their country?

Taking the governor out too would be a bonus.

"If Doud wants to make headlines around the world, he's chosen the perfect venue."

"Yeah." Nick exhaled. "This isn't just a random act of terrorism."

No, it wasn't. It was a well-thought-out strategy, designed to send a powerful message of hatred to America by killing scores of her staunchest defenders.

"I agree." Luke flexed his fingers on the steering wheel to restore circulation to his bloodless knuckles.

"We're going to need some additional personnel to handle this."

"I'll call County and get mass casualty teams on alert and coordinated with dispatch. I'll also talk to my boss and have him ask Patrol to send officers down here for traffic control around the perimeter of the park."

"That works. Stand by while I connect with the park and get some details on the location of the event and ranger personnel on-site." The line went dead.

Luke zoomed up the ramp to Telegraph, hung a left, and accelerated north as he made his calls—including one he hadn't mentioned to Nick.

Hopefully Sarge would cut through the red tape and get him the gear he'd requested.

The banquet center registered as he zipped by, but the retirement party on the marquee that was scheduled for this afternoon was small potatoes compared to a gathering of military veterans.

Unless they were way off base in their assumptions, Doud was closing in on his target.

He spotted Nick's car a few vehicles ahead as his cell rang again.

"The event's at the outdoor amphitheater. Most of the veterans were bussed in from the convention hotel, but the locals attending filled the lot. That will work to our advantage. After we enter, leave your car on the side of the road and ride with me. I can give you an earpiece that will help with communication."

"Got it. Has the governor arrived?"

"No. We're diverting him."

One piece of positive news, anyway.

As they ended the call, he pressed on the gas, hugging Nick's bumper.

And praying harder than he'd prayed since the hours he'd spent in the emergency room three years ago, waiting for the doctor to come out and talk to him about Jenny.

That day, he'd known even before the solemn-faced physician approached him that he'd lost his wife.

Now he could lose Kristin too.

The harsh reality slammed into him with the same breath-stealing impact as the blow to the solar plexus that had sidelined him once during a soccer game in high school. The inability to catch his breath was as potent and terrifying now as the day he'd lain on the field struggling to suck air into his lungs.

Clinging to the wheel, he tried to follow the instructions the coach had given him two decades ago.

Stay calm. This will pass.

Didn't work.

Because this might not pass. He and Kristin might never have a chance to explore the future he'd been convinced lay ahead for them.

Fighting for air, he looked toward the heavens.

God, please! Don't let her die! Please!

The desperate plea bubbled up from the depths of his soul.

Yet even as he sent it hurtling to the cloudless sky, he knew it would take a miracle to save the woman who'd stolen his heart.

· · · · ·

Jefferson Barracks?

Kristin stared at the small road sign as Ryan flipped on his turn signal.

Why would he pick a location like this for a suicide bombing?

But as soon as they swung into the park, the large electronic sign at the entrance gave her the answer.

WELCOME MISSOURI VETERANS
Follow the arrows to the state VFW convention picnic.

Ryan was going to detonate the bomb in a park filled with American heroes who'd fought the country's enemies in numerous wars?

A wave of horror rolled through her.

No.

No!

Stomach churning, she swallowed past the bile rising in her throat.

Waiting had been a mistake.

Yet when could she have made her move? Detonating the vest on I-44 or I-270 would have killed scores in the heavy Friday afternoon traffic. Every car around them had been filled with innocent men, women, and children.

Still . . . there would be many more casualties here. Hundreds of people might be in attendance.

Hysteria threatened to shut down her brain —but a firm inner voice yanked her back from the brink.

Stop it, Kristin! Pull yourself together. It's too late for regrets or second thoughts. Work with what you have. Do the best you can to save as many lives as possible and steal this victory from Ryan.

Gritting her teeth, she straightened her shoulders.

Okay.

She could hold it together long enough to do this.

Maintaining her grip on the dash, she scanned the park. There was too much activity near the entrance, too many cars coming and going. The best place to detonate might be the parking area. If the picnic was already in progress, there should be few people wandering around.

And the lot had to be close.

Meaning the clock on this drama was ticking down to the end.

A bead of sweat trickled past her temple, and she swiped it away. Strange to be perspiring when she felt cold and clammy.

Stranger still to know her life would end in a handful of minutes.

If ever there was a time to pray, this was it.

She bowed her head and closed her eyes as Ryan guided the car down the narrow road, following the arrows.

"Talking to your God?" Derision scored his question.

Kristin ignored him.

"You Christians are a curse on the world." He spat out the condemnation, his hatred almost palpable. "As is America."

She remained silent. Trying to convince a fanatic to change course was futile, especially at this late stage. She'd rather devote her final few minutes to prayer.

And as the car rolled toward the parking lot . . . as she centered her thoughts on God . . . her fear gave way to steely resolve and an almost out-of-body calmness.

Only one regret shadowed her heart.

The tomorrows she'd envisioned with Luke that would never be.

·　·　·　·　·

Inside the park boundary, Luke jammed on the parking brake in his Taurus. After pulling a pair of binoculars from his glove compartment, he sprinted to Nick's car and slid into the passenger seat.

"Here's your coms." The agent handed him the earpiece.

He fitted it into place, pocketed the power pack, and clipped the mic on his collar as Nick peeled off the shoulder and sped down the road.

Half a minute later, the agent ignored the arrows for the picnic that pointed straight and hung a right on Grant.

"Why this route?"

"Grant parallels the road to the amphitheater and the parking lot. I was patched through to the ranger in charge at the scene. He said the road is hidden from view by a small hill—making it an excellent staging area."

"Does he know what's going on?"

"Yes. We need someone already inside the park to help pull this off. He's going to intercept Doud at the entrance to the lot and instruct him to continue onto the adjacent service road at the far end and park on the grass."

"Won't Doud get suspicious about the diversion?"

"He shouldn't. The ranger says the lot is full of cars and buses. I also asked him to keep Doud talking as long as possible."

Luke flipped on the power pack for the communications gear. "Does he know we're dealing with a suicide bomber?"

"Yes."

"What if he gets nervous? Clues Doud in?"

"I think he can handle the assignment. He's a former Green Beret and longtime park employee. Besides, we have no choice. He's here, he's in uniform, and there's no time to get one of our own people into position."

Hard to argue with that logic—even if the setup left a lot to be desired.

"Where's your sniper?"

"He and his spotter passed us on the approach road. They're going to park in our staging area and find a position with a good line of sight. There's a copse of trees at the fringe of the blast zone that should give them reasonable cover."

"So the plan is to take Doud out after he parks and leaves his car."

"Yes."

"What's the backup plan if your sniper can't get a clear shot at him?"

A tic in Nick's cheek confirmed Luke's suspicion even before the agent spoke. "We have an armed bomb technician suiting up as we speak. He'll approach from the other side of the parking lot once Doud drives onto the grass. If Brett can't pull this off . . . the agent will move in. Doud can't protect his back from every direction."

"He'll detonate as soon as he spots him."

"I know." He glanced over. "We have agents preparing to herd the crowd back the second Doud drives past the open area where the amphitheater is located. But moving a group that size with a high percentage of people who are older or disabled isn't going to happen fast. We have to minimize the loss of life."

Luke understood that.

As incident commander, he'd make the same difficult call.

But it punched a gaping hole in his gut.

"So we need to . . ." His words rasped, and he cleared his throat. "We need to deal with Doud as soon as he gets out of the car—as far from the amphitheater as possible."

"Yes. Some of the crowd may still be in range of projectiles from the explosion, but it's the best we can do." He executed a U-turn and pulled onto the shoulder of the road, behind another car.

Luke surveyed the empty vehicle. "Your sniper's?"

"Yes."

Luke's earpiece crackled to life. "Brett here. In position. Excellent line of sight to target area. Over."

Nick spoke into the mic clipped to his collar. "Copy that. Expect the subject to arrive momentarily."

"Doud will be parking on the other side of those trees?" Luke motioned toward the brushy, wooded area topping the rise beside them.

"Yes. From the crest of that hill, there's a long, gentle slope down to the service road where the ranger will direct Doud." Nick retrieved his own binoculars from the back seat. "You ready to do this?"

No.

Not even close.

The mere thought of seeing Kristin strapped into a suicide vest turned his stomach.

Nor did he want to stand by and watch while a terrorist played with a detonation button.

Or witness the carnage if the sniper missed or couldn't get a shot and this went south.

But he couldn't wait on the sidelines, either.

"Yeah." He opened his door.

When Nick touched his arm, he paused. "Remember we're borderline close if the bomb detonates—and the projectiles are like bullets."

"I know exactly what we're up against. That's what big trees are for."

"Agreed. So let's use them. And we're only going close enough to get a view of what's happening. Seeing detail is what *these* are for." He lifted the binoculars.

Luke locked gazes with the man. "I don't take chances that have no reasonable expectation of producing results."

After a moment, Nick dipped his head. "Are those anti-reflection equipped?"

"Yes." Glint and glare from optical surfaces could be deadly—the very reason he supplied his own binocs.

"Okay. Let's go."

They set off at a jog for the thick cluster of large trees and bushy shrubs that would offer them a view to the adjacent service road—and a modicum of protection from flying projectiles if any happened to travel that far.

Somewhere among those trees, Brett was also hidden—ready to take out a terrorist.

And as they crested the hill and the narrow road came into view . . . as he and Nick tucked themselves behind two large oaks . . . he prayed the sniper got his chance before it was too late—and that his aim was true.

31

The amphitheater was packed.

As Doud drove past the gently sloping terrain that led down to the stage, Kristin's stomach lurched. Hundreds of people were gathered around the raised platform in the distance, swaying to the big band sound of "In the Mood" being played by an orchestra of uniformed servicemen and women.

In a handful of minutes, Ryan planned to wade into the midst of the festive group and sow destruction.

But she wasn't going to let him.

Pulse accelerating, she curled her fingers into tight fists as he continued past the crowd, toward the adjacent parking lot.

As far as she could tell, it contained only vehicles. No people.

The perfect place to implement her plan.

A ranger stepped out from the side of the road as they approached and lifted a hand.

The car slowed, and Ryan dropped his hand to his lap. Wrapped his fingers around the button.

Her heart stuttered.

If this ranger caused them any trouble, Ryan might not wait to plunge into the crowd to detonate the bomb. Despite her skimpy knowledge of explosives, she'd read enough suicide-bombing news stories to know that such a blast had a wide radius.

And many of the people in the amphitheater were within the danger zone.

Ryan braked and lowered his window halfway.

"Afternoon, folks." The ranger leaned down and smiled into the car. "You here for the VFW event?"

"Yes."

Despite Ryan's terse response, the man's genial demeanor didn't waver. "It's quite a party. And you're getting here at the perfect time. The band just started playing. We had a big backup trying to get into the park about an hour ago, but you missed all that."

Ryan's leg began to jiggle. "So where do we park?"

"Well, that's the one downside to arriving a little late. The lot's pretty full. Those buses took up more space than we expected." He waved toward the six motor coaches that filled the whole first row.

"We can squeeze in somewhere."

"There are only two more rows, and they're mostly full except for a few spots we're saving for handicapped people. With a group like this, we have quite a few of those. If you folks don't mind a short walk, we're asking able-bodied visitors to pull down the service road and park on the grass alongside." He motioned to a small road that veered off the parking lot on the far end.

A few cars were scattered on the grass—and that location was even farther from the crowd.

Better.

With every yard they put between themselves and the open expanse in front of the amphitheater, fewer people would be affected by the explosion.

"Fine. We'll park down there." Ryan started to close the window.

"One other thing." The chatty ranger's amiable smile held despite the abrupt response.

A muscle twitched in Ryan's cheek, and Kristin held her breath until he lowered the window again. "Yes?"

"A tip for when you leave. Instead of coming back this way, continue on the service road. It will hook you up to the street that leads to that picnic shelter." He pointed out the pavilion at the end of the road, on a small height. "That will take you to Grant, which will get you out of the park. You'll have much less congestion going that way. It's no fun to fight traffic at the end of an enjoyable evening."

"Thanks." Ryan activated the electric window again. It rolled up and shut tight, sealing them inside. "Like I really care about driving out of this place, you moron."

As he muttered the derisive comment, he drove forward and took a right onto the service road. A couple hundred feet down, he swung in beside another car parked on the grass and shut off the engine.

"Finally." He gave the peaceful, bucolic surroundings a slow sweep.

Kristin did the same. The green rolling hillside was empty save for some wooded patches in the distance. Behind them, the other side of the road was dense with trees and undergrowth. All seemed quiet.

He turned to her. "Open your door."

As she did so, he grasped her upper arm in a steel grip, clutching the detonation button in his other hand.

"I thought you w-wanted me to get out?"

"I do. But we're doing this together. From now on, you and I are joined at the hip. Swing your legs out and scoot to the edge of the seat."

He was getting out on her side?

"Move!"

She eased around and lowered her feet to the grass. A few seconds later her seat sagged as he moved behind her, so close she could feel his body heat.

She tried not to retch.

"Here's how this is going to work, Kristin." His hot breath scorched her ear as he spoke. "After we're out of the car, I'm going to wind the cord into my hand. Then we'll walk toward the amphitheater. I'll be behind you, my hand in the small of your back with the coiled cord and the detonation button. And I'm going to keep shifting us around as we walk."

"W-why?"

"In case anyone is watching us. I think we're clear, but if we're not, it's always harder to hit a moving target. All you have to do is keep walking and follow my lead. Got it?"

She gave a jerky nod.

But as he urged her out of the car, she planned to do a lot more than follow his lead like a sheep to slaughter.

She was going to *take* the lead.

Ryan might be willing to die in order to kill other people— but she was willing to die to *save* other people.

For all his careful planning, she doubted he'd factored that kind of sacrifice into his equation.

But if her courage held, in less than a minute he was going to find out that for all his hatred of America and Christians, the values of her country and her faith were going to prove more powerful in the end than his ideology of hatred and intolerance.

. . . . .

They were getting out of the car.

From his concealed position behind a large oak tree in a thicket of greenery, Luke tried to steady the binoculars he'd trained on the duo.

Hard to do with the quiver in his fingers.

Nick's curt voice spoke in his earpiece. "Brett—status report."

"Subject is too close to hostage. Waiting for clear line of sight."

"You've got thirty yards. Max."

"Understood."

As Luke listened to the conversation, some of the stiffening went out of his legs.

Thirty yards gave the FBI sniper a very small window in which to work—and Ryan was sticking tight to Kristin.

Even worse, he was on her far side. And he was tugging her around, weaving back and forth, scanning the surroundings. Like he knew he was being watched—and was doing his best to make it hard for anyone to get a clear shot at him.

"I think he might have spotted us tailing him." This from Nick. "All that bobbing and weaving is suspicious."

Luke spoke into the mic clipped to his collar. "Or he's being cautious."

"Doesn't matter the reason. If we don't get a shot, we'll have to go with plan B."

The one involving the guy in the bomb suit, who was approaching from the other end of the parking lot.

The one that guaranteed Kristin would die.

"Not the best solution." He snapped out the words as his control slipped, the binoculars glued to his face. "With a sniper shot, at least she has a chance, however small. The other way, she—"

He frowned.

Zoomed in tight on Kristin's face.

She had a nasty purple bruise on her jaw—but that wasn't what made the panic alert beeping in his mind go berserk.

There was no tension in her features. No fear in her eyes. She appeared calm. Resolute. Almost as if she'd switched to autopilot for some predetermined sequence of activity.

But what kind of activity? What options did she . . .

His heart stumbled as the truth slammed into him like a punch in the gut.

Kristin sold candles to support monks who helped those in need. She'd donated two years of her life to service in the Peace Corps. She ran a shop that gave an economic assist to people struggling to make a living in less developed countries.

This was a woman who cared passionately about others.

Who would never put her own needs above the needs of someone else.

Who would sacrifice her own life to save the lives of innocent people.

"Luke? What's going on?" There was an edge to Nick's voice.

In his peripheral vision, he saw the agent edge out from behind the nearby tree where he'd secreted himself.

Kristin fisted her hands.

"She's going to detonate it herself!" His words came out ragged.

Kristin lifted her chin.

His pulse began to gallop. "Brett—take your shot!"

Kristin's chest heaved.

"Nick—give the order!"

As he barked out the command, Kristin wrenched free of Ryan's grip, swung around, and yanked at the cord in his hand.

"Kristin! No!" Luke bellowed the desperate plea.

Two shots exploded in rapid succession.

Ryan jerked.

Blood spurted.

And Kristin went down.

■ ■ ■ ■ ■

What had just happened?

From the kneeling position she'd dropped to when her legs gave out, Kristin sank back on her heels and blinked.

Blinked again as she tried to put together the pieces.

There had been a shout.

An explosion.

Blood.

She studied the bright red spatters on her shirt.

Odd.

Nothing hurt.

Or was she too numb to feel pain?

She lifted her hand and examined her fingers.

Everything appeared to be intact.

Yet Ryan was lying in a twisted heap on the ground beside her.

He was dead . . . but she wasn't?

Nothing was computing.

All she knew with absolute certainty was that she was still strapped into a suicide vest.

"Kristin!"

The voice again.

The one that sounded like Luke's.

She lifted her head. Searched the surrounding hills.

There.

In the distance, a male figure waving at her.

It *was* Luke.

He cupped his hands around his mouth. "Help is on the way, Kristin. Don't talk. Don't move!"

Not a problem.

Her muscles had turned to mush, and her vocal cords had shut down.

Besides, since by some miracle her attempt to blow herself up had apparently failed, she wasn't about to finish by accident what fate—or God—had derailed.

Luke disappeared over the crest of a hill, but she followed his instructions and remained motionless beside Ryan's lifeless body.

Time passed. How much, she had no idea. But at last someone

in what looked like a space suit approached her from the direction of the parking lot.

No, not a space suit.

A bomb suit.

She'd seen photos of them on TV.

The figure drew closer but didn't speak until he was less than twenty feet away.

"Ms. Dane, I'm Special Agent John Lawrence with the FBI." His tone was calm as he continued to walk toward her, like they were having a chat at Starbucks. "I'm a bomb technician. We're going to get you out of that rig as fast as we can. Okay?"

"Okay." Her acknowledgment squeaked out.

Somehow, despite the bulky suit, he managed to hunker down on one knee beside her. "Before I touch anything, tell me what you know about this vest and how it was put on."

Somehow Kristin managed to walk him through what she'd found in Ryan's kitchen and how he'd strapped her into the vest, answering all of his questions as best she could.

No, he hadn't mentioned anything about a timer.

No, there were no locks on the vest, just straps.

No, as far as she knew there was only the one detonation button that had never been far from his hand.

"It's right t-there." She flicked a glance to the button at the end of the wire that protruded from the bottom of her vest and snaked across the grass.

As he angled sideways to size it up, she began to shake.

Hard.

Her stomach bottomed out.

No! She had to remain motionless! Ryan had warned her that too much movement could set the bomb off.

"Agent L-Lawrence." He refocused on her at once. "I can't stop shaking. I-I'm afraid I'll make this blow up."

"If you haven't set it off yet, I don't think we need to worry about that." He continued to speak in a smooth, reassuring tone. "But we're going to get it off of you fast. I have an assistant on the way who will help with that task. I think you know him. A detective by the name of Carter."

Luke was going to get up close and personal with this bomb?

The taste of fear soured her tongue. "I don't want him anywhere near this thing."

"He'll be suited up, like me."

"I don't care. It's too risky." At this range, those suits wouldn't offer sufficient protection if the vest detonated. It was bad enough she and this technician could be blown to bits. Luke didn't need to put himself in the danger zone too.

"As I understand it, he wouldn't take no for an answer. He had some guys from the County unit haul their equipment out here, and his bomb squad background gives him the credentials to assist."

Kristin stared at the FBI tech.

Luke had a background working with bombs?

The man was full of surprises.

Including the fact that he planned to put his own life on the line instead of staying on the sidelines until Agent Lawrence disposed of the vest.

Pressure built behind Kristin's eyes as the implication of his choice sank in—and despite the explosive vest strapped around her body, warmth overflowed in her heart.

As did hope.

Because only a man whose feelings ran as true and deep as hers would take such a risk.

And if God had brought her this far, surely he was going to keep her safe until she could step into Luke's arms and give him a proper thank-you.

32

"What in blazes is going on?"

Luke picked up the helmet for the bomb suit as Colin flashed his creds, ducked under the inner perimeter yellow crime scene tape, and barreled toward him.

He did *not* have time for this.

"We'll talk later."

"Kristin isn't answering her phone. Tell me she doesn't have anything to do with this suicide bomber/hostage situation that's been all over our secure police channel."

"I wish I could."

The color leeched from Colin's face. "She's the one in the suicide vest."

"Yes."

His Adam's apple bobbed. "What's the status?"

"The vest-maker is dead. We're getting ready to free Kristin."

"You know how to deal with these kind of explosives?"

"I've had experience with bombs—but the FBI tech agent is taking the lead. I'm just assisting." He lumbered toward the service road as fast as the bulky suit allowed.

"Does he *need* your help?"

Luke kept walking. "Extra hands never hurt."

"Hey!"

He glanced over his shoulder without breaking stride.

"Thanks. And good luck."

With a bob of his head, he continued toward the road.

A minute later, Kristin came into view, still sitting on her heels, the front of her shirt splattered with Doud's blood. She hadn't moved an inch since he'd called to her from the top of the hill before racing around to the staging area and the waiting County bomb crew.

Thank goodness Sarge had come through for him and he could suit up fast.

As he put on his helmet and started down the road, Kristin's gaze latched on to his—and remained locked there while he trudged toward her in the heavy suit.

The FBI bomb tech stayed on his knee beside her while Luke completed his trek and hunkered down on her other side.

"You're gonna be fine." He laid his fingers—the only exposed part of his body—on the back of her icy hand.

"You didn't have to do this." The warmth in her eyes seeped through the layers of the protective suit and filtered into his heart.

"Yes, I did." Through his visor, he looked at her for several long, intense beats before shifting his attention to the bomb tech. "What do we have?"

"It appears to be a rudimentary detonation device." He motioned to the cord that ended with a button. "However, I don't want to touch anything until we get her out of the vest. Ms. Dane, can you unbutton the shirt or would you like us to do that?"

As she lifted her hands to examine them, Luke understood the reason for the man's question.

They were shaking badly.

"I-I'm not sure I can manage it."

"No problem." Luke edged around in front of her. "I'll do

it." His own hands were none too steady, but they were in better shape than hers.

"I'll work on the cuff of this sleeve." The agent bent down to ease the button out.

As soon as Luke finished the front of the stained shirt, he went to work on the other cuff. It too was bloody—but the splotches weren't as fresh.

Once he opened the button, the crusting slices in her wrist revealed the source.

Keeping his tone as even as possible, he traced the edge of one slash. "What happened?"

She inspected the abrasions. "He used wire to restrain me. I tried to get f-free, and it c-cut into my skin."

"And your jaw?" He gently touched her chin.

"He hit me."

Rage bubbled up inside him, as turbulent as a rumbling volcano, and Luke had to call on every ounce of his self-restraint to keep it from erupting.

Kristin didn't need his anger.

She needed his support and encouragement.

And after the FBI agent parted the shirt in front and the bomb-studded vest came into full view, Luke had no difficulty redirecting his thoughts to the more immediate, life-threatening challenge.

"Ms. Dane, do you recall if the front and back of the vest are the same?"

"I-I think so. It seemed like a mirror image, with a hole in the middle."

"Okay." He produced a pair of scissors from a toolkit beside him and moved behind Kristin. "I'm going to cut the shirt up the back and we'll slide it down your arms."

He did the job with quick efficiency, examined the back of the vest, and repositioned himself on her other side.

Luke worked his half of the shirt off while the agent did the same.

"I think we have basic straps and ties under the arms." The agent laid the shirt aside. "Let's verify that. Ms. Dane, would you slowly raise your arms a few inches?"

She did as he asked.

Luke examined his side of the vest. It was a simple garment, cinched with canvas straps affixed with plastic buckles that clicked into place. Like the ones on the car seats Becca had for the kids. "I think we can open these without any issue."

"I agree. I've got three on this side."

"Same here."

"Let's do it."

With a gentle squeeze, he released them one by one.

After the agent finished his side, he carefully repositioned the cord with the detonation button so it was out of the way. "Let's remove the vest. You take the front, I'll take the back."

After giving Kristin's fingers one final stroke, Luke rose and grasped the bottom of the vest.

The agent did the same in the back. "Pull it straight out, then lift it up and over her head. We'll set it flat on the grass, to your right. Ready . . . up."

Luke synchronized his movements with the agent's, maintaining the same slow, steady pace as they removed the vest and lowered it to the grass.

Kristin was free.

But she was still in the danger zone.

As if reading his mind, the FBI bomb tech spoke again. "You can both take off. After you're clear, I'm going to see if I can disconnect the detonation cord."

"You need any help?" Much as he'd prefer to walk away, Luke had to offer. This guy had put his life on the line for Kristin.

He grinned at him through the mask. "Disconnecting a cord isn't a two-person job. If it gets too complicated, I'll let the robot take over. We'll need to bring it in anyway to secure the explosives in the vest. But I'd rather not have this go boom during that process if we can avoid it."

That made sense.

Luke leaned down and held out his hands to Kristin. "Let's get out of here."

She grasped his fingers and he pulled her to her feet, holding tight when she swayed.

"Sorry. My legs are s-shaky."

"I can carry you."

"In that getup?" Somehow she dredged up the flicker of a smile. "That might be difficult. I'll make it as long as I can hold on to your arm."

He crooked his elbow. "For as long as you need to."

Together they walked down the service road to the parking lot, Luke setting a fast pace.

Too fast, based on her tight grip.

But he wanted her out of bomb range ASAP.

Only when they were fifty feet from the emergency crews did he shorten his stride.

"Colin's here." She stared at her childhood friend waiting on the other side of the tape among other law enforcement personnel and emergency crews, fists clamped to his hips.

"I know."

"Is that the safe zone?"

"Yes."

A shudder rippled through her. "Half an hour ago, I didn't think this was a remotely p-possible outcome." She looked up at him. "I have a lot to say to you."

"I have a lot to say to you too—but it's going to have to wait awhile. Can I interest you in a pizza later?"

"If it's takeout at my place."

"Consider it a date."

When they were ten feet from the tape, Colin ducked under and charged toward them, lifting Kristin off her feet and into a bear hug as he carried her to safety.

"Luke." Nick motioned him over.

Since Kristin was in excellent hands, he joined the agent on the other side of the tape, removed his helmet, and waved over the County bomb crew. "I need to ditch this get-up. It's not made for St. Louis summer heat."

"Not a problem. I know we've both had a long day—and night—and day, but after we get Ms. Dane some medical attention, we'll need to do a fast debrief with her."

"I'll let her know."

Five minutes later, free of the suit, he jogged toward Colin and Kristin.

"Yes, you do need medical attention." Colin glared at her while two paramedics hovered in the background.

"No, I don't. I already told you. I have a few cuts and bruises. That's it." She glared right back.

"What's the harm in letting them do a fast evaluation? That's their job."

"Only for legitimate patients. I'm fine."

Colin spotted him. "She won't let the paramedics check her out. Maybe you can talk her into it. I'm getting nowhere." He scowled at Kristin, exasperation oozing from his pores.

Luke draped an arm around her shoulders. Up close and without the helmet and visor impeding his view, the bruise on her jaw was much more pronounced—as were the cuts on her wrists. But otherwise she appeared to be unharmed.

Thank you, God.

He picked up one of her hands and examined her wrist. "It might not be a bad idea to at least let them put some antibiotic

ointment and bandages on these." He gave her his most persuasive smile. "It would make their trip worthwhile and keep
your friend happy."

She maintained her rigid stance for a few moments—and
then every muscle seemed to go limp at once. She leaned into
him, and he tightened his grip, absorbing her weight.

While she might not be hurt, her adrenaline was dipping,
and exhaustion was setting in. What she needed most was to
put her feet up, chill out, and spend a quiet evening—with
him.

Coming up soon on their agenda.

"Fine." She exhaled, and he felt a quiver run through her.
"They can treat my wrists. That will save me from doing it after
I get home." She angled toward Colin. "Satisfied?"

"As long as you follow through."

"She will." Luke squeezed her shoulder.

"I need to get back to work." Colin raked his fingers through
his hair. "I'll give Rick a topline, but call him as soon as you
get a chance, okay? He's been bugging me every ten minutes
for updates."

As Colin pulled her into another hug, Luke caught the attention of one of the paramedics, tapped his jaw, and tipped
his head toward Kristin. The man nodded.

Over Kristin's shoulder, Colin mouthed a silent thank-you.

The next hour passed in a blur as his own adrenaline bottomed out and weariness sapped his last reserves of energy. The
paramedics did their stuff—much more than Kristin had agreed
to, in their subtle, persuasive way—and the two of them found
a quiet corner to talk to Nick. The part of her story about the
tap on her cell raised both their eyebrows, but the rest fell in
line with their assumptions.

Nick stood as they wrapped up. "That's all we need for
now. We'll examine the phone and get it back to you as soon

as possible, Ms. Dane. Luke, why don't I drop you both at your car? With the VFW crowd milling around, you should be able to slip out without drawing any media attention."

"That would be great. I don't think either of us is up to having a microphone thrust in our face."

They wove through the crowd, slipped into the back seat of Nick's car, and did a quick transfer at the Taurus. Before anyone noticed them, Luke was pulling out of the park and driving toward the highway.

Keeping a firm grip on the wheel, he reached over and took Kristin's hand, weaving his fingers through hers.

She squeezed them and shifted the paramedic-provided cold pack against her jaw. "What a day."

"I'll say."

She studied the sun beginning to dip toward the horizon. "An hour ago, I didn't think I'd be here to see another sunset." Her voice hitched. "It's like a second chance at life."

"I know—and I don't plan to waste a minute of it."

"How so?" She gave him a curious glance.

This wasn't the time or place for soul-baring. They were both exhausted, the trauma was too fresh, and his mind was too muddled to do justice to the topic he wanted to discuss.

"I'll tell you what. Let's table that topic until we get to your place, order our pizza, and chill for a while."

After a few moments she gave a slow nod. "I think that's smart. I have some things to say to you too, but I'd rather do that after I feel a little more normal." She leaned her head back against the seat and held tight to his fingers.

The remainder of the drive passed in silence.

And that was fine.

Just holding hands was more than sufficient for now.

Besides, as the miles passed and the reality of their near miss began to fully sink in, Luke needed the quiet interlude to get a grip on his wobbly composure—and to send a heartfelt thank-you heavenward for answered prayers.

· · · · ·

"Wonderful. There's a news van in the parking lot." As Luke drove toward her condo, Kristin grimaced.

Microphones might be in their future after all.

She was so not up for that.

"Is there a back entrance to your unit?" Luke surveyed the parking lot.

Of course. If her brain wasn't stuck in slow motion, she'd have thought of that herself. "Yes. Circle back to the main road, turn into the next drive, and we'll hoof it to the back door. They won't be able to see us going in from where they're parked."

He followed her instructions, and five minutes later they slipped unnoticed into the rear door of her condo.

After he shut and locked it behind them, Luke pulled her close and cupped her face in his hands, his fingers gentle on her bruised jaw. "I've been wanting to do this ever since I took off my helmet."

Before she could respond, he leaned down and touched his lips to hers.

Melting against him, she put her arms around his neck and held on tight.

Who needed words, anyway?

The kiss was tender and sweet and careful—yet brimming with a barely-held-in-check passion that sent her pulse back into overdrive . . . for much more pleasant reasons than earlier in the day.

She was in no hurry to end the embrace—but at a sudden vibration against her hip, she jerked back.

"Sorry." He groped for his phone. "I'll turn it off."

"No." She stole one more quick kiss and drew back. "With all that's happened today, you better see who's calling."

"Yeah. I guess." With a resigned sigh, he pulled out his phone. Rolled his eyes.

"What?"

"It's my sister. She always did have rotten timing."

"Or she suspects you might be involved in what's going on. The media has to be all over this. Go ahead and call her back. I need to touch base with Rick and my dad anyway. I don't want either of them worrying, and Dad could hear about this on the news."

"Are you always this logical?"

"No."

"Glad to hear it." He winked at her as he tapped in a number. "Don't go far."

"I'm not planning to." Ever.

But she could share that in a little while, once they both made their calls.

Ten minutes later, after reassuring Rick she was fine, filling her dad in on the events of the day, and ordering a deluxe pizza with the works, she found Luke sprawled on her couch.

"When did you last sleep?"

"I don't remember." He sniffed his shirt. "But I think I need a shower more than sleep. I should go home, freshen up, and come back."

"No way. I have a clean bathroom, plenty of towels, and a T-shirt that will fit you. I wouldn't mind a shower myself."

He waggled his eyebrows. "Is that a proposition?"

"Nope. Ladies first. Give me ten minutes. I'll call out after I'm finished and leave your shirt and a towel in the bathroom."

"You're no fun."

She smiled. "I think I'll enjoy disproving that comment down the road."

He gave her a slow, wicked grin. "I think I'll have fun letting you."

A delicious quiver of anticipation zipped up her spine.

Down, girl. You'll have plenty of opportunity to explore the electricity zinging between you. No need to rush this.

Right.

She cleared her throat and backed away. "I won't be long."

"Good."

At the parched-man-who's-stumbled-upon-a-desert-oasis look in his eyes, she fled before the situation got downright dangerous.

Standing under a cool spray in the shower helped restore her equilibrium, and as she slipped out of the bathroom and Luke took her place, she felt almost back to normal.

Almost.

He showered even faster than she had, emerging from the bathroom as the doorbell rang.

"About this shirt. Seriously?" He pinched the tee between his fingers and plucked it away from his skin like it was a leech.

Hmm.

Maybe the reaction of her Treehouse Gang buddies to the *Alice in Wonderland* cast and crew shirts hadn't been over-the-top after all.

It wasn't the most masculine garment, with all that swirly type against a powder-blue background.

"That's Rick's T-shirt for this year's show. Colin's wife made him take his, but Rick refused to wear the one I had made for him."

"Smart man. If I wasn't desperate, I'd follow his lead."

The doorbell rang again, and Kristin started toward it. "That's the pizza."

"Or an aggressive reporter. Let me answer it."

"In that?" She motioned to the shirt.

He hesitated for an instant, then picked up his pace. "I'll survive. What are the odds I'll ever see this guy again?"

She watched from the sidelines as he opened the door. The kid gave the shirt a dubious once-over as Luke dug out some money, then beat a hasty retreat.

"You owe me." Luke carried the pizza into the living room. "And I'm not referring to a monetary reimbursement for this pizza."

"I always pay my debts."

"Hold that thought. I'm starving."

"How long has it been since you had any food?" She ducked into the kitchen to retrieve two sodas.

"Can't remember." He set the box on the coffee table, tugging her down beside him as soon as she returned. "By the way, you're invited to dinner at my sister's house on Sunday."

"I accept."

"That was easy."

"I'd like to meet your family." She wound a stringy piece of cheese around her finger and deposited it on top of her slice of pizza. What she was about to say might be premature, but after everything that had happened today, she wasn't going to waste her second chance at life, either. "If you'd like to meet mine, I'm flying to Boston next weekend. I told my dad about you, and he reminded me their townhouse has two guest rooms."

"I'd be honored. And we might as well get the meet-the-family ritual out of the way up front so we can concentrate on each other."

"I like how you think."

"If we finish this pizza fast, we can practice that concentration."

"Then let's not waste time talking." She took a huge bite.

The pizza disappeared in record time.

But the dessert was better.

And it lasted much longer than the pizza.

When they finally came up for air, Luke touched his forehead to hers. "I prayed harder today than I've prayed since the day Jenny died. I couldn't even fathom the thought of losing you too." His whispered words were hoarse.

"You didn't. You won't. I'm here. I'll always be here."

He backed off a few inches. "I don't want to rush you into making promises."

"You're not. I've known almost from the day we met that you were special—and I'm smart enough to recognize a keeper."

"Me too. I already knew you had a tender heart and deep compassion and a host of other fine qualities, but when you tried to detonate that bomb today . . ." His voice choked, and he swallowed. "You're a bona fide hero, Kristin Dane."

So he'd realized her intent as she'd lunged away from Ryan. Thank heaven her plan had failed.

"You are too. And not just for what you did today. The FBI tech told me you were once on a bomb squad."

"For eighteen months in my distant past. It freaked Jenny out, so I quit."

"I can understand how she felt. Promise me you'll never get anywhere close to a bomb again. Your job is already plenty dangerous without adding more risk."

"I promise. If I never see another bomb again, it will be too soon." He surveyed the waning sunlight filtering through her half-open blinds. "It's getting late. I should go."

She snuggled against the solid warmth of his chest. "I know."

He settled deeper into the cushions and pulled her close. "Ten more minutes."

But in less than five, fatigue took him out. His breathing deepened and steadied, and slumber erased the last vestiges of tension from his features.

Kristin's eyelids grew heavy too.

And as she drifted off . . . as a deep sense of contentment settled over her like a cozy comforter on a cold winter night . . . her lips curved up.

Life didn't get any better than falling asleep safe in Luke's arms.

Where she belonged . . . for always.

EPILOGUE

"Don't you feel a tiny bit guilty about lazing around on a white sand beach in the Caribbean while our families and friends are battling a December blizzard?"

At Kristin's question, Luke smiled without opening his eyes. "Nope."

The double chaise lounge they were sharing in the cabana shifted, and he turned his head to find his wife perched on her side and propped on her elbow, chin in palm, an impish grin curving her mouth.

"I don't either."

He chuckled. "Maybe we should stay on Antigua forever."

"I like the sound of that—but honeymoons have to end."

"Ours doesn't."

"Nice to hear." She traced the line of his jaw with her fingertip, her touch elevating his pulse—as it always did. "This has been an incredible ten days, starting with the wedding."

He captured her hand and kissed her fingers one by one. "I agree. Did I mention you were a beautiful bride?"

"Only a few dozen times."

"It bears repeating. When I saw you at the back of church on your father's arm in that amazing dress, I . . . wow." As long as he lived, he'd never forget his first glimpse of his bride, her face radiant as she walked down the aisle in a stunning white lace gown that hugged and dipped in all the right places.

"I'm glad you liked it. I had a blast shopping for it with your sister."

"Who wouldn't give me the slightest hint what it looked like."

"She was under a solemn oath to keep the secret. But the pearls you gave me as a wedding present were perfect with it."

"That's what Becca said when I ran the idea by her."

"She has excellent taste. I like her a lot. In fact, I like your whole family." She leaned closer and brushed her lips over his cheek. "You know, I think your dad was really touched that you asked him to be your best man."

It was hard to focus on their conversation while her kiss was sending his mind in a completely different direction. "He, uh, deserved the job—though it was a rather odd wedding party with Becca as a groomswoman and Colin and Rick as your men of honor."

"My mom thought it was creative."

"I'm glad she approved. I'd hate to start off on the wrong foot with my mother-in-law."

"No worries there. You won her and Dad over with those Ted Drewes packed in dry ice that you brought on your first visit."

"I'm not above a little bribery if it earns me points with my wife's parents."

"They're partial to toasted ravioli too."

"Duly noted for a future trip. But on a more serious note—I'm glad your mom was well enough to enjoy all the festivities. She's made remarkable progress since our first trip together to Boston."

"I agree—and I'm happy they're going to carve out more time

for a personal life after all the years they've single-mindedly devoted to their careers."

He shifted onto his side too, so he could face her and play with a few strands of her silky hair. "I intend to carve out plenty of time for a personal life in the *midst* of my career. What happened in June gave me a very clear sense of priorities."

A shadow crossed her face. "I still shudder to think how close . . ."

"Hey." He cupped her cheek in his palm. "No shuddering allowed on a honeymoon."

"Sorry." She gave a rueful shrug. "Sometimes the memories creep up on me."

"I know." More than she realized, after her middle-of-the-night thrashing that had jerked him awake their first couple of nights as man and wife. Only after he'd tucked her close, stroked her back, and murmured soothing reassurances had she quieted. "Scars from a trauma like that can run deep. Why didn't you tell me you were still having nightmares?"

She bit her lower lip. "Have I been waking you up?"

"Only twice."

"Sorry. I thought . . . I hoped . . . after we were married they'd go away."

"You haven't had one the past five nights."

"That's a positive sign."

"Does that mean they've been more frequent at home?"

She shrugged and played with the ruffle on her swimsuit. "Sometimes."

"Kristin." He waited until she lifted her gaze. "Whenever I ask how you're doing, you tell me you're fine."

"I am."

"Not if you're having frequent nightmares."

"They'll go away. Faster now that I have someone to snuggle up with in the dark." She ran her fingers through his hair, letting her hand rest at the base of his neck. "And you always have a full plate at work. I don't want you worrying about me."

He leaned close and stole a quick kiss, staying a whisper away while he spoke. "Goes with the territory. And for the record, I'm not complaining. I'm grateful to have someone I love enough to worry about."

A sheen began to glisten in her eyes. "Thank you for that. And the feeling is mutual."

"Good to know. Now, why don't I go get us each a papaya smoothie and we'll toast to that?"

"I'm willing to indulge my sweet tooth if you are."

"Isn't that what honeymoons are for?"

"If ours is any indication . . . yes." She gave him a frisky nudge.

"Any complaints?"

"Not a one."

"Don't go anywhere without me."

"Never."

After one more kiss, he swung his feet to the sand and ducked out of the cabana.

As he walked away, the soft West Indian breeze rustled the palm fronds overhead, the surf lapped against the sand in a lulling cadence, and the sun illuminated the deep blue sky and brilliant tropical flowers.

Inhaling the fragrant air, Luke paused to look back at the secluded hideaway on the beach where he and Kristin had spent a sizeable part of the past week, tucked away in a world of their own.

Unfortunately, she was right about the actual honeymoon having to come to an end.

But every day of all the years God granted them together would be a honeymoon in spirit.

He'd see to that.

Because the incredible woman who'd given his life new meaning, who'd chased away the shadows in his heart and filled it with sunshine and laughter, deserved no less.

. . . . .

"Here you go. One papaya smoothie coming up."

As Luke rejoined her in their cozy cabana, Kristin raised the back of the chaise lounge to a sitting position. "Perfect timing. I was beginning to miss you."

"I was gone less than ten minutes." He handed her one of the tall fruity drinks, complete with an umbrella.

"It felt like ten hours."

"Music to a new husband's ears." He sat and clinked his glass with hers. "To us."

"To us." She took a sip of the frosty concoction. "Mmm. Very refreshing." After another taste, she lifted her glass again. "Now I have a toast. To happy endings."

"I'll drink to that." He touched the lip of his glass to hers and took a drink, watching her over the rim. "That one's for more than us, isn't it?"

She stirred the slushy drink with her straw. Why pretend? If Luke had witnessed her nightmares, he knew the traumatic events of six months ago continued to hover on the fringes of her mind.

"Guilty as charged."

"Let me guess. You were also thinking about the Bisharas with that toast."

Bingo.

The father and son had often been in her thoughts these past few months. A man caught in impossible circumstances, who'd been shot, felled by a serious illness, and almost lost his only offspring. And a young man held captive by terrorists for two years, who bore scars no one could see.

How could she not think of them?

The horror she'd endured was nothing compared to what they'd gone through day after endless day.

"Kristin?"

At Luke's gentle prod, she sighed. "You know me too well."

"Not yet . . . but I'm working on it." He gave the tip of her nose a playful tap, then grew more serious. "They had about the best possible outcome, you know."

That was true.

Yusef's cancer appeared to be responding to treatment, the FBI had agreed not to prosecute because of his cooperation on the case and his willingness to advise on similar investigations in the future, and the art museum had hired Touma after Yusef decided to step down.

"I know. It was a win all around."

"True—and I got the grand prize."

As he smiled at her in that warm, intimate way of his that always melted her heart and played havoc with her respiration, Kristin took a sip of her cold drink.

It didn't cool her off even a fraction of one degree.

"When you look at me like that, I get all hot and bothered."

"Ah. Mission accomplished." He took another sip of his drink, scooted to the bottom of the lounge, and dropped the privacy flap on the cabana.

"What are you doing?"

"The view outside is too distracting. I'd rather focus on you." He lowered the back of the lounge chair, set his cup in the drink holder, and stretched out.

She angled toward him, twirling the tiny umbrella between her fingers, feigning innocence. "Sleepy?"

"Nope." He propped his head on one palm, plucked the umbrella from her, and twined their fingers together. "Thinking about ways to distract you from unpleasant memories."

She sipped her drink through the straw as a delicious tingle raced through her. "I take it you have some ideas."

"A few." He gave her a gentle tug and eased onto his side. "Want to see if they work?"

"I suppose I could be persuaded." She set her drink down and stretched out beside him until they were face to face, mere inches apart, his hand resting lightly on her hip.

"Can I tell you something, Mrs. Carter?"

His husky question sent a quiver of anticipation through her. "Uh-huh." It was all she could manage.

"I am the happiest man alive. And if I live to be a hundred, these past few days with you will be the standard I measure the world against."

Oh my.

His face blurred, and she blinked to clear her vision.

"That is the most beautiful thing anyone has ever said to me."

"A beautiful compliment for a woman who's beautiful inside and out." He skimmed the pad of his thumb across her lips, his touch featherlight—and far more intoxicating than the alcohol-infused froufrou drinks so many of the guests at the resort seemed to enjoy. "So what do you say we make some more warm, tropical memories to take back with us to cold, snowy St. Louis?"

"I'm all for that. But you know what? For the rest of my life, even on the coldest days, my heart will stay warm because of you."

"I love you, Kristin." His irises darkened to the color of burnished jade.

"I love you too." That emotion-choked whisper was all she could manage as he pulled her close.

And in the fleeting moment before she lost herself in his embrace, Kristin sent a silent thank-you heavenward.

For all the yesterdays, good and bad, that had led her to her own happy ending.

For the gift of today in this amazing man's arms.

And for the deep, abiding love that would grace their lives for all the tomorrows they were blessed to share.

READ ON FOR AN EXCERPT
FROM IRENE HANNON'S NEXT
Hope Harbor Novel

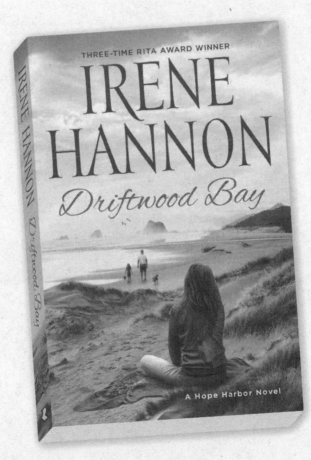

Chaos.

That was the only word to describe his new home.

And his new life.

Logan West ran his fingers through his damp hair, exhaling as he surveyed the mess in the kitchen.

Shredded paper towels covered the floor like springtime petals from the Bradford pear trees that had lined the small Missouri town of his youth.

Eggshells were scattered about, the residual whites oozing onto tile that had been spotless when he'd stepped into the shower less than ten minutes ago.

Soup cans, peanut butter jar, bread wrapper, OJ carton, the open container from last night's take-out dinner, and other sundry food packaging items rounded out the inventory—all of them pristine. As clean as if they'd never been used.

Meaning Toby had gotten into the trash.

Again.

The happy-go-lucky beagle might be cute as the proverbial button, but he was wreaking havoc on a life already in disarray.

Logan wiped a hand down his face.

What on earth had he been thinking when he'd decided to add a dog to the mix?

Or maybe the problem was that he *hadn't* been thinking.

Not straight, anyway.

Because getting a dog was flat-out his dumbest idea since the day he'd convinced his kid brother it would be fun to jump off the porch roof into a mound of raked autumn leaves that wasn't nearly as cushiony as it appeared.

Man, their parents had never let him forget *that* escapade—or the subsequent trip to the ER to get Jon's broken arm set.

Skirting the mess on the floor, Logan edged toward the counter as a familiar sense of panic nipped at his composure.

How could his well-ordered existence disintegrate into such bedlam in a mere four months? ER doctors were supposed to be pros at dealing with turmoil.

However . . . hospital trauma centers were *managed* chaos, with protocols for every kind of emergency, while his new life in this small town on the Oregon coast hadn't come with a procedure manual.

But who would have expected to need one this far away from the hustle and bustle of San Francisco and the complications of big-city living?

Go figure.

All he knew was that based on his first thirty-six hours in Hope Harbor, his dream of a quieter, simpler life in a small seaside town seemed destined to remain just that—a rose-colored fantasy with no basis in reality.

With a resigned sigh, he retrieved a garbage bag and began collecting the debris. Once the kitchen was clean, he'd have to round up Toby and—

A swish of movement in the doorway caught his attention.

Smoothing out the frown that more than one intern had deemed intimidating, he straightened up and turned toward Molly.

The five-year-old stared back at him, eyes big, expression solemn, feet bare, her strawberry blonde hair in desperate need of brushing, her ratty baby blanket clutched in her fist.

"Hey." The sticky goo from the eggshell in his hand leaked onto his fingers, and he tossed the fragment into the trash bag.

Or tried to. He finally resorted to shaking it off. "I think you forgot your shoes." He forced up the corners of his lips.

Hers remained flat as she watched him in silence, then stuck a finger in her mouth.

His stomach twisted.

If there was a secret to coaxing a smile out of a grieving little girl, he'd yet to learn it.

He set the garbage bag on the floor, crossed to her, and dropped to one knee. At the thick fringe of lashes spikey with moisture, he swallowed past the lump in his throat.

She'd been crying again. In private—like he and his brother had always done. One more trait she shared with them, in addition to the distinctive cleft in their chin and wide-set blue eyes.

He took her small hand and gentled his voice. "Did you brush your teeth?"

She gave a silent nod.

"Why don't you put your shoes on and I'll tie them for you? Then we'll go down to the beach. Would you like that?"

She slowly removed her finger from her mouth. "Can Toby go?"

Not if he had his druthers. One glimpse of the leash at the end of their outing and the beagle would race off in the opposite direction, sand flying in his wake. After their stroll yesterday, it had taken ten minutes to corral the pup, who seemed to think they were playing a game of tag.

But if Molly's request meant she was beginning to warm up to the new addition to their family . . .

"Sure. You get your shoes while I clean up the kitchen." He stood. "Is Toby in your room?"

She shook her head.

A quiver of unease rippled through him, and once again he furrowed his brow. Come to think of it, the playful pup was uncharacteristically quiet.

"Do you know where he is?" He kept his tone casual.

Her gaze slid toward the back door.

Uh-oh.

"Molly, sweetie"—he dropped back to the balls of his feet—"did you let him out?"

She dipped her chin and wiggled her toes. "He wanted to go."

Great.

With his luck, the dog would come back covered in mud and dragging another gangly plant, as he'd done yesterday.

"We talked about this, remember? Toby needs to stay in the house unless we're with him. He could get hurt if he runs around by himself."

The finger went back in her mouth.

His stomach clenched.

Again.

He was so not cut out to be a single parent.

"I'll tell you what. After you get your shoes, we'll look for him together, okay?"

Unless the dog responded to his summons, eliminating the need for a search party.

Like that would happen.

"'Kay." The soft word found its way around the finger that didn't budge.

She retreated down the hall, trailing the bedraggled blanket behind her.

As she disappeared, Logan moved to the back door and called Toby.

No response.

Of course not.

That would be too easy.

Shaking his head, he shut the door, dampened a fistful of paper towels, and dropped to his hands and knees to scrub at the stubborn egg whites clinging to the tile.

They were stuck as fast as the glue he'd used in the ER to suture minor cuts.

In fact, stuck pretty much described the situation he'd found himself in four months ago.

But he'd made a promise—and he'd honor it.

Whatever it took.

· · · · ·

Aha.

She'd found her culprit.

Yanking off her garden gloves, Jeannette Mason kept tabs on the dog intent on digging up yet another one of her flourishing lavender plants.

The plants she'd nurtured from tiny starts, potting and watering them with TLC until they were sturdy enough to be tucked into the beds she'd painstakingly prepared.

Based on the pup's location, the lavender now under siege was a Super French.

Lips clamped together, she tossed her gloves on the workbench in the drying and equipment shed and stormed toward the door.

Enough was enough.

If that dog kept uprooting her stock, Bayview Lavender Farm would be out of business less than three years after she'd opened her doors.

And that was *not* happening.

She'd invested too much effort in this place to let anyone—or anything—jeopardize it.

Snatching a long-handled trowel from the tool rack as she passed, she charged out into the light rain falling from the leaden sky. She should have grabbed her coat too. Now that the sun had disappeared, it was cooler than usual for mid-April.

But coastal Oregon weather could be capricious in any season—a lesson she should have learned long ago.

Brandishing the garden implement, she sprinted toward the tri-colored dog, weaving through the symmetrical beds.

"Hey!" She waved the trowel in the air. "Get out of there!"

The pup lifted his dirt-covered snout. Started to wag his tail. Reconsidered the scowling woman racing toward him with weapon in hand and skedaddled toward the tall hedge that separated her farm from the adjacent property.

Within seconds, the white tip of his tail disappeared as he wriggled through the dense greenery.

Huffing out a breath, Jeannette gave up the chase. The dog was gone—for now. Her time would be better spent repairing whatever destruction her unwanted visitor had wrought.

She continued to the bed, muttering as she surveyed the damage. Two of the plants had been uprooted, and the pesky beagle had started in on a third.

This was as bad as the last attack—except he hadn't absconded with one of her plants this go-round.

Gritting her teeth, she stalked back to the shed to retrieve a shovel. The ripped-up plants had to be her top priority.

But once they were back in their beds and watered, she was going to march next door and have a little chat with her new neighbors.

Shovel in hand, she retraced her steps to the pillaged bed, casting a dark look toward the hedge that hid the small house on the adjacent lot.

She should have inquired about buying that property too, when she'd purchased this one.

But the three acres she'd purchased were already more than she needed for her plants and tearoom. An acre or two would have sufficed.

However . . . none of the other parcels of land she'd viewed had had a path at the rear of the property that led to the dunes, which provided access to the vast beach and deep cobalt sea of Driftwood Bay. Plus, the microclimate in this particular, sheltered spot was perfect for lavender.

So despite the excess acreage, the location had been too good to pass up—especially since the land on one side had never been developed, and the house with new owners on the other side had been occupied by an older man who kept to himself as much as she did . . . and who'd long ago planted an insulating privacy hedge.

She dug into the bed she'd augmented with truckloads of rotted fir bark and aged horse manure, casting another glance toward the shrub border.

Strange how she'd had no inkling her former neighbor had sold the property until the moving van showed up a week ago. And he'd done nothing more than flick her a brief, disinterested look as she'd driven past while he was directing the moving crew from his front porch.

Then again, she'd never gone out of her way to be sociable, either.

A twinge of self-reproach niggled at her conscience, but she quashed it as she resettled the first lavender plant in the fertile earth.

There was no reason to feel guilty. On the few occasions their paths had crossed, he'd barely acknowledged her.

And just because she didn't attempt to engage people didn't mean she was antisocial. She was always polite to her customers at the town farmers' market and in her tearoom, and she smiled and waved at familiar faces in town . . . even if she rarely stopped to chat.

But she was never *un*friendly to anyone.

Although that was about to change.

She eased the second traumatized Super French into the hole

she'd dug and doused the roots with water. If fate was kind, all of the plants would recover from the shock of their abrupt extraction.

Wiping her palms on her jeans, she detoured back to the workshop, snagged her jacket, and cut across the gravel parking area at the front of her property that was empty of customers' cars on this Wednesday morning.

At least the pup hadn't launched his sneak attacks on a weekend while she was busy serving afternoon tea to a roomful of people paying a hefty sum for a couple of hours of peace and genteel elegance.

She circled around the end of the hedge that lined her drive and strode through the adjacent yard, toward the front door of the small bungalow in need of a fresh coat of paint and some landscaping.

Maybe it was better she hadn't known it was up for sale. The temptation to buy it—and protect her privacy—would have been strong.

And she did *not* need more maintenance cluttering up her already too-long to-do list.

As she approached the door, the muffled sound of yapping penetrated the walls.

Apparently the dog was a barker as well as a digger.

That figured.

She stepped up onto the porch, took a deep breath, and pressed the bell. It was possible the new owners would be nice. Apologetic, even.

One could hope, anyway.

Confrontation wasn't high on her list of favorite activities.

But these people needed to get control of their dog—and she intended to make that crystal clear before she returned home.

Whether they liked it or not.

AUTHOR'S NOTE

Suspense books laden with technical information—like this one—require countless hours of research. While the stories may be fiction, much of the backdrop and the law enforcement and military protocols are real. And I'm a stickler for accuracy.

During the writing of a book, I use many sources as I dig deep into my subject matter, and I always consult with professionals about questions unique to my story. With this book, I want to single out one particular source who went above and beyond.

FBI veteran Tom Becker, now chief of police in Frontenac, Missouri, was my go-to person for all things law-enforcement related this time around. Since he's had careers with both the FBI and local law enforcement, he was able to provide insights into both. Thank you, Tom, for sharing your unique expertise with me; for your thorough, prompt, and patient replies to my queries; and for helping me make my books as authentic as possible. You are the best!

In addition, I want to offer a special thank-you to my husband, Tom—my real-life romantic hero; my mom (in heaven now, but always in my heart) and dad, Dorothy and James Hannon, the world's best parents; all the readers who buy my books, thereby allowing me to tell my stories; and the amazing team at Revell, especially Dwight Baker, Kristin Kornoelje, Jennifer Leep, Michele Misiak, Karen Steele, and Cheryl Van Andel. Cheryl, who recently retired, was the guiding force behind all of my fabulous covers for Revell. A total pro, she was always a joy to work with. I will miss her!

I hope you'll join me in April 2019 for another trip to Hope Harbor in *Driftwood Bay*, when a woman who runs a lavender farm/tearoom crosses paths with a man who's in over his head juggling a new life, a grieving little girl, and a rambunctious dog that happens to like digging up lavender plants. And next October, I'll conclude my Code of Honor series with Rick's story—which also features the newest investigator at Phoenix Inc., the PI firm from my Private Justice series!

Irene Hannon is the bestselling, award-winning author of more than fifty contemporary romance and romantic suspense novels. She is also a three-time winner of the RITA Award—the "Oscar" of romance fiction—from Romance Writers of America, and a member of that organization's elite Hall of Fame.

Her many other awards include National Readers' Choice, Daphne du Maurier, Retailers' Choice, Booksellers' Best, Carol, and Reviewers' Choice from *RT Book Reviews* magazine, which also honored her with a Career Achievement Award for her entire body of work. In addition, she is a two-time Christy Award finalist.

Irene, who holds a BA in psychology and an MA in journalism, juggled two careers for many years until she gave up her executive corporate communications position with a Fortune 500 company to write full-time. She is happy to say she has no regrets.

A trained vocalist, Irene has sung the leading role in numerous community theater productions and is also a soloist at her church. She and her husband enjoy traveling, long hikes, Saturday mornings at their favorite coffee shop, and spending time with family. They make their home in Missouri.

To learn more about Irene and her books, visit www.irenehannon.com. She is also active on Facebook and Twitter.

Bestselling and Award-Winning Author
IRENE HANNON
Will Capture Your Imagination with a
MIND-BENDING STORY

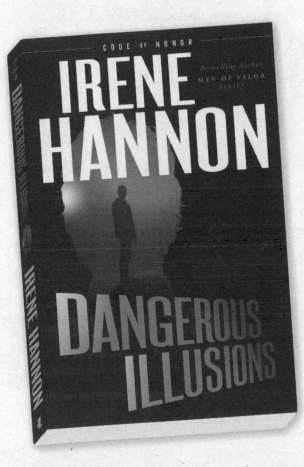

Detective Colin Flynn investigates a tragic death that's been linked to a grieving woman with apparent memory loss, but it quickly becomes clear there's more to the case—and the woman—than meets the eye.

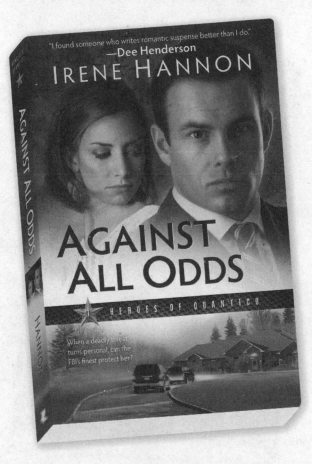

Want More of Mark's Story?
Check Out **BOOK 2** in the
HEROES OF QUANTICO Series!

Award-winning author Irene Hannon brings readers another fast-paced tale of romance, suspense, and intrigue in the can't-put-it-down second installment in this exciting series.

MORE ADVENTURES FROM NICK IN
HEROES OF QUANTICO BOOK 3!

A bestselling author brings readers another fast-paced story of romance, suspense, and intrigue as worlds collide and family connections are uncovered.

DANGER LURKS AROUND
EVERY CORNER . . .

"An engaging, satisfying tale that will no doubt leave readers anxiously anticipating the next installment."

—*PUBLISHERS WEEKLY* ON *TRAPPED*

Love Cole? Get His Story and More in
***LETHAL LEGACY* and the Other**
GUARDIANS OF JUSTICE Adventures

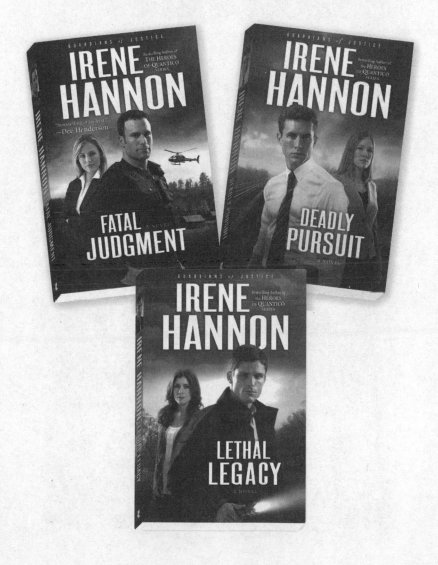

Come home to Hope Harbor—
where hearts heal . . .
and love blooms

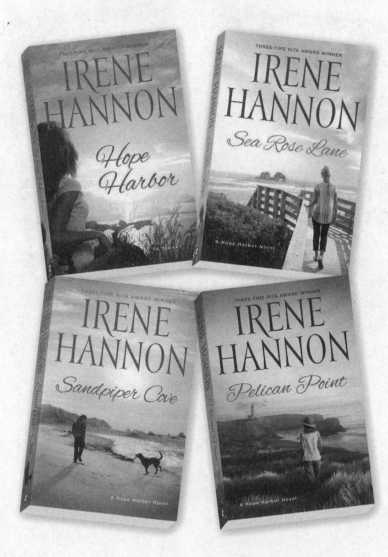

Meet
IRENE HANNON

at www.IreneHannon.com

Learn news, sign up for her mailing list,
and more!

Find her on 🐦